I0615705

RED TAINTED
THREADS

MAXIMILIANO SALAMONE

Red tainted threads / Maximiliano Salamone.

– 1st ed. – City of Buenos Aires, 2018.
Digital book, Amazon Kindle

Digital file: download and online
    ISBN 978-987-42-9492-0

1. Mythology beings. 2. Fantasy literary. I. Title.
CDD 398.4

To humanity,

that never ceases

to surprise me.

PART 1: THE SETTLED MEETING

Nothing stranger than the wind that blew that night. The treetops moved at an uneven pace, bizarre, unnatural. Only one figure severed the cold winds. At the side of the stone road, over the hill, a humanoid shape was bent, sitting in a rock, playing with a beautiful cane between his hands. He patiently looked at the night sky and the Moon in waning quarter, with an expression in the face impossible to define with exactitude, a few light wrinkles at the side of his eyes that denoted experience, and a careful trimmed beard. He wore clothes that gave the appearance of coming directly from the XIX century, although absolutely pristine. A golden brooch hung with dignity from his tie, a fine top hat crowned his temples, the final touch of an air of majesty hard to find in anyone else. Seen through the veil of the night, it was an old fashioned gentleman, unequaled.

He lowered his gaze for a few seconds, while still playing with the cane, decorated with a finely carved dragon head.

_You happen to be late, Kad.

Far, by the stone road, a second figure approached walking slowly. He was a man of size, broad shoulders, elegantly dressed with a suit and a heavy black overcoat of peculiar texture, same that could be observed in his shoes, and every piece of his odd imitation of clothes. These did not have any insignia or markings, nor did he carry any ring or decoration of any kind. The moonlight flashed stifled over his blond short hair, and his color-changing eyes. He approached nearer with tranquil, no change in his pace. By his movements, it was impossible not to notice his radiant aura of confidence, of having traveled and witnessed. His face expressed an artificial joviality.

_My apologies, roman. I was distracted on the way here.

_It is tolerable, do not worry. Last time you were delayed by three days, being it only one this time around is a vast improvement.

Kad smiled, like he always did. His countenance seemed kind and full of vitality, at least on the surface. To know what dwelled behind that well-crafted social mask was more complicated that trying to see the ocean floor from the shore.

_How have you been, Perius? I see that your taste for fashion remains unchanged.

The gentleman chuckled to himself, while inviting his strange guest to sit by with a hand gesture.

_You already know me, I like classics. I am not suited for useless amendments.

_I don't know, in my opinion you overshot it. - said Kad, while sitting in a rock a few meters apart, without letting his smile slip away, and sustaining a sudden fierce stare.

_What about you? Any adventures worth of your renown in this last fifty years? - soothed the gentleman.

_Nothing extraordinary. I have been roaming through America, catching up. I know what you mean, and no. At least I haven't made anything explode.

_A shame, because I was expecting exactly that. - both men laughed, relaxed.

Perius continued. _And what about your famous list of the thousand amusing things to do? You mentioned it once.

_I accomplished it, of course. - he answered as he put his hands in his pockets of unusual fabric - I repeated some because they were especially entertaining. Others were changed, and I added some new ones, so it ended up being about a thousand and five hundred.

_Do you recall when you blew up the Fenris Palace? That was included, right?

Kad let go a short laugh, followed by his interlocutor.

_Yes, it was number one actually. That night was great. I should do that again, a pity that they no longer invite me to Council meetings...

_I would expect no less, they got quite irate at the time. - Perius giggled, only to gradually change to a serious tone - Those that are like *us*... cannot have friends, that is well known. But even then, I consider you a great partner of mine. On my way here I was thinking, how long do we know each other?

_Can't say, I'm terrible with dates. - Kad shrugged.

_Could it be... four or five centuries, give or take? I cannot evoke the first time we crossed roads. The oldest memory I recall right now is the boat trip to Toulon that we made together. You should not have sunk it, by the way.

Both laughed again, with little desire.

_You can't deny it was fun, partner Per. - said Kad with an accomplice smile.

_No, I cannot, that much is true. The captain's look when he found a barrel sized hole in the hull was priceless, no doubt.

For a few moments, they remained in silence, observing the dark mantle of the sky, speckled with shiny pearls over their heads. The cheerful look vanished from the gentleman's face, as he lowered his gaze and kept toying gently with the carved cane. _Those have been good times, do not they?

_Certainly, but now it seems very to be different. - The atmosphere between them darkened noticeably.

_You have heard, huh? - said calmly, as he raised his gaze searching Kad's flaming eyes.

_I heard rumors, I assume are real.

_Oh yes, very real. Caucasus is dead, and a successor is needed.

Kad sighed and kept observing the sky, as if he could see something invisible to a normal human eye. _You know I couldn't care less about politics between *us*, I find it extremely boring. They know too, that's not a novelty. Frankl-

_I get it, Kad - interrupted his partner - I know you well enough. But you do not break loose of being the oldest one alive. In my... humble opinion... they will come after you. Both factions. - the gentleman's voice became suddenly hardened.

Kad stared fixedly at Perius, his calm attitude unaffected. _What do you mean with both factions?

Perius placed the cane over his knees. _I have been doing something of an investigation on the matter. I find Caucasus' passing to be rather strange. - Kad nodded - There is a big fuss in all this, and the currents are divided. Some think that the Mandate must be recomposed immediately, naming León in his place, even himself being the prime suspect. The others believe that customs must be followed above all, and the next in antiquity must be named while the Mandatary's dead is investigated, and León mainly.

Kad crossed his arms. _And the next in line happens to be me. How convenient...

_That is right. They have means to find you. - Perius looked sideways at his partner - Both sides have. - remarked again.

They remained silent, for seconds that seemed eternal.

_Well, I don't give damn about the Mandate, León and the whole business. The only thing that makes me curious is how they managed to kill Caucasus. - Kad spoke, with a slight sadness.

_He was very skilled, and smart. I cannot come with a way to explain it.

_There are a thousand ways to kill one of *us*. - Kad told with an ironic grimace. - But to get someone of his level, I count them with the fingers of one hand. And rumor-wise so far have it, he didn't do it himself.

Perius stared seriously, wordless for a minute. _I believe you should consider it...

The man sketched a grotesque grimace, with pale red inexpressive eyes, pointed at the gentleman. _I won't. I'm not interested.

The wind continued to blow abnormally, whirling the dead autumn leaves over the floor in an erratic pattern.

_Do you remember what would I do once my thousand amusing thing list was finished? - uttered Kad.

Perius looked down, with an unconcluded mixed expression between sadness and impotence, over a tapestry of absolute tranquil. _Yes, you said you would end it all.

_I haven't changed my opinion. This world bores me, *comitem*. - the punctual use of Latin did not seem at random - I have done everything I wanted, and more. Seen more than I needed, and whatever happens nowadays matters to me less and less. I can sink every ship I want and topple every palace, but it still is an old sensation in the back of my mind.

Perius took a while to reply, maybe afraid of the answer. _And what is left to do?

Kad put his hands on the rock, stretched his legs, and leaned his head backwards, eyes on the sky. He paused a few instants before speaking. _Wait the dawn. I haven't seen it the way it should for some years. Be incinerated. - he took various long seconds more - It seems like a worthy ending to my long life.

Perius' face remained unmoved, like a marble statue. _A painful ending. And a shame, comrade.

Kad smiled kindly, like he always did. _You are going to miss me, right?

_In truth I will – Perius cleared his throat, something really unusual, making in the process a seemingly unplanned pause. – Is it true that there is nothing left for you?

_Well, within the limitations, I have done everything I could and wanted. – he dropped, with something alike a genuine opinion.

_I understand. Beside the limits of imagination, of course.

_Sure. – responded Kad laughing– Many of my antics were suggestions of yours.

Perius shadowed appearance suddenly lighted up with a more cheerful color. _Maybe I could find a deed you have not done yet, that would result entertaining.

Kad grimaced with some light sarcasm. _I'm all ears.

The gentleman stood up, walked a few steps looking at the horizon, and leaned heavily on his cane. _Have you ever been a God? – he asked, while subtlety turning his head, gesturing with a fist up.

Below the peaceful quietness mask of Kad, surged the strange blaze of something similar to legitimate curiosity. In the past he reckoned Perius as a smart man, worthy of his respect. He crossed a leg over the other, before speaking. _I have been king, prince, witch doctor, and many even worshiped and flattered me uselessly, if that's what you mean.

Perius turned around, while walking again towards his partner, with a halo of mystery. _No, I mean something deeper, to be a Deity.

_I can't divide the waters, or make it rain frogs. - responded with a wave, now clearly poignant.

_Then you have not, and it is a worthy challenge for you. - Perius pointed at him theatrically.

_All right, you have my attention. How do I do it?

_It is simple. - Perius continued - Become yourself into a God tha-

_That really answers. - Kad interrupted him.

A casual observer would have sworn that the gentleman was more animated, although getting into his mind was impossible. _This is what this deal is about. You could... choose a human for starters. Fulfill that one's prayers, or something along those lines. Then you will need more followers.

_And who do I choose? - In Kad's voice a new nuance of moderate interest could be noticed.

_I have no idea, whoever you fancy. I guess someone whom has lost his faith. That is up to you.

_Could be interesting, yeah. I'm thinking about all the stupid things that a human can ask for, and how easy are to accomplish. And I'd play with that one... until I get bored.

_Would you be so kind, please take at least fifty years to get bored of that. So you could be on time for our next meeting. - Said Perius, with a faint smile, between sarcastic and conspiratorial.

_I will think about it. Maybe I send you a letter too. - replied with a similar expression - If I'm still in the land of the living, where shall we meet next?

Perius stood seriously again. _I was thinking in London, it is a city that very possibly will still remain in existence and is worth a visit. As always, the tenth day of the tenth month, of the year that ends with double zero or fifty.

_So, year 2100 in London. Very well. Where are you going now? - Asked Kad, inquisitively, covered by his calm and empty smile.

Perius stared fixedly at Kad, like reading a hidden intention behind such an innocent question. _I have not decided yet, I suppose Rome, to speak to The Cardinal, and see if he knows something about the Caucasus' subject, albeit he probably knows as much as we do.

_The Cardinal has many contacts, undoubtedly seems a good place to follow.

_And you, have you decided where you will go? – Perius didn't cease to pierce Kad's eyes.

_No. Maybe I will walk along the coast, while looking for the ultimate place to sit and wait for the Sun.

The gentlemen put a hand in his pocket, and extracted a wooden pipe, carefully crafted and with a fancy design, along with a tobacco box.

_I hope for you to choose well for that place, but please take my words into account. – he slipped as he prepared the smoking pipe.

_I will, partner. Until next time, then. – Kad stood up – My apologies for not having news, I promise to blow up something big before coming, so we can talk longer – he stated with an innocent smile.

_This has resulted in a short meeting, but as always, it is a pleasure speaking with you, Kad. – he paused briefly before continuing, helped by a hand gesture – Something tells me that we are to cross roads before the agreed upon.

_I thought the sensation was mine alone. – Kad bowed his head cordially – Goodbye, Per.

He began to walk away on the road, nailing his usual friendly smile in his mouth.

Perius greeted back, and sat down on the rock again. He crossed his legs, and lit up the smoking pipe with a match. The smoke rose slowly while he gave puffs, slowly paced.

He spent several minutes seated, following Kad's figure with his gaze, until he could no longer be seen in the darkness of the night. He placed his eyes above the treetops, which were beginning to stir at a now natural rate, as he continued letting smoke out.

A section of the road started to emerge and change shape. Stone over stone, semi liquefied, placed one over the other, until they adopted the structure of a humanoid. The features of its face accentuated, carving shrewd eyes, a mouth of thin lips and a square jawbone. His rocky skin became continuous and tanned artificially, with clothing slowly drawn over it, changing the consistency of the skin into a hard, cracked black leather. Black hair began to emerge from his head, stopping at a few centimeters in length. It took a few more seconds for him to look like a whole person, when his garments were also complete, resembling trousers, a shirt and a black jacket, all of a texture that resembled seamless fabric. Perius quietly watched the scene, as he threw away the burnt tobacco and put in new one. _Do you think he noticed you?

The man finished adjusting the last details of his fake clothes with his hands. Then he combed his hair back without too much care, and took a few steps toward the gentleman. _I doubt it. I don't know anyone who can detect me.

Perius looked at the man sideways as he lit the pipe again. _Kad is no fool. I have no way of distinguishing if he suspects anything or not.

_I'm going to follow him. We need him alive.

Perius took another puff. _If he decides to take his own life, there is nothing we can do. It is a real shame, I enjoy our meetings... and the shaking he causes. – he smiled slightly.

_Do you believe he'll follow your idea, of being a deity? It struck me as pulled out from the sleeve.

_Yes, I pulled it out of my sleeve. I really consider him a valuable partner, it would sadden me if he died. But at the current rate of things, if he does not do it himself, they will come for him and try it. I still do not grasp how they do it, but they are obviously capable. The world is changing and I do not know what is going to happen.

The mysterious man remained completely serious. In his gaze and way of acting, one could only notice a constant search for perfection, in not leaving a single movement to chance, in pursuing the goal efficiently and brutally. _Let's say he goes after your idea. What kind of individual do you think he'd choose?

He took a few seconds to answer, sitting on the rock. _I suppose someone who inspires him pity, and whom he believes would be willing to have him as the new savior. Someone who had hit rock bottom.

_I understand. I'll make sure to find such an individual, once I know what he's looking for, and then proceed with the plan.

Perius withdrew the pipe from his mouth to laugh inwardly. _Evidently, my good Lykaios, you do not understand... Kad is... chaotic. He could do just about anything. If he finds it fun to raze a city to the ground, he will, or if he decides it would be comical to witness a homeless man rise to power, he will. He is capable of whatsoever. And is patient too, so he spends decades playing with something, or someone.

The man raised an eyebrow in true confusion. _If that's really so, why was I ordered to follow him? What's the use of it? He seems like a lousy leader.

The gentleman looked at him with a mischievous eye, that of an old man who had lived, in the face of the inexperience of a young man. _Because as you see him, with his serene attitude, Kad can tackle with half of *ours* if he desires so. And we want it to be the other half. After him, we will elect a Mandatary who respects the customs and the line of Caucasus, which, although it has been... a debatable one, is undoubtedly better than León's. - he smiled, looking down - Kad is not a leader, he is a workhorse.

Silence took over the scene, not even the crickets sang. Only the wind dared to disturb it.

The former stone man turned around, and walked away at a steady pace along the way. _I'll get on with the mission, then.

Perius continued smoking, taking puffs of smoke. He turned his gaze to the distant lights of the city, and sighed.

PART 2: FROM THE SHADOWS

It was not difficult for Lykaios to follow Kad on his trip to Spain, making a long stopover in Barcelona. During the first week, he divided his time between keeping an eye on his movements, and finding a place that would serve as a base of operations, that would be modest, easily accessible to him, and above all, that would have a basement. The second night was devoted to spying, as always, while capturing some humans from the street, those who were not important to society and that nobody claimed, to leave them chained and doped in the basement of the new lair, absorbing just enough blood so that they would not die. And in case he needed something extra, he'd eat their flesh. They'd help him avoid wasting time having to hunt from then on. He made sure to get three, as he had to meet a high energy demand from his constant transformations into inanimate objects, those that caught the eye the least.

By this milestone in his mission, he had already managed to sketch out the psychological profile of his prey. Even within the chaos, there is a pattern of order, and he believed he had found it, thanks to direct and meticulous observation, and of course to rumors from *others like them*. He knew that Kad, the last of the Akkadians, spent three to four months in a city he had not visited for a long time, to wander around it completely on his night walks, and that if he liked it or found something (or someone) to play with, he would stay longer, up to ten years or more.

However, he noticed that he was "off" as far as his present actions were concerned. Of all the things he had been told about him, he didn't seem interested in repeating any of them. Maybe what he heard about the conversation between him and Perius was true. He was bored with the world, and all he had left to do was disappear. That could not be allowed it or his assignment would fail. Fortunately, no one else had tried to get close to the target. The side of León had made no move, which was suspicious.

In parallel, he devoted himself to an extensive investigation of a subject who would serve as a faithful follower of Kad in Perius' far-fetched plan, which much to his regret, was the only one available. He detested not having an alternative plan in case the first one failed, and had no choice but to prepare the "A" as best as possible, and make no mistakes. He made a list of twenty possible candidates, which he came across during his investigations, including the necessary changes he needed to make to their lives to make them as miserable as possible, and thus fit in the predicted pattern, which would be most appealing to Kad. Of these, he selected the ten most likely to occur, and began to introduce small variations in their lives. One of those ten should work.

He discovered a predilection of his main prey for a certain beach, which he visited four times, among the many times he wandered on his night walks. It was likely that he had chosen it as his final place, but he needed to confirm it. He had to push him to a meeting, not a simple matter.

Among the people the Akkadian spoke to (those like *them*) was a gypsy woman. She was relatively young, less than a hundred years old, but she had a talent for visualizing future events, or so she claimed. It was a good place to start.

He spent two nights following her, to come up with a profile of her. The task in general was infinitely easier than the other. On the third night of the second week he set out to contact her. It was time to place his bet.

_You're Crista, right? – he stopped her, with authority.

The young gypsy woman looked with obvious surprise at the figure that had appeared in front of her out of nowhere. _Who's asking?

The alley in which they were both standing was empty, except for a few bags of debris and a couple of vermin crawling across the floor. Crista was wearing an usual attire in her community, with a long cotton skirt up to her ankles, sandals, a multi-colored coat and a scarf decorated with golden metal beads tied around her head, contrasting with her pale skin. A bundle of bracelets decorated both wrists. The alley was one of the places she hunted, usually unfortunate men with too much lust in their minds.

_My name is not important, but you can call me Shadow.

Crista watched him from head to toe, quickly, trying to get as much information as possible out of him in less than a second. His outfit was the same uniform that he had created before, but his face was slightly different, the shape of his nose was more pointed, his eyebrows more distant. His hair this time was long, reaching almost to his shoulders, maintaining its dark color.

_Look, Mr. Shadow, I have no business with you, so if you'll excuse me, I'm going to leave.

The man didn't move a muscle until he spoke again. _I'm part of Crest. I have followed you these days, I know you have no affinity for León or any high-profile issues, but perhaps I could interest you in a small job with a good return.

The situation made her tense. _That's right, but I'd rather stay neutral on the whole thing. – Crista continued to watch the strange man, with artificial calm, as she settled down the brown hairs that had fallen softly on her forehead.

_I can imagine. Even so, I'm able to offer you a deal, where you'll get... "benefits".

The girl's light blue eyes flashed fleetingly as the headlights of a car passed down the side street. _All right. Explain, you can never have enough "benefits".

_We can offer you a considerable sum of money, twenty thousand euros, and an exclusive hunting reserve for the term of two years protected by us.

Crista raised an eyebrow. _It sounds like too much money, the job must be risky... I'm not interested in exposing my neck in the middle of a civil war. I'm sorry.

_It's not dangerous actually, but it is... important. We need you to push a certain man into an encounter that will keep him alive long enough to be useful.

The young woman was intrigued by the curious offer. _A man? Who's this about?

The Shadow crossed his arms, and leaned his back on one of the walls. _Here he introduces himself as Carlos, but he is better known as the Akkadian among *our own*. You had a few words with him last Thursday. He was wearing a black coat, dark hair and a beard.

Crista kept her composure. _Yeah, I kinda remember who he is. And what am I supposed to do with him, in case I'm interested?

_It's very simple. You will meet him again, as if by chance, at the place and time I'll indicate to you. There you will tell him that you dreamt about him, or that you had a vision, whichever you prefer, and that you saw him on the beach that he always visits, and that he must go there again that same night, because he must talk to someone.

An expression of suspicion wrapped over Crista's face. It took her a few long seconds to speak again. _And... that's it?

The man adjusted his back against the wall. _That's it.

The woman put her hands together, touching her wide skirt, and gently bit her lower lip. She finally broke the silence. _I find it too simple for the "benefits" you offer, Mr... Shadow. It's obvious there's something hidden in the whole thing. I'm risking too much here.

Lykaios separated himself from the wall, and put his hands in the pockets. _The offer still stands, and it's non-negotiable. If you think it's convenient, we'll meet tomorrow right here, at this time. Even if your answer is negative, please present yourself. I have my tricks to get you out of your lair, so let's save ourselves the trouble.

He didn't wait for her answer, and walked out of the alleyway. Crista, on the other hand, stood there, her gaze moving nervously without looking at any particular place. Then she remembered that she was still hungry, and had long before she had to answer that strange offer.

Crista appeared again the next night, this time dressed in a crimson skirt, a white shirt and a wool coat of the same color. On her head she wore the same scarf, which was like her lucky charm. During the day, in her confinement, she told her own fortune with tarot cards, and had not been warned of any danger or any major change in her life, which was ambiguous. She was thinking of asking them to double the offer, as it was "so important", but it might not work in her favor in that way. Having the exclusivity of hunting in a village or an area in a city was a great relief to her famine, she could even sell some of her preys and make profit. It was promising, and the task did not seem difficult at all. She remembered the light chat she had had with "Carlos", who didn't feel odd at all, just a very kind and handsome guy who admired her special gift. Of course, she didn't know anything about him at the time. A call to an acquaintance alerted her about that person. He wasn't what he looked like.

Even so, she would accept the offer, she was ready to turn her life around, which she considered pathetic, even if the cards kept it from her. And there she was, waiting for that Shadow dude to show up. Until he did, she just couldn't see where he had come from, he just appeared behind her back.

_All right, what have you decided?

Crista turned as quickly as she could, extremely surprised. _Hey! I didn't see you coming.

The Shadow stared at her, waiting for an answer to his question. She breathed and exhaled several times until returning to something somewhat normal, and continued. _I don't know, I'm not convinced by the situation. It *really* is a risky business. I showed up because you're a skilled person, who can give me a hard time if you want to... actually–

_Gypsy, I'm not good at haggling. – he interrupted her without any social tact – The offer is still the way I said it to you last night. – he handed her a piece of paper, and she took it.

Crista looked at the paper, a check, and the amount written in it. She didn't know much about checks because nobody used them anymore, but she knew she could convince some human to go to the bank and leave with the money without even sweating a drop. She made such an effort to keep her face still that a poker player would have applauded her.

_So... it's this amount, plus a hunting ground of my choice, right?

The man shook his head. _No, we'll assign you which one, once you finish your task.

Crista could no longer contain the faint, deep red smile on her lips. She could already feel the magnetism of the money in her fingers. _All right, I accept. Give me the details of what I have to do.

Both parts of Lykaios' plan were in motion. On one hand, he had to make sure that the woman did her job, and that she did it right. Then it was no longer in his hands, but he was confident that it would be successful. On the other hand, he had already discarded half of the ten chosen humans, and of the remaining ones, he had selected two as the most likely. He had to select one of them in less than two days, when the gypsy's part would develop. He took action. For Case number 1, he made sure that it was left homeless, as the last step in a series of miseries that fell on the subject in few days, all of them manipulated. For Case number 2, his last move had been to eliminate its only immediate family member so that it would appear to be an accident.

Case number 1 took its own life the next night, discarding itself. Case number 2, on the other hand, caused destruction in the place where it lived, particularly destroying the religious images in its possession. He closely watched Case Number 2 until almost dawn, wrapping up the final details and planting the right trigger in its unconscious. He finally retired to his hideout. The victim was ready.

PART 3: LIKE CLAY IN THE HANDS OF AN ARTISAN

Amelia woke up with irritated eyes. She'd been crying all night and half the morning. Her life was overall a wreck, but in the last week it had become an unbearable hell. Her father had passed away. An accident, she was told at the hospital, a huge portion of a balcony fell on him as he walked.

They didn't get along at all, but he was the only family she had, and although she never said it, she loved him. That fact broke her heart, because he could never hear it ever again, no matter how loud she screamed or kicked, he wouldn't listen. Actually... he never ever listened, but this time around, it wasn't his fault.

She got out of bed reluctantly, to sit while rubbing her eyes still with some dry tears on her cheeks. She glanced around, her room looked like a garbage can, smelled like one, and there was not a sound behind the insulation of the walls. The apartment seemed like an open tomb, where she lived as master and mistress. On the walls hung some posters of rock bands, half torn up by the rage of the previous night, some books on the floor, a few torn dolls, a statue of the Virgin in pieces, a broken chain with a cross, pieces of magazines, and the other halves of the posters that had not resisted gravity. Through the window came a faint light, which made her sick. She didn't want to see the light. She didn't want anything at all.

It crossed her mind again to kill herself, but she was too cowardly to do it, she couldn't imagine trying for real. Whenever she made up her mind, her body just wouldn't respond, and would just stand motionless. She hated herself for it, along with a thousand other things. The fatalistic thought was overtaken by a torrent of memories, of moments in which she could have acted differently, and didn't, whether out of shyness, cowardice, or plain, flat stupidity. That time she could have talked to the boy she liked at school, when she declined the scholarship to study abroad, even that one when she refused to go to the park with her father as a kid, the time she fought with her best friend over a trifle.

Then she recalled all the misfortunes that had happened recently. When she was unfairly expelled from the university for a threat to a teacher she didn't make, when she lost her job as a secretary when the office closed because of debts (she wasn't even aware of the company's financial problems), when her supposed friends turned away one by one, for the most part without understanding the reason, and finally a death. It was too much for her, more than a person could bear. But what could she do? Praying again? Not an option. If there was a God up there, obviously didn't want anything with her miserable life.

She rose to her feet, and stood where she was, for several minutes, unable to move, plunged into the negative thoughts that invaded her. Nothing to do, no one to ask for help. Just an abyss, into which she would soon, very soon, fall.

She spent the whole afternoon and evening sitting on the floor, picking up some of the broken objects, moving the clothes to the bed or back to the chairs, eyeing some pages of the books that had fallen, not really reading them because she was unable to focus on anything with her wet eyes. She turned around, wiping her nose, and saw a poster she didn't remember having. It pictured a bay with lots of light, and people bathing, as if it were paradise itself, underneath it said in giant letters "Mermaid Beach, Barcelona. Summer 2050". She felt an unstoppable impulse, the urge to go and contemplate the sea, which was just a few minutes away. Perhaps the fresh air would take away some of the horrible thoughts that inhabited her head. She left the poster on the floor, put on a pair of shoes and left, unable to stop.

She walked slowly down the street, her eyes and steps lost, heading for the ocean. Twice she received honks from motorcyclists crossing the streets. Amelia barely noticed, just kept walking.

She arrived at the beach, and headed south, walking on the sand, with her shoes in one hand and a dirty handkerchief in the other. On the horizon, far out at the sea, she could see the Sun setting to the west. The night was a little cloudy, so the only lights available were the city's streetlights, and the nearby buildings.

She stopped walking, and sat on the sand, the murmur of the sea gradually calmed her down. From the frenetic rhythm of thoughts crammed into her mind, she moved into a quiet void, as the minutes passed and the Sun disappeared completely. She looked around, there was no one near. She noticed that it was a particularly cold night, so she held herself, trying to keep her body warm, losing track of time, in the sway of the waves. Sadness took hold of her, and she could only weep again, looking up at the cloudy sky, blaming the fate of her misfortunes.

Not far from there, Crista sat on the front steps of a house, on the corner of the streets that had been pointed out to her by that strange guy who called himself Shadow. She tried to stay calm, but impulsively bit her lower lip, as usual, like every time she got nervous. She told herself all the time that she had to be relaxed, that it was a very easy job, that it would only take a few minutes, and then she could go and extract the funds with the check just as she looked up earlier in internet. Probably the next night, she'd move into her *exclusive* hunting ground. That thought drew a smile over her smooth lips, this time without any particular color. As she moved her gaze back and forth, paused to smell her perfume, which she had enjoyed so much when she bought it. That thought remained unfinished when she saw in the distance the reason for her commission. A few hundred meters away she could see among the crowds the alleged Carlos that they had told her about, who was wearing the same black overcoat as a few days ago. He walked slowly, strolling and glancing around with an enviable calm.

Crista had never lived calmly, not even when she *changed* and ceased to be human, to become *that other thing.* She thought that it would be great to be immortal, that that it would be the end of her worries, that her new power would be enough to trample over the world. And it wasn't like that, not in the least. She discovered that all that supposed power came with experience over the years, and that there were real *horrors* in the world that preceded in status and capacity. She also discovered that was no longer possible to go out and enjoy the day without feeling the light and heat burning down, and that the food was no longer filling. She felt very useless, this time in a new world, as rancid as the old one. And now, she was a few meters away from one of those horrors. He was no different from her, but so skilled that he could undo her in seconds, no matter what resistance was put up. That thought disfigured her graceful face, as she desperately tried to maintain her composure and finish the task she had, to then run away in search of safety, just as a child.

She stood up, and took a few long seconds to recover, before marching on to meet him. Time to shine, Crista.

Kad followed her with his eyes as the girl walked towards, pretending not seeing him, until a few steps later they crossed paths. This time he wore his hair black, a bit of a beard, as if it were neatly messy, with his jaw slightly more rectangular, but keeping his forehead wide, and the same confidence of the world on his broad shoulders. The color of the eyes was also different, faintly gray. Crista would have been attracted to him if it hadn't been for her panic to know what he was capable of.

_Hello, Mr. Carlos, what a coincidence to meet you here.

Kad shook his head as he sketched his characteristic smile and stared at her.

_It's certainly a great coincidence. - he replied in perfect Spanish.

_What a beautiful night! I like the cold nights. And it's cloudy, it invites to the hunt.

Kad put his hands in his pockets, which had a strange leather-like texture, as did all of his fictitious clothing. _I actually haven't been on a hunt in a long time. When you've walked enough, you get bored with the same routine.

That answer took Crista by surprise, at that moment she did not imagine how one of her *own* could go by without hunting.

_Ah... w-well - she stammered, losing her balance. Something strange was up, terror was suddenly taking hold of her chest. Her heart kept pumping desperately, looking for an extra milligram of adrenaline to allow her to run faster than him. - I can't imagine how you do that, Mr. Carlos, I think you're a wonderful person. - she scolded herself for such a stupid answer.

Kad laughed to himself. _That's what I've been told. And how you've been... - he seemed to be struggling to remember her name.

_My name is Crista. - she smiled falsely.

_Ah, of course. Crista. Well, how have you been?

_Spectacular Mr. Carlos, in fact it is very good that I am meeting you, since I have something to tell you. - she bit her lower lip very hard.

_I figured so... What's it about? - Kad's tone of voice resembled that of an adult talking to a small child who is just learning to draw with crayons.

_It's just... I had a vision a few nights ago. In it I saw you visiting a beach, and in there you found a person. That person seemed important to you, sir.

_How interesting, Crista. And... what beach would that be?

The girl hesitated for a moment. _It seemed to be one that you like very much, and that you visit often. Mermaid Beach. - soon she realized that she shouldn't have let go of that detail.

_Oh, I understand. Thank you very much, Crista. You've done very well. - Kad placed his right hand on the gypsy's head in a quasi-paternal gesture and slowly continued his march.

Crista could only remain with her eyes wide open, looking towards the end of the street in the same position she had remained in, completely still. She wasn't sure of what terrified her more, if it was the way he said that last sentence, or the loving gesture an angel would have with a soul that has been condemned to an eternity of suffering. Slowly, a small voice inside her head rose up, shouting to leave at once, to collect the money she had been given, and to wait for Shadow where she had been told. When the voice occupied her whole mind, she was finally able to unlock her legs and run down the street, as far as she could, as fast as she could. She ran until her lungs and legs couldn't continue.

On a nearby roof, a grey column changed shape, ready to move to follow its prey. The ex-column was increasingly concerned about the effectiveness of his methods, were they obvious to a prey of this caliber? The Akkadian exceeded him by more than three millennia, and he had probably learned things he was completely unaware of. For a moment he envied *all* that experience and skill. He would become better and in much less time, because he was applied and left nothing halfway. Oh yes, he'd definitely outgrow him soon enough. That thought floated through his mind as he leapt quickly between the roofs in a westerly direction.

Kad arrived at the beach he'd been frequenting. He seemed to like it, though there's no way to know why. Perhaps it is similar to the place he envisioned for a long time as his dignified finale, having his ultimate experience, watching the sunrise, absorbing so much energy from the King Star until his body could not tolerate it and begins to disintegrate, as each cell, overflowing with power, reaches its maximum expression to die afterwards.

The beach was empty, except for one silhouette sitting on the sand, trying to occupy as little space as possible. One of Kad's eyebrows arched infinitesimally. He raised his head as if the moon behind the clouds was shining just for him. And he began to walk forward.

PART 4: SAND AND SALT

Kad stood up, facing the sea, beside the girl who sat there in the same place where she had been for hours. She simply followed him with her eyes, still wet with tears.

For a moment, the gentle, distant sound of the waves banging against the dock mediated between them. A few salty drops jumped over them, mixed with the dew of the night, falling in an oddly timing, as bizarre as the swirling wind, which was simply not normal.

_The ocean is beautiful, isn't it? - Kad said, unraveling the omnipotent aphonia that surrounded both.

Amelia cleared her throat repeatedly before she could speak. _Yeah, it's pretty.

The stranger's voice had a enthralling effect on her, and her heart began to work faster.

_Do you mind if I sit down?

_N-not... not at all. - that short sentence was not even completed, that Kad was sitting on the sand, with his hands together on his legs.

_I know both sides of the sea, but I like more from this one. This beach pleases me, one day, when my adventures are over, perhaps I will sit right here, and with the ocean behind me, I will be blessed for a last time by the rays of the Sun. - the phrase was losing volume as he said it.

Amelia looked up at him, as he was at least one head higher, while she wiped her nose with the handkerchief and shook the surprise off her. She let out the only words that managed to accumulate in her tongue. _Are you... sick of something?

_Let's say that no, but everything must have an end, doesn't it?

She nodded her head apathetically.

_What's your story? - Kad asked.

Amelia took several seconds, and responded. _My life sucks, that's all... - and took a deep breath - a lot of things have happened and I don't know what to do.

_I'm sure there's a solution to everything.

_No, it doesn't. Suddenly I'm... - she rasped again - alone, unemployed, uneducated, and my father has recently passed away. - a thick veil of shade fell softly over her eyes - There is no solution.

Kad stared at the horizon, at the foam that came and went over the water. _Almost everything, then.

Amelia tried to take up even less space, beginning to feel uncomfortable with the conversation. She never trusted strangers, on the news there are stories every week about girls who should have run and didn't. However, she felt anchored to her place, and couldn't figure out the reason.

Kad took a deep, forced breath. _If it's all right with you – he continued- I can solve your problems, as long as they are within my scope, of course.

She frowned in a suspicious gesture. She really had to start pulling the anchor soon, and run away. _And why would you do that for me? We don't even know each other.

_It turns out that some... mysterious force... – he said with obvious irony – has brought us together, and I am curious to know who, and what for. Besides... I'm in a position to help, and I find it entertaining.

Added to the frown, a grimace was appended in her mouth. _I don't understand, what do you mean?

_Let's say I'm a God. Well, almost a God... I can do a lot of things, and some I cannot.

Perhaps she could make time with her words as she finished pulling the anchor. The fellow seemed a little crazy to her, but possibly not dangerous. On the other hand, he was very attractive. She was distracted for a second by the fact that she could not determine his age, seemed young and old at the same time. Amelia loosened her hard features, to give way to a sharp expression. _Are you some kind of genie? Do I have three wishes?

_I hadn't thought about it but it sounds like a good idea. Yes, I grant wishes, and from now on you have three. - Kad's soft tone of voice was unshakable.

Amelia smiled as she shook her head. _You're out of your mind, sir. - she had definitely been unlucky enough to run into a guy with a few nuts missing from his engine. Now she was concerned about the dangerousness of the subject. She decided to be more polite, that would work for the moment. _Do you have a name at least?

Kad stretched his legs on the sand, resting his head on the ground with his hands behind it. _I had a name a long time ago. To be honest, I've forgotten it. But never mind, you can call me whatever you want.

She laughed this time. The nameless stranger had at least distracted her for a few moments from her inner darkness, and even made her smile, after so many days without doing so, it didn't seem so bad. _I don't know what name I can give you... How do your friends call you?

_The closest person to what I might consider a "friend", calls me Kad.

Amelia reached out to him, as if she was trying to make friends with a hyperactive toddler. _Nice to meet you, my name is Amelia.

Kad accepted the greeting, not dropping his gentle, calm smile. _The pleasure's all mine, miss. So, what's your first wish?

As she let go of Kad's hand, she began to stand up, shaking the sand and salt from her body. She had finally made it! By the time she looked up, he was already standing facing her, and to her surprise without a grain of sand between his heavy clothes of strange texture. Her face expressed itself properly.

_H–How are you so clean...

_I'm willing to wait... for you to think it over, because it's only three wishes. I'll see you again tomorrow night.

_I'm sorry, Mr. Kad, but I'm not sure if I'm coming back here tomorrow. I don't want to disappoint you. – Amelia's mind was a beehive of things that came and went.

_I didn't mean for you to come back to this place, I'd better get close to wherever you are.

Amelia laughed out loud this time, a response that did not quite faithfully combine the agglomeration of thoughts that ran through her head. _I'm not going to tell you where I live...

Kad shrugged, hands in his pockets. _No need, Miss Amelia. Amelia – he repeated, as if he was looking for a way not to forget a name, even if only for once.

And he evaporated into thin air in a second, leaving a red trail that was carried swiftly by the wind. And after that, there wasn't a single visible trace of him. Amelia's face twisted in sudden terror at the disappearance of her interlocutor. When the initial sensation was over, a barrage of questions began to fall on her already tormented mind. What was that? Who was that guy? How did he disappear? Is he really a genie or something? And most importantly, does he know how to find me?!

After several minutes without finding answers of any kind, she picked up her shoes from the floor and trotted to her apartment. It took her some time, however, to recover her breathing and a more normal expression.

The unnatural wind ceased to blow, and the fine drops of sea water were regularized. A stone from the pier rose suddenly, slowly but steadily taking on an anthropomorphic shape. The surrealist vision was crowned with the consummate conformation of a being, dressed in eternal black, one who constantly moves in the shadows of the world, whose mission was still on the move. The fact that his prey was suspicious continued to fill him with doubts. It was not possible for it to detect him, however, the message was directed at him, at the "mysterious force" that was controlling everything behind the scenes. He quickly pushed the questions out of his head, as he had to continue the mission. He was to inform Crest's leader, Eylem, of the news, as well as keep up to date with the movements of León and his side. The war had not yet gone into direct action, but it was on the brink. It could even have already started while he was there, finalizing the details of his clothes.

He set forward. As the custom dictated, the meetings were to be held in person. The new technologies were susceptible to failure or intrusion and were not his specialty, but León and his group were, so he did not trust their use. Travelling incognito would take him a few hours longer than usual to reach the Crest quarters in Marseille, he had to hurry before the sunrise that would make the matter more difficult.

As a first step he returned to his temporary den, to eat and kill the humans he did not use, to collect his personal effects, which fit in a handbag. A Shadow of his rank could never afford to carry too many items, only those that were exclusively necessary: a handgun, armor-piercing ammunition, two knives, a map, a notebook, pen, rope, credit cards, cash and an old–fashioned mobile phone, the only one that did not inspire him any security and used the less. He left the place completely clean, removed all the bloodstained plastics from the floor and incinerated them, and after transporting the bodies into the trunk of a stolen car, threw them into the sea in the darkest area he could find. He left the car in a street with little traffic, and chose another one to steal, the one he would use to travel to the French border, where he would get rid of it to get another one. He set out, with only a few hours to go before dawn. It caused him displeasure to leave his deal with the young gypsy woman unfinished, but his assignment was a higher priority and there was no time to waste.

PART 5: IN THIS HOLY LAND

_Greetings, Priest Filippo. - Perius said in correct Italian, while bowing slightly.

_Blessings to you, Brother Perius. - hc replied.

A few doves fluttered near the majestic fountain in the small courtyard under the Cardinal's chambers in the Vatican. Framed by tall white columns, the inner square gleamed beautifully under the light of the lanterns, a perfectly maintained garden, full of life.

Both men walked forward under the balconies as they talked quietly. Perius, perhaps for a major cause, had put aside his old clothes, wearing instead a modern, fine but very modest suit, a white shirt and a grey tie. His shoes showed an almost perfect gloss. The cane, in contrast, was conspicuous in its absence. Beside him, Filippo wore a large black cassock, and a white embroidered shirt poking out from underneath. The religious man's dark brown hair was carefully cut and combed. A pair of glasses crowned his air of solemn seriousness, on a face sensibly exhausted, pale and with consumed features.

Filippo continued. _You haven't been here in a while. Have you confessed lately?

Perius smiled broadly. _No, Father. I have not. I have been quite busy, with all the excitement that has come up.

_Oh yes, a regrettable episode. Really regrettable. – Filippo lowered his gaze with a look of genuine concern as he rubbed one hand nervously against the other.

_No doubt, that is why I have asked for an audience with The Cardinal, I need to find out some details.

_Of course, Brother. And I'm sorry I took so long to offer you an appointment, but the Cardinal's agenda has been busy lately. He's already been told of your arrival, so he's waiting for you in his quarters.

_Thank you very much, Filippo, and it is no problem, although I am in a hurry today.

They stopped in front of double oak doors, decorated with taste and grace, with rhombus-shaped gold appliques. The knobs on both doors were exquisitely crafted, pretending to be two angels reaching out to one another to join hands, but ironically, they would never succeed. Filippo knocked twice the golden hasp, which had the face of a winged person, between whose fists was the hoop.

In the night's silence, footsteps were heard. The bolt made a metallic sound, and one of the doors opened heavily.

Filippo gently peered in, whispered a few words, to walk away later.

_You can go in, Brother.

_Thank you again. - Perius replied quietly, a few steps away.

The priest stopped him with his hand before he entered. _If you'll be so kind, could we exchange a few words when you finish your dialogue with The Cardinal?

The gentleman squinted, suspiciously. _Yes, of course.

Filippo shook his head politely and let him pass, opening the door further.

Perius took just a few steps inside, when he turned to greet again. _Good evening, Sister.

The nun answered the greeting with only a slight bow, but without mentioning a word. Then she waved indicating him to the next room.

The first and second chambers were splendidly decorated, with shades of wood and gold. The walls were papered in a muted purple color, with a pleasant, soft texture to the touch. The carpeting had a similar but more intense coloring, as did the curtains. The second room had a huge oak desk, carved and detailed to the finest detail. Several plates of fine ceramics with leftovers seemed dislodged from the scene. The smell of food permeated every surface. Behind the monumental desk stood a slim, small man in a white cassock with small pearl appliques and a purple stole hanging over his shoulders. He had the same consumed and exhausted expression as Filippo, but more wrinkled, which was especially noticeable on the back of his hands.

He circled around the enormous desk, with a laboriously affectionate gesture. _Perius! What an honor to have you here. Please, have a seat. – the voice was remarkably hoarse and muffled.

_Giuliano, I thank you for accepting me here. – Perius replied, with equal pomposity, as he took a comfortable seat in one of the oak armchairs.

Giuliano slowly seated again. He stared at his guest through his glassy, light gray eyes whose edges were undefined, and mingled with the white of the sclera.

_Have you by any chance improved your sight, Cardinal?

_Yes, I've improved, but not too much. – he marked out every word as he twisted the huge ring on his finger.

_Oh, I understand. It's a lengthy process, you have to be persistent.

Giuliano took several seconds, keeping his eyes down, and playing with his ring. _You well know... I became... *this*... for the fear of being left in the dark. – he opened his mouth to continue, but no sound came out – The idea of going blind almost made me lose my faith. Neither medicine nor the Church provided me with a suitable solution at that time. – Perius nodded his head – And I came upon this other *reality...* but it becomes so challenging, Perius... so challenging.

_Well, nobody said it was easy, and the cons are many at first, as you distinguish by now.

_In this Holy Land, I am regarded as a person with strange habits, and only respected for my rank. I'll never become Pope, that's for sure. And what's more, in a few years I will have to leave this place, and move to another where I won't raise suspicions because of my age. But it's all about my sacred duty, isn't it?

Perius kept quiet. Giuliano continued. _I ask forgiveness every morning for not being able to go out and receive the blessing of the light. I ask forgiveness for my condition, which was my decision.

The gentleman grimaced and closed his eyes momentarily before speaking. _My dear friend, indubitably it's difficult to amalgamate *this* with the creed. Throughout my life I have believed in many things, and I also stopped believing, to be frank about it. For now, I just let things happen, not worrying whether or not is there a Divine plan, or whether there is a punishment for my actions, but about what I can do to help and what I can stop doing. – he remarked these last words with seriousness, but relaxed later adding. – No offense meant, I am just not a religious person.

The Cardinal watched him with a sad, yet empty, look. _None taken, Perius. Maybe you are not aware, but... for many years I asked for my humanity back, undeniably my prayers were not answered. It seems to be... really irreversible.

Perius looked sideways at the religious before answering him. _Oh my... I... I do not know of any credible case in which it could have been reversed, no. - he paused – How long have you been like *this*?

_Two hundred and ninety-three years.

_I see. And in that time, you have done quite some good deeds, Cardinal. And met a fair number of remarkable people.

_Yes. I've also traveled, and studied. - he spoke with even greater sadness.

_And most important, you have made a name for yourself among *us* in that short time. Even sat at the right of Caucasus as the Virtuous of Loyalty, no less – he took a watch with a chain out of his pocket, to look at the time – We are going through some tough times, and we all need you.

_Yes, of course. - Giuliano leaned against the backrest and folded his hands in his lap.

_I am terribly sorry but I seem to be in a hurry, so forgive me if I step right into business. I have been told - he

47

began – that you are acquainted in the circumstances of Caucasus' death... you were very close to him, his favorite I would say. And being in the Council, a person of your intellect surely has connected some dots in this mystery. – he inquired, tucking the watch back into place and feeling the hilt of his dagger, which he kept hidden and ready for action.

The Cardinal slowly scratched his eyebrow. _His favorite... – he repeated quietly, with a blue smile – I've been told a version. More than one, clearly.

The nun passed by quietly, and began to remove the dishes from the desk. Perius looked at the Cardinal, waiting for a signal. _Don't worry, you can talk with confidence. I didn't know you were so interested in the Mandate and the Council, Perius. It surprises me, actually.

_Of course I do, it affects all of us. If it is no trouble, can I ask some questions?

Perius continued, as his eyes burned and his hand rested tightly, because the ship had arrived to turbulent waters. _First of all, I have a question: How is it that we are so short of a confirmation in an issue of such weight?

_It just so happens... there's no body left. Nor has his alleged killer been seen. Attempts to Seek him, or contact him, have failed. – the voice of the religious had become hard.

_As far as we know, Caucasus was not skilled in the arts of concealment. Where was he last seen? - Perius left behind his kind tone, which became suddenly threatening.

_At the Aegis Palace. He had retired to rest during the day, but by early evening he was no longer found. No signs of a struggle, or notes were found.

_Enigmatic... - Perius crossed arms and legs, with a thoughtful expression - Is there an official word in the Council?

_None. We don't have even a single evidence, only reports of the consequent failures to locate him. And they fight uselessly, and defame themselves. Thank the Lord the hostilities have not yet begun...

_Oh, I am afraid they will soon. I am certain that León will do his second injury before justice is done.

The Cardinal played nervously with his ring of gold and diamonds again. _León's attitude is fishy, I guess it's not completely wrong to be suspicious of him. Whoever is behind this, what do you think their next move will be?

Perius focused steadfastly on the Cardinal's weak eyes. _In my humble opinion, they will use the same trick, whatever it was, to eliminate the Akkadian, who would succeed him as Mandatary, despite the fact that he is not interested in the least. But once out of the board, Crest's loyalists would probably shrink, split in two.

_Well, there's still one more in antiquity before León...

_Yes, I admit. The long lost Garim, but has not been heard from him in many centuries. Unlike Caucasus and any of us, he was a master of concealment, so it is believed that he is still alive, somewhere. But you cannot count on him.

_Of course. - he made a great effort to get up, walked to one of the windows, drew the curtains a little and with his hands behind his back, looking out. He finally spoke up - It seems that the most beneficial situation would be, and I'm terribly sorry to say it, since he's a Virtuous too, for León to disappear... - he put his right hand to his forehead and made the sign of the cross.

Perius let out a sardonic laugh as he loosened his fingers from the hilt. _I can say I agree with that. It would surely soothe the situation. But he is hiding, if I did not hear wrong.

_Oh indeed, that's been discussed a lot. Since the last Council meeting he attended about two months ago, he has only sent out statements. The most skilled Seeker at the service of the Council says she can't find him.

_The so called Beatrix? - Perius interrupted, politely.

_Exactly. But it's known that she works for him. Or is rather his prisoner by now, so she's lying. We consulted another one, from the Crest ranks, named Ginebra Annet. Crest does have the motivation to know his whereabouts, but she stated that she couldn't find him, getting confusing readings when she tries. Either that or, that he's moving all the time. – Giuliano turned around and walked over to the desk.

_Which would not be completely odd...

_Possibly. And... there's been another rumor.

Perius raised an eyebrow, perhaps pushed by the air of secrecy that the Cardinal had suddenly gained.

_I got some information about a new armed group under the tutelage of León, or someone from his faction – he continued – Almost nothing is certain, just conjectures. On Crest they call them "The Menace", and they are very agitated on that matter.

The gentleman waved a negative gesture with his hand as he uncrossed his legs. _If it is so new, is it really a cause of concern?

_Let's hope not, Perius. Let's hope not.

The gentleman rose slightly. _Giuliano my friend, you have been extremely helpful, I will not take up any more of your time.

_You are welcome whenever you wish. I'm sorry I can't give you any more information that would be of value.

_No need to apologize, please. I hope to visit you soon in a happier occasion. It is been a pleasure nonetheless, Cardinal.

Giuliano set out to shake his hand out of habit, but then remembered that it was against the custom for physical contact between those who are like *them*, so he stopped. _The pleasure has been mine, bless you, Brother Perius.

Perius walked out the door, accompanied by the same woman who had let him in, and like before, she did not say a word. Filippo was waiting outside.

_How did the meeting go?

_Very picturesque. - the gentleman said - What did you want to tell me?

The priest noticed his diligent attitude, so he set about getting to the point. _I'm concerned about the Cardinal's situation. He is constantly plagued by hunger. It plagues us both. - he corrected himself quickly - but that is secondary, our faith allows us to continue like this, for now. The problem is his sight. The fact that he cannot be cured of this illness by his own is making him stagger, and I fear that it will end up... affecting him, and he will fall prey to his more primitive instincts. - he persigned himself twice as he completed the sentence. - He started this... journey to find a cure, and it still evades him, after all this years.

Perius remained silent, his expression unchanged.

_My question is: Is regeneration really that difficult? We've been studying biolog-

_It is certainly not a trivial matter, Brother. - he interrupted, noticeably in a hurry now - Studying the body helps, but true knowledge is obtained through experience, receiving wounds and healing. And the process is slow. Very slow. I am afraid that in his present situation he is even more delayed, as he is relegated to a peaceful life, and evidently has no talent for this complex art. Science would have a better answer to his ills, I estimate.

Filippo looked down, letting a sigh slip by. _I see. Thank you very much for the advice, Brother. And... something else if I may.

_Yes?

_I thank you for... understanding our position on the matter. We remain loyal to the Council and we know that Crest looks after our interests. Always loyal. - Filippo looked down at the gentleman's hands.

Perius watched him from top to bottom, as he probed his hidden edge covertly. He quickly regained his courteous and helpful demeanor. _No need to thank, we are all on the same side, I wish you all success with your endeavor. - He waved his hand, then walked away.

_Go with God. – He persigned himself twice more, while giving a blessing in a low voice to the newly departed.

Already in a rented vehicle heading for the airport, Perius took a personal assistant from his pocket, which vibrated incessantly.

_*Aló!*

_Mr. Perius, I have the information you requested. I sent it to you a minute ago – announced a voice in an odd monotone.

_Excellent news, I will check it right away. You have very done well.

_Thank you sir. I'm here to serve. – bowed Thomas Hicks, the US Secretary of Homeland Security.

PART 6: A MONSTER

Amelia went up to her apartment, trying to leave behind her fleeting encounter with the man who evaporates in the air, removing the sand that still resisted in her soles. She convinced herself that it was just a madman. A madman who knows magic tricks, of course. After all, she had too many problems to worry about. Unsolvable problems, the worst kind. As she entered, she was first pressured by the loneliness that had been dwelling there until her arrival, and that refused to leave. Secondly, because of the thick atmosphere, but it had more to do with her mood than with the environment. Her room was just as she had left it a few hours ago, messy and full of broken things. The drowsiness made its way through, so she quickly cleaned her bed, left the things on the floor, to lie down. It didn't take long to fall asleep.

She woke up distressed with the arrival of the late afternoon, but could not identify why, and strangely vital. She looked around for any sign of that sudden change, but only found the wall clock that indicated that it was 18 hours into October 23rd, a day like any other. In the back of her mind she felt that something had been done right, even though didn't know what. She was left with that feeling, pictured as a pearl floating in the mud. She decided to start different, from a new angle. After cleaning up and getting dressed, she visited a digital newspaper.

How hard could it be to get a job? She did it once, and could probably do it twice.

She went through the classifieds section from head to toe, and marked the ones that fit best and seemed interesting, updated her resume, and mailed it from her diminutive computer. She tried to sort out the mess around her, but it was especially difficult. Most of the things she had broken were of sentimental value, and just couldn't be thrown away. She got rid of the statuette, the posters, and even the clothes she wore the day before, but hesitated on whether or not to throw away the cross. It was a gift from her mother many years ago, when she was still alive. She decided to put it in a drawer, just out of respect for her.

Once the cleaning was done hours later, she was relieved. She retained her inner drive, with a little help she could make it bloom again. A small voice in her head reminded that she was only sweeping the darkness under the carpet, but quickly silenced it. It was not the time to think but to act. She wondered if she could make a phone call to one of her friends that argued with her recently. She sat there with the phone in her hands, checking the contact list over and over again, but found only an army of doubts, and gave up. Outside, seen through the window, the Sun was falling, painting the nearby buildings in orange tones, and reflecting intensely on the glass. She realized that she hadn't eaten anything for hours, and prepared something quick to go to bed. With a bit of luck, the one who had gracefully dodged her these days, they would call her in for an interview. She needed a job soon, the bills didn't pay themselves, and the savings were alarmingly low.

Already in bed, ready to sleep, she was assaulted again by all the unfortunate events she had lived with. She paralyzed herself, on purpose, to shed no more tears. There she was, caught up in that inner struggle, when the sound of her windows violently opening distracted her.

She couldn't have opened her eyes any more even wanting to. As the only defensive reaction, she pressed the sheets to her chest and shouted a drowned cry.

Kad peered in, as calmly as usual, wearing a dark gray suit and an unbuttoned shirt of the same shade under his large coat. His hair had become lighter again, the shape of his nose and cheekbones were slightly different, and the skin tone was slightly darker. He didn't have a beard now, and his haircut was carefully messy.

_Good evening, am I interrupting something? – he asked cordially and with a hint of sarcasm.

Amelia began to release a series of monosyllables for a few seconds before regaining her ability to utter complete sentences. _What are you doing here? How did you find me? – She tried to ask a third question, but didn't know which one.

_I followed you, of course.

Finally found a new one to ask, as she focused on remembering an object that would serve as a weapon for defense, that would be blunt enough, and above all, within her arm's reach. _What do you want from me?

_Well, I was expecting you could tell me what your first wish is.

She discarded a dozen things that were not suitable for wielding on the stranger's head: clothes, a pillow, a piece of the bed frame, a pin stuck in the wall, a teddy bear, a slipper, among others. _I wish you'd leave!

_Nah, that's too easy, and useless to you. - he said, putting a chair down to sit down. - Perhaps you should calm down a bit first...

He stared into her eyes, which flared intently. _I really think you need to calm down, don't you agree?

A strange sense of calm invaded Amelia's body as she listened to each word in slow motion, echoing back and forth in every corner of her mind. _Y-yes, I agree. - the answer escaped his mouth, barely with control over it.

_Much better. - Kad seemed to hesitate for a few moments - I apologize for the abrupt entry, next time I'll be sure to knock first.

_Th-there's no problem. - Amelia couldn't stop looking into Kad's exotic eyes, everything else was on the background.

_Let's get started, then. - he slammed his fist into the plastic door of the closet. The sound reached the girl's ears like a distant outburst, awakening her from her hypnotic phase.

_I hope you've already thought about what you want. - he continued.

_N-no, I didn't really think about it. - Amelia simply decided that the state of shock had triumphed, and let herself be carried away by the current.

Kad picked up a book and started browsing it. _What a shame...

_Who are you really?

_That's... a good question, but the answer's truly a long one. Let's just say I'm a person who has lived a long, long time, and knows some interesting things. The rest are details. - he spoke slowly, as he continued to turn the pages.

_How did you disappear last night? Is that a magic trick?

_No, it's not magic. I went up into smoke, and moved quickly out of your sight. - he continued to flip through the pages.

Amelia took a few seconds while breathing slowly. _Could you... do it again? - "Outward and not back" she thought to herself.

Kad left the book on the floor, and right there, where he was sitting, a cloud of fine red drops replaced his head, shoulders and then the rest of his body. The drops were bound and unbound all the time without ever becoming disconnected, dancing to an unnatural rhythm. They quickly moved to the other end of the room, falling to the ground, to form a solid body again from the legs of a bipedal creature, in a grotesque and unrealistic vision. False clothing formed on the body as it took on a humanoid form. Kad, restored to a solid form, stood, now dressed in the same black clothes he had worn the night of his meeting with Perius. He opened his coat, and looked at his suit. Gradually and in areas, it began to lighten, until it formed a gray tonality, similar to what it had previously had. _Mmm... I forgot that part.

Amelia was simply stunned. She had witnessed a life-changing event. Not in a bad way, though. She was genuinely impressed, arousing within her an unstoppable curiosity, as if she were trying to guess the tricks of an illusionist. _That was... - she didn't know how to describe it - fantastic... How... no, really, what are you? Was that blood, or what?

_Among other things, yes. - he walked to the same chair from where he came out, and sat with his legs crossed and his hands on his lap. His figure, so imposing, no longer made her afraid and she didn't understand why - I can travel short distances like this, or let myself be carried away by the wind if it is favorable. As for my nature... *those* like me... we have been called many things throughout history. Angels, demons, vampires, ghosts, zombies, druids, witches... *monsters*... and a lot more. People have told millions of stories about what we do or don't, more than half of them are bullshit.

Amelia didn't know whether to continue the talk or try to keep the monster away with the innocent cross in her drawer. She sought to regain control of her face and return it to normal. It was certainly the strangest thing that ever happened to her, but she felt no danger. _There are more like you then?

_Sure, lots of *them*... and right now they're fighting each other. - he made a mocking gesture with his hand - I'm not interested in those matters.

_Can everyone.... do that red smoke thing? - she helped the expression with a circular motion with one hand, while she carried the other, almost without knowing what she was doing, into the drawer next to her.

_Oh no, just a few. Only a handful. - he looked up slightly, up to the ceiling, with an air of sadness - Most of the time they crawl through the cities, butchering people.

_Wh... why are they killing people? - Kad's answer flabbergasted her, she didn't really expect thousands of creatures like this one to be out there, while she squeezed the cross in her hands. Now she didn't know if she took her out to feel protected by her mother, or to see if it worked like the vampire stories she knew.

_To feed. But enough talk, it's getting boring. – the man in black and grey moved his foot impatiently. – Are you going to make that wish or not?

_It means that, if I show you this cross, nothing's gonna happen to you? – she lifted the metal object towards Kad, as if they were in an exorcism film. She felt rather foolish as doing so, and blamed herself under her breath.

He smiled broadly, and waited a few moments before speaking. _No, nothing. Is it a gift for me?

_Mm-hmm. Yeah?

He stood up, walked towards her, and took the cross from her hands. He watched it for a few seconds as he held it in the palm, then put it in one of his pockets. _Thank you. – he replied in an ironic tone. – Well?

The girl took several seconds to answer, now somewhat annoyed that she had given up her cross without thinking. If he insisted so much on the subject of the wishes, perhaps that monster was really willing to fulfill them, and what did she needed the most at that moment, besides being five thousand kilometers away? – All right, I want to find a job. No – she corrected herself quickly – that is, having a lot of money. Being a millionaire.

_To find a job and have a million then. That'll be easy. You'll see how I'm a God who keeps his promises. – Kad's smile became malicious – Where would you like to work?

She remembered some of the places where she had sent emails that very evening, and the one that she really wanted to be hired over the rest. _In... Sinolta, it's a compa-

_Never mind, where is it? - he didn't let her finish her sentence.

_On La Guardia Avenue, eight blocks from here. It's the building with the triangular dome.

_That'll be all for now, first thing in the morning, introduce yourself by name. At night I'll come back for your millions thingy. See you soon. - he approached the window, placing one of his feet in the window frame, ready to jump.

_But I didn't tell you my last name.

_There's no need. - he pointed to the cover of the book on the seat, which stated "Property of: Amelia Alba." He jumped into the void, and disappeared as quickly as he arrived.

PART 7: THE SHADOWS OF THE CREST

Lykaios journey to the border had been smooth, except that he had to make a detour to avoid what he believed was one of his *own*. He disposed of the car as planned, leaving it on the side of a road through the dense foliage, and walked a couple of miles to a hotel outside Marseille. He lamented that he had not been able to make it all the way in time in the same night, stopping like that for so long was exasperating. But if something happened during the day on his trip he would be at a clear disadvantage on a sunny day, there was no choice. He slept for a few hours, and spent the rest polishing his metamorphic abilities. Those are not only the capability to change appearance, but also texture and color. But most of all, doing it fast. Changing from one state to another requires great concentration, practice, energy and a great deal of self-knowledge. He did not let a single day go by without practicing any of his arts.

Behind his conscious mind, he continued to worry about his prey's suspicions, which made him doubt his own abilities. But it wasn't the only thing. In Marseille, he would probably cross paths with Anzhelika Petrova. He hated and admired her at the same time. Ever since he met her centuries ago, she's always been ahead of him. Her talent and skill as a Shadow were simply superior, even being so "young". He used to say and repeat to himself that he would overcome her one day, when the generational gap shortened and time passed.

What infuriated him the most was that she took his rivalry as a game, something humorous to have fun with, while he had her as a role model to follow and surpass in the last half of his life. And the worst part, she never saw him as a man. Although learning to change shapes renders appearance worthless, his mental image of Anzhelika was always one of radiant beauty, enveloped in a coldness he felt in no other person. She was one in a trillion. And she would never be his.

As the afternoon fell, he mobilized again. When he left the hotel, he changed the form of his face, added some facial hair and skin tone, but left the rest the same, especially his classic black uniform. He took a taxi with a driver - a relic that resisted oblivion - with which he traveled to a few streets away from his destination. He hesitated to pay or feed with the taxi driver, but remembered that he had already given him a service, so he handed over the sum indicated on the meter and left on foot. He came across an old, discolored mansion with a neglected garden and dead trees. Some of the columns of what was once a large house were broken and split in the middle, the tiles cracked everywhere, as were the walls, where there was hardly any trace of paint. He opened the iron gates, which squeaked horribly, and walked in to the front door. There he stopped, and knocked four times. A piercing voice was heard on the other side, speaking in French.

_Go away, there's nothing to see here.

_That's what I'll do as soon as I can get the flowers. - he answered with the keywords.

The old iron bolt made a dull metallic sound, and the heavy, aging door opened. Behind it was a large, hard-bodied man, dressed in jeans and a tight T-shirt, careless about the low temperature. A small medallion with the figure of a wing with sharp feathers, the Crest emblem, hung from its neck. _Welcome, Mr. Lykaios.

As only greeting, he made eye contact with the man, to continue his march inside the house, while behind him the door closed again. Inside the darkness was almost total, only a few lamps lit up the enormous room. He headed for the kitchen, where two more men were sitting at a table playing cards. Hanging from their necks was the same winged medallion that indicated an Initiate. Lykaios had long ago been able to do without it. They turned to examine the newcomer thoroughly and with little decorum, and then continued their game. He bent down and pulled a huge rusted metal hoop, which opened the entrance to the basement. From the inside could be seen that it was much better lit than the rest of the place. He stepped down the narrow staircase, closing the small door behind him.

The basement was not only better lit, but infinitely better preserved. The concrete walls were fresh. Above them hung neon light tubes, and underneath these were huge military green cabinets. The place was divided into four compartments, the entrance, two at the sides and a central one. He was heading for the middle one. A few steps before reaching the door, a female voice resonated from the inside. _Come in.

He opened the door, and entered. The underground room, though small, was overflowing with objects. On the north wall was a library that ran from the ceiling to the floor, filled with books. The south wall had a shelf, as high as the library, with objects of all shapes and sizes. Items that a collector would give their family away to get hold. These were piled up, without too much care, to give room for another series of objects that had been placed more recently: ammunition of various calibers. On the east wall was a giant picture of Caucasus with his most known facial features. Underneath it, on the ground, several boxes of weapons were piled up. In the middle was a modest wooden desk with a chair. Sitting behind it was Eylem, leader and founder of the Crest faction. Her slim, relatively short appearance contrasted with her energetic personality, while the soft, rounded shape of her nose betrayed her stabbing character. Her short and straight hair shone in the light of the neon lights on the ceiling. She had always kept her body small and agile, and her appearance had not interested her in the least for way too long. At Crest she was judged for her leadership, power and intelligence, and nothing else. Thus had she taught her disciples.

She stared sternly at the guest. _Lykaios, we are going through hard times, we can put aside this face-to-face summaries until the situation normalizes... - she let out a short sigh - What news do you have?

Lykaios stood in front of his interrogator. _As ordered, I followed Perius in his scheduled meeting with the Akkadian. They both showed up, and I witnessed their conversation. Since then, I followed the Akkadian to Barcelona, Spain. There, the parameters of my mission changed, as I was forced to fabricate an encounter with a human woman that would serve as a toy for him, to buy enough time.

_Typical of him. - Eylem smirked as she leaned on the back of her seat.

_As far as I could perceive, the improvisation was successful. As expected, he refuses to participate in the conflict in any way. He just seems interested in letting himself die.

The woman folded her arms as she twisted a pen in her hand. _Perius warned me about that. The bastard couldn't be more useless... in the state of things he chose the worst option.

_Do you think he'll let himself be murdered, if that's the case?

_Of course not. The Akkadian is a war machine, if someone dangerous faces him, he will enjoy tearing them to pieces. The problem is that maybe he won't win this time around.

Lykaios waited a few moments before asking. _Should I continue my assignment?

Eylem placed her hand on the chin in a thoughtful gesture. _Yeah, follow him. Your mission will also be to disarm any attempt of Menace to contact him, if it has not already occurred. Last thing we need now is for them to convince him to attack us... You are allowed to kill the contact, as long as you are able to do so quietly. Otherwise we'll send someone more qualified. And in any case, *please* contact me directly by phone. You'll have to learn to be more flexible. The devices we have are safe.

Those words particularly hurt Lykaios, but he remained impassive, not reacting at all.

_Any questions?

_No, ma'am. That's perfectly clear.

_Superb, you can go now.

The Shadow stepped out of the cabin, and once out of sight of his leader, let the anger escape as quietly as he could. Again, he felt that all his work was not received as it should have been. He deeply respected Eylem, she was the voice of order within the anarchy that reigned. Crest was a very recent organization, just a few centuries old, but he felt attached to it. Its supporters faithfully followed the customs, which had maintained peace and equilibrium for millennia, as it had been during the prolonged rule of Caucasus. Now all that staggered from its foundations, by a clear blow. And he would do everything in his power to prevent the fall. If only they would acknowledge his merits...

He climbed up the ladder one more time, and again the men playing cards examined him. As he continued through the main room, he noticed a new presence. Some object, among those present, was a Shadow, and one not too skilled. It took him about ten seconds to identify it. He glanced with marked disdain at a strangely uneven-looking wooden box under an old table. He did not recognize the author of such an obvious deception, but he did not need to. He was angry that that one had the same rank as him.

The big man opened the door again, this time without a word.

As he mapped out a travel plan to resume his assignment, a voice interrupted his thoughts. _What? Were you planning on leaving without saying hello, little boy?

He turned in alarm to both sides, but found nothing. Now he was angrier, he really fancied that he actually managed to get out of it, but didn't. And he had walked into her trap without noticing anything for the umpteenth time. _Lika, good to... see you. – the tone of his voice was a mixture of powerlessness and reluctance.

_*See me* you say? You don't even know where I'm hiding.

From a tree a few steps away, the bark began to mold into a human figure. It was completed noticeably faster than it typically takes him to complete. Anzhelika was recreated as a tall, slender woman with straight black hair, which fell wavy on her face with fine features and manufactured beauty. A black uniform was also created, adjusted to the body, with the same strange and indescribable texture similar to leather as his. The cold aura around her was practically palpable, while the tone of her words was mocking and hurtful. _Looking good, cub.

_Thank you very much. You're still as crafty as ever.

_The missions I am assigned are getting more and more complicated, they keep me sharp.

_You don't seem too worried about it. If you're in the middle of one, shouldn't you leave?

_That's right, but my flight leaves tomorrow, I have to wait until then.

_Oh, I understand. I, on the other hand, have to get going. Right now.

71

_Are you still spying on the Akkadian? It sounds monotonous... except he discovers you, in which case you'll probably end up in a boom... - she wrapped up the sentence with a scornful smile, snapping her fingers simulating an explosion.

_He won't. - the curiosity ended up beating the desire to get out of there quickly. - Can you talk about your mission, or is it a secret?

_It is a secret, but it doesn't matter if I tell it to you, wolfy boy. - Anzhelika put her hair back in place, then started braiding it. - I'm going to Berlin to investigate the new Menace's combat cell.

_...What's so special about it?

_We don't know, that's why I'm going to investigate it. But Eylem thinks it's critical.

_I wish you good luck then. - he shut down tight.

_You too, little boy. - she winked one eye smiling mockingly.

Lykaios continued toward the exit with a steady pace and evident moodiness. Among all the things he hated, the biggest was losing his imperturbable and professional character. He walked several streets, until he put his head in order and regained balance. He used a taxi to take him to the outskirts where he would repeat the same plan, but along different routes. Next time he'd use the assigned phone, he learned his lesson.

The subject of Menace remained floating in his mind, and how he would manage to subtly ask about it when he returned.

PART 8: THE GENIE IN THE BOTTLE

Amelia woke up very early that morning. The events of the previous night were so insane that they resembled a dream more than reality. As if on autopilot, she washed, applied makeup and formally dressed in a skirt, a pink blouse and black jacket. She doubted Kad's words, but what harm could it do to show up anyway? In case they didn't hear from her (which was most likely) she could pretend to leave a paper résumé and retire. It was a strange plan and it felt like twenty years in the past, (who used paper nowadays?) but it was better than looking like a fool. She finished with the last details, which ironically took longer than everything previous, and left.

She walked the few streets that separated her from the destiny company, and before arriving she armed herself with strength. Sinolta's building was ultramodern. In the middle of the reception hall was an asymmetrical statue made of metal, illuminated by a circle of spots projecting different holograms. The floor was entirely carpeted with this new self-cleaning material, and on the walls hung pictures with surrealist art, or with landscapes of beautiful and non-existent places. Two women were waiting behind a very elegant counter, taking calls. She approached, once she found an "Information" sign in front of them.

_Good morning... My name is Amelia Alba. – she hesitated for a brief moment and wondered if she was really going to say the following – Is it possible that I was asked for an interview today?

One of the secretaries left the phone on a side, a crystalline tablet with a transparent screen, resting on her neck to answer her. _One moment please. – she typed on her computer, but because of her expression, she couldn't find what she was looking for – Alba told me?

_Yes. – Amelia had already begun to think of a phrase credible enough to get out of there with dignity.

The secretary left the call on hold to make another. _Mr. Ruberte? There's one person, Amelia Alba, she says she has a... yes, all right, I'll let her know. – she turned to her – Yes, you have an appointment with the Human Resources Manager, he's on the third floor, by the elevator over there. – she pointed to the left.

_Thank you very much. – The girl's astonished expression didn't go unnoticed.

She headed for the elevator, went in and out, this time a lot more nervous. Knocked on the door and she was received by another woman, who kindly told her to wait. No more than twenty seconds passed when she heard his name. _Miss Alba, please come in.

Now she was very, very nervous. She didn't know what the hell Kad had done, but suddenly she had a real interview with the manager. What was she supposed to say? "Hi, how are you, maybe a guy who looks normal talked to you last night, but can go up in smoke and change the color of his clothes". Too late, she was already inside.

The office looked similar to the rest of the building, refined, modern, with a lot of money invested. Behind the desk sat a chubby-looking, gray-haired person in his fifties. He looked elegant, however, with a gray striped suit and a lush red fluorescent tie. As she arrived, his gaze met hers. She noticed something strange, as if both eyes were made of glass, virtually expressionless. Like a puppet.

_Come in, miss, we finally met!

_Mmm... yes, thank you. - Amelia didn't really know what to say to that, she just sat down and listened.

_Good, good... I'm very happy to see you. - he began to shuffle maniacally through the files on the computer - Here... here! This is your contract, miss, from this moment on you are my personal assistant. My... another assistant... will help you with the rest. - he extended the contract to her, with an empty smile on his face.

Amelia could no longer contain her disconcerted face, which simply sprouted outward.

_Read it carefully, you can ask Roxana any questions you have. Welcome aboard! - he extended one hand to her.

She accepted the handshake with the same expression as before, and walked out slowly. Behind her she could hear the man speaking quietly to himself, repeating over and over again, "This was a good idea, oh yes, a very good idea, an idea very good".

She turned to the woman who had previously attended her.

_Are you Miss Roxana?

_Yes, no need for formalities, please have a seat.

Roxana was a girl of her age, thin, with a round face, short, red hair and a bow tie. _Well, that was a quick interview. – she turned around to search in her screen.

Amelia lost to her curiosity. _Excuse me for asking, but is Mr. Ruberte always... like this?

Roxana turned her head, but it took her a long second to answer. _No, he's been weird since this morning. He mentioned to me three times that someone important was coming.

She took the time to read the contract carefully, finding the working conditions very favorable, and the salary excellent. Throughout the whole process a small voice constantly distracted her, telling her that she couldn't believe what was happening, while another one answered that yes, it was right to disbelieve. She finally signed.

_That's it, you'll start tomorrow, in this office. Early in the morning I'll take you on a short tour, so you can get acquainted with the place. All right, welcome, Amelia. - they greeted each other with a quick handshake.

Once outside, she set out for her home. All that was beyond her. She couldn't believe it would have been that easy, and pinched her cheek comically, smiling from ear to ear.

She spent the afternoon cleaning her apartment completely, except for her father's room, which preferred to leave until later. A lawyer had contacted her hours earlier to assist with the accident trial and the family inheritance, which was not much more than the place where she lived, and a few assets, but served to remind her of how lonely she had been left in the world. At least... some of it had been put back together, thanks to the strange smoke-man.

Before the Sun went down, she discovered herself getting ready for when Kad arrived. She was not sure if she liked him or not, but the voice of reason announced that such a subject was not acceptable, so she gave up. Hours passed, and no one showed up or rang the doorbell. She made herself dinner and ate. When finished, she heard several taps in the window, and then a loud one. The sudden wind came in and got to her. A voice was heard from the room. _Hey, where are you?

She ran away, with sudden distress. To find him snooping around her things on the shelves.

Kad continued to look at the shelf as if nothing had happened. He wore his usual overcoat, the suit of the previous time but darker, and his eyebrows slightly more populous. _Here you are. How'd it go?

_Hello Kad... - the same feeling of fear she had last night came back as a tidal wave over her head.

He turned around to look at her. _Did I scare you again? I knocked before coming in this time.

_A little, yes. - she made a huge effort to calm down, and decided to start somewhere - Thanks for the job, I've been hired. I start tomorrow, actually.

_Congratulations. - Kad took a book off the shelf and started to browse through it.

_How did you do it? Do you have any friends there?

He sat in the same chair as the night before. _No, I don't have any friends there. I just asked nicely for the manager's address, went over there and talked to him. We agreed that it would be a *very good idea* if they hired you, and then I left - he looked up to look at her and smiled hypocritically - Quite easy, no?

Amelia raised an eyebrow. _Was that it? Did you threaten him with something?

_No, we had a very affable chat. I can be convincing when I want to.

_How... how do you do it? Is it hypnosis?

_Exactly. – Kad put the book down and took another one.

Amelia didn't really expect that answer. One more trick added to the strange, kind monster that came in through the window whenever he felt like it. A dozen questions came up, but she knew he would only answer one or two before he lost his temper and changed the subject. _Is it... hard to do?

_Not when you know how. It took me a long time to learn, but it is useful.

This was problematic, she disliked the idea that anyone could come and play with her mind, but if he said that it could be learned, she could too, right? She folded her arms and narrowed the eyes as she took a breath to drop the question. _And... could you teach me how to do it, or how to defend myself so it can't be used against me?

Kad responded with a calm but flaming look. _I could... is that your second wish?

She deliberated with herself for a few moments. _I'm not sure, I'd really like to learn how to influence people.

Kad closed the book tightly, stacked it with the others, and placed his hands on the arms of the chair. _You have to keep in mind that you will not reach the same level I have, you would need some... no, *a lot* of practice time. But, if you turn out to be talented and practice every day, you might become good. It would be a strange wish though, it's more up to you than to me.

_I dunno, but it sounds very interesting. – a little doubt fell soft as an iron hammer in her head – Wait a minute... did you ever use that on me?

_Yes, twice.

She was perplexed, unable to determine when.

_One when you were on the beach and the other last night to calm you down. – he continued, standing up to go to the window – Well, if you want to learn about it, you have to start with something basic. Get a mirror and put it in a comfortable place. What you are going to do is look into it, and convince yourself of a lie that is not too obvious, until you believe it to be true. Pay attention to how you do it and what you think about it. You can write it down somewhere if it helps you. That's where you begin, learn to deceive yourself and know when this happens. I'll be back in a few days, and we'll continue... but you'd better think of something else to ask me. – he closed the sentence looking at her sideways.

_O-okay, I'll do that. Thanks...

_Oh, I almost forgot. – Kad took a piece of paper out of his pocket and handed it – I took the trouble to arrange a bank account for you, don't ask how. This transfer was made a few hours ago, now you own a fixed term, and it's at your name. The manager has been very kind in this regard. If you look it up, you'll find that it adds up capital month by month. You're not a millionaire now, but you will be in about two years. With this, your first wish is fulfilled. - He smiled broadly, showing his teeth. See you soon.

In no time at all, the blood-red cloud formed again and quickly slipped away.

Amelia looked at the numbers that were printed on the paper in her hand. It took her some time to understand what it meant. She made a quick calculation with the annual percentage rate listed there. She opened her eyes wide, until they hurt.

PART 9: PANDORA'S BOX

Kad returned to the solid state on the rooftop of Amelia's building, standing with his hands in his pockets. _So, when are you going out?

On the adjacent roof, a figure appeared. It stepped out from behind a small room, wearing an elegant tuxedo, shiny shoes and a bow on his neck. He was a tall, stocky man, his hair carefully combed backwards. He held his hands one on top of the other in front of him, appearing relaxed, looking down at Kad from above.

_Good evening, I hope I'm not inconvenient, but I have a few words to cross with you.

Seeing no reaction, he continued. _Can I take a few minutes of your time?

Kad kept looking upward, calmly and with a delicate but not very subtle mocking tone. _Yeah, sure. Come closer.

The tuxedo man approached the edge of the roof and jumped to fall a few meters from Kad, who continued to watch him unfazed.

_I shall introduce myself, my name is Pierre Chambeaux, it is a great pleasure to meet you personally Mr. Akkadian. Your reputation is admirable to me. - he extended his hand, in a rigid and formal gesture, far from the tradition.

Kad looked down briefly to observe the unusual greeting, to stare mercilessly into Pierre's eyes. _Why are you here?

_I have been sent to make a request, appealing to your well-known generosity. - he said, quickly withdrawing his hand - The Council needs you, sir. We want you to present yourself as the new Mandatary and, if you do not wish to remain in power, resign. In this way we will avoid a major conflict among *our own*, the transition will be peaceful without regretting any victims.

_What a nice plan, who sent you Pierre?

_Mr. León, of course. We are very interested in keeping the peace, unlike the faction that calls itself Crest, which unfortunately seeks an escalation of violence, with no good end in sight.

_How wicked are those guys from Crest, huh? But there's a problem with all this, Pierre. I'm not interested in political games. If you want, go tell them I gave you the Mandate, I don't care.

_I'm afraid that's not possible. Neither party will accept... - he paused for a moment - my word instead of yours. It will have to be in person, at the Aegis Palace.

_I don't feel like going there. Maybe someday I'll pay a surprise visit.

Chambeaux squeezed his jaw slightly, looking noticeably thoughtful. _No need to answer my request today, sir. You might answer me tomorrow, after you've thought it over. At any place you like.

_There's no need, you can have my resp-

_Please, sir – he interrupted quickly – if you give me your answer tomorrow, I promise I'll never again bother you in any way, what do you think?

_I could have taken care of that myself, but to wipe out a diplomat is dull. – Kad shrugged.

_Excellent, how about us meeting right here, in this very spot?

His flaming eyes flickered suddenly, as he became serious. _No. It's preferable on that rooftop. – he pointed his chin toward a nearby building a few stories higher.

_We are in agreement then. Have a good rest during the day. – he walked away to the staircase, which he stepped down at a steady pace.

Getting to Barcelona was easy for Lykaios. He was almost worried that no one had even tried to follow him in any way. He doubted whether his stay there justified hunting several humans as the previous time, or whether it was more efficient to do it one by one as he needed them, so he set about finding a place of similar characteristics to the old one, with the infallible basement. He found one where only one person lived, who served as the first easy victim. He made sure to remember his face, to imitate it in an emergency. He conditioned one of the rooms by covering its windows and openings so that the light would not pass through, and left when finished, to find his prey again. He roamed the places where he was most likely to find it, but without success. Asked for "unusual" moves from his *own people*, that had nothing to do with both sides, trying to be as subtle as possible and paying the right amount. Just as he could ask for someone else, someone else could ask for him, and also asked about the gypsy woman, but no one had seen her. He noticed that he had made a mistake, wasting too much time following traces he already had. Excessive prudence led him to jeopardize the mission. Eylem was right, he should have used the phone, but he just didn't trust the security of the communication. The night was over, and had to leave. Internally, he felt a little disoriented and disappointed not being able to find Kad, but regained his strength by convincing himself that he would make it the following night.

During the day, in addition to resting the body, he traced the points where it was most likely to be found. If he had no results by midnight, he would be forced to phone and ask a Seeker to locate him. Seekers were strange people, they could locate anyone they knew, some needing only a garment or a personal object. Most of them were frauds, but a handful of them were excels. But that option displeased him completely, and it was a mockery to his tracking skills. He devoted himself to the practice with knives until it was time to go out again.

With the nightfall of the 25th he went out to some of the places closest to his new lair, and then went to the apartment of his Case number 2, his tailor-made victim. From the shadows, he saw something. There was a man standing, not too hidden, on one of the nearby rooftops. That must have been León's contact, just as he and Eylem suspected would appear to contact the Akkadian, and had to prevent it at all costs. He stepped stealthily into the twilight, making sure the loaded pistol in his jacket and the knives in his pockets were ready for use.

When he was close, he discovered that he had been reckless in his movements. There was someone else watching, crouched in the night, and he'd been seen. The man, warned, hurriedly ran to his left, leaping toward the adjoining building. There was no turning back, he had to pursue him as quickly as possible, and then hunt down the observer. Fired a few shots as he ran, and two of them struck the tuxedo man, who was clearly affected by the pain. Lykaios jumped one more building with great agility, continuing to fire another burst, this time without hitting. Leapt at great speed toward the rooftop where the mysterious man had remained, and saw him crouching down, pulling something from under a sheet and seeking refuge from another burst. He could see his face covered in sweat as he pointed that hidden object at him. It was a huge rifle. The shots sounded like thunder as he tried to sneak behind a column. He understood in a split second that these were explosive munitions. If any of them caught him, he'd be knocked flat until he could reform. He ducked instinctively when he heard another series of shots. The second figure in hiding was shooting from somewhere. He had lost the initiative again, and had to get out of there. The difference in firepower was gigantic, and he doubted the damage he could do with his weapon. The only chance was to get closer and thus double his effectiveness. He blinked heavily, and let out a sigh.

He changed the clip of the gun, and after throwing one of his knives against a wall as a distraction, he threw himself at the tuxedo man zigzagging along with the speed of a cougar, surrounded by the cement dust from the shots. A first shot could be heard hitting away from him. He fired three times at the tuxedo, and turned to make another three as suppressive fire at the concealed shooter. A second shot went by whistling into his ear, and finally a third. He couldn't hear it, only felt a discomfort in his belly as he looked face to face at his enemy only two meters away. With his head hyper accelerated he managed to shoot him once more before the charge finally exploded. Horrifying pain overwhelmed him completely. He fell to his knees to the ground, trying to cover with one hand the hole that had suddenly appeared in his side, only to receive two more explosive charges, this time on his chest and ribs. His senses failed him, and rushed all the way down, lying in a pool of blood. With his last strength, he tried to collect as much of his flesh and blood with his arm to reabsorb it, but the bleeding was excessive. On the brink of death his ear heard nothing but echoes. Several wobbly footsteps sounded loud as they approached. It was the end.

Blurry images began to parade as mistimed flashes, of his adolescence when he was human and lived in poverty on the island of Crete, and swore that one day through his efforts he would become someone in the world. The day he met Eylem, the person who made him what he was. He remembered his hated rival and impossible love, Lika, and the few times she smiled at him with less coldness than usual. And that was the last thought left in his mind when a final shot came to him.

Chambeaux fell to his knees on the blood of his recent victim, leaning on the enormous rifle that still fumed at its end. He was totally exhausted, and the wounds were causing him stinging pain. His restorative ability was very poor, and consumed by the nerves as he was at the time, he could not concentrate. He wiped the sweat from his forehead as he recalled the intensive survival training at *Prima-Gestalt* that could save his life, as long as he could begin to close those wounds.

_Are you okay? - a voice in French was heard from behind him.

He turned suddenly to the voice, and it took him a few moments to realize the source. Between gasps he could weave an answer. _No... it's hard for me to... concentrate.

_If you don't do it soon, you're gonna bleed to death. I guess this is it... we've opened Pandora's Box. This guy here must be a Shadow - she said, pointing to Lykaios's body - and I doubt he is alone. They must have an informant in town, and even if they don't, when this one here fails to report, they will know that he was involved in a small accident.

_I didn't... expect this... Soleil. - Pierre's face was constantly twisting from the punctures.

Soleil stood with a similar rifle in his hands, looking around. She was a young-looking woman, with long hair and a ponytail combed back, cold and coarse eyes, as if she distrusted absolutely anything that could move. She was dressed in a dark blue uniform, heavy boots, a beret of the same color on her head and safety goggles that protected her eyes, her most precious gift. Her ability to detect traces of people's aura was the reason she was recruited at *Prima-Gestalt* in the first place. There she was given military training, especially in telecommunications and remote sensing. At that moment she felt anxious, and happy? Because of the chaos that was approaching.

_You expected this. You told the Akkadian you'd see him today, to give *Speerspitze* time to get to the city. We must now warn of the failure of this mission, so that the next one can begin, and get out of here as soon as possible.

_No, Soleil... don't call... please. - Pierre dropped the heavy weapon, to sit on the floor. - It's still... it's still possible.

Soleil laughed with some malignancy. _No, Chambeaux, look at you, this has already been decided. - she was distracted shaking some dust off her trousers - On the other hand, this corrupt world could use a little action. - She took a satellite phone out of her belt and dialed a number.

_No... there's still time... I can convince the Akkadian... please don't call... - he stopped for a sudden coughing fit, spitting out some drops of blood.

_Keep quiet, will you? You're such a dumb-

Soleil was going to say something else, as she held the phone to her ear, but could not. She felt a chill running down her spine, and a few drops of sweat on her temples. Something horrible had arrived.

_You've been having fun, little darlings. - Kad's voice rang out behind both their backs, standing quietly with the hands in his pockets.

Soleil's eyes slowly injected with tears of terror as she turned to look at Kad's imposing figure, his wild and overwhelming aura, his black intentions. She could barely move. Her ears were blocked by the pressure. From the phone a voice was waiting in anticipation.

_Please, sir... stop her, don't let her communicate... – Pierre's breathing was more and more forced. – Please...

Kad turned to face the young woman. _You're not going to put that down, are you? – with a quick movement of the arm, it stretched out unnaturally in circles like a whip, on whose tip his hand had hardened like bone, and sharpened like a sword. He wiped away cleanly Soleil's hand holding the telephone, falling to the ground both flesh and technology. A loud scream tore through the night veil.

That monster's intentions were clear. He wasn't going to let her live. She hated with all her might the commander who had entrusted her with this mission, that idiot Chambeaux and his illusions of keeping the peace, and the horror that was about to kill her. It wasn't the end she pictured, not at all. She lifted the weapon to fire, but the monster had already moved behind her and held her by the throat. Squeezed the trigger as hard as she could, and some ammunition got stuck in Kad's feet, causing a dull burst and a cloud of dust and blood, but no real damage. The hammer struck several more times before she realized there was nothing left in the clip, but her finger was still stuck on the trigger. There was nothing she could do now, but perhaps she could give one last gift to the treacherous world she so loathed. Between tears and pain, she observed that the communication was still open. She glanced sidelong at the aberration and knew she had to shout and do it quickly. _Mission failed! Mis–! - was all she could say before Kad choked her.

The diplomat made an enormous effort to check whether the satellite phone was still working, and was greatly discouraged when he found out that it was, with a voice on the other side giving verbal confirmation. He had been very self-confident when he was assigned to the mission, he knew that if he was successful it would mean his entry through the front door to the new Council of León, where he would begin to forge a new order for his own and for humanity. And now it was all over. Even his own energies had betrayed him.

He continued to cough up more and more blood, the same that gushed from his wounds unceasingly. _It's... it's late... they'll come for you now... and the war will start.

Kad watched the young diplomat condescendingly as he continued to hold Soleil's throat, agitating in pain and lack of oxygen. _Man, you really are passionate for peace... but you won't achieve it dying in the process. Hold up.

Pierre collapsed completely on the ground beside Lykaios. He tried to formulate words, but they just wouldn't come out of his mouth. Along with his hopes to save them all, he had lost the will to fight the life that was escaping through his open arteries. He stood there, as approaching heartbeat to heartbeat to the unknown.

Kad stomped the device down, released the girl from the neck, making her fall to the ground. He pierced her with a stern look in his eye. _Speak, who are those supposed to be coming after me?

Soleil coughed several times until she was able to recover. Her wrist had already stopped bleeding, and the wound was beginning to close. _Those who killed Caucasus are close. – she coughed again – You won't be able to handle them. –A smile full of revenge surfaced in between the tears of terror.

Kad bent down to meet her face to face. _Good, good. I was hoping they'd show up at last. – he returned a similar expression and raised a hand threateningly. He stayed like that for two seconds that seemed like an eternity, as if he doubted the real value of a life. Finally he rose to his feet, stared at the Shadow's inert body, that of the dying Pierre, the young woman's horrified eyes. He grimaced weirdly, and vanished with the wind.

PART 10: SPEARHEAD

As soon as the wheels of the plane touched the runway of Berlin's Schönefeld airport, Anzhelika set in motion. Disguised as an elderly woman, she stepped steadfastly into the bathroom, ignoring the stewardesses' warnings. Once inside, she transformed her hand into a hard bone cone and her arm into a huge muscle mass. She pierced a hole in the fuselage, and snuck down through it almost liquid, bringing a small black bag with her. She carried even less than any other Shadow, only a mobile phone, as everything else she might need was held in her memory or supplied with her own skill. That gave her a greater ability to quickly transform herself into whatever was required, and leave little behind that betrayed her. Again in human form she ran into the darkness, barely broken by the lights of the nearby towers. The snow was slowly falling over the whole place, as if the whole world had slowed down, giving the sensation of fantasy rather than reality. She leapt over a cold wire fence, changed form to a voluptuous young woman with few clothes, and waited on the side of the road. A motorist stopped at her signal, smiling and inviting to get in. Anzhelika broke his neck, and hid him behind the grove a few meters away. Getting a vehicle has always been easy for her. She drove in automatic, adopting the face of the recently deceased to go unnoticed by the other cars, which would otherwise be alerted of a manual car.

She left the car parked with the battery disconnected so it wouldn't send location signals, and started walking, she knew the tricks of the trade well. The facility she was heading was far from the city, in the exact place where she had been informed. From the main trail there was a dirt road leading into a wired field with several "private property" signs. A hundred meters ahead the road was paved, leading to a complex of several low buildings, surrounding a maneuvering area where some cargo trucks were stationed. Soldiers in camouflaged arctic uniforms and machine guns surveyed the unloading of several boxes from one of the trucks. She took a few minutes to plan her entry, filling her lungs with the fragrance of the sap of the trees around her. She left her small bag hidden in a mound of snow behind a low wall, took the form of a soldier and walked absently towards the nearest building. Passed by one of the soldiers guarding the entrance, with which she exchanged a few words, noticing that he had recently been *transformed*. It was straightforward: beginners are often euphoric, eager to experience their newfound state in whatever comes to mind. Then they discover that it is exactly the same as before, only now they have much, much more time to do it. Everything except for the food of course, which serves less and less to relieve the dreadful hunger every day. Being a beginner clearly sucks.

She persuaded him to escort her to watch away from there, which the guard couldn't resist. Once away, she murdered him, adopted his face, quickly buried the body in the snow after removing his gun and identification. A piece of cake. First suspicion: no a security aircraft in sight. Strange nowadays.

She retraced her steps and finally got in. That particular building was two stories high, about fifty meters long by thirty meters wide and was of very recent construction. It was the tallest of the buildings in the area, and the only one that didn't look like a vehicle hangar. Inside it looked like a hospital, or a medical center of some kind equipped with state-of-the-art technology, all of which the astronomical amount of money that León and his group could buy. People wearing white overalls and writing on their touch screens walked down the aisles. Two who passed by stared at her sideways. She assumed it was rare that one of the soldiers would get inside the facility, so she had to change form again. And not only that. Both were human, but they had an absent expression as if someone had been poking around in their minds at a deep level for a long time. She figured it was necessary so they wouldn't run scared at *dinnertime*.

She followed them quietly until they split up and chose one to stalk. He was a fat man, with beard and a lot of gray hair, wearing his inevitable white coat. She waited for him to enter one of the offices, which he did, but only after swiping a card, entering a code and being accepted by a retinal scanner. The chubby man seemed to have access to some interesting places. Bingo. Like lightning, she went behind him and pushed him so hard that he fell to the ground. The office was relatively small and separated into two sections by a mirrored glass. In one there were several monitors and computers of the latest generation, the other one was empty, undoubtedly for observation of something, or someone. Against the wall opposite to the door, a filing cabinet clashed with the high-tech environment of the place, accompanied by a gleaming aluminum water dispenser. The fat man stammered in place, clearly nervous about the situation.

Anzhelika disguised as the late soldier glanced darkly at him as she made sure no one came and closed the door. _Quiet.

The man tried to scream, but no sound came out of his throat.

_You're going to be very still and very quiet while you listen to my voice. Very still. Very quiet.

The effect was almost immediate, the man was unable to move or make any noise, he just lay flat on the ground with the same expression a wounded deer would have.

_I want you to tell me what place this is and what you do here.

After a few seconds, she got an answer. _Prima-Gestalt. We're training the new ones.

_What is your personal password?

_...34692001.

_Is it the same one that gives access to the computers?

_...No.

_What is it?

_Capital M, g, g, g, h, hyphen, 431212.

She logged into the computer using the ID name and password. She started going through the files with the man still trying to move his muscles without success. She copied the ones she was most interested in, using a memory stick she found on the desk.

_Does it bother you if I snoop through your e-mails? I hope not because I'm already doing it. – she said smugly as she entered the user's mailbox.

She stumbled upon something interesting: A speech on the need for the installation of a new scheme that would be pioneer in the world. She turned to see her hostage and after checking that he was not going anywhere, sat down comfortably. She felt comfortable making fools out of her enemies. What she read surprised her quite a bit.

In short, *Prima-Gestalt* was a prototype establishment for the transformation of humans with "special talents" into what they call *neomensch*. Basically, she thought, one more name to refer to her *own*, nothing special by the way. There are trained in various disciplines depending on their development, in addition to studying their behavior. They have created two branches, a scientific and a military one, which in turn is divided into conventional and non-conventional military, while the other into several sections, most of them quite regular except for the *neomenschgenetik*, which involved development from embryos created using genetic engineering. She didn't find any more about it among the other files, she had to search through someone else's. She copied everything, closed the session, and left to find a suitable hiding place. She found it two doors to the right, a small room where boxes of thousands of papers were stored, probably backup copies in case of an extended blackout. She returned to where the scientist was. He was still paralyzed and helpless from a mixture of fear and superficial hypnosis, which she considered to be pathetic of him. She snapped his neck, and when assured no one walked down the aisle, she carried the body and took him to the paperwork room. He was heavier than she thought, and smelled of lack of hygiene. Before she left and dropped him off, remembered that extra help was needed. She stretched out a nail until it was sharp and stout. Took his right eye out and put it in her pocket while taking the shape of the deceased. The blood already bathed the wretched man's clothes, so she was careful not to step on it. She plunged the eye into her socket, emptied especially to accommodate it. It felt weird, next time she'd come up with a better method.

She closed the door and continued her mission. Now that she had left a body in a place that was not completely hidden, there was not much time for it. She quickly checked her surroundings, and guided by instinct, followed a corridor with security cameras. At the end of the hall there was another biometrics reading machine, so she passed the borrowed eye, the card and entered the code. On the other side was a long hallway with more security cameras. Maybe it wasn't convenient for her to be seen passing by. If someone discovered the body and checked the security cameras, they would know what had happened and there was only one escape route.

It amused her to wonder what Lykaios would have done in that situation. He probably would have taken the form of a box and moved slowly in, praying that they wouldn't see him. When back, she was gonna play a little prank on the good wolfy cub. She tossed the identification, memory and eye rolling across the floor, transfigured into the shape of the smooth white tiles on the wall, and began to move relentlessly through the floor socket until she reached behind the line of sight of the devices. She went through another door again, this time asking only for a magnetic identification. Evidently the building and security had not been designed to stop someone like her, serious mistake, and second suspicion. Not that León didn't know what a well-trained Shadow can do. Inside the office were several servers that made a bestial noise. The light was dim and bluish. A single person was sitting in front of one of the monitors, who was surprised to see her arrive. He was a human male over forty years old, thin, wearing a pair of glasses with quite a bit of magnification, bushy eyebrows and a moustache, all recently dyed black. Of course he was dressed in a white coat.

_Hahn, what are you doing here at this hour? - he asked her in German turning around.

_I came to ask you a few questions, and you're going to answer them all, while you sit quietly in your place. - again the victim was unable to reuse the orders.

Anzhelika, disguised now as the stout Hahn, grabbed him by the throat and made a threatening enquiry. _What's your name?

_M-Manfred.

_What are you doing here?

_...I keep track of... activities.

_Of everything in this place?

_...Yes.

_Tell me what you know about the *neomenschgenetik* section.

_...it's a section... that... takes care of... things... - the answer was taking longer and longer to come, without a doubt he had more willpower than the fat guy.

_Don't resist, Manfred, what are they doing there?

_...create *neomensch* with talent... and train them.

_What are you training them for?

_F-For the divisions. – Manfred made an enormous effort to resist the spell that now possessed him.

Lika frowned. She had to ask more specific questions if she wanted to win in the strange mind game she created.

_Are any of these divisions part of the unconventional militia?

_...yes.

_Did any of these divisions have anything to do with the death of Caucasus?

Manfred closed his eyes tightly, trying to stop thoughts from escaping his head. _Yes.

_Which one? What's its name?

_*Speerspitze.*

_How is it composed?

This time Manfred did not answer, he had bitten his tongue and a little blood was squirting from the commissure. Anzhelika grimaced, sensibly annoyed. _Stay absolutely still, bastard.

She sat in front of one of the computers, and with Hahn's user searched on *Speerspitze*, but the system denied the results.

She read Manfred's full name from the ID hanging off his coat, and entered it into the system. _What's your password?

_...53...16...a...d...- he babbled, spitting out some blood.

_Go on.

_...19...p...p...p...hash.

She tried again, this time successfully. While copying all the contents onto the small stolen memory device, she snooped around.

Speerspitze - from the German: Spearhead - was the result of years of research on the human genome, specifically on effects considered "paranormal" by conventional science. *Neomensch* embryos with certain characteristics were created to work in conjunction with a specific combat tactic and to resist and encourage the effects of contagion from an early age. She disliked the idea of calling a "contagion" what she *was*. She continued reading. The triplets that make up Speerspitze were ranked as the most efficient of a set of eighteen trios once they all reached the age of six, when they became available for further specific training, while the others were either discarded from the project or passed on to alternative units. The order and cataloguing of the archives was impeccable, excellent for cases of espionage with little time.

The first individual in the trio is a man whose codename is "Fender". In addition to having an above-average intellectual and physical level, he had developed a high capacity to regenerate both his own body and that of his twins, as they have an identical genetic structure. A whole set of tables and graphs showing the results of the tests carried out were skipped. There were more than two hundred videos recording the "training" he underwent. She opened only one at random, "Test_97", quickly skipping through several scenes where black-clad men tortured a little boy with sharp elements, fire, gunshots, among other worst things. A horrible way to learn to heal quickly from an early age. She continued.

The second is a woman under the code name "Konnex". Her physical abilities are similar to those of her brother, with the difference that she is an extraordinary empath being able to instantly communicate sensations to anyone, or understand those of the individuals around her. Attached to the report was a score of magnetic resonances that had been done on the brain, and a video highlighting her in bringing down with mere sadness a group of apes, by just approaching them. She wondered what advantage empathy provided over hypnosis. She closed the files and continued.

The third in the group is another woman known as "Lohe". Physically she shows unique characteristics, which are listed as classified. She was subjected to prolonged doses of daylight throughout her life. Although she is not capable of metabolizing it, as happens to all of them, can resist and accumulate potential and then dispose of it, thanks to martial arts training and the handling of body energy as if it were a capacitor. There was a special mention of her obedience. The first video of hundreds was a short film of a man in a white coat talking, and then a girl in an iron-clad room breaking half a dozen cement blocks with her bare hands. Intriguing.

She went on to the next point. Manfred continued to watch with his eyes wide open, and now he was releasing guttural sounds as he slowly forced his arms to move. Lika came to a part where it listed the missions that had been assigned to *Speerspitze*, and skipped them quickly to get to the last ones. The sixth turned out to be the demise of Caucasus, marked "Accomplished". It named a seventh, whose target was the Akkadian, and was "In progress". They were already on their way... she had to warn Eylem urgently.

The Hahn disguise began to get up when something else caught her eye. There was a direct link to view the missions that were underway at that very moment.

In addition to *Speerspitze* there was a group of operations assigned to that same mission as support, under the name of *Iluminieren*. Two conventional Alpha and Gamma military groups were on the move for an invasion of the Aegis Palace, and two Meteor demolition divisions were targeting for the destruction of the old Athens Palace and the Hall of Notables in Austria.

The war has begun! She lost her concentration for a moment, and portions of her Hahn costume deformed. Any one of the items was vital information for Crest, and she didn't know where to start. However, there was no time at all to decide, as the monitors suddenly turned off. Some scandalous red lights flashed up and began to spin, painting everything with emergency. Evidently they found any of the bodies, so she had to get out of there as soon as possible. She turned to look closely at Manfred's anguished face making sure to carry the copied information in her pocket, and quickly imprinted his features to the unmoving man's surprise. She winked at him with his own face before running away, closing the door behind her.

Through the loudspeakers the intruder alert sounded continuously, piercing her ears as she advanced. A dozen armed soldiers were taking all the scientists to a huge room, where she believed they were being interrogated. Getting caught there would be a lot of trouble. She made sure no one saw her enter an office full of desks, computers and microscopes that was now empty, and took on the appearance of a soldier. Walked out of there and took a steady step toward the exit. More soldiers entered through the only door to the outside, severely complicating the escape. She decided on a risky move, taking advantage of the fact that the texture of her costume was difficult to see under the red lights. They really hadn't thought this through. She trotted up to whoever looked like the sergeant in charge. _Sir, the civilian personnel are already contained and being questioned. Still no sign of the intruder, sir.

_All right, keep searching.

The sergeant and his men renewed their march, and she stood to one side, trying to hide a smile that wanted to emerge. She stepped out of the building cautiously, and headed for the darkness of the night. A jeep stopped a few hundred meters away, turned and undertook again, this time in her direction. Alzhelika noticed this, and redoubled her pace to then run. The jeep increased the speed of its pursuit firing a large machine gun, which lightened and illuminated everything around it.

She reached in a leapt with a few shots taken behind the low wall where her phone was hidden, which she quickly took to run away again.

Between the trees and the darkness, she hurled to the ground and dyed herself white as the snow around her trying to close the recently awarded wounds. Now more jeeps were searching her, but they'd lost track. She dialed Eylem's number once she made sure no one was around, and waited.

_Hello?

_Bronze bells.

_Report in.

_Hostile units on their way to Aegis, the former Athens Palace and the Hall of Notables, and the same group that killed Caucasus is now after the Akkadian. – on the other side of the phone there was a sepulchral silence – Eylem?

_I was already counting on Aegis, I've sent enough elements to defend it... but I wasn't expecting the attack on the other two targets. If they take over Aegis and destroy the old centers of political power, there will be no way to stop the Council from appointing him Mandatary... what am I saying? They won't even care about the Council, they could do whatever they want.

_How did you knew about the invasion of Aegis?

Eylem waited a few seconds before answering. _I assumed that it would be the next target of León once any member of either side fell. I commanded Lykaios to contact me... and he hasn't. – Anzhelika's face, still as white as the snow that kept falling, was paralyzed. For a few moments her mind was empty, while the frozen air hurt her nostrils – and an hour ago I asked a Seeker to find him, and she couldn't do it. Now that the shock troops are on their way, I realize he's dead.

If Anzhelika had taken the trouble to recreate functional tear ducts in her eyes, she would have shed a tear. She had a special feeling for Lykaios, as if he were her little younger brother, such as the one she had many centuries ago and whom, like him, had died. *Those* who are like her rarely feel close to anyone, (let alone are capable of loving) but he woke up a protective instinct that she didn't even know she had.

_We can't do anything for the Akkadian, he knows how to defend himself better than we can. - Eylem continued - The only thing left to do is not losing the Palace. You did well, Lika, go back to Marseilles... please. - and she cut off the communication.

Anzhelika held the phone in her hands, letting the cold gradually seep into her, lying on the snow and darkness. She was haunted by memories that came to her like a demonic torrent, memories of the death of her blood brother, and of her little false brother whom she would never have near again. Nothing left to do. She felt powerless, just like then.

She gathered strength to get up and run again, arriving later at the vehicle she had previously traveled with, to set it up, heading to the airport when she was sure no one was following. A risky move, but she didn't mind. As soon as she arrived, she'd change her shape and they couldn't find her anymore. While running away from an army or the police could be easy for her, escaping from memories was impossible.

PART 11: OF GODS AND MEN

An ocean away, a bored guard looked up from his personal assistant's screen, a small smoky acrylic plate filled with gold and carbon nanotubes, only to find a huge entourage of uniformed men from his own base surrounding an unknown man in a suit. General Fisher received visitors constantly, but none so garrisoned. He rasped before he spoke.

_Good evening, gentlemen...

One of the soldiers in the procession that filled the lobby stepped forward and replied in a monotone that was difficult to ignore and with a slightly misguided look on his face. _Mr. Perius... is coming to see... General Fisher... let him know... he's here.

The guard stood still, doubting what to do, feeling an army of eyes judging him silently. To some extent he tried to resist, but it was unfruitful. He knocked on the door, and walked in. Suffocated as he was by the situation, he took a deep breath before addressing the secretary. _There's a garrison outside escorting a fella named Perius. I don't know where he's from, it seems he has an appointment with the General, is that possible?

111

The secretary was a young woman in uniform who was obviously not cut out for the battlefield, perhaps not even office work, or any work at all. She looked up with a mixture of weariness and need to justify that she had many things to do even if it was not true, and let out a slight sigh. She activated her calendar and turned a few pages. _No, Peyton, I don't have an appointment for this hour.

Peyton grimaced as he thought of a quick excuse to say that would appease the dozen and a half soldiers who had been accompanying the guy in the suit, and threw a few insults inward.

He went out and closed the door behind him. _I'm sorry, sir, General Fisher doesn't have an appointment.

The armed party seemed confused, and they turned to look at Perius. Peyton noticed that everyone moved in a peculiar way, but could not identify exactly why. Perius tilted his head slightly, as if he were tired of continuing with the same routine. He reached out to him to greet him, and when he had the soldier's hand on his, he squeezed it tightly. _Good evening young man, tell me your name please. – he spoke politely and jovially.

The stranger's eyes incinerated him from the inside out, burning him almost literally. The right hand was being compacted and the pain impulse quickly reached an uncoordinated brain. He squirmed his face like exposed to fire. _C-Corporal Luis Peyton.

_Nice to meet you, Corporal Luis Peyton. It is very, very important that I speak to General Fisher. It is clear that I must be allowed to pass, as this is a very important issue and must be dealt with urgently. It's urgent, Peyton. Very urgent.

The soldier's mind was completely convulsed. The only thing that sounded clearly within such confusion was a loud foghorn warning indicating that he must act immediately to allow the strange and suddenly extremely transcendental subject in front of him to pass. He was released, and a hand on his shoulder pushed him in with a few friendly pats.

The secretary looked at him with a gesture similar to the previous one. _What's all that peo-?

_Mr. Perius... must come in at once, please tell the General. - Peyton interrupted in a bad way to her surprise.

She picked up the phone slowly, but stopped before dialing. _What am I supposed to tell him?

_That the... - it took a long second to accommodate the phrase - Mr. Perius is coming on a very important and urgent matter...

Upset, the young woman pressed the corresponding extension. _Sir, I'm sorry to bother you, outside ther-

_What is it, Christina? I'm busy right now.

_There are a lot of men outside, they're escorting Mr. Perius and he's coming for a matter that seems to be urgent. They're from the base, sir. Sir? Are you there? - She hung up slowly, a little bewildered - Tell him he can come in.

Peyton nodded slightly and emerged, mechanically opening the door wide.

Perius entered the small room, greeted the young lady gallantly and moved on.

The heels of his shoes emitted a spectral sound against the wooden floor as he advanced to the office, time itself flowing abnormally in his path.

The General's office was austere, but decorated with grace. The mahogany furniture was recently polished and shone under the effect of the chemicals that were used to treat it every morning. On a wall there was a portrait of a soldier with a hundred decorations and some diplomas. On one of the corners was a mast with the flag of the United States shining with its golden sconces. And behind the desk was General Carl Fisher. He was a brown-skinned man, full-bodied but in good shape, perfectly shaved and with an unblemished hairstyle. The lines on his face showed both age and experience. All along the scene, the only shocking feature was the air of deep uneasiness that surrounded the General, in the face of the figure who had just entered to dominate everything with his mere presence.

114

_Have a good evening, Carl, I hope you do not mind my surprise visit.

Fisher was out of his element. _Exactly who are you?

Perius laughed warmly and slightly. _I figured you would know by now, oh well. The important thing here... is that I have a proposition for you, Carl. And no, do not tell me you are not interested before you hear it.

Fisher breathed slowly as he clutched his hands at the sides of his armchair under some strange influence.

_Maybe are you aware or not, that I can convince you of whatever I may fancy, play with your mind as I please, make you believe you are a daisy in the garden if I wish so, but that is not the point. That does not last for long, at least not long enough. Before coming here, I paid a visit first to Secretary of Security Thomas Hicks and then to Admiral Longcastle, both of whom have kindly helped me in everything I asked for. I went to a lot of trouble to see all three of you, I embarked from Rome especially for that, it is a matter I had to do in person.

Fisher opened his eyes wide. He immediately suspected the purpose of this Perius and his nature, a fierce demon of what he thought for many years was just a myth, folklore, stupidity. And now here he was. _I think I know what is it about and I have no interest. Leave now, please.

Perius snapped his lips several times, disapproving of the soldier's attitude, and carried his hands behind his back, both holding his beloved dragon cane, to stand by the window and watch some troops running and vehicles rolling, while the orange clouds quickly turned blue, and the blue ones black. _Well, it is not too hard to guess why I am here, but I will not be leaving yet.

The General, in a sudden change of attitude, appeared serene, loosening his features and intertwining his fingers on the desk, on which were a few files, a framed photograph of a smiling woman with a girl in her arms, and yellow folders with the inscription "Classified", on paper, as he liked it. _I deem to understand what your skills are, your intentions too, what I don't understand is why you take the trouble to talk to me. I refuse to help. If you have any way of convincing me, use it and leave.

Perius turned, while pulling his pipe out of his pocket, and slowly transforming his illusionary modern costume into his exquisite but old-fashioned attire, made from his own modified skin and will on the spot. _Would you object if I smoke?

_Go ahead. - he managed to say after shaking off the initial surprise.

_Thank you. - he said as he lit the pipe and started to smoke - I will cut to the chase since I do not like to steal my hosts' time. You have already realized that what I am looking for is something of magnitude. Access to this nation's nuclear arsenal. - if Fisher could cast lightning bolts out of his eyes, that would have been the closest he ever came. – What you may not know is that I have it practically in my hands, thanks to some sly moves, information, and well... hard and honest to goddess work.

Fisher made a great effort to remain impassive, as he searched his head for 101 ways to escape this dangerous situation. _Impressive, but it doesn't answer the underlying question.

A puff of smoke remained in the air. Outside the darkness was quickly winning the battle of each night against the light.

Perius continued. _Carl, do you see what is out there? It is a new world. One I distaste, and so do you if I am not mistaken. – Fisher raised an eyebrow – An event has happened recently that has not transcended to the public, and never will. I doubt that you are aware of a certain... organization... that has been in charge of maintaining order in this blessed world since before it became a world. – there was no response from the other side. He continued – For better or worse this organization is going through a severe crisis after the death of its former leader. Now, there are two sides fighting over the crumbs of what was his power, one that has been in sharp decline for centuries. The high–profile decisions have long since emanated from there, they do not want to see it. But this also provides an opportunity that should not be missed. – he turned around to throw the burnt tobacco into the basket and then fill the pipe again.– What I want to do is get things back to their natural state.

Fisher wet his lips to talk. _I don't know what you're talking about.

_Do not play the fool, Carly boy. - he gesticulated with his index finger, disapproving again. - I will explain why I need access to the weapon with which men like to play gods. In approximately sixteen hours there will be a skirmish that will decide the fate of this organization of which I speak. And neither side should be victorious. Both must end up losing, by a whole heap. An attack with one of these divine atrocities will not only achieve disastrous losses, but will initiate a New Age. - Fisher put all his attention on Perius' words, not giving credit to his ears or to what was happening at this bizarre meeting.

_To do this - he continued - as you should realize, I do not require your help. I just need to know the last third of the code and who the operator to dictate it to is. But I need you, my friend Carl, for what is coming next.

He fixed his gaze on the soldier to finish that sentence, then lowered it down to his lit match. A faint, triumphant smile loomed from his mouth. In the office the aroma of fine tobacco was renewed. _After the hit, it must be spread that it was a terrorist attack by a totally unknown, powerful and widespread group, which has access to many of these ravaging weapons. That will cause a surge of fear, yes. It is a pity but it is also a fundamental part of the plan. The whole operation needs to be kept secret, under seven keys. Are you following me, right?

Fisher watched in awe, as if listening to the insanities of a dictator with too much power. _That is madness!

_No, old sports. There is a reason for everything. Think about it... what effect would it have on the world if my plan were to become reality?

The General looked down nervously as he demanded himself to think at full speed of the brightest thing that ever came out of his head, a string of words that might convince the monster in front of him to stop. _That... – he took the probably most unpleasant seconds of his life – would change the rules of the game, nations would react immediately by strengthening their borders, it would alter alliances. Personal civil liberties would be lost for at least a decade, international trade would collapse. A desolating crisis.

_That is a correct but a somewhat negative view, Carl. Who will take the reins of that troubled and scared world? – Perius pointed it out with his index finger – You and I. We will make this nation the standard that others must follow to be safe, in the leader nation once again.

The soldier wiped the sweat from his forehead with a handkerchief. This was getting out of hand at an astronomical speed. _I don't understand, for... for what? Why?

_Carl, I know you better than you think. I know what kind of person you are. You long for the golden years, when values were standing strong and issues marched the right direction. I do as well, the difference is that I am able to get them back where they belong, and I am going to do it. I see this world corrupted by money, warring over stupidity, great countries falling to their knees in front of ships full of poor quality products that flood their weak markets. What have they become? Garbage! That is right, garbage. - he suddenly turned around - Look at you, Fisher! Bent to technology. I know that at some point you feared being replaced by a machine, one that would devise better strategies than you, that would be faster, better, that would never get tired. - Fisher squinted when he felt a sensitive fiber touched - Science advancing unrestrained, creating bestiality, useless and meaningless things, it is barbarism. Everything is tinged with corruption... everything.

Perius continued. _The bonds have weakened, the whole world is adrift. - he made a violent gesture with one hand - It has become so small that anyone can walk it in less than a human life... and that is why it loses its richness, nobody respects this planet anymore - he let out a sigh - I am an adventurer, friend Carl, that is why it hurts me especially where the fates are heading. I want to correct it, to venture back into the world of old. Think about it, are you worried about those who may die in the attack? They are like *me*, nobody is going to regret them. From then on, no one needs to be sacrificed, no more lives are lost.

Fisher couldn't take his eyes off the floor. _I still think it's insane. It's... it's over-exposing.

_Tell me the truth, would you not like for things to return to the way they were before?

_I... yes. I guess so, but not like this.

_Do you think it might not work?

Finally he could raise his gaze, trying to focus it on the ancestral monster of such refined manners. It wasn't unworkable if what he thought of Perius was real, and given the evidence he has witnessed so far, it was *very* real. The truth would never come out. _With you behind it all, it might. That's what I'm afraid of.

_Excellent. I do not expect you to cooperate immediately, it will surely take time for you to understand the implications and benefits, both for yourself and for the country you serve. It takes a leader, Carl Fisher. People need to be led the way. - he crossed one leg over the other after taking seat. The theatrical performance seemed to be finally concluded - but for now... the first step must be taken.

Fisher made a profound grimace of displeasure at a situation he did not call, an operation he did not want to carry out, the unfeasibility of refusing, and the fact that his mind was altered by that... individual so despicable and yet so charismatic. He assessed his options, and spoke in a tone from beyond the grave. _Tell me the other two parts of the code, I'll arrange for the destruction of the target. What are the coordinates?

Perius pulled a piece of paper out of a pocket inside his jacket and read it.

_Here it is. 44° 31 minutes, 10 seconds North, 9° 3 minutes, 55 seconds East.

_That must be... northern Italy.

_That's right. It's an elegant but faded palace in a region called Montoggio on the outskirts of Genoa. - he extended the paper - These are the other two parts of the code.

Fisher glanced at the paper that reached his sweaty hands. It had handwritten the coordinates he had previously dictated, and two sets of characters with numbers and letters. He picked up the phone quickly, but hesitated to dial. He finally did. _Rogers, this is General Carl Arthur Fisher, get me Hendrich. - and after a few seconds - Hendrich, I have orders for you. Pay close attention. This is a matter of national security, not a drill...

PART 12: THE THRONE OF THE PUPPETEER

The steps sounded dry between the empty corridors. The shadows, long and enigmatic, danced under the influence of the candles. A silhouette advanced calmly, causing dozens of echoes which spread in all directions. The Aegis Palace, hidden in Montoggio, had always looked like a monumental tomb, fit of a pharaoh, but that night it was especially phantasmagorical. The style of the place was strongly reminiscent of the Greek classic, with its huge carved white columns, its pale gleaming marble floors, its walls covered with paintings of great artists of all times, its finely decorated domes, its countless passages and halls, all of which bear witness to the passing of the centuries in its cracks. Aegis was the crown of a world without a king, the faceless power, the throne where the puppeteer pulled the strings, and had been for almost a millennium. Its symbolism had and has an unimaginable strength. The personal jewel of Caucasus, now coveted by everyone. From a room at the end of the hall, a series of screams and laughter crashed violently against the sober majesty of the place. The figure continued to advance toward the room. The screams ripped through the air, the laughter pierced the silence like projectiles. The echo of the footsteps was gradually lost amidst the sea of screams of fear, and the laughter. The horrifying laughter.

_Well well, look who's here.

A good-looking young man sat at the side of the imposing door of the hall, with one foot resting on a table in front of him, filled with alcoholic bottles of all kinds. An extinguished cigar hung from his lips, and beneath his nose could be seen clear traces of cocaine. On his naked torso were tattooed some winged skulls with thorny vines, and some Latin phrases. Pants and leather boots were his entire wardrobe, not counting a metal piercing that shone on his right eyebrow.

_Deios, what a... pleasure to see you again. – the figure who had just arrived gestured nicely. He wore a thin white coat over a linen shirt, light grey trousers and white reptile leather shoes. A hat of the same color as his coat dangled from his head covered in golden hairs down to the base of his neck. His features were well proportioned, his gestures full of confidence, false harmony and hospitality, each of his fingers adorned with thick gold rings. The pallor of his skin matched his attire – Did you arrive long ago?

_Most of us arrived last night, MacOwen and Chandresh arrived today. Also another guy I don't know.

The man in white raised an eyebrow in surprise. _If those two came together, it would be the strangest event of the century.

Deios laughed slightly as he searched his pockets for a lighter. _No, no. They arrived separately. Your imagination is going haywire for sure! – his tone was erratic and euphoric.

_Besides, if he hears that you don't address him as "Lord " he will get angry.

_Oh, you're right! I don't want to fight him, tonight's the night to celebrate. With any luck, the Lions will come and we can kill a couple of them. In a little while we'll drink a toast to "Lord" Chandresh and the damned whore who gave birth to him... hmm, how old is he?

_I don't know, but it must be more than half a millennium. – he said as he checked the dirty crystal glasses in front of him.

_Never mind, we'll toast anyway. To his health!

_Cheers. – he raised a makeshift glass – Abe must have come with you, right?

Deios looked to the back of the room, where there were several like *him*, gossiping and laughing aloud both standing up and on the floor, or sitting down. In the adjoining room there were others who were having sex, and a third one, where the cries of intense pain came from. Bloody footsteps came and went, along with a nauseating feeling of death and cruelty. He pointed his index finger at the latter. _He must be there. They brought some women from the village and they're having fun with them.

_I figured Abe would have more fun with men...

Deios smiled with sadism. _Where there's blood, he's happy. The first thing is that he's happy, ain't it?

_Of course. If you don't mind, I'll go say hello to MacOwen.

_Not a problem, Vogel! Pour yourself a drink on the way. Surely he's on the other side of the palace, the bastard doesn't like to spend time with his colleagues.

Vogel greeted politely taking off his hat and turned around. He disliked all that, although at some point, a hundred years ago, he did similar or even worse things. When he thought he was the sovereign of the night, master and lord of the human vermin. Until he met one of the true owners of the world, a terrifying entity that had always wandered the earth. She opened up a new universe of political games, of extensive and profound networks of power. She showed him the Palace, the Council and the Grand Caucasus. It was a hard blow that filled him with due humility and a new meaning. To climb up. Climb as high as possible, and dodge any obstacles in his path. And he would remain with Eylem as his ally, for the time being at least. He got rid of the glass, trying not to make any noise.

He continued to walk through Aegis's sepulchral corridors, with some screams still filling his ears, and memories floating in his mind. He recognized that feeling that his "wild stage" was over only served to protect his ego. Deep down he still wanted to drink blood from the open flesh of an unfortunate woman, but he could not allow himself to do so. He was better than that now.

As he arrived at the main hall, he noticed a dim light coming from one of the corridors on the upper floor. He climbed up the sumptuous marble and bronze stairs and headed that way. Some musical notes blinked subtly, gradually covering up the faint howling. The doors of the enormous hall were open. Inside, a beautiful ceiling spider with several dozen electric candles hung splendidly. An old white wooden piano delicately adorned was in one of the corners, and behind it a large painting representing an old man in red rags inside a dark room, writing in a desk, alongside an incomplete skull.

Sitting at the piano was a woman with short, jet-black hair and dressed in the same color, focused on her task. She didn't even flinch at the arrival of Vogel.

_Good evening, beautiful lady.

He waited a few seconds and, in the absence of any response, continued somewhat confusedly into the adjoining room where voices were heard. He knocked on the solid wood door and entered when allowed.

_Welcome, newly arrived? - he was greeted by a bald man with glasses and hard features. Some wrinkles appeared on his forehead and the sides of his sunken eyes.

_That's right, I don't think we've met, sir. - Vogel was puzzled to run into strangers here. He looked at the person next to him. It was MacOwen, a thin but fibrous man with short brown hair and a quiet expression. He had a little beard under his chin, and wore a brown leather studded shirt and shoulder pads of the same material. It looked as if he had jumped from a window leading to the 15th century. He was known to be a man of peace most of the time. Otherwise he was occupied by being a religious fanatic. It was difficult to maintain a transcendental dialogue with him if you were afraid of literally losing your head. Beyond that he was versed in various sciences and arts. A picturesque inclusion to Crest's lines.

_Welcome, Drescher. - MacOwen said curtly as he pointed at the bald man with his gloved hand - This is Charles Dipson, my travelling companion for some years now.

_Nice to meet you. - Vogel bowed slightly.

_Likewise, would you like to take a seat?

_No, thank you very much. I'm curious, who's the woman at the piano?

_She said her name was Syra, but wouldn't give any details. She's a Shadow, these people don't like to socialize nor care about anything but the art of war.

_Oh, I understand. Any news?

_No, nothing of importance. – answered MacOwen – We are still waiting for a movement from León's men.

_We will have to wait, for now. The calm before the storm can be felt. – Dipson concurred.

_Let's be prepared, then. I was looking for Lord Chandresh, have you seen him?

MacOwen watched the newcomer from top to bottom, with some indignation. The bald man instead took off his glasses to clean them, trying to hide his sudden discomfort. _No, we haven't seen him.

_I have a question for him, since we are gathered here. I wouldn't dare talk to him under any other circumstances, he's a despicable person.

Both men loosened their expressions. _He's probably outside.

_Thank you, and see you later, gentlemen. – Drescher bowed goodbye with his white hat in one hand. Before leaving the room, a generously proportioned sheathed sword caught his eye. He could recognize an ancient symbol on the hilt that he has seen before.

As he passed through the piano room again, he spent a minute listening to the sad melodies that came out of it. He simulated great taste in what he heard. _You play charmingly, Miss Syra...

Again there was no response of any kind.

_Will you join us in battle? - the question remained frozen in the air for a few moments - Well, I presume so, it would be an honor to be on your side in that case. My name is Vogel Drescher, don't you forget.

The Shadow continued in its task without even returning a glance. Vogel shrugged, put his hat on the head and walked out. He wasn't sure if the antisocial pianist would survive or not, but that should be enough if she did. Now he had to concentrate on finding Chandresh and leaving the Palace immediately. He trotted down the stairs, when he remembered that the place could be crowded with hidden Shadows without him noticing. He grimaced at the need to change plans. He tucked his coat in and headed for the exit. Detection and concealment were definitely not his strong suit, but he decided to try his luck.

_Hello! Anybody out there? I'm looking for Lord Chandresh... - the vapor from his breath was slowly dispersing while he waited for the answer from something that shouldn't be there.

A voice answered from the top floor, but he could not determine the source. _He's in the back grove. - the mysterious voice sounded masculine and with a significant degree of hostility.

It made him shudder to know that there were definitely Shadows hiding *somewhere*. Some may have even convinced him that they weren't there with a weird trick, how should he know? He thanked his invisible interlocutor and continued on his way to the grove of trees along a narrow, poorly lit path that bordered the Palace. On the outside it looked rather dull, to attract as little attention as possible despite its size. Several columns were cracked and invaded with vegetation. The back grove was difficult to define, as the foliage was abundant in either direction. The night dew was frozen by the low temperatures and covered the grass that still fought the frost death. The flowers and the leaves of the canopies had long since lost the fight against winter, remaining under its soft and cruel spell, until spring brought them back to life.

He didn't need to seek too much, a huge presence was sitting against the trunk of a tree, where it barely gave the light of the lanterns of the Palace. He approached calmly, as usual.

_Good evening, Lord Chandresh, I hope I'm not disturbing you with my visit.

The enormous big man looked up for a brief moment and continued his work. In his hands he held a knife and a piece of wood, which he was giving the shape of a four-legged animal. The tone of his skin was strangely brownish, somewhat atypical among his own, but common in the Indian subcontinent, where he was originally from. He was also covered in scars of all shapes and sizes, more than certain as a way of bragging about how many battles he had been in and out alive. Everyone knew of his enviable regenerative and biomass management capabilities. He was dressed in tight trousers and a shirt of strange textures, the constant of all those who change their physiognomy at will. On his neck was a long string with carved wooden beads, each representing the head of an animal. More famous perhaps was his personality and his way of facing life's challenges. With violence, and a great deal of it. He thrusts forward like a beast, a creature from another world, a rather unorthodox way of dealing with a fight, repulsive to most.

_I have just arrived from my trip and I was greeting all my brothers and sisters, in this raw undertaking that awaits us shortly.

In response he only received a low grunt. Small fragments of wood fell to the ground as the knife shaped the figurine.

_...well, I think I'll leave you alone. Farewell.

None of *his own* had a bond with social life as they used to before the conversion, but this was too much. It angered him to see the black side of what he *is*, or was, maybe. He was distracted by the cold from the atmosphere that was already beginning to bother him, so he decided to go inside. He had to be among the first to receive word if León's forces appeared to take over the Palace. He looked up at the few clouds that protruded from the mosaic of celestial stars, it seemed impossible that on such a quiet night could happen something... so atrocious. The Moon, almost full, suspended majestically, bathing the place in a dim light.

But that's how Isabella had warned him. After Eylem's order to defend the Palace with half of the elements of Crest, he consulted her about his fate. Vogel had learned to trust the visions of the beautiful young woman, as most of them were fulfilled with dreadful accuracy. She was the most talented clairvoyant he'd ever met, so he kept her hidden as best he could with... unfriendly guiles, so that she would remain in his care in this ferocious world they inhabited. It was not wise to let her go, such a tool must remain with him. Plus, he provided everything she needed. Even an unfounded fear of strangers, a very healthy one.

And the vision she had was especially terrifying. She saw the Palace wrapped in a shroud of fire, burning everyone inside. Death. Death everywhere. But unfortunately, no details of how it would happen. That probably meant that León's troops would strike with full force, and that he should be far, far away when that happens. The problem was that the survivors would tell the details of the fight, and it would be known that he was not there, automatically losing Eylem's support, and all of Crest's. It was a substantial price to pay for security. Instead, he resorted to an alternative solution. To go and make sure to greet in person those he considered most likely to survive and to leave his presence on the record. And as soon as the episode begins, run away in the confusion. With so many Shadows present he had to make sure that they were *very busy* before he flew away. He had to measure the exact moment accurately so as not ending up under the flaming threat, whatever it was.

He walked again to the entrance of the Aegis, trying to see some sign of a hidden shadow, but was unable to do so. He really had no talent for it, and prayed he had enough to run when needed. He was warming his hands when a strange, persistent buzzing sound came to his ears. A nearby statue and a broken column changed shape until they adopted a humanoid to his amazement. Both ran to the outside, and returned within seconds at full speed. _They're here! It's an air raid!

PART 13: *COUPE DE GRÂCE*

Kilometers from there, the afternoon was already giving away its last rays of the imposing star radiating once again its particles of life, as it has done for eons. The luxurious mansion in Barcelona was preparing to enter a temporary universe of darkness, which would fall in a few minutes when the Sun sets over the horizon. Inside, only one person walked it. Kad had been using it as a small personal castle for a few days, since he convinced its owner that it was an excellent moment to travel with his family while he protected the property. The innocent ruse would last only until they realized how illogical the decision was and returned, probably with police forces. Of course Kad would no longer be found there, and even if they did, they could hardly stop him.

The manor was old on the outside but suitable for modern times in its interior. A beautiful front garden served as a stage for half a dozen stone lions along a short stone path. Kad was attracted to this decoration, probably as a sort of mockery if he was attacked by León or whoever was behind the death of Caucasus, or perhaps because the house was dim in the daytime with its curtains closed. The main room was generously decorated with pastel tones, a huge (and probably expensive) Persian rug, a seductive life-size replica of the Venus of the Nile, and elegant gold foil moldings. A giant television set occupied almost the entirety of one of the walls and in front of it, a comfortable four-seats armchair. Nearby, another single-seat armchair was next to a high-end stereo and a shelf full of discs of various generations of technology and genres. The whole house transpired material wealth and the peace, also material, that it conveys. Kad stopped his steps in front of an impeccably framed picture hanging on the wall opposite the TV set. It showed a man in rags and on his knees begging a woman in fine clothes, the "Shepherd and Princess" of Dirck van Baburen. He stayed there for a few moments, perhaps admiring the baroque style, perhaps because it evoked some memory of his own past. He then stopped in front of the stereo and turned it on. It began to sound from the powerful speakers The Peacocks, a melancholic jazz ballad composed by Jimmie Rowles. Kad was silent as he listened to it standing, as he glanced at the musical fortune that lay before him. He then pulled some discs off the shelf, set some aside and left them on a small round table to one side, while carelessly tossing the rest on the floor over his shoulder. From those he had set aside, he chose one after a brief deliberation. He opened the tray and put it in. This time the Prelude of *Tristan und Isolde* of Wagner took over the hall. He sat placidly on one of the couches, with a singular smile planted on his lips and his head thrown back, while he accompanied the compasses with a finger.

A tiny, almost horizontal beam of light slid through one of the closed windows. Kad led his hand into the light, until the beam was focused flat on his palm. A small stain of burnt skin appeared, it vanished and then reappeared while fighting cell renewal, leaving a ghostly trail of grey smoke that rose lightly.

_It's almost time.

Outside, two entirely black vans parked one behind the other. The metal in the plate flashed under the dying rays of the Sun like a leather shroud. The back doors of one of the vans opened wide and four figures descended from it quickly and synchronously. All four wore black garments that covered them completely, mostly opaque except for portions of lustrous alloy on the helmets, mask, chest and shoulder pads. A belt full of magazines with explosive ordnance completed the outfit. In their hands they carried peculiar weapons. They were of a coarse, rectangular design, carrying a square, bulky section underneath their high-caliber barrel, as if the weapon itself had been structured around that box. In low relief, the name *Lichtbogen II* was engraved on the side.

The *Illuminieren* quartet glided quickly with a lapidary silence around the mansion, crossing the beautiful garden and leaving in its wake trampled flowers, the first victims of the day. At a signal from the leader of the operation, two of them stood at the sides of the main entrance, one at the back, and the rest climbed the balcony of the upper floor with the agility of a feline. The leader grabbed a small device from one of the pockets and slid it gently under the door. A miniature monitor placed on the inside of his forearm recorded the images obtained from inside the mansion, confirming the target. He removed the device and gave a new signal with his hand while giving a brief radio command to begin the second phase of the operation. With impeccable coordination, all of them placed plastic explosives in the main openings of the house, remaining crouched in their places. The roof and windows of the second van opened. It was divided into three parts, the driver's cab, a second part that remained sealed and the rear part, where one person was located.

She was a young woman, with a calm expression and delicate features that contrasted with her torso, shoulders and arms of fibrous and delineated muscles. The upper half of her tender body was naked, while the lower half was covered in black combat pants and heavy boots. Her short, blond hair gleamed briefly in gold as it received the warm rays of sunshine that seeped in. With slow movements, she stood up and extended her arms and hands upward, completely at the mercy of the star. Small specks appeared on her smooth skin, spreading as the seconds passed. The young woman's impassive face grew into one of deep pain as her upper body burned again, as it had every day of her life. Her knees ran out of strength, shaking until she staggered and finally fell. Doors and windows were closed quickly and automatically, while the second sealed section was opened. Inside, two more individuals had been on the wait, dressed in the same way as the first squadron. One of them took off one of his gloves and helped the blonde girl to stand. Where he placed his hands, the burns disappeared as if they had never existed. At the end of the miraculous healing, he stayed behind his dark visor and watched her. She opened her blue eyes, then shook her head. Equipped on the rest of her apparel and gear in a few seconds with a fixed schedule, just as she had been trained. She tightened the helmet straps and lowered her visor. Lohe was ready.

The Spearhead Triad got out of the van and headed for the door, still guarded by the leader of *Iluminieren* and his escort. The leader raised his left hand above his head, and stopped there for a few dramatic seconds when not even the wind dared to blow. As he lowered it, the fury of all the explosives was unleashed simultaneously. The dust was still not filling the space when flash grenades were thrown into the interior, saturating it with light and mist. Exactly one second later, both groups rushed inside. Each member of *Iluminieren* guarded one of the holes in position, while the trio moved in over the rubble.

Kad waited inside, in the same chair beside the stereo, while The Prelude continued to play at full volume. His silhouette cut against the background of dust in the room. Kad tried to stand up, but a blast of explosive ammo prevented him from doing so. The bullets exploded against the walls of the mansion with violence and rumbling, stained with the blood and flesh of the Akkadian.

A brief pause was taken, during which the seven combatants stopped firing in order to assess the situation. Kad stood slowly, with no signs of apparent damage, a warm smile on his lips and hands in pockets.

Lohe threw her weapon aside, and went into combat posture, Fender and Konnex placed behind her in a triangular formation, as they flipped a small knob on their weapons that enabled the main function of the rifles. The fourth and final phase of the onslaught had begun. The Iluminieren group surrounded their target and approached at optimum distance in a matter of instants.

The motionless Kad finally raised his jaw and looked around. The situation seemed to amuse him, perhaps it was something he had been waiting for since he learned that there was something capable of eliminating someone of his class, and now it was developing in front of him. It was the right time to unleash the horror.

A new burst of explosions pierced his figure, one that was no longer human. Irreal tentacular extensions now filled the spot where Kad had been, soon covering walls, floor and ceiling in overwhelming numbers, dripping blood from wounds that closed almost instantly. The vision in the mist was the closest thing to something taken from the nightmares of a deranged psychotic. The two closest members of *Iluminieren* doubted for their lives, until their military training took responsibility of the situation. They advanced with their rifles high, this time using in their real function. Beneath the muzzle, from a protrusion of the narrow box, fan-shaped electric arcs emerged, extending almost two meters to the front, electrocuting and incinerating everything in their path. Both did their best to contain the beast from the flanks long enough, but failed. The tentacular nightmare was quicker, slicing them up like loaves of bread. The smell of blood and burning had long since covered the smell of cement dust. The remaining members of the command opened fire as they relocated to take the place of the fallen, keeping the monster as far away as possible. They had to buy enough time. Just enough time. But it was not possible to keep him in line. It zigzagged forward in an inconceivable way and in times that at first glance could not be possible, driving everyone back. Only Konnex remained in place, trying to attack from a completely different angle. Ever since she entered the house she'd been trying to break through Kad's mental barriers, so far without success. His mind was a maze of desert dunes in which she found no point of connection. She was pushing herself to the limit and time was running out.

Fender shouted an order, and the edge of the spear came into action. Lohe charged into the terrifying mass with incredible speed. Her lightning movements were impossible to follow as she leapt past the sharp tentacles, the voltaic arcs and the bullets that were constantly flying through the air. However, few of her blows reached their destination, and if they did, had poor effect. When a tentacle was destroyed, it liquefied quickly and returned to the main mass, which changed shape at all times.

A huge biological mass shot out into one of the corners of the roof, and came down like a rain of long, sharp bones and tendons on the remaining members of the support squad, immediately beheading one and filling the body of the other commando and Fender's body with holes. In this cruel way, the well-prepared group of proud *Illuminieren* soldiers was eliminated, leaving behind them only grunts of pain and death. Fender stood up. His uniform had holes all over it, but underneath the body was intact, courtesy of his superb cell regeneration. Inside his head, the question was different, as dozens of plans paraded, discarded one after the other in the face of the Akkadian's power. He was superior. Extremely superior. There was only one tactic left available other than to flee. Was it even possible to make a run for it? The Akkadian clearly did not intend to escape, he might as well be having fun. Everything now depended on Konnex and her wonderful ability to break anyone down.

The battle had become practically a duel between Lohe and Kad, on the one hand a lightning bolt of omnipotent agility and drive, and on the other a beast that could not be destroyed, but damaged with every move. Lohe was full of superficial and some deep cuts on her extremities.

But somewhere, well hidden, an ancient screen fell, a barrier shattered, exposing a receptive mind for the first time in probably millennia. Konnex had accomplished her task with an atrocious effort, managing to implant an idea in the depths of his psyche. Just one feeling, but one that changed everything: Despair.

Despair.

Despair.

Despair.

The tentacular mass stopped moving for a moment, and then gradually regained a relatively human form as it retreated in surrender. A face emerged from the whole, one infinitely tired. Kad's smile had evaporated. Fender shouted another command at Lohe, who turned to him. It took him a brief moment to heal all her wounds in the same miraculous way as before.

Lohe got on her guard again, drew a wide circle with her arms, carried her right hand behind her, fist firmly stuck to the waist. She paused, while concentrating all her vital force in one tiny point, all the scientific effort and all her life of soulless training. It had to be that one and there'd be no more chance. She had to concentrate it all, even if she fainted. She rushed to her stationary target with redoubled speed. And struck.

An explosion broke through the entire mansion, shaking to the ground. Parts of the ceiling of the mezzanine that had remained during the battle crumbled, the dust from the air dispersed in a fraction of time.

Lohe fell to the floor, totally exhausted. Every muscle and joint in her body hurt, the helmet preventing her from breathing. She made a great effort to remove it and look up, until she did. Kad was gone, and The Prelude wasn't sounding anymore. In its place, there was only a scattered compendium of strange organs, blood and stones. It was finally over.

PART 14: BEHIND A SMOKESCREEN

Carl Fisher was confused and crestfallen. He gently pulled his head back as he let the cigar smoke out of his mouth, forming shapes in the air in front of him. Sitting down to smoke one of his *Cohiba Pirámide* in the dark helped him relax and think. He had not slept through the night, meditating on what had happened since Perius' arrival at his office. That office that now disgusted him, where he was forced to lower his head in the first place, and that was the reason why he had moved temporarily to the basement of the headquarters. His new, makeshift, windowless office was ideal for him to sit in the dark and think of something to get him out of the mess he had gotten into. Hardly a lamp in a corner and the tip of his cigar emitted light in that site. A slight buzzing sound could be heard from the wall behind him, and on the other side several dozen computers controlled the traffic on the base. That buzzing was a firm reminder of how fast things were moving forward, of how the fear of feeling superfluous was fiercely on his heels. He actually knew that they would never do without whoever was in the position of commander, but there is a huge difference between who decides what to do, and who only signs under a sheet of paper delivered by a machine. And the operation he now had in his hands was strangely similar. This time he had no choice but to sign below, but the sheet came from the hand of an incredibly dangerous being.

Everything was already in motion. For a moment he hated the part of himself that planned *for* the monster instead of rebelling, but it was too late and knew there was no other choice. A nuclear submarine was awaiting his orders, and Intelligence was already drawing up a plot to serve as a smokescreen for the operation. And that's as far as his role went, and wasn't planning on lifting another finger.

He clenched his fists as he rebuked himself for lying to himself. It was clear that this would not end here, it was only the beginning of the calamities. He failed to see any escape. If he disappeared from the scene he would have to go underground, but also have half the army looking for him to try and convict him. If he stepped aside, someone else would discover the farce and he'd end up sentenced. The only way out was out in the front, into the mouth of the abyss. Unless he fought back, and became the hero of the story.

The train of his thoughts was cut off by the piercing sound of the phone. He almost thanked the event that brought him out of the horrible place that was now his head.

_Fisher here.

_General, the presentation is ready. Mr. Perius is already here.

_...I'll be right there.

He reluctantly put the cigar out on a modest glass ashtray, took his hat off his desk and stood up to go out. Outside the room two soldiers with lost eyes waited. They turned at an unusual and almost clumsy pace, saluting.

_Sir, would you like us to escort you?

_No, thank you, soldier.

_But sir... Mr. Perius has ordered us to accompany you at all times.

Fisher was getting fed up with that little game. _Tell me... Bobland, that Perius has any military rank?

_N-no, not that I know of, sir.

_Is he the President?

_He's not.

_Then can he give you orders? – Corporal Bobland was speechless, utterly enmeshed in his inner confusion.

_I am *your* General, and I *order* you to stay here with your partner and guard my office. Understood?

Neither of them said a word as Fisher turned around to leave. He did not even manage to make three steps that he heard they were following him. It is useless, he thought, they really can't resist. And continued the march with his compulsory escort.

A hundred meters ahead on the same basement, Intelligence was in a state of turmoil as the final details of the plan were being worked out. About twenty men came and went with photo folders and digital tablets, typing on their computers or making phone calls. In the middle of the room a huge oval table dominated the scene, along with a large screen that was suspended in front of it, similar but larger than another one embedded in the table. On one of its tips, a calm, old-fashioned gentleman sat with his pipe between his fingers as he gently held his fine, beautifully decorated cane. Behind him four well-armed soldiers waited with blank minds, ready to fulfill the wishes of the eminent Lord, but mostly as a slight demonstration of power before the newly arrived General.

Some officers, those closest to the door, greeted Fisher firmly as he and his escort walked through the room.

A man stepped forward and extended his hand after the proper greeting. _General Fisher, it's a pleasure to have you here. Have a seat, please. - Hendrich pointed out a comfortable armchair upholstered in black leather at the opposite end of Perius.

Carl Fisher was powerfully struck by the fact that Thomas Hendrich spoke and acted normally while the rest of the base was influenced by the beast. Chief of Intelligence Hendrich was a tall, black man with square features and an outstanding chin. He had a small scar on the side of his neck, caused by some sharp element. His black eyes inspired tranquility beneath his fine eyebrows. His personality was energetic, radiating vitality and intelligence.

_Thank you, Hendrich... are you all right?

_Perfectly, sir.

_In that case, after the presentation, I'd like to cross a few words with you. - Fisher pointed his index finger at him.

_Surely, no problem. - he replied, with an unchanging air of professionalism.

Hendrich shouted out some orders and sat in his place to the right of the General. A dozen officers left their reports on the oval table to take their seats immediately afterwards.

The Chief of Intelligence at the base waved his hand slightly, and the lights in the room dimmed. Both screens lit up, showing a map of Italy and the other one of the island of Manhattan.

_Well then, General, gentlemen present, Mr. Perius, welcome to Intelligence. We've been working hard under the circumstances but at a good pace. My congratulations go out to all my staff. Operation *Bullseye* is classified as Class S and is highly confidential, starting today, October 26th. The personnel present, Admiral Sherman Longcastle and Secretary Thomas Hicks, who have given their express consent, constitute the only persons with full access to it. Without further introduction I will begin. *Bullseye* will be composed of three phases. The first one is already underway. The USS *Poseidon* is armed and ready to run, with visual support from the *Compass III* satellite. The *Poseidon* will launch a tactical nuclear warhead at 44° 31' 10" North, 9° 3' 55" East. The number of human casualties per direct impact will be zero, while within the area affected by the residual radiation the estimated number of humans affected will be approximately two thousand until evacuation tasks are completed. Fatalities among those affected by radiation are estimated to be less than three hundred, provided evacuation begins immediately. - Hendrich's voice didn't flinch when he mentioned the numbers - The number of non-human targets in the area unknown, but it is expected to exceed one thousand five hundred, with a survival rate of less than 1%. - on the monitor embedded in the table, the graph of a reddened area was spread over a portion of the map, while another green area showed the expected effects of the wind carrying the radiation. – On completion of the attack, the second phase begins. Dickson, if you please. – he addressed a bald man sitting in front of him, who stood up. The soldier looked like a ball of nerves. His cheekbones, usually red, were pale. His hands did not stop shaking as they barely held a bunch of notes. His gaze, empty of content, could not focus on any particular place. _Gentlemen... the second phase has been dubbed *Decoy*.

The tone of his voice revealed something abnormal, as did the imperceptible pauses between words. _During this phase which will begin at 0600 hours tomorrow... the unit of Sergeant Perez and his men is already affected to take position at ground zero as soon as the highest amount of radiation is dissipated. They'll be carrying samples of enriched uranium from... Erongo, Namibia. – he carefully read the notes on his hand – ...where they have orders to plant it as evidence to... disengage the US Navy's missile strike. The uranium records... have already been erased so they can't be related to us in any way. – a long pause was taken to continue, while looking at his notes – Perez has also been instructed to seal off the area, prevent the passage of civilians and military personnel, and prevent analysis by the European Union for fourteen days. We assume... we'll be able to replace his unit once we're authorized to send massive troops in about two more weeks. At the same time a specialized unit will be sent to the island of Manhattan, where they will find in these coordinates... – both screens changed content. The map of the island was present on the table, with a small blue dot on it – ...a low-priority al-Qaeda cell. On... the 31st, the targets present will be eliminated, and a container containing uranium from the same source as the previous one will be planted, along with... plans and digitized information for an operation with nuclear arsenal. – Dickson turned the page slowly – Five hours after the attack, the press will be informed through a White House conference about the successful deactivation of... a terrorist operation that sought the destruction of a vast portion of the city by... – he breathed heavily a couple of times – a new organization widely spread around the world. Details about this new organization will be vague on purpose, releasing infor...mation about it over the months. First of all... it will only be mentioned that this is a group with strong funding from religious extremists, who seek an end to the Western way of life through... terror tactics and the use of weapons of mass destruction, under the name of "*Al-Jannatu*", whose approximate translation is... "The Paradise". – he turned another sheet of paper, and stared attentively in silence.

_Dickson, please continue. – Hendrich hastened.

_Yes... *Al-Jannatu* will be classified as Maximum Danger, and will serve as a scapegoat for military maneuvers anywhere on the globe. From now until...

the period of one year, three deactivations of cells will be made known to the public, and from then on the rate of appearance of cells will be sporadic and will depend on... - he stopped to read the exact words - the political necessity of the moment.

Fisher couldn't sit still anymore. _This plan is leaking all over the place, it's too bold, it leaves too many loose ends! How can you fake an organization like that, started out of nothing, one that the United States never mentioned even a thing to the international community? It's almost idiotic.

Hendrich left the papers in his hand and cleared his throat before speaking. _It doesn't really come from "nothing," General. We are basing the behavior and composition of this new organization on *Al-Qaeda*, renaming it and giving it more attributions, perhaps, but it is not coming out of thin air, if that is what you mean. I assure you that the professionals who have accompanied me in putting this plan together are among the most capable and best trained in the world. The plan is solid. And in the event that a minor fault is found, it will be resolved quickly.

_Let's see then, Hendrich. Where do they get their funds? Where have they been hiding from the eyes of the major powers all this time? Why don't they keep attacking targets elsewhere?

_Step by step, please. We will inform that the main influx of capital comes from the illegal sale of arms in Central Africa and South-East Asia. There is no way to discuss this point, as there is no unquestionable record of arms trafficking, only conjectures. About the next issue, they were hidden under the umbrella of non-aligned governments and better yet, hiding as if they were part of other terrorist organizations. Hence their dangerousness, they can be anywhere at any time. On the last issue, they do not continue to attack because we have discovered and infiltrated them, which is why they are holding back until determining what happened. We will probably need to let another attack to pass, to reinforce the idea of their power.

_You already talk as if they really exist.

_For practical purposes, they exist. They provoke terror. For theoretical purposes, they are a tool.

Fisher let out the air he kept in his lungs, and with it his desire to keep questioning.

_You're probably wondering what action we'll take against them. We already have that covered. Ashton, go ahead, please.

This time Ashton stood up to talk to everyone. Ashton was young for his position, but his analytical skills (and some political favors) earned him the status of Hendrich's right-hand man. Nothing unusual was noticeable about him, as it was about his direct boss.

Fisher raised strong suspicions. There were some edges of the situation that he knew nothing about and that deserved his immediate concern. No doubt he should talk to Hendrich and try to get as much information out of that fox as possible.

Henry Ashton, yellowish in complexion, with brown eyes and long limbs, slowed down before he began, noticing that Dickson was still standing in place without moving. Hendrich intervened. _Dickson, have a seat so Ashton can get started.

A deep, powerful voice was heard from one of the sides of the table. _Is there anything else you want to tell us, Roy? - Perius turned to Dickson, who suddenly reacted.

_Yes, I... I don't like this plan. I don't... li–like it.

_No worries, Roy, everything will be fine. Have a seat if you will be so kind. Henry, please continue. - Dickson sat down immediately, and Ashton began.

_Gentlemen, the last phase of the operation is called *Liberty Wings*, and it will be the basis of American foreign policy in the next quarter century if everything is as we expect it to be. First of all we will call for an extraordinary meeting of NATO - North Atlantic Treaty Organization - plus NPV - New Warsaw Pact - in view of the new threat. In it, we will set out the new scheme for detecting and destroying *Al-Jannatu*, a task that will require a firm and determined command from the unified forces of all Allied forces, under the command of the United States Army, the force most prepared and capable of doing so. – Ashton cleared his throat – The new guidelines will include an increase in the military budget for the modernization of ordinary and intelligence equipment. We will highlight the benefits of our newly developed system, the OPTER 12, to be the standard of both organizations. We doubt that the United Kingdom will comply with the 12 as they have a similar one in power and performance, mostly i–

_Ashton, those details are not vital at this time. – Hendrich interrupted.

_Of course, my apologies, sir. – he turned a couple of pages on his tablet and went on. – We expect our allies to acquire our technology, which will help finance the costs of the operation. The following measures will also be required: One hundred and twenty–day closures of international airports, doubling of border personnel in each country, and the immediate and indefinite transfer of ports and airports to military jurisdiction. All three of these measures must be complied with in full. At the same time, we will temporarily increase the current personnel for the control of the border with Mexico and Canada, both of which will be transferred to purely military jurisdiction within a period of twelve months. The Congress will be asked to increase the number of personnel for European bases by 100% as the primary objective, and by 50% in the Middle East and Asia.

Fisher, who had been drumming his fingers against the table, raised his voice, staring at Ashton. _You understand that you intend to militarize an entire continent with our troops, right?

_I... yes, that's right.

_Where will the funds for such a budget increase come from?

Ashton looked down. _It will probably be necessary to create a special tax and reassign it to National Security. Given the scenario, it shouldn't be difficult to put pressure on the Congress for that.

_That's bullshit, there's no way to sustain that spending on time. You just can't, it'll sink under its own weight. - he spoke wearily as he cleaned the sweat off his forehead.

Hendrich looked sidelong at Perius, who was still in his seat, cross-legged and listening attentively. He looked back at him, and with a smile answered his unspoken question. _Thomas, you can explain to the General how we will get the funds.

Hendrich glanced at all the people present, and declared. _The reach of Operation *Bullseye*... extends beyond what has been mentioned so far. We want Europe, America and the Near East to be under American protection, and for their economic, political and security affairs to pass through Washington. In short, the future operations will be funded with money from our protégés.

_I don't believe it, you want to blackmail the world. - lamented Fisher - You're crazy, Perius.

Perius laughed quietly. _Again, do you think I will not be able to do it?

_The whole plan is compromised, it's in danger of being discovered at every moment. Even... *your people* will know it's a lie.

_For every difficulty there is, I will take care of it. Carl, I came here with solutions, not problems. I like the plan you lot have in mind. - he said to everyone - I congratulate you. Personally, I would change a few details, but there will be time for that. I am anxious to get started. What is the situation, Thomas?

_Armed forces of unknown origin approaching coordinates. - he checked his watch, whose timer was running - Estimated time of arrival in three minutes.

_Excellent, then everything is ready. - he wrapped the sentence up with a wide smile, while playing with his cane - Carl, are you willing to continue then? Your command is needed.

Fisher seemed to shrink in size, wedged in his now enormous armchair. He was cornered, it was time to decide his immediate future, whether to follow the monster and let it weigh it on his conscience forever, or whether to rebel and be brainwashed. He was surprised that his instinct for self-preservation was overshadowed by the idea that his wife and daughter might suffer. No, the road was only one. It has always been just one.

_Authorization granted, you may execute *Bullseye*. - the drops of perspiration kept falling on his face.

Hendrich nodded his head, and an operator a few meters from the conference table typed the entire code encrypted to the Poseidon.

PART 15: IN A HOUSE OF CARDS

Vogel Drescher looked up in sudden panic. It couldn't be happening, he'd been warned, he was smarter than the others. How did his hand of four aces fail? He hurried off stumbling down the cold marble steps into the interior, desperately seeking more time to think. Inside, the Palace looked like an anthill kicked by an infant. Dozens of Shadows were positioned in their places, not quite ready for an attack with air support. A woman in black pushed Drescher to the side, and threw several insults at him before continuing her hasty march out. A huge explosion was heard dangerously close by, blowing window panes everywhere. Some fell on Drescher, causing a superficial wound to his left hand. He watched a solitary crimson drop sprout and fall to the ground in silence. Another deafening explosion brought him back to reality. He turned to face the front of the Palace. And didn't like what he saw. Some "Menace" troopers in blue and black uniforms and huge alloy weapons had entered. In the background, some helicopters were fluttering, firing lead on to the top floor. The winged Lions had arrived.

If even a burst reached him, it would be the end. His dry mouth and the sweating that ran down the back made him terribly uncomfortable, he struggled with himself to stay focused. He had to get to safety somehow, and began to dig around frantically to find a lifesaving idea, but the only thing that caught his attention was a staircase to a lower floor that led into a dark hallway. He made sure there was no attacker behind him, and slid awkwardly over there. The corridor seemed to him to be the Limbo in comparison, devoid of movement and hardship. Obviously, it had no tactical significance for anyone, at least for the time being. Saw a small, semi-destroyed window on one side, slightly above the line of his head. He analyzed the possibilities of following the path, going out through the small opening, trying to get to the upper floor or staying there. Some sort of certainty was extremely needed, even if it was minimal. He looked again at the window to see if he could fit, and climbed up to observe. Any information he might have was better than ignorance, said to convince himself. The blackness of the snow-covered forest was interrupted by the movement of troops descending from the helicopters, trying to surround the entire building. The forest road was the best he had and it was dangerous.

Something caught his eye. There was something else, waiting crouched in the foliage. A grayish fright suddenly moved at great speed toward the column of soldiers. The guns screamed in unison, but they could not contain it. The giant specter moved among the trees, plucking wood and meat equally at its wake. The blinking lights of the bombs revealed its cruel nature in flashes. It was a beast of six limbs, each with three or more joints, with what appeared to be a strong shell of scales covering it completely. On its head shone four eyes and at least a hundred teeth within its huge, ghostly jaws. Drescher had never seen Lord Chandresh so focused on his primal instincts as to unveil such a creature from the confines of his mind and body. His stomach could not tolerate all the killing in front of his eyes for long, so he leapt back to the ground. The last scene gave him hope, though. Chandresh had clawed down one of the helicopters and scattered the survivors, so at least the back of the Palace would not be a hell of a troop when he got there, that was the path to escape!

He continued to trot through the ancient passage of lustrous stones, continually attacked by the sounds of war and the piercing screams. The passage turned into a hall with enigmatic black and white ceramic floors, huge columns, a penumbral beauty of refined taste. Not a soul in sight anywhere... it couldn't be that simple. He let himself be fooled by a sense of empty victory. What if he just ran to the back at full speed? Who would notice him, a single man running away from the conflict? He accelerated, this time with a wide smile on his face as he held his hat. He painstakingly lifted the wooden board that secured the wide double doors of oak and iron and threw it aside. Opened one of the doors loudly, and looked outward. He was greeted by a draught of icy air against his temples, the darkness of the night and some immaculate snowflakes.

Vogel panted a few times, even more convinced of his luck and wit. He managed merely one step out when a stabbing pain squeezed his right arm, as he was stunned by a dull echo. A torrent of blood stained his clothes and he rushed down. He observed the wound, and instantly understood that it had been an explosive ammunition. The confusion sublimated with speed. A second projectile struck the door within centimeters of his head, sending shrapnel in all directions and his faithful hat away from salvation. He leapt backwards to the ground, feeling betrayed by his austere fate, feeling the burning of the new wounds on his forehead. He checked his injured arm with the touch, which was in poor condition, but attached to him for the time being. In the midst of the cruel anguish, he fleetingly remembered Isabella's face, her eternally rosy lips, her deep, innocent honey eyes. He wanted to be back in her warm refuge, undressing and hugging his beloved Isabella. That thought was interrupted by a big jumble of emotions, did he feel anything *real* for her? He surprised himself greatly. Outside, in the winter cold, voices were heard ever closer. The shooters were going to enter shortly. There was no time for nonsense. He climbed to his feet in pain and ran down another corridor, into the house of cards once more.

Charles Dipson and MacOwen stood up immediately when they heard the alarm coming from the ground floor. They looked at each other without saying a word, and set about collecting their belongings as soon as possible. They left the room, to find the silent Shadow still chanting a sad melody on the piano. Outside, the first explosions shook the melancholy atmosphere.

_Miss Syra, the enemy is at our gates, we must face them. - Dipson anticipated with urgency.

_She's in a trance and won't listen. We can't afford to waste our time here, we have to go out and face the Menace. -MacOwen seconded, as he prepared his opaque sword.

They walked across the room, but interrupted their departure at the sound of an awful, out of tune note of the piano. They turned around, to find Syra completely still. For the first time she laid her eyes on them. _We've got to run! We're all going to die here!

_What are you talking about, hav-? - Dipson couldn't complete the sentence.

_Finally I can see through the veil. - she held relatively calmly- We will be attacked with a terrible weapon, and must escape. We don't have more than two or three minutes.

_A terrible weapon? Can't we face it? - MacOwen resisted the idea of giving up the fight.

164

_No way. - the Shadow expressed as she jumped over the furniture. - I intend to get to safety in the catacombs of the Palace, it's the only chance if I have one.

MacOwen looked out to see what was happening downstairs. _We can't seem to repel them, if we get to the catacombs we'll have to go together. I'll take the front. In other circumstances I would not have intended to put you in danger, Miss, but I understand that your skill can get us out of trouble. You'll be in the back. Charles, follow us to a safe distance, but don't miss the beat, we may not be able to get back.

_I agree. - Syra said.

Dipson summed up his acceptance by nodding his head as he persigned.

_Now. - MacOwen hurriedly charged out, as he persigned himself with one hand, hold his weapon with the other, as they all walked down the majestic steps.

On one side, half a dozen soldiers were gaining territory inside the Palace. On the ground lay heaps of undecipherable debris, glass and biological remains. They were momentarily distracted by the appearance of a Shadow that had remained hidden, pretending to be a portion of the ceiling. He rushed toward the fighters with a machete in each hand, severing the heads of two of them and the leg of a third. The others opened fire, failing every discharge. The Shadow had turned into a pool of thick blood, to resume humanoid form behind the soldier who remained bent in pain at the loss of a limb.

MacOwen in turn jumped down behind one of them, inserting his steel in the torso of an unfortunate recruit, while Syra slid almost liquidly behind the other two, killing them by burying her sharpened and abnormally long fingernails in their throats. The mysterious Shadow recreated his legs completely and continued to march outward, where the explosions repeated themselves ceaselessly, and another, larger group of Menace lined up in his direction.

_Let's continue. - Syra said, heading down a wide corridor. The two men followed her. They emerged into a large hall with ample windows and columns of ancient Greek style.

_There seems to be no resistance for this wing. - Dipson cried out, panting heavily.

_Don't get confident, Charles. Eyes always open.

They ran until Syra surprised them with a sudden scream. _Stop! Get down! - she glanced outward throwing herself on the floor and flattened almost impossibly. The incessant murmur of turbines and blades increased abruptly, announcing the arrival of an imposing combat helicopter. It maneuvered low and turned, scattering ammunition left and right, demolishing concrete and glass alike. Several rounds of ammo were stuck in the chest of MacOwen, who had taken a courageous step forward, sending him off against the wall and leaving a red, viscous trail in his path. The helicopter completed the circle, and flew up again, trying to dodge a duo of Shadows that had jumped over it. For a moment, only stone dust, the smell of burnt blood and the roar of engines disturbed the bloody scene.

Syra watched MacOwen's wreckage, undisturbed. _It's unfortunate, but we must continue. - she commanded.

_Wait, please, he needs time to recover! - Dipson asked.

The dazed Irishman regained consciousness as his wounds miraculously closed, leaving his clothes as the only remaining gifts of the strike received. _I'm... almost ready. - MacOwen spoke with difficulty as he stood slowly and retrieved his sword. They went through the room into a narrow corridor. Stopped again, this time listening to loud, irregular footsteps. MacOwen gestured silently with his finger, and they waited as the steps grew closer. From the other end of the corridor loomed a figure, clad in white and stained with blood. Drescher looked at the trio as if he were witnessing an apparition and shouted a short cry.

_Drescher! How did you get here? - Dipson asked genuinely surprised from behind.

_I... I was in the fight, I got shot. - he paused to catch his breath - Then I got lost, I can't go back there, I'm really hurt!

_Let's not waste any more time, we may have barely seconds. - Syra hastened.

_Where are you going? May I join you?

_To the catacombs. Stay with Charles and stick close to him. - MacOwen's imperative tone became urgent.

They ran down another corridor, full of doors on the left and right. Syra slammed the last three doors before she found the right one. _Here.

They went into a small service room. The room was completely dark, the slight light revealed little of its interior. In the center, an old trap door could be hardly seen. _I don't know where this entrance leads, but we can't look for another one. - explained the Shadow, as she lifted the lid, which protested with a shriek.

Dipson and Drescher went first down a corroded iron ladder, followed by Syra and MacOwen, who closed behind them. A sullen electric light bulb glowed in the middle of the gray basement, activated by an antique switch at the entrance. A few shabby shelves with old boxes populated the faded walls. In the back, a heavy metal door remained undisturbed amidst the dance of lights and shadows that the light bulb, hanging from its cable provoked around it. The perception of time seemed different under the earth, with the seconds stretching like rubber bands. Syra stood motionless facing the door, again in a trance, as the others searched the place. A few moments passed that felt eternal, before speaking. _It's not safe here either, keep going.

_What do you see? I don't understand. – Drescher snapped.

_I see fire... blazing fire.

The answer upset Drescher enormously. _Is there a way out of that door? We need to check it out!

Dipson approached the rusty door, and after two attempts he managed to open it. A new corridor presented itself before them, descending into total blackness. Only the first section was covered with paving stone, while the rest was made up of bare rock. Four torches hung on the walls, three of which had their wood rotten, falling apart when taken. Only one, in its precariousness, was fit to be used. Dipson pulled a pack of matches from his bag, cut off his sleeve to tie it at one end and lit it carefully. An endless array of brown rock was waiting for them underneath.

_Let's move forward, but don't let your guard down. – MacOwen warned.

On the surface, the fighting was raging, dozens and dozens of bodies lay inert on the ground. The invaders continued to advance over the wreckage, into the Palace, while the survivors of Crest were entrenched as best as they could in the face of the overwhelming attack. Not far from there, the voracious ocean opened up. The waves constantly crashed against the walls of the ship, illuminated by the selenite light, without disturbing it at all. A mechanical gate opened, and the fire and the smoke floated momentarily over the waters.

Thus, the Hammer of the Gods ascended in all its splendor, rising from the depths of the sea, leaving behind it a trail of greatness and withered corruption. It sailed across the black skies with speed and certainty, flying over heaven and earth. It formed a perfect arch to descend on Aegis, the Palace of Eternal Decadence.

For a brief moment, silence became absolute emperor, leaving chaos, in its purest and most elemental expression, as its heir. The earth, razed to the ground, burned like never before, becoming in seconds a horrifying wasteland, crowned by an imposing mushroom cloud that denied all life at its feet.

PART 16: THE GIFT

The dust was slowly settling over the destroyed furniture in the unfortunate Barcelonese manor, improvised battlefield of *Speerspitze's* most difficult mission. Outside, in the garden, the sounds of the night gradually usurped the place. Fender took off his helmet and tossed it next to him, physically and mentally drained. He had blue and tired eyes, some very short blond hair extremely sweaty surrounding his rounded head, and a wide mouth without shade crowned by a straight nose of almost perfect proportions, identical to those of his sisters. He did a quick panning around. The blackness of the night had already filled the house, and the interior could only be seen by the reflection of the city lights and the park lamps. His sense of smell was totally saturated with the scent of death that permeated everything. He wanted to get out of there as soon as possible.

There were only two issues left, to evaluate the state of the group, to confirm the demise of the target, and they could leave. He breathed out the sinister air that was still inside his lungs strolling angrily back and forth. Closed his eyes to reward himself with ten seconds to relax and let his body reabsorb the torrents of adrenaline that his now undone armored suit had released into his blood. Hung his rifle over the shoulder, and tried to loosen his knuckles, which were attached to the hilt like the jaws of a crocodile to its prey. He inhaled a few times near the destroyed window, picking up the soft scent of the trampled flowers, and returned inside, as things had to be taken care of. Walked to the place where the Akkadian had been until a moment ago, tried to turn on the lights but it seemed useless, so he pointed his flashlight and checked the remains. Indistinguishable chunks of bone, flesh and red liquid crowded the floor, the walls and what was left of the furniture. Everything was covered with a thin layer of dust and small pieces of cement and brick.

The blow had really been lethal. He felt a mixture of relief and pride in his sister. For both actually, and for him, too. The whole team. He turned in his footsteps, flashlight in hand. The next priority was to assess the status of *Speerspitze* and *Iluminieren,* and to leave as quickly as possible. He started with Konnex, who was in a fetal position against a corner, still affected by the mental stress of having drilled the subconscious of the Akkadian. He took her helmet off carefully. Tears streamed down her soft, colored cheeks, and her lips, thin and smooth, whispered the word "despair" over and over again. She wasn't going to come out of shock for at least a few more minutes. He'd give her two minutes, no more, then give her a calming injection if necessary, and stroked her short, sweaty hair before continuing. He turned then to check on Lohe, who was still trying to catch her breath kneeling on the floor. The muscles of her right arm were twisted and torn from the tremendous force applied in her last blow. He knelt beside her and healed her wounds again.

_Are you all right, little girl? – Fender asked quietly, in German.

_Yes... yes... give me a moment. – Lohe's breathing was heavy and slow.

_I'm going to check on our teammates, I don't think I'll be coming back with good news.

He walked past the headless wretch and examined the other one's pulse. Nothing. He advanced a few more meters to where the last two were. The bodies of both were in a pitiable state, no effort would return them among the living. He took his radio from the belt and informed the drivers of the vans waiting outside about the situation.

_Fender here, mission accomplished, four casualties. Call the cleaning crew. *Speerspitze* extraction in one hundred and twenty seconds.

He heard confirmation from the other side and returned to Konnex.

_Are you better, sis?

_It was awful, Fen... I can't explain it in words, I was about to give up many times. – she paused – but I carried on, for us.

_I know, you were fantastic. You took the honors in this mission. Lohe's fine, the others didn't make it. We gotta go, ninety seconds tops. Can you stand up?

_I think so, yes. – she staggered and would have fallen if it hadn't been for her brother's help.

_Hold on to the wall, I'm coming.

He went to Lohe and assisted her in getting up, raising her arm above his shoulders.

_The extraction is... what's that? – Fender turned around, terrified of what he heard.

Something was moving, hidden within the confines of the manor. The triplets stood still, focusing all their attention on their ears. It was heard again, and again afterwards. That something was crawling in the rubble.

_I MUST SAY I'M SURPRISED, AND PLEASANTLY. YOU HAVE SO MUCH POTENTIAL. – the monstrous voices came from three, four, maybe more places at once.

_Where are you? Show yourself! – Fender shouted with all his might, lifting Lohe up with his shoulders and assisting Konnex with one hand, while his mind

174

sank deeper and deeper into the confusion. Was the Akkadian alive? It was impossible, it had to be someone different. Who else could have walked in without being seen? He pointed his flashlight in all directions, unable to illuminate any answer.

_THAT TALENT... IF YOU COULD JUST USE IT TO YOUR LIKING, THINGS WOULD BE SO DIFFERENT, WOULDN'T THEY? - spat out the voices. Several entities continued crawling around the corners in the dark interior of the semi-destroyed house.

_Who are they? Who are they? - Konnex, not yet fully recovered, had clearly panicked.

_IN A FEW HUNDRED YEARS... YOU COULD BE THE NEXT LEGEND. DID YOU NOTICE HOW YOU TOTALLY LET GO OF YOURSELF... WHEN ORDERED TO? - the sadistic voices now sounded in different places from the previous, far away, close, from five, six, seven different sources, causing a vibration that resounded in what was left of the crystals. They were everywhere, they were nowhere. - DID YOU FEEL THE FREEDOM... THE POWER OF BROKEN CHAINS?

_Wh-what do you want? - Fender unconsciously began to go back step by step, pulling his sisters with him. He turned his head quickly, the garden outside looked like a sanctuary of paradise, illuminated by the

175

lanterns and flooded with the scent of destroyed roses. At the front, instead, the demon himself seemed to have risen from hell to claim the entire site.

_I'M GOING TO GIVE YOU A GIFT. – the inhuman and grave tone said, from the left and right, from the front and back. -SOMEDAY... THANKS TO MY GIFT... YOU WILL BE FREE FROM THOSE WHO IMPRISON YOU.

Fender pushed Konnex trying to get her as close to the garden of Eden as possible and save her, but her legs failed, and she fell to the ground. _Get up! Run, Lohe! His eyes were totally out of whack, injected with blood and terror. Lohe took a few poor leaps, still exhausted.

_Get up! We have to es–!

Fender left his sentence incomplete. A tentacular force tore his head cleanly off and dragged it through the air into the Avernus. Lohe and his brother's inert body fell slowly to the ground. The silence was so dense that it could be cut with a knife.

_No, no please, please... – Konnex's drowned cries rang. Her sobbing ended suddenly, suffering the same fate, her head severed from the neck rose slightly to disappear into the darkness forming a pendulous path of blood drops, where invisible entities continued to creep about.

Lohe watched in horror and blurred eyes at the inanimate shells of her most beloved ones in the entire world, in total panic, swallowing her shrieks several times.

_Now, run away! Maybe we'll run into each other again, child. - Kad's kind voice suggested.

Lohe's legs responded halfway, but enough to get up and try to run. Each step took her further away from the nightmare. She crossed the yard as quickly as she could and hit the back of one of the black vans twice with her fist. The door opened and she threw herself in, utterly defeated and unable to hold back her tears. In her confusion she didn't notice until several minutes later that the vans were already underway returning to the base.

Kad left the mansion making sure not to damage the lawn of the garden covered with pieces of glass and debris. His stature was noticeably reduced, his body now thinned, rickety. He no longer had his usual black overcoat made of compressed biomass, instead he only formed an improvised tight shirt and pants of indefinite color. He slowly transformed the bare skin of his feet into crude shoes as he walked, and they glowed in a subtle black tone a few seconds later. Looked up at the cloudy sky with some bitterness in his expression. Moved a few meters away from his temporary home, before stopping suddenly and returning a few steps. He watched the mansion, now little more than beautiful ruins, still with its lions guarding the park. Seemed hesitant for a few moments, then he walked toward one of the walls that bordered it, and extended his index finger covered in firm, sharp bone.

He traced the word "*PERDÓN*" - sorry, in Spanish - on the wall, sketched out an enigmatic smile, and left, passing among the few curious neighbors who went out to snoop.

PART 17: PATRIOT

Fisher played nervously with a pen in his hands, looking sideways at Hendrich and Ashton, but not even daring to lay eyes on the alien. The waiting was suffocating him, little by little he felt as if the walls of the bunker were closing in on him. Everyone there was acting so strange... with that artificial and impure serenity they had been infused. His ears were still not used to the soft, invasive buzzing of the computers around him. For the umpteenth time he annihilated the impulse to get up and run away, in each scenario he saw himself lying on the ground with more or less violence involved. The pen bent to the limit of what the plastic's resistance could offer, being tormented under his restless fingers. Suddenly it happened.

_We have visual confirmation of *Compass III*, successful attack, target destroyed at 0.502. – the monotonous voice of an operator punctured the stillness of the Intelligence Room.

Hendrich quickly clapped his hands, followed by the rest of the crowd, with the exceptions of Fisher and Dickson who remained still.

Perius raised both hands in satisfaction. _Excellent. Gentlemen, we are inaugurating a new world era, you must feel joyful to have been here at this historic moment, and to be a fundamental part of it. My applause is for you.

Hendrich was particularly euphoric about it. _I want to extend my thanks for your support. At 2000 hours my assistants will have the report ready so you will be able to read it after dinner. In the morning we'll close *Decoy's* details, but by then our men will be on their way. You are dismissed.

Fisher slowly counted to ten, as the zombies present gathered their things and left. A tiny plastic shrapnel flew out of the pen, which shattered when the count was over. _Hendrich, don't forget our talk, when can we meet?

_If you give me half an hour I'll be at your disposal, General, how about in my office? - he replied, while packing a stack of reports into his briefcase.

_If you don't mind, I need a little sunshine on my skin, being underground is no longer for me.

_What do you suggest?

_Nothing unusual, outside your office, in front of the A3 barracks.

_Well, all right. In thirty minutes. - Hendrich saluted with a cordial but stiff greeting.

The Chief of Intelligence left with an escort, followed by his lackey, Ashton. That, that one would follow later, as soon as he finishes with that fox Hendrich. Fisher was sure that Perius had done no tricks on them, yet they were the two most cooperative in the base. He imagined several questions and answers in his head, entire conversations he could have with Hendrich, because he knew he had to be very cautious in the questionnaire, to get as much information out of it in exchange for as little as possible, and to elucidate his secret agenda.

But first, one small step for a man. Recover his own office. Daylight will surely help regain it and leave his defeat in the past. He was about to leave, when two soldiers flanked him.

_What do you intend?

_Escort you, sir.

_Bah! – he let go, significantly less angry than he was a few hours ago. Now he had a plan, or at least the beginning of one.

Before he left the room, he couldn't help but keep an eye on the demon. Perius followed him with his eyes, with the poise of someone who has already read the script and knows the end of the play.

He arrived at his office, but it took him a moment to cross the doorway of his office. It looked different now, illuminated by the divine sunlight. He took two steps inside, claiming his domain again. Called his faithful secretary Christina and asked for a cup of coffee while waiting for his meeting. Caffeine always managed to activate him, even on the longest days. He reviewed over and over again the questions he would ask, the correct order and tone of each one, to best cover his knowledge gaps in one go. His coffee arrived and he rushed it in a few sips.

_Christina, I'm going to the barracks, if anyone asks I'm doing a surprise inspection, I'll be back in about an hour. - He walked out of there with determined steps as he put on his coat.

_You two - said to his compulsory escort - I am on my way to talk to Hendrich, you may accompany me, but when we get there you will wait for me at a safe distance. Under no circumstances you are allowed to listen or participate in the conversation. Agreed? This is a private conversation. That's an order, soldiers.

He assumed that as long as it wasn't an order that went against the programming, it would be effective. They both nodded, and the trio got going.

Outside, the morning cold reigned. A platoon ran around the barracks to the sergeant's rhythm, spewing steam in unison from their exhausted mouths.

They arrived at the site, and waited. A few minutes later, Hendrich's figure was seen leaving his offices.

_Stay here. - this time the soldiers obeyed.

Fisher approached and both men greeted each other.

_Well then, what did you want to talk about? - Hendrich's voice sounded calm. He was wearing a solid black jacket, a vest and a tie of the same color. A badge with the logo of the base hung around his neck.

_Hendrich, I don't like to beat around the bush, so this will be a short and intense meeting. I know you're willingly collaborating with this Perius guy, you and your advisor. I also know that this monster has half the base under control, or more, including Dickson. What I want to know is why you're helping him.

_I doubt that Mr. Perius would like to be addressed as a monster, I would say that he is a very resourceful person.

_Anyway, it doesn't answer the question.

Hendrich let out a faint, sneering smile. _Do you know Fisher, what Perius *is*?

Fisher tipped his hat. Hendrich was skipping questions, but he was also interested in that subject. He tried to give no more than the essential information. _Well, I have a slight notion. I know that at some point there was a project that involved quasi-mythological beings to create supersoldiers or something similar, that seemed ridiculous and a little nonsensical to me. Until one of them broke into my office yesterday.

_No, Perius is not a supersoldier, nor a nonsensical project. I'll trust you with this information. There are at this very moment - he paused - an unknown number of entities that cannot be considered human, which we call in Intelligence, precisely, non-humans. It's not a whim. These entities have very different capacities from ours, among which are some properties that are adverse to them, but also the capability to modify their physical structure to their liking, among other surprising feats. But the most important fact is that they have been accompanying the development of humanity since ancient times, and that this has allowed them to attain structures of political and economic power so deep that, for practical purposes, they dominate the planet. - Fisher tried to keep his composure while listening.

_Are you telling me that nations are controlled by things like that? - he said, incredulously pointing his index finger at his interlocutor. The previous answer had shaken his script. Hendrich knew more about the subject than he had imagined.

_Yes, but not only that. Multinational corporations too, secret lodges, and organizations that I have no idea about. You may have noticed that they have no difficulty in dominating, even with the mere word.

Was Hendrich trying to play with him? He did not detect however, that he was lying, at least there was some truth to a greater or lesser degree in all that. But with his words he indicated that these things were more intrusive in world affairs than he originally believed.

_If they are in control of the United States, why come here personally? The order to attack could well have been given from above, without setbacks.

_I can't give you too many details, unfortunately, but I understand that there is currently a little commotion in the command of these entities, with two opposing sides.

_I see. And which side have we been forced to adopt?

_That Fisher, that's the best news. None. Don't you understand? For the first time, one of *them*, a high-ranked one, has approached us for genuine interest in this nation, rather than to mediate in their internal power struggles. – Hendrich was accentuating his words with a wave of his hand – *Bullseye* has dealt a hard blow to these sides, and yes, for the first time in... hundreds of years! America is free from their influences. Their power structures are faltering, it's time to step up and take our true place in history. Perius is going to help us with this.

Fisher looked at him with some condescension. _Do you really think you can trust him?

_Yes, I believe so. Know this, I have had to deal with these entities on several occasions, and they always have an agenda that favors their party interests. But Perius... he's a free agent, he doesn't have a side or anything to tie him down. He does what he does to see the world transformed and to bring true order. And he has chosen us to be the guardians and makers of that change. - Hendrich's frown remained static.

_Where did these beings come from? - Fisher tried to deflect the focus.

_From nowhere. From ourselves, more like. - he corrected himself - If you're asking, they're not aliens or whatsoever. I don't have the authority to inform you with technical details, but you can obviously ask for them. With your rank it shouldn't be difficult for you.

The feint upset Fisher greatly. _Don't take this the wrong way, Hendrich, but I believe you think you're a patriot when you're actually a fool, and all this business is going to weigh on our country for generations.

_I believe fervently that it will not be so, and that after meditating on it you will understand my reasons and cooperate with Mr. Perius. Why don't you talk to him personally about this subject? I'm sure he'll be able to answer your questions better than I can. - Hendrich's professional tone remained intact.

Fisher was tired of the situation, and the time was appropriate to turn around and end the questionnaire. And so he did, with few certainties. He was about to leave, but first he had to ask his last and most important question. _How long have you known about these entities, and Perius?

Hendrich was more surprised by the attitude than by the question itself, but he answered anyway. _About non-humans, long ago. From Perius... relatively little, about three years.

_I must assume that the first time he contacted you was then, wasn't it? And that this plan is nothing new to you, you've known about it for a long time.

Hendrich looked him straight in the eye before he uttered a word. _Have a good day, General. – he made the necessary salutation, and left for his underground offices.

Fisher stood by, watching the Chief of Intelligence walk away. That *Bullseye's bull-shit* had been in the oven for quite some time, under everyone's noses. How many others agreed with that, from the start? How to ask Longcastle and Hicks without being exposed? His escort stepped forward again, and they remained standing by his side.

He watched them both with tired eyes. _You again, Bobland? And... Suarez, the dynamic duo. – Fisher felt like doing harm, even if he was only armed with his words. – Did you even know that Perius is a monster? That's just been confirmed by Hendrich.

_No, sir! – they replied.

_Well, he's a monster, and got us in his claws.

PART 18: HOMELESS

_Enough Akkadian, your damn rock is gone, why don't we go now? - Argosio said, very annoyed - There will be a bloodshed here again soon and I don't want to be here when it happens. Wars don't interest me, I prefer to spend my nights with women and drink, not burying my sword in the chest of folks I don't know and risking my own.

Argosio was a robust, slightly hairless bear-like man with a bald head and scars on his face. He had a slight uneven beard, and an intense listlessness in his eyes. He was dressed in a studded leather harness and sandals of the same material. From his belt hung a short sword that had seen better years, within its ruined sheath. A bronze shield full of holes rested on the ground nearby. Above, the sky was clear, only the stars lit up the night in those nameless lands.

_I tell you, I'm about to get out of here and leave you alone, huh? Akkadian!

Kad looked up at his partner furiously. His face looked very different then, in a different time, many centuries ago. His nose was more curved and short, his brown hair covered part of his face, long to his shoulders and very dirty. He wore a torn, mud-stained camisole, a makeshift rope as a belt, from which dangled a faded bag of coins. One of his feet was bare and full of calluses, while in the other he had a leather sandal, though not in the best condition. He also had the lower part of his face and his hands covered with blood that was not his, as was the man beside him.

_Argo, shut the hell up! I didn't ask you to help me, you came because you wanted to, since you were bored in the tavern. Spare me your complaints.

_Buddy, your wretched stone is no longer here. Look, see? – Argosio pointed to the walls of what used to be the city of Ficana, from where huge columns of smoke climbed up ceaselessly – They used them all to hurl against the citadel. Rained all day long, they even threw dead mules when they ran out of rocks.

Kad stood up and put both hands around his waist. He looked back with nostalgia at what was a beautiful citadel, a ruby on the green meadow, now turned into shapeless rubble. He shook his head several times. _I still can't believe it.

_That's the way it is, Akko. I'm not happy either, huh? I liked the warehouse over there, they served good wine. I've got an idea, what do you say we go in and do a little run? We'll pick up some valuables and leave to Rome. We'll also see if I can get you something for your filthy feet. – he pointed out mockingly at Kad's feet – I know you don't like Rome, but it's close by and the people are meek.

189

Kad let out a sigh. Argosio became unbearable at times, but he was a good traveling companion, skilled with the sword and shield, and did not shy away from combat. He had also taught him how to repair weapons in the forge, which was useful if they camped in one place long enough. He was fond of him, even if he never told him.

_It's that there's nothing there, just peasants... bah, all right, come on. I can't think of anything better to do.

He took one last look around. A pair of bodies were lying on the ground, dead hours ago and cannibalized, beside various wheel marks from the siege machines that had been there all day. They carried their meager belongings and left.

They walked towards the citadel. Kad's gait was very different to the present: energetic, marked, ready to leap into action in the face of danger, even now that he was slowly approaching the ruins of his favorite village. Some flames resisted being extinguished on the straw roofs of the buildings, some soldiers ran through the streets, ending the lives of the elderly, children and women who had survived the initial attack. The screams filled the cruel scene.

They were already a league away when stopped.

_Are you sure about this, Argo? I thought you weren't in the mood for a fight.

_We'll do the usual, as soon as we see a small group with some loot, we take it out and escape before they see us. Let's go that way. - he said, referring to a portion of the wall still standing. The wall was made of cold, stacked stones, and had recently taken a few clear blows, scattered in all directions.

Crouching, they ran to the wall, without drawing attention. The troops within the city were too busy burning, destroying, and stealing to pay attention to a couple of moving shadows.

Kad, leaning out of a crack in the wall, watched the scene with bitterness. Ficana was more than just a citadel. It was the place he had called home for over two hundred years. All his adventures, unconsciously, began and ended there. The longest journeys, to the ends of the known world, were to return to Ficana, rest, and undertake the next one. It was the place where he could close his eyes in peace, take a deep breath and just stay. No one asked uncomfortable questions, no one interfered in his life. Found them kind, even. He had seen it grow, stagnate, fall and grow again. Seen the fashions come and go, the buildings built, aged and be demolished to use the materials in different ones. Sometimes he believed that it was his personal project to keep it the same, always radiant and vital. The riches he earned (if he came back with any) he would use to keep his favorite places running, the Tavern of the Pike, near the main entrance, the Traveler's Inn, where he had spent so many times hidden during the day, the market by the river, where he always found someone to buy his trophies and get some coins in exchange. And Ficana never ran out of ruffians, the kind that nobody was interested in, and that he could hunt without anyone seeing or suspecting. He loved to go back there.

Kad mounted above his eyes a memory, lost in there, of his happiest moment in this place. A festive night full of lights, of children dancing in the streets, of couples flirting in the dark, of laughter and wine on every corner. But nothing lasts forever. And he would no longer call "home" to any other place. He had grown tired of losing again and again that precious place to which one returns, instinctively, to heal the wounds of the soul. That port where you can anchor in the troubled sea. He had already had many dwellings that he called home, even small villages, all lost in time. He dared to call home to a person, a family, a company. But none of them survived with him. Finally, he dared to call an entire city his home... to end up the same way. He took a few moments to bid farewell to his Ficana and memories, which would rest peacefully in the boundaries of his mind.

A strong tap on his shoulder woke him up.

_There, those two. The tall one and the dwarf. Anybody's a mercenary these days, huh? Getting half a wage? – Argosio laughed loudly, until he realized that had to remain silent if he wanted to strike a clean blow. He cleared his throat. – They're carrying an interesting bag, I think I want to take a look at it, what do you think?

_Yeah, that'll be our loot and then we'll be gone. I don't want to stay here one more knot. – Kad's seriousness was total.

They moved as close as they could, until they were about thirty feet from their target, two men tucking shiny objects in a sack. Both had a brown leather shirt over their torsos and a bronze helmet on their heads. At their feet, two swords of good luster slept awaiting the renewal of hostilities. The tall man was on his back, with his head inside a window full of soot, with one hand he pulled out wooden, copper and lead cups, which he passed on to his tiny companion, who threw them in his sack after a brief examination. Argosio took a stone and flung it behind the dwarf's back, which turned around alerted.

_Hey! Who's there?

He crouched down to pick up his weapon from the ground, but it was his last move. Kad had slit his throat from side to side. The tall man pulled his torso and head out of the building to find himself surprised by the scene. He wanted to scream, but the edge of Argosio's weapon stopped him.

_These guys forget to pay attention, that's why they die young, huh? – Argosio laughed softly. The two men picked up the bag and took it to a dark place. Quickly

193

browsed their contents, removed out the least valuable and heaviest, leaving only what was easier to sell.

Argosio hung his sword in the sheath and carried the sack over his shoulder. _The tall fella has some nice sandals, don't you like them?

Kad retraced his steps, looked at the deceased's shoes and his own, incomplete. With quick movements, he pulled out his new spoils and tied them tightly together. He jumped a couple of times to test them. _They serve me. Let's go. Argosio, aren't you taking your shield?

_Bah! It's useless now, it's got more holes in it than a net.

They ran along the side of the wall, seeking distance from the citadel. Once away, Argosio turned to look. _What a view, huh? Too bad I can't carry a keg of beer. Akkadian dog, won't you turn around and say goodbye to Ficana one last time?

Kad didn't answer and just managed to keep walking. The big man drew a grimace on his mouth. _Don't take it like that, I liked the people here, nice women for the region. – they walked in silence for a while, and he seconded– You never told me why you wanted that rock of yours, was it a lucky charm or something?

Kad took a moment to respond. _No. Every ten years, or whenever I could, I would make a mark on that rock, counting the years I've been alive. Now I don't know exactly how many I have, nine hundred... seventy... and a few.

Argosio laughed out loud. _Is that all? But you do remember more or less how many. What difference does it make if they're three too many, or three too few?

Kad turned to look at Argosio, his eyes indignant and tired. _It's true, it doesn't really matter to have a hundred more or a hundred less... what's the point of keeping track? If my existence is a gray continuum, like a flowing river that never stops.

_The akkadian dog knows poetry! – he thundered a couple more laughs – Don't be sad, partner. And don't get too tired, I'm not going to carry this bag for more than ten leagues, then it's your turn, you slacker!

PART 19: THE SEED OF AN EMPIRE

Kad looked into the distance, and for a moment hesitated to be on the right path. _Is that Rome? - he asked rhetorically.

_I don't know, I never visited this city. - replied the woman accompanying him.

They both rode a horse, her in front and him behind, under the light of the Moon on a flattened earth trail. In the distance, some watchtowers stood up, each one crowned by a flame, and in the middle of them a beautiful arch serving as a portal. Thirty years ago, when Kad last stopped by with his lost comrade Argosio, it was a shabby peasant village where they had barely made a coin out of their stolen belongings. Now it had high, imposing walls. It is not that they had quarreled with his old companion, they simply chose different paths, something that is recurrent in centennial travelers. For the moment, he was in better company. More voluptuous at least.

_This used to be a hamlet until recently. - Kad was surprised.

They continued to move forward, riding a Lusitanian horse, mottled in grey, black and white, with fine limbs. Behind them, held by a rope, a second horse of the same breed, white and dotted with grey specks, was advancing peacefully. It carried several packages and bags on its back.

Kad looked happy. He had shoulder-length, copper-colored hair tied to a tail, wore a well-tailored linen outfit, decorated with a few golden threads and a red band around his neck, and a thick brown leather belt from which a brand-new sword hung in its sheath. A heavy brown wool blanket with a hood covered him. On his feet he wore high leather sandals down to below his knee, painted with black figures and some metal appliques. His companion wore a white woolen shawl with a hood, sandals covered with wool of the same color, a quiver full of arrows hanging from one shoulder, and a short bow from the other. She was a brunette, with long, jet-colored hair, fine, delicate and sensual features. Her lips were curiously shiny, crimson in color, and full of joy. A charming mole rested beneath her lower lip, which seemed to move on its own every time she spoke. Beneath her shawl, an ivory robe covered her shapely figure, and two bags of metals, coins, and precious stones dangled from her waist.

_We could spend a few more days, and see how much it's grown. You never told me why you're so fond of this region, Jano. - she said, using the unusual name she dubbed him in the absence of a proper one.

_It's a long story, Circe, and it's quite sad. - Kad replied.

A guard dressed in leather armor and armed with a spear stepped into their path as they approached the entrance. _Stop there, travelers. Are you merchants?

_We are just passing through, but yes, we might sell our belongings if possible, and buy some if we like. - Kad said.

_In that case you must pay for the entrance, it's five sesterces or a dinar. The lady doesn't pay admission.

Kad and Circe were surprised. _Why is this policy favoring women, kind guard?

_You'll see when you enter, there are few women in the city nowadays. The kings think that way more will come on their own. - he replied, following the speech to the letter.

Circe took a dinar out of one of the bags and handed it to him. The guard made sure it was genuine, and left the way open for them.

Most of the buildings were new, sturdy and made with good judgment. They were surprised that late at night some traders were still selling their products and knick-knacks. The trading center at the entrance was full of life, buyers shuffling the drawers with goods, discussing the "right" price, traders exposing the goodness of this or that mystical object.

_This is great! – Circe exclaimed – Do you mind if I take a look?

_Not at all, take your time. I'll go find some tavern to catch up the news and rent a bed.

Circe handed Kad one of the bags of coins and kissed him goodbye on the cheek. She stepped off her horse with grace and agility, and quickly lost herself in the crowd.

Kad dismissed her with a smile. He was only hoping she'd come back with enough coins to pay for her residency. He rode aimlessly through the streets, bringing up to date his memories. Rome had changed a lot and in a short time. He instinctively kept an account of all the guards who now walked the walls and the streets, and that as the subject at the entrance told them, the ratio of men to women was six to one. He moved away from the most commercial area and entered a residential area. A few torches on the corners shed light on the alleys, where the rascals crowded, away from the eyes of the authority. He consulted a couple of men sitting on one of the corners for a place to stop, and was given several options to spend the night in exchange for a coin. He decided on one and rode there.

The Hungry Man's Inn did not seem particularly promising to him, but of those available it was the closest, and the recommendation for good wine weighed heavily on his dry throat. Later he would see if he was in the mood to hunt some lowly crook. In one corner a sad troubadour sang of sorrow and pain, and a small crowd listened to him, asking for poems to be composed and recited on the spot.

A few steps closer and with a much smaller audience, a puppeteer with one leg missing, sitting on a sad litter on the floor, made two battered puppets dance by pulling some red tainted threads. One of the dolls, made of sticks, rags, and little imagination, moved acting in awe of Kad's attention, and made a great, pompous bow by waving its bound hand. The puppeteer smiled with black teeth, waiting for a coin. Kad crouched down and placed a sesterce in the dirty sack in front of the man, and facing the puppet, he could only feel a bitter sensation behind his throat. He almost felt his own threads that had, since forever, been pulling him. He decided to walk away.

Tied both horses, tipped the short, bony man sitting in front of the inn generously, and he walked determinedly to the counter to sit down and ordered the best wine in the house, paid in advance. The tavern was in gloom, a few sorrowful bait candles shed the light needed to see inside. Some folks in the background were throwing tabs and gambling while getting drunk. He managed to have a good drink when he was stunned by a scream. _It can't be!

It was a familiar voice, but he could not immediately identify whose. Kad turned his head to see a huge man approaching him.

_Argosio?

The big man gave him a strong hug, a strange greeting for two beings like *them*. He wore leather armor just like the rest of the soldiers, but with a red badge on his chest and back.

_By the beards of the gods of yore, it's the wretched Akkadian! What are you doing in Rome?

_I can't believe I found you here, can't I ask the questions at least once?

They laughed sincerely, forgetting the bitterness of their lives and drinking more wine. They tried their best to catch up.

_Now, let me get this straight. Are you a damned guard? – Kad asked.

_No no no, I'm the Chief of the Guard, which is very different. – Argosio defended himself.

_Sounds the same to me. And who's the chief's chief?

_The chiefs, you mean. - he replied, hurrying his drink - Aren't you surprised that Rome has grown so big? That was two of *our own*, they've been attracting people and building for decades. They pay well and some outstanding builders have come forward. I don't know who those guys are, but they work wonders.

_Doesn't it surprise anyone that they don't go out in the daytime? - Kad asked, already a bit affected by the alcohol.

_Nah, nobody asks anything. What people do love is spreading rumors. Now it is said that they are brothers and that they are descendants from a god, or that they were raised by wolves. Everybody knows they were born to smelly pigs. - he laughed - It's like a contest to spread the wildest story.

They both laughed again, and asked for a new round.

_Don't tell me you came alone, Akko.

_No, actually, I'm traveling with a partner, Circe. She's beautiful as a pearl.

Argosio exclaimed loudly, his cup in his hand. _That's what I wanted to hear. Is she good in the sheets?

Kad smiled mischievously. _The best. - he said, receiving a friendly elbow in the ribs.

_Let's drink to women! Oh, wait a minute... is she common, or *carries the blood* like *us*?

_She's got *the blood*. I wouldn't dare travel with a common one. The times I've done it... it hasn't been beneficial to them. – he paused, thoughtful – Do you know how she calls me? Jano. Says it's because I look like a guy named like that.

_It's a terrible name! ...Jano – Argosio laughed out loud – If everyone agreed and remembered you as the "akkadian dog" it would be easier. – he received a strong punch in the shoulder from his comrade – Come on, don't be angry, dog. In fact, I have a proposition for you. Why don't you go talk to the kings? Maybe they have something interesting to say.

_What could it be? – he asked, filling the cups with more wine.

_I don't know, but they're very convincing folks. They made me a good proposal and I accepted it. Like I told you, I've been here fifteen winters and I like what they're doing in the city. It's been a good change to our adventurous lives, huh?

_And will I be welcome here?

_Of course, man! You were my partner, so you're more than welcome, you and your woman.

_Speaking of which, why are there so few women, have they been eaten?

_It's not that there are few, there are the same ones as always. There's more men out there. It's not right for me to confess to a newcomer, but the hell, I'm a little drunk. The truth is that we are organizing certain "maneuvers" to solve this problem. Well, we've basically been looting neighboring towns and bringing some down here. The people know or suspect it, but they don't say a thing because they know that slaves are needed.

_Are you stealing women? How come Rome isn't on fire at this point?

_Thanks to me, of course. The Sabines and the Aequi hate us and have tried to rescue them on some occasions. But I keep my boys well trained, and each of those raids has cost them dearly. That's why they're quiet for the moment. I know they're plotting to get them back and stick my ass in a pike, but they're not gonna make it.

_It seems like a delicate situation, and that you could use a hand.

Argosio extended his palms upward, making it clear that this was his point. _Exactly, what we are needing is a skillful and handsome fella to sneak into the neighboring villages and see what he gets out of it. - he said, pointing his big, fat index finger at him.

_All right, let a wraith take me away if I can't help a partner in distress. I'll pay your bosses a visit.

_Kings, dog, kings!

_Whatever, you dumbhead! I'll go get Circe, and tomorrow night you'll take me to the palace, okay?

_It's a plan. I'll meet you here. – Argosio paid for the numerous jugs of wine and they separated.

The next night Kad and Argosio met again and rode to the palace. They were received with discipline and kindness, although with a certain coldness. Argosio was respected and feared among his men, and few dared comment on his activities. Of course they were dedicated to the local favorite sport: spreading rumors. The palace of the kings was large, elegant, but very practical and minimally decorated. The architect evidently had in mind to expand it in the future, but in the plans there were more urgent things to draw and work on, something that did not bother the inhabitants. Stone upon stone it was a beautiful place to live, work and prosper.

The floors were covered with carpeting and skins over the well-polished tiles. The rooms were spacious and with comfortable seating available. A guard with two purple feathers on his head declared the arrival of the newcomers and asked them to wait.

_You could tell me something about these so-and-so guys, don't you, Argo? – Kad asked, sitting down.

_Of course. One calls himself Remo, said to come from a place called Troy, a city that fell into disgrace many years ago. He's rather quiet but good-natured. The other has called himself Romano since he arrived, but before that he was known as Romulas, and before that as Caucasus. There are conflicting versions of where they do come from and where they don't, but they're both older than you, so they probably went through them all.

_Interesting, I haven't run into anyone older in a while. - Kad quietly looked around, he liked the place.

_Great, huh? And you haven't seen the barracks yet, you'll love it. - Argosio said as he settled into his chair.

_Very nice. I'll have one like this, maybe bigger.

_Yeah, with whores and kegs in every corner.

_And full-time acrobats.

_And some comedian to throw rotten food at him.

_Or some juggler out of tune, you can never have enough!

The opening of the huge door in front of them interrupted their ravings. A man in a white robe with violet sleeves told them they could enter.

They went through the door, and didn't really expect what they saw. Two men were in a big pool of hot water. The steam from the water filled the room. Some slender, naked women carried and brought fruit, goblets of red liquid, and cuts of meat that could not have belonged to an animal.

_My kings. – Argosio greeted with an elaborate bow – He is the person I told you about, the famous Akkadian.

_Welcome you are! – one of them politely greeted – Would you like to join us? The water is delicious.

Kad looked at his companion in perplexion, but he was already leaving his objects and clothes on a bench, so he did the same. They went into the pool, and let the water cover them.

_So, the Akkadian. – held the other man – I've heard a lot about you. You were a lord and a vagrant, a soldier and a farmer. What do you do today?

Kad didn't know what to expect from the meeting. In case of emergency, he could always escape sword in hand, rescue Circe, their things, and leave quickly. The point was, what could he make from it. He noticed how hot the water was and how uncomfortable it made him.

_I am committed to venture into the world, to know its goodness and its misfortunes. Walk to the end of the world and back.

_Excellent, as you may have heard, we are also adventurers. My name is Remo, and he is my faithful companion, Romano. - Remo was tall, stocky, with beautiful, masculine features. His jawbone was square, and he had it covered with a neat black beard, as the color of the short hair on his head.

_Nice to meet you, Akkadian. Tell us, did Argosio comment you about our anguish? - Caucasus had a very different face at that time, his eyebrows were straight and bushy, his eyes piercing. The chin protruded lordly outwards, and his shavings were impeccable. He was slightly taller than Remo, though less stout. He wore his head shaved in a military style, a single strand hanging from his back to the shoulder line.

_Briefly. -he observed at his side. Argosio wasn't having a good time immersed in the hot water. Neither did himself. He was surprised at how well the two kings endured it. Didn't they carry *the blood*? Were they puppets set for him? He could hold out for a few more minutes, but his body was already absorbing the excess heat.

_Then we'll fill you in. - announced Caucasus - What you see around you, the beautiful Rome, is but a seed germinating, the seed of an Empire. Soon Rome will be the center of the world. - he looked sidelong at Remo, who was watching closely. He stood up, dripping hot water. His skin was not red from the effort, looking normal – What we are building, my good friends, is an empire that will last a millennium. What am I saying! It will last for eternity itself. Our desire is to unite all the folks of the earth under our reign, a perfect amalgamation, a concert of souls. Every man will bring his best effort and skill, and will get justice, prosperity and respect in return. With such a strong foundation, it can't possibly fall. – he made a perfect pause – No matter how vile the enemy that faces us is, how powerful the storm that strikes us, how big the world and its dangers. Rome will survive, eternal and beautiful. – Caucasus shook his fists spectacularly in the air. – We are living in a different era, we can now enter the sea and take possession of its treasures. Go deep among the savages and civilize them. Enter into Hades itself and conquer it. Who, perhaps, is in a position to stop us, if not even death is capable of reaching us?

Kad listened attentively, but was plagued with questions. He had to put them aside, as the scene apparently called for his intervention. He decided for a sarcastic way out. _The millennial empire... Gilgamesh already tried it eons ago and failed, why would it succeed this time? Because it's two people? – he mentioned pointing to them.

Caucasus smiled, but let his colleague answer. _Gilgamesh was a madman. He asked to be killed with his restrictive policies. How can you govern with a crowd of ignorant people screaming for your head? The key, gentlemen, is very simple. Keep the populace working and content. As long as that golden rule is followed, we will not fail as has been done in the past.

_Sounds logical. – Kad took an abnormally long pause to continue. Something strange was going on. Many, many people for hundreds of years had wanted to convince him of different things, but not like now. It was having too much effect. He was immediately committed to the Roman cause, which set off an alarm in his mind. What was going on? – I'm interested, I'd like to hear more. – he finally decided to wrap up. His skin was burning and he wanted to get out of there by any means.

_All right. – continued Caucasus. He made a sign, and several naked women came with tunics for the kings and their guests, and finally they all came out of the pool. When the women withdrew, Remo told two of them to stay. Those were the losers of the day, Kad thought.

_I'd like to invite you to another room, where you might be even more comfortable.

Argosio leapt to his feet, took off his tunic, gasped, and began to put on his attire again. Kad, on the other hand, kept the garment, and just managed to fit it better and take his clothes under his arm. More comfortable? What trap was he falling into without noticing? He could not help thinking that, contrary to custom, he had not been offered anything to eat or drink. For a brief moment he felt unworthy, but could not determine exactly of what.

The four of them advanced to an adjoining room, from whose walls hung more lighted torches than necessary. It had wide columns, decorated in light blue and blue tones. Furs from several wild beasts were lying down, and felt comfortable to Kad's feet.

On one of the corners, four stone benches surrounded a low table carved from the same material. All the pieces were covered with fine purple fabrics. The kings asked them to sit down. It seems that they intended to move on to more intimate negotiations, and close the deal, whatever it may be.

_Your Majesties, how can I be of any use to the city then? - Kad wanted to know, as he continued his inner struggle.

_In many ways - said Caucasus - perhaps you are aware of certain... imbeciles... who are not allowing our development. The Sabines have been resisting being part of the Great Rome. The Aequi despise us for our greatness... the Etruscans ignore us, and we still have no official answer from any Samnite. All that must change. Everyone must be part of Rome, no matter how. By force, by word, by friendship. That would be your own choice.

_We propose you to work for the prosperity of Rome, for a lustrum. - Remo seconded - If the task is to your liking, we will renew the deal for another five years. In return you will have a permanent place in the city, wealth, land, servants, animals, your own home. - that last point displeased Kad, and he struggled not to show.

_Is it possible that I give you my answer tomorrow?

_Of course, although we really hope it to be a positive one. If it's convenient for you, tomorrow we'll close the details to be polished. Until then. - Caucasus smiled mysteriously at him. He made a sign, and a man gently escorted them out.

Argosio and Kad advanced several steps outside the palace before speaking. It all ended very quickly, and he was eager to begin the task. It was definitely not normal, but he gave up on giving a negative answer. Something that no one said, saw or felt, was what most caught his attention.

_Pal, what was that all about? - Kad asked.

_I don't know, but I feel a little dazed. - Argosio's reddened skin had already recovered - Still, you could tell they were two great guys, huh?

_I can't stop thinking about something. I couldn't tell at any time if they were lying or telling the truth. I couldn't read them in the least. How do they do it?

_Ah, you noticed. I have no idea, Akko, I have no idea.

_I'd like to learn how to do that.

PART 20: THE SECRET OF THE ORDER

_It hurts! – Vogel Drescher lamented, sitting against the side of a tunnel with no apparent end, under the radioactive wasteland of what used but yesterday to be the Aegis Palace. His shoulder still bled a little after the attack, staining his coat with red, over the already brown of the mud.

_I know, Mr. Drescher, as soon as I can see again I'll check it out. I'm sure I can help you with something. Don't worry, you won't die from it. – Charles Dipson replied, who was sitting in front of him in total darkness. MacOwen and Syra had taken away the only torch they had as they explored the endless number of underground passages in search of a way out.

Drescher was agitated and couldn't calm his nerves. _What if I die here? I was never good at closing wounds... well, neither good at fighting... to be honest. Why must I be so brave? – he gasped several times before completing the sentence.

_If it's any consolation, neither do I. That's why I've learned to stay in my place, and let act those who know. A wise advice, if you ask me.

The gentle murmur of a stream of water splashed into their ears constantly, flowing from one place to another, into the dark immensity of the underground. Above their heads, the tunnel through which they had descended was out of their reach. The heat that emanated from there was suffocating, so they had to go down a long distance until they were cool. Now they were surrounded by cold rock in all directions, with passages going north, south, and east, horizontally and downward. Some were carved, others were natural, but none had a mark or sign, except for the first one they tried, without luck, so it had received a crude X with a stone on its side.

_Charles, may I call you Charles? Are you a doctor or the like?

_Something like that, I've learned medicine for many years, with many teachers too. Unfortunately, the art I'm looking for is still far from me. Ah! Yes, you can call me Charles. If you don't mind, I'll address you as Vogel.

_No, it's no bother. And... What art is that you're looking for? Neurosurgery?

Dipson laughed kindly. _No no, you see Vogel, for half a century I've been trying to... well, actually trying to heal. Just as the healers of yore did, with their bare hands and their conviction as their only medicine. But it is a hard and difficult road that is still elusive for me today.

_I don't think I understand, healing someone using nothing?

_Yes, that's right. To be able to heal another person, without any elements.

_I've never heard of that, except from the mouths of phonies, of course.

Dipson lost a sigh. _It's a lost art, I'm afraid. But I know it is possible, I have found documentation that proves it, even though it is very much based on the faith of the writer at the time.

_No offense, Charles, but... - Drescher settled against the wall. - I understand that not to be possible. Know that I am a man of the world, I have visited many places throughout my life, I have met true geniuses of medicine, and I have been told that no one can regenerate another, because for that you should perfectly know the structure of the other person, I mean, at an unconscious level and force with... how to explain it... with your own vitality... or will? to recover that of who is injured.

_That's true, yes. You have been informed correctly. But here I have found a way... - Dipson's voice had become deep and mysterious – a way to pass my will, through my cells, to someone else's cells.

_Wow, sounds... complicated. So you can cure?

_No, not yet. I have achieved small effects. Cut off the circulation in a vein, open up muscle tissue. And my greatest achievement, for which I am proud, is to begin a purification.

_A what?

_That's the name I gave it. What I do is to "instruct", let's say, the patient's cells to annihilate foreign bodies. I activate their autoimmune response, and I can direct the leukocytes in the process, effectively fighting off an infection.

_That's excellent, I congratulate you Charles! How do you do it?

_Using water. I fill the water with my own lymphocytes, and pour it into the wound. I reabsorb that water, and then my body learns to fight the infection. Then I pour my blood into the wound, and the process begins. At the same time, it helps me to destroy bacteria in the water and make it drinkable, if I don't have anything to boil it.

_You surprise me, you're certainly an incredibly talented man. – Drescher smiled. He was happy to spend time with extraordinary people, it was one of his favorite pastimes. The best part was collecting anecdotes to tell later and become the heart of the party. Suddenly a thought came to him. – What a fool I am, I have my assistant in my pocket. So much has happened that I forgot about it. – he removed a small, oval, translucent device with his healthy arm. When it lit up, it illuminated the whole cavern intensely. – No signal... but it works.

_We'd better not waste the battery unnecessarily, look, it seems they're coming back.

At the end of one of the tunnels, a light flashed, accompanied by two figures. The Irishman and the quiet shadow approached at a slow pace. Apparently they didn't bring good news.

_Anything new? – Drescher asked impatiently as he covered his eyes from the flame.

_We found what looks like a way out, but as we approached we discovered that the water falling from that direction is hot, and probably radioactive. If we have to go out that way, we'll probably be dead in no time. We need to find another one that's further away. – MacOwen said, his voice tired.

Syra was standing a meter behind him, with the same neutral expression as always. No doubt she disliked completely the circumstance she was in.

_I think we should move, but first we ought to treat Drescher's shoulder. I couldn't help him without light, and we don't have much left. - Dipson was watching the torch, which was burning out at every second. - Fortunately Vogel has his phone with some battery, it will be very useful.

_Why didn't you mention before that you had that? - Syra spat out.

_I'm sorry, I completely forgot.

_Can't it wait? We need to keep looking for a way out. - MacOwen got impatient.

_No, no! It can't wait, it hurts too much and it will probably get infected and I'll lose my arm! - Drescher exaggerated.

Syra turned, exasperated, putting her arms akimbo. _He's useless...

_Hey! This is what I get for wanting to help my teammates, despite my... inadequate combat experience. - Dipson was already near Drescher inspecting the wound.

_It's not that bad, it won't be long. - Dipson took a small plastic cup out of his bag and picked up some water that was falling down the wall. He cut off one side of his finger, from which a drop of blood sprouted and fell into the cup. He poured the contents over

Drescher's shoulder and waited a few moments. He ran his cut finger through the wound, absorbing the water slowly. He clenched his fist, carried it over his head for a few seconds, and returned over his shoulder. This time enough water and blood flowed from his finger to cover the wound completely.

_I'm almost done, patience. Take off your clothes, please.

He took some bandages out of his bag and used them to wrap the affected area completely. Finally, he helped Drescher put his dirty shirt back on and got up.

_It still hurts, is that normal?

_Nobody said it was a painkiller, just antibiotic.

_Thank you very much, Charles. - Drescher thanked with a slight grimace.

_You're welcome. May I have a light?

In the light of the device, Dipson put new cloth on what was left of the torch and lit it again. The four of them set out, and chose another of the passages at random, after marking with an X the one that did not serve them. The journey became monotonous, buried under the rock, always advancing to find larger amounts of grey, black and brown.

_Vogel, aren't you worried for ignoring how to defend yourself? - MacOwen asked, with real concern.

Drescher was surprised by the question and the sudden confidence. _No... I mean, I'm not talented for the arts of violence. Instead I've been gifted in diplomacy. I'd rather negotiate than fight, I've always been like this.

_But not all conflicts can be resolved by speaking, Dutchman. Without going any further, we just came out of one where the words didn't do any good. Would you have stayed to talk to one of the Menace invaders, to share a drink?

_I don't know what to tell you, the time for words may have passed, but it certainly existed. A perceptive diplomat would have avoided all that mess. I don't know your first name, MacOwen.

The shadows paraded under the torch held by the old Irishman. _Liam. My name is Liam MacOwen. No doubt you will understand that if you get caught up in another of those moments where words no longer work, you could perish.

Drescher was silent as they walked. The tunnel curved downwards, so they went down with a little difficulty. _Yes, I understand. – he squeezed his face in pain – It's just not in me.

The tunnel became horizontal again, and split in two. A quick run through one of the partitions revealed only one wall, so they continued on to the other. They continued walking to find a carved section with adobe brick arches. On the walls, there were small niches, filled with bones and skulls. Strangely enough, no inscriptions on them.

_Who could they be? – Dipson asked.

In the absence of a reply, Syra made a statement. _They have no name, so they could be Shadows. I didn't know they used this place as a final resting place.

_Why are Shadows denied their names? – MacOwen turned to Syra with a frown.

_Nobody denies us anything, names are just a tool we use. When we begin training with Eylem, we discard any pride or calamity tied to our past to start from scratch. That's when we gain real power.

_Leaving behind the pain of the past sounds interesting, but it also dilutes the person; how do you keep your word without a reputation?

_Promises? – Syra drew a tiny smile on her pale lips. – They are also tools, in my opinion. Not everyone thinks so, though.

_Word and honor are everything to a man. I wouldn't even dare look my rival in the eye if my name is stained. – MacOwen's tone of voice was severe.

_There is no need to agree, everyone chooses how to be and how to survive. Let's move on.

The heterogeneous group set out again. MacOwen had trouble restraining himself. _I understand survival, but you don't have to resort to dirty tricks to achieve it. Being brave, going straight ahead and upright has always been my way of life.

_And that's what a Templar says?

MacOwen suddenly stopped, forcing everyone to stop. He stared at Syra with an angry expression, which was at least a full head smaller in height. _No Shadow without honor will question my actions and those of my brothers in arms.

_Ladies and gentlemen! Please, don't ignite the passions. There's still a long way to go to get out of here. – Vogel had stood between them, trying to appease the waters.

_What do you know about the Templars? You have no idea what we went through.

_I know enough. I know you have to live with caution after surrendering and submitting, at the risk of losing your neck if you anger the wrong person.

_MacOwen, please calm down. – Dipson asked – Promise me you won't use your weapon against anyone here until we leave. You owe me one, remember.

MacOwen turned to Dipson, and snorted. Charles continued. _And you too, miss. I'd prefer we didn't use violence until we got out of this granite tomb.

_I agree, I'm not motivated to fight in such a horrible place.

They continued at a steady pace, soon leaving the niches behind. Drescher, however, was consumed by curiosity.

_Liam... dammit. - he smiled nervously and couldn't control his curiosity - I hope I don't screw up, but I'd like to know more about the Templars. I've never run into one before. What's your story?

MacOwen fulminated him with his gaze, but quickly calmed down as he understood the greed for knowledge of his obliged companion. _I am of the second generation of Templars, before the Great Fall. The former were judged as traitors, and hunted down as if they were wild animals. Of the first generation, only two remain. Of the second, barely seven. There's a third one, but they don't have a reputation, and frankly I don't know how many there are.

_But, why were you considered traitors?

_For hundreds of years we kept a secret, and those who didn't know it accused us of blasphemy.

_And that secret... may I know it?

MacOwen turned to see Dipson's expression, but he did not return any particular one.

_It is said. – he began – that there was once a person, a man, who was like *us*, but by God's divine intervention, his humanity was restored to him. And not only that, but his blood could turn *ours* back into normal people, allowing them to walk under the sun and die properly and in time, surrounded by their families. He was also a healer and a prophet. He left us, after his execution, a chalice of his blood as a legacy. That chalice converted many, even hundreds of years later, until it gradually lost its effect. We kept that grail zealously guarded for millennia.

Drescher raised an eyebrow and dropped his jaw in surprise. _It's not possible... really? It's the first time I've heard of such a thing. I have nothing for or against religion, but anyone capable of removing... *this*? I find that very hard to believe.

_Unfortunately, I never saw that miracle with my own eyes, since the grail lost its power long before I was born. But I believe in my brothers who have lived at that time and in their sayings, since they are men of word and honor. – he marked those words as he looked sideways to the Shadow, that ignored the situation.

The end of the tunnel led into a chamber, and the chamber into an underground river that ran south.

They went down to it, and with the water up to their knees, they continued. Time passed slowly, as they splashed step by step, and the cloth of the torch consumed more and more.

_Liam, can I ask you a favor when we can get out of this cave? I'd like to learn how to defend myself, something basic, if possible.

The Irishman turned to Vogel, who looked at him with a certain plea and a pinch of appreciation. _All right, why not. I'm already teaching Charles a few things, it doesn't hurt to have another apprentice.

Drescher smiled broadly. _I'm grateful, then.

PART 21: A TRUCE

The elevator reached the thirtieth floor and stopped with the softness of a feather. The gleaming steel doors opened, giving access to the suite of the luxurious Cynatech Tower, the center of the world's largest pharmaceutical multinational commercial emporium. A man in a suit walked slowly inward, took off his tie and carefully placed it on an armchair. His gaze was completely neutral, which was the only thing that remained static, while his entire appearance changed. His height varied making him increase a few centimeters, his facial features were severely modified. A carefully crafted moustache sprouted under his nose, his cheekbones receded, as did his eyes' orbits. The shade of his hair became darker, his ears changed shape and position on his sides. León's best-known appearance tidied his clothes a bit, and he sat down heavily in front of a beautiful meeting table that ruled the room.

The suite was wide, illuminated diffusely by lamps that varied in intensity, becoming more intense if someone was nearby, and darker when no one was there. Black and silver were the preferred colors, mixed with a delicate aesthetic taste. On one of the walls hung a modern giant Vitromarque, which continuously passed images of works of art, being at times The Mona Lisa, and two minutes later, The Temptation of Saint Antony, all with an unparalleled quality of reproduction, better than the originals in some respects. The room also overflowed with life, each column of marble, silver and diffuse light was accompanied by three delicate pots with ferns, which floated in the air by the effect of electromagnets, giving a set of exquisiteness and applied technology. The center of the room was dominated by a huge meeting table in matte black and silver legs, whose height was automatically adjusted depending on the average height of those present and the quantity, an exotic inclusion to the set. A hand gesture on its surface ignited the holographic interface. Along with his pending agenda, balance reports and miscellaneous logs, a window was waiting for his confirmation to start the conference. León took a deep breath, settled into his chair, and accepted. Immediately, three ethereal panels took up positions in front of him, each with the image of a person. The meeting had begun.

_Good evening, gentlemen. - León solemnly greeted, his voice deep and rich in nuances.

The three people greeted each other politely. None of them were too happy. They were the three claws of León, who handled the real concerns, and the cover that had been the exponential emergence and growth of Cynatech. They looked at each other digitally, with remarkable nervousness in the background. The leftmost face was the financial advisor and CEO of

Cynatech, formally known (as today) as Luca Di Gennaro, and among *them*, simply as The Genoese. On the ethereal screen in the middle, the military adviser and Commander of the clandestine military branch, Matthias Weissman, who still kept his birth name for pride. To the right was the image of Budem Edelstein, scientific advisor, and the mind behind the vast majority of the technology that had put the pharmaceutical company at the forefront of the industry, and who had made the *neomensch* units a reality that would soon revolutionize the war.

_There is no need for introductions, we all know the current situation after yesterday's events, so I will concentrate on the news. – León continued, calmly – I just had a nice talk with Eylem. It has become clear that neither they nor we know who the perpetrator or perpetrators of the attack on the Palace were, even if the reason is quite clear, to deliver an accurate blow. I knew the risks when I sent all those brave people, I knew there was a chance that many of them would not return, but with the right strategy and intelligence behind it, that would not happen. Unfortunately, the plans did not work out.

León paused to stare at the holographic version of his Commander. _Weissman, I don't blame you for what happened. You managed the operation with your maximum operational capacity, I have been monitoring it and it has exceeded my expectations, not to mention

229

the final result, which could not have been foreseen – the tone of voice revealed absolutely nothing.

Matthias Weissman was a consecrated military man, and had been one throughout his human life, when circumstances changed and he was mobilized by the unstoppable whirlwind that was León and his *new existence*. His gaze was penetrating, showing a high level of commitment and cunning, worthy of being the Commander. He knew he was oddly young in relation to those around him, despite his century and a half of military experience. His lips were tightly clenched, listening to their leader. He had some hair on his narrow chin, and his cheeks were sunken. That little comment, almost as it passed, had calmed him down halfway. Perhaps León still trusted him and his ability, despite the defeat. But he knew it wouldn't be free. The anxiety of the news he was about to hear kept the hairs on his neck stiff as wires. He had a question on the tip of his tongue, but he dared not let it go, waiting for the right moment. He only shook his head slightly.

_The day has certainly been a complication. - The Genoese said, with a somewhat worked-out attitude, like if he had anticipated the events years ago - But I must say that it was not total wreck. The information obtained from *Speerspitze* is valuable, and I am sure Edelstein is already working on a revised version. I'm optimistic, under the circumstances.

Edelstein didn't say a word. He barely moved his lips to his side. He was an extremely thin man, unchanging in many respects, behind his halo of complete confidence in his intelligence. He wore reading glasses for two reasons, because he had not been able to heal on his own, and because he thought the surgery required precious time that could not be wasted. He was at this moment strangely distracted in his attention to the conversation.

León looked at Edelstein's image for a few moments before continuing. _I agree with that. We must plan the steps ahead. The truce is firm, but only for now. There is no way of knowing how long it will last, and that is the window we have to restructure. Initially there is the *Prima-Gestalt* issue. – Weissman swallowed strongly, feeling the looks of those present on his reflection – I find frankly... unforgivable a security breach of such magnitude. I understand, Weissman, that General Krupp is in charge of the security of the base, a man of your confidence.

Weissman opted for an offensive as the best defensive method. _General Krupp is indeed a man of my entire confidence, yet he did not carry out the security improvements I recommended. Until two days ago when the gap occurred, these improvements were implemented at sixty percent, but they were clearly not enough. Even now I have full confidence in him, as with an extra week to work on I am sure that the improvements would have been completed in full. –

the question he wanted to ask almost slipped out of his mouth. But now he saw that the situation was zero-sum. Krupp has been a close colleague for almost fifty years, and would have entrusted him with his children if he had any. He had to save it, but couldn't. So he apologized silently for his next sentence, for he would no longer ask if Krupp could be forgiven - I cannot answer for him, as the schedule demanded the work to be speeded up, which was postponed. It's not in my hands, but as his superior, I would recommend a disciplinary sanction.

León listened attentively, his hand on the chin, swaying in his comfortable chair. _A sanction? No doubt about it. But Matthias... - Weissman, hearing his first name, prepared himself for nefarious news - To compromise the security of our most important base, is a milestone in our organization. I fear that in this case, an exemplary sanction will have to be applied. A high responsibility - León panned with his eyes to all the virtual presents - carries a high risk. I think it would be very judicious of me to propose for Krupp to be removed from charge, without honors. And give his story some closure. - León burnt Weissman with his eyes.

And Weissman got the hint perfectly. He wanted Krupp dead, silently and without witnesses. And the man in charge of that task was himself. One of his dearest companions. He answered in automatic mode. _So be it, sir.

León continued, in perfect calm. _That's settled, let's move on to the next one. I am very pleased with *Speerspitze's* achievements, even in defeat. I have no way of knowing why the Akkadian left the Lohe component alive, probably because of some of his sadistic whims. But it's still a fortunate one. Once it's operational, I'll reassign it to the *Grüne Wiese* base. I'm interested in the next generation drawing on its combat experience. I suspect no one better than the old Lohe to train the new ones.

The Genoese nodded his head, while Weissman looked down, and Edelstein continued suspiciously silent, glancing sidelong. In the sudden silence, Di Gennaro noted. _More than anyone else I like the idea of a complete division of *neomesch* like it and its twins, but so far I think we should recruit more conventional troops, given the fragile peace we have achieved with our declared enemy, and we still have no information on–

_Is something amiss, Edelstein? – León suddenly interrupted.

Edelstein stared at León, but made no sound for several seconds. Then he looked up for a few moments, and finally spoke, behind his tarnished glasses. _One minute, please.

The transmission from the scientist's side was cut, leaving a waiting phrase. Weissman and Di Gennaro watched each other curiously, while León waited patiently. A little less than a minute later, the transmission was renewed. The man no longer wore his glasses.

_Sorry for the delay, León. Nothing unusual happens, the events of the past date have given me a lot to think about, that's all.

_I see, and what's your opinion on this? - observed the leader.

_I agree with my colleague, we need to reinforce our lines as soon as possible. I would like to focus on another matter, if I may, gentlemen.

No one said anything, inviting to continue. _The circumstances that led to the break-up in hostilities with Crest, when we did not yet have confirmation of the Akkadian's response, the security improvements already discussed had not been completed, and that ultimately accelerated the events we know about, have not been completely clear to me. I want to know exactly what happened.

_We've already talked about this, Budem. The operation failed and a Crest agent was killed in action. - replied The Genoese- I don't think th-

_What are you getting at? - interrupted León again, this time stunning his advisor.

_The people in charge of that operation must also be sanctioned. Who are they? I don't know their names.

_Pierre Chambeaux who has passed away and is beyond reprimand, and Sergeant Antoinette Soleil who is returning to Germany, having carried out her orders. – León kept piercing Edelstein's eyes – It's not a matter of concern at the moment. Those were the most important issues, I have some personal matters that require my attention, so I say goodbye to you. At about this hour tomorrow we will continue, there is work to be done. Good evening, gentlemen.

_Good evening. – the three advisers replied.

The transmissions closed. The last thing Edelstein saw before closing the session was León's magma eyes chasing him. He took a deep breath and exhaled, relaxing on his couch. The room was mostly dark, if not for the light on the screen, and a couple of spotlights near the balcony. He made a conscious effort to release his stiff hands from the armrests. Drummed his fingers on the desk for a few seconds before turning away and standing. Just a meter from him, lying on the ground, rested Budem Edelstein's inert body. The standing Edelstein approached, as he shifted radically. A brief chill ran down Anzhelika's body as she finished her transformation to her most common figure and gathered her hair in a ponytail. With her arms akimbo, she made a quick pan around her, to make sure nothing was out of place before she left. Half a dozen sad pictures hung on the walls, on the wooden floor was now stained almost completely by all the blood flowing from the open jugular. Suddenly behind her back, the screen reactivated. A conference request, this time one on one. León was calling.

Lika was surprised, as she didn't expect such action from him. She hesitated for a while about what to do. Eylem would probably be furious when back to the base of Crest. The truce had also been a surprise, what she considered a clean entry and exit from enemy territory, was now a clear breach of the ceasefire. And it was her fault. Not only that, but what she was doing had suddenly become but a personal crusade, one to avenge the memory of her beloved false brother Lykaios. The ringing sound continued, waiting for a response.

She acted accordingly on what thought was the least worst of her options. Again adopted the face of the recently deceased scientist. Looked up at a mirror on the wall to wrap up the details of her impersonation. She rasped and repeated Edelstein's name a couple of times, until the tone of voice seemed as faithful as possible, sat down and answered.

_Yes, I'm here, did something happen?

León did not open his mouth, he stood still, scanning from top to bottom. _Who are you? – he finally said, with authority.

Lika cut the transmission. Her hoax had been uncovered, though at least her identity remained hidden. She hurried down the hallway, changing shape on the way to an innocent old woman. Finally reached the street and closed up after herself. What would she do now?

Was she a free agent or still with Crest? That depended on whether or not Eylem knew about her latest affair, and the most likely answer was yes. On the other hand, she could not afford the luxury after the fiasco of the Palace, to leave aside one of her best elements, but without a doubt she would be in a rage worthy of an Epic. Worst of all, she now had a new target to pursue before going back. Antoinette Soleil was the only person between her and revenge. Only one life, and she would return to continue her flawless trajectory as a Shadow. Could she afford to go after her?

As she walked through the quiet streets, the same feeling of helplessness invaded again as before, but why? She wasn't the same person she was a few centuries ago, things had changed. Maybe, just maybe, she could forgive herself for not being perfect, for not being able to be everywhere and for saving everyone she esteemed. But certainly she couldn't handle with Lykaios soul on the shoulders.

She waited for a bus, wrapped up in the cold night, and boarded with feigned difficulty. She picked a lonely seat, and resumed the plan. Pulled Edelstein's mobile assistant out of her fake pocket, unlocked it using the victim's cut finger, and browsed the contacts for the one that looked most promising.

Elsewhere, not too far away, a military officer was also closing the recent transmission. Weissman stood up and poured himself a whisky-filled drink, which ended up halfway through in one go. He snapped his lips and played with the glass in his hands. No doubt what he was about to do would put his entire career, and perhaps his life, between a rock and a hard place. Suddenly his modern apartment disgusted him, surrounded by so many modern comforts. He missed his tent, a practical piece of cloth that gave him security and rest. It was the only thing a real man needed. He threw his glass still half full to the side, making a shrill noise, and remained silent for a moment as he stared down at the ground, ordering his head in revolt. Finally he had not dared to ask. How is it possible that no one had seen this outcome? León had a Finnish seer named Beatrix Virtanen of renowned talent, whom Weissman knew very well, with whom he had so far overcome all kinds of dangers thanks to her visions of the near future. And what happened in this case? How didn't she see the Palace? Something didn't add up. As soon as he solved (if it could really be solved) his most immediate problem, he would find out from Beatrix herself. But first things first.

_Call... Alex Krupp, secure line. – he said, and his computer obeyed. It began, this time only as a voice transmission.

_Matthias, I was expecting your call. What did he say?

_Man, this is bad news. León wants you dead. And to do it myself.

_It's terrible... I don't know what to say. But why? I've done as he asked.

_What do you mean?

_I followed the update schedule to the letter, I wasn't late! I don't have the file here, but you must believe me, Matthias.

_I believe you, Alex, but that doesn't change the fact... we must... we must fake your death. I can't think of anything now, but I had to tell you right away. The best thing is for you to disappear and hide.

_Yes, yes. I agree, yes. – the General paused. – Thank you, really, my friend. – both knew that disappearing from a Seeker who knows you is extremely difficult, so hiding was unlikely – I'll call you in an hour, okay?

Weissman cleared his nose and answered. _Yeah, all right, 'till later. – and he cut with a wave of his hand.

He exhaled all the air left in his lungs, bitterly. Walked over to the broken glass, but stopped. He raised his head, looking up at the ceiling. Would he risk his head or Krupp's?

_It was true what they say... how can you have friends, among *us*?

PART 22: WINGS OF FREEDOM

Lohe awoke startled, and took her a few moments to understand what was around her. She was in a hidden bunker somewhere in Spain, surrounded by concrete walls from ceiling to floor, with faint lines that simulated brick separation. Lying there on a bunk bed that was not too nice or too clean, still in her black attire. At the sides, soft lights officiated as the only illumination of the place. The rest were off, as were the red emergency signals. They indicated that it was probably daytime outside, but she didn't know for sure. Sat up, with some pain in the legs and a dazed head, searched one of the metal cabinets that were embedded against the wall, where she found equipment, a *Lichtbogen II* rifle, a handgun, boots and a helmet. She checked her watch for orientation. It was the day after the horror, not even fifteen hours had passed since she lost her siblings, forever. She left the sophisticated watch in the closet, and walked around the room tired, distressed, and nervous. She knew the room, as had been there the day before while preparing to strike, along with her siblings and the support group, which had also fallen in combat. She sighed out loud, as if she could shed bad memories just like that. In one of the corners there was a washbasin with a mirror. It was in better condition than the bunk bed and had recently been replenished with hygienic items. She washed herself a little and watched the image returned to her from the cruel mirror. She had dark circles under her eyes, her short hair all tangled and dirty. The eyes were a mixture of the blue or the iris and the red of the blood. She felt awful, the sleep far from helping, made her even more fatigued.

She turned around, quite upset and searched the other cabinets. There was an urban camouflage uniform, some civilian clothing and another black suit, all of her size. She took some clothes and opened the door, walking exhausted down the aisle. The lighting there was more intense, and it made her punished eyes burn. She continued on to the other end of the bunker, crossing no one. Took off her black suit, noticing that each piece had huge holes and cuts, yet underneath her skin was intact. The last act of Fender, who had healed her before perishing. She got into the showers, and let the water that fell on her slender body take away all the frustrations and sadness. She finished washing herself and changed clothes. New boots, a white shirt and camouflage pants would do for now.

She could not consciously stop all the events of the last mission passing through her mind, as if it was a film that repeats itself without stopping. Sometimes she was the villain for having survived, sometimes the Akkadian for being the terror in the flesh, at times León for sending them to their death. She looked around for distractions, but found nothing, and came out of the showers still drying her hair with towel, steam floating on her back. Something stopped in front of her and she couldn't move forward.

_What a failure, huh?

Lohe looked up, without a hint of good humor. The woman in front of her had extremely pale skin and wore a dark blue uniform, which regular militia officers wear when on special duty, with a beret over her dark hair and purple glasses.

_I have no desire to speak now, Soleil.

_I can imagine. – Antoinette Soleil looked up and down at her in a derogatory way. She, the little star of *Speerspitze* (and probably of the entire of León's army) had proved to be nothing more than a failure, a lie, plain and simple – It must be difficult to deal with that flop of a mission.

Lohe forced her way through, and pushed Soleil aside with lousy tact.

_What a temper... wait, I have something to report. – Soleil continued – We have a new command. Looks like some heads rolled after yesterday. Krupp was removed and we are now under Weissman's direct orders until he is replaced. Nor are we going back to *Prima-Gestalt*, but to the *Grüne Wiese* base.

Lohe finished with the towel and left it on one shoulder, stopped her pace and turned around. A handful of things had happened and she had to find out, reluctantly.

_Why not *Prima-Gestalt*?

Soleil folded her arms. Her missing hand had been fully recovered. _Looks like they're dismantling the base, but I still don't know why. I'll know when we get back to Germany. By the way – she looked at her watch – we leave in four hours and twenty minutes.

Lohe closed her eyes with disgust. _One flight, just the two of us?

_Yes, one flight. But there are also coming along all the agents stationed in Spain.

_What do you mean, everyone? – some detail was missing – What happened?

Soleil raised an eyebrow, then remembered that the little star had been sleeping all this time. _Not yet..? There were no survivors of the attack on the Palace, not one. So in one stroke of the pen we lost two fifths of the army. Looks like the order from above is to regroup and hide until we strengthen our numbers.

Lohe looked down. She didn't know what to think. _I'm going to... rest until then.

_Don't be late, or we'll leave you behind. - Soleil wanted to be hurtful, but her victim seemed defeated enough for that, so her tone of voice betrayed her. She adjusted her glasses and headed for her gray room.

Lohe did the same. Threw her boots to the other side of the cabin, set the alarm, went to bed and tried to sleep in vain. What happens now? The army was half destroyed, the much talked about masterstroke, which had been planned for years, had failed catastrophically. Suddenly she got a bad feeling. What would she do? Years of training and experimental education had blocked her individuality. From an early age she had moved as a unit, she and her twins, all pointing to the same place and fulfilling exactly what was asked of them. But the unit was gone. She instinctively touched both sides of the bunk, to see if she was indeed more alone than ever. It felt so strange now that she had no direction or companions. Did she really have nothing to do? Remembered her sister's voice just before she was silenced, and shed a couple of tears that she could not contain. Felt her stomach in a knot and her soul in pieces. Stood still, barely moving to breathe and sob. Who was the villain in the story?

Who? Had she struck better, stronger, more accurate, her twins would be alive? Had León not been a deranged megalomaniac, would her unit been spared? Had the Akkadian not been a demon from hell itself, could they have triumphed? She hated herself. Hated Krupp, Weissman, León, Edelstein, the Akkadian, the bastards of Crest, Eylem. All of them. She passionately hated the bitter tears that now covered her cheeks and seeped down the corners of her lips, tears that could not be stopped. She cursed her luck, for giving her a life of suffering and hardship. And finally, she felt a lot of fear, knowing herself to be small and without destiny. She struggled with those hordes of negative thoughts, until exhaustion forced an interval, and fell into a deep sleep.

She woke up again in a shock. The alarm indicated that it was almost time to leave the bunker. She had been dreaming, but those memories quickly disappeared and couldn't focus on anything. Changed clothes without wanting to, this time in the black suit, and made sure she carried everything useful for the trip, carried the rifle and backpack on the shoulder, handgun on her belt, and the helmet under her arm. On one of the shelves she found syringes with Proteplasm, a thick, colorless liquid that had everything needed to feed in the field. She injected one in the arm, put two in her pocket, and then headed off. She was thankful that her internal strife had not yet resumed.

Left the room and walked down the hall to the stairs. Went up one floor and approached the exit, where everyone was waiting. There were seven officers sitting, tucking stuff in their backpacks and talking on the quiet, all dressed in black. She only recognized Soleil and the two drivers who had driven the vans of her unit and *Iluminieren* the night before. One of them greeted her and informed that the helicopter would arrive in a few minutes. She sat there, checking the inventory, noticing that Soleil was looking at her sideways. After a few uncomfortable seconds, she had to ask.

_Why are you ogling me?

Soleil answered seriously. _You're different.

Lohe looked at her with her palms up, not understanding the point. _I don't know what you mean.

She pointed her finger at one eye. _I can see things, you know? Your aura is different.

Lohe ignored it and unilaterally cut the chatter.

The helicopter didn't take long to show up. It made a big fuss before landing. The eight of them put on their helmets and came out. The Sun still refused to surrender its kingdom to the darkness for the time being, and it fell softly on the horizon. All the agents climbed up and the artifact took off immediately. The noise of the engine was a relief for Lohe, who wanted to avoid talking to anyone present. Fortunately, none of them made any effort to engage in any conversation. The helicopter continued to fly across the border into France.

Now she was accompanied only by herself, it was time to solve her dilemma. The hours of rest had helped, and she felt her mind clearer. The "new" individuality ceased to displease her, but she could not help but feel that she was stepping into new territory. Above, the Moon baptized with its pale face the vegetation on the banks of the Moselle River. She liked the image, it looked beautiful, no doubt. The tallest trees were covered with a thin layer of snow that shone brighter than the rest, more opaque. She shifted her attention back inside the craft. Seven black figures surrounded her in silence, holding on to their seats. They looked like lifeless wraiths. She saw her hands, and the weapon between them, feeling sickly restless, what did it all mean? Why couldn't she just stay calm and wait? Maybe Soleil was right and she had changed.

She wondered again who the villain was. It was León, for believing himself the new master of the world, only for having sent her to finish the previous one. The Akkadian was too in his own way, even though the war knocked on his door and not the other way around. Was he guilty of wanting to defend himself? No, but still couldn't forgive him for being the executioner of her loved ones. And finally herself. No doubt she was also the wicked one in the story. The difference is... she could do something about it.

She looked up. Was really willing to do it? She waited, looking for a shred of wisdom to help her, and couldn't believe it at first, but yes, she was actually ready. She glanced to the side. Her breathing got a little faster. The helicopter flew over forests and hills with speed. Her fingers practically moved against her will. *What am I doing?* She wondered without being able to give a convincing answer. Untied her seat belt and stood up. All eyes turned to her. Felt a hand clinging to her arm, and screams that told her to return to her seat. She saw the opportunity, and jumped. The ground approached her in slow motion, frame by frame. The sound of the roaring engine was getting softer. She was flying, downwards. She could even tell the dull green from the grasses at close quarters. Very, very close. Suddenly, the hit.

Lohe rolled down the hill at high speed, but the jump had been fairly well executed. When she stopped after countless rolls, she no longer had the rifle and her right elbow was killing her with pain. She looked up at the starry sky and saw the helicopter turning around to follow her. She sought her weapon quickly but did not find it nearby, and had to run. And she ran with all the strength of her legs into the trees. When sure she could not be seen from the air, took off her watch and shattered it with her bare hand. Let them try to chase her now. The helicopter's powerful luminaries grew farther and farther away, as her tracks became more difficult to follow, until they no longer pursued.

She waited almost two hours in a makeshift hideout, panting and feeling her heart almost popping out of her chest and her elbow pain becoming more intense.

249

There was no one, anywhere. Giants of wood in front and behind, and the blackness of the night that covered everything. She started laughing at the nerves, something amazing about her. Since when did she get nervous? No longer recognized herself. She was going to fix everything.

And she was happy. So happy that could ignore that she didn't even have a tiny clue of where to start. But now she had time to think and decide, all the time in the world. She felt free, incredibly free.

PART 23: A PERFECT TOMB

_Do you really believe what he said?

_Believe in what?

_About the secret of the Order of the Templars.

Syra looked at Drescher with deep disdain. She now had two pairs of eyes, one under the other, with hyper dilated pupils to help her perceive better in total darkness, only pierced by the soft light of Vogel's assistant's screen, which threatened to soon run out of battery due to continued use. They had been walking for hours now, looking for the elusive end of the tunnel. Everything was going well, until the Dutchman thought that the silence had to be broken.

_No, I don't believe a word he said. They were all wiped off the map for some good reason, no doubt, but I don't believe any of that nonsense. Maybe because they opened their mouths too wide. - she scored meanly, especially directed at his obligated companion.

_When we gather again I'm going to ask him more about it. I have to admit, it's a compelling story. - he finished saying and hit against a protruding wall.

_We'd better focus on what needs to be done, find the way out.

Drescher decided to shut up about the lady's lack of tact, and kept pointing his assistant forward. The tunnel seemed infinite. _How long have we been trapped?

The four eyes focused again on him, and then on his sophisticated device impatiently.

Drescher laughed, nervous. The situation, between the eternal rock roof and the woman who accompanied him, probably also made of rock, was pushing him to the limit. He thought himself as an adventurer, but not in *this kind* of adventure. Only the ones where he'd end up with the clothes clean. He looked at the clock and the calendar and did a quick calculation.

_It must be about... forty hours, or a little longer.

Both of them suddenly felt the pressure of hunger from within, despite not saying so. Fortunately, an event distracted them.

_That, there's something there. – Syra pointed out.

The dreary tunnel rose suddenly, and the light bounced differently at the end. They went up a hundred meters, all the way to the end. Or almost.

_Another cavern! It must be a joke. – Vogel protested.

The tunnel through which they were going led to a huge limestone void, worn down by millennia of constant dripping. The ceiling was covered in stalactites, but the background was not visible, only the occasional glow of light over the water trapped in puddles. But, perhaps the most important fact, on the other side a huge gaping mouth could be seen that continued to rise, at just a small jump of five hundred meters.

_Isn't it strange that there aren't any creatures around here? Besides the insects, of course. - the Shadow kept ignoring him.

Syra squatted and more seriously than usual, as she assessed the possibilities. _The bottom should be about three or four hundred meters down. We might go down and explore the other side, it looks promising. But it will take a long time to do so, and there is a possibility that it will not help us at all. We'd better get back and let them know before going any further. - she looked up at Drescher, with his suffering face and injured arm, like someone who has to grudgingly deal with an arthritic old man - Dipson has a rope, you're not going to stay trapped here.

_Shall we go back?

Syra was sorry she had chosen him as her companion when they split up to investigate. Dipson talks too much, and she probably would have had a fight with

MacOwen, but they were both infinitely more useful than this runt. She turned around and looked down the endless rocky corridor they had come down, overwhelmed by the situation and by the hunger that kept on attacking.

_Phew! – Vogel snorted comically, trying to alleviate the black situation – Maybe... if I scream and the others turn out to be close, they'll hear to us and we'll save the trip.

_Don't be ridic-

_Hello! Hello! –he interrupted screaming, echoing everywhere.

_Drescher, is that you? – was heard in the distance, somewhere undetermined by the constant echo. But it was definitely Dipson's voice.

_Yes! Where are you? – answered with a scream.

_Looks like in the same place, but lower down. – the reply rumbled.

The cheerful Drescher and the surprised Syra searched the dark immensity until they saw, on the same margin, to their left and far below, the tiny light of a torch beckoning.

_We've saved ourselves several hours of travel, miss. How do we get to them?

_Jumping.

_I... I don't think that's convenient!

Syra looked at him with clear weariness. _No, really, how old are you?

_I don't know how that fact is relevant to our situation... this year I will be three hundred and eighty.

_And all that time what the hell have you been doing? – Syra continued, now outraged.

_Traveling the world, getting to know cultures. Becoming wiser, I hope. – Vogel replied, angry to see his lifestyle criticized.

_Nothing useful if you don't think you can take a four hundred meter fall. I can't explain how you could have survived this long. Haven't you ever been stabbed or poisoned? Even a domestic accident could have killed you. – she pointed at Drescher's injured shoulder – You couldn't even control an infection.

_That is not true! – he was already upset about the direction the discussion had taken. No one had objected to his decisions for more than three centuries. More precisely when he lived with his mother. What was wrong with pursuing luxury and a good living? – You've followed a path of hostility and I haven't, why should yours be better? And for your information, yes, I've been stabbed more than once and here I am. You must be convinced that I'm some kind of useless individual, but I'm not. Violence doesn't solve anything, I've... I've lived long enough to know that. Yeah, you'll probably get rid of an enemy by killing him, but another one will come along for revenge. It is not a long-term solution in any way.

The four eyes of the shadow pierced him fiercely. _So why did you come to the Palace? To chit-chat with the Menace blokes?

_I... eh... - he hesitated a few more seconds than recommended, and lost the proper momentum to continue the lie. He was physically and mentally exhausted, and his hunger was stomping on him - The truth is, I came here because - he rasped - I am loyal to the old ways and to Eylem, but - he breathed out making a lot of noise, not believing what he was about to say - I thought I would escape as soon as the problems came up, because I don't know how to fight, okay?

For the first time since they met, Syra laughed, albeit briefly, to Drescher's astonishment. _To add insult to injury, you're a coward! Well, at least you're not a liar. - snapped her lips - not a chronic one, that is.

They were distracted by a voice that sounded directly beneath them, it was MacOwen's. _Having trouble getting down?

Drescher looked anxiously at the Shadow, but faced with doubt, he asked. _You're gonna leave me here, aren't you? Why don't you jump?

_No, I'm not leaving you. Just because you made me laugh, it's been a while since I've been taken by surprise with a stupid gag like that. Don't make a habit of it, you'll be on your own next time. Light up the wall with your thingy while I go down.

Instead of jumping to the cave floor, she slid down the wall with the help of several rock protrusions with superhuman agility, until she was close to the men below. She told Dipson she needed the rope and he threw it at her. Climbed back up again, with enviable speed, and tied one end of the rope to a firm rock so that it could be released later. She finally jumped.

_This will do, thank you very much, Miss Syra! Drescher shouted, as he struggled down the rope, trying not to hurt his shoulder any more.

After a few minutes of slow descent, the four of them were back together on the floor of the large cave.

_This whole set of caves and caverns is huge, I didn't know they existed underneath the Palace, how come nobody explored them? - Drescher asked, recovering from the effort.

_Maybe some of the skeletons we saw were from unfortunate explorers. - Dipson commented, tucking the rope into his bag – You know the hermetic politics that prevails in Aegis. Prevailed. – he corrected himself.

_That opening – Syra interrupted – we could see that it continues to rise, possibly leading to the surface.

_We've observed it and we agree, I propose we go over there and try it. – said Charles Dipson, busy tying a new piece of cloth to the torch – Although there are no bats, which is suspicious.

Drescher laughed mockingly. _Yeah, I noticed that already! Although they may have escaped after the explosion. – he added later, thoughtful.

_We'd like your opinion on something, Vogel. – MacOwen said, as they walked towards the opening – Are you versed in modern weaponry?

_Yes, I like to be informed of such novelties.

_We were discussing with Charles about the battle we have witnessed, and we were both drawn by the weapons used by the infantry.

_Yes, I understand. I don't know exactly the model of weapon, but they used explosive ammunition, and have long range accuracy as well.

_The strange thing is not that, but the helicopter that hit me – continued Liam MacOwen – used instead... normal ammunition, so to speak.

_.50 caliber.

_You know why I use a sword these days, Vogel?

Drescher pointed his assistant to light the sword hanging from the Irishman's belt. _Tradition?

_No. Bullets don't do enough damage to *our kind*. Anyone who is moderately literate in combat recovers from a shot quickly. On the other hand, severing a limb causes great damage in most cases, which could take days to recover. Generating more damage than the opponent can bear is the key.

_Eylem would make a full recovery in less than two seconds. – said Syra as she walked along.

_Yes, Eylem's abilities are a particular case. I doubt I can even strike a blow against her. But even so, an old-fashioned sword gives me an advantage that cannot be achieved with conventional firearms.

_It's odd now that I think about it – Drescher continued – Why use ammunition that is not effective? A distraction? To reduce the damage done? It doesn't make sense.

_That's exactly what we're trying to get to. – Dipson stated – If they wanted to keep the structure, they wouldn't have used bombs, which they did. And to eliminate the most dangerous elements of Crest, it would have been convenient to use the improved ammunitions. Since they used at least a dozen of these ill-equipped aircraft, we conclude that they tried to reduce the damage in some way. It couldn't have been a mistake.

Drescher raised both eyebrows in genuine stupefaction. _True... but I can't think of a reason. Any previous pacts? León does not exactly have a resource problem and would not leave such a detail to chance.

_Quiet! - Syra shouted, stopping the group from marching. She crossed her gaze with MacOwen, who had suddenly drawn the sword.

_There's someone here, everyone on guard! - Liam opened his arms and tried to establish a defensive position with him in front. Several seconds of intensity passed, but nothing was revealed.

The light of the torch and the mobile assistant made the shadows dance, passing from here to there among the stalagmites of the ground, and provoking fleeting mirages with the brightness of water and the humidity of the bare rock. A few more seconds passed, and the tension was not breaking.

_Don't let your guard down, there's someone else here. - MacOwen ordered - Show yourself!

_You don't have to be so alarmed, partners. - a macabre voice sounded from somewhere behind their backs.

_Impossible... Chandresh? – MacOwen was greatly surprised.

_Lord Chandresh. Shocked to have me with you? – the figure approached them walking slowly but suddenly changing direction to pass behind the spectral rock formations.

_Don't come any closer, I'm warning you! – shouted MacOwen, putting the group behind him.

_Lord Chandresh! It's a... miracle you survived. – Drescher made a desperate attempt to decompress the situation – I saw you fighting fiercely in the woods, how did you manage to get down here?

Chandresh stopped the pace, placing one of his hands on the side of a stalagmite. Now that both light sources were focusing on him, it was noticeable that he had lost a lot of body mass. He looked tiny, thin, but still kept his skin full of his characteristic scars, and his ruthless gaze. _The Dutchman, if I'm not mistaken. Yes, it's true. I fought bravely against the invader. I fought until I sensed the danger. I tried to escape, but there is no escape from that attack. So I dug, I dug with all my might, through the earth, through the stone, to the catacombs. I had to leave behind much of myself to save the essential, what you see here in front of you.

_That's amazing! – Drescher replied with superficial kindness, sweating intensely.

_No doubt, the last time I saw him he must have weighed more than half a ton, and now he's just a fraction of that. - Dipson noted.

_What surprises me is that he's so verbose. What do you want? - cut MacOwen.

_Same as you, getting out of this perfect tomb. - he replied, making strange guttural sounds - But I'm suffering and I don't know if I can go on. - he began to march towards them, slowly. - I am struck by a voracious hunger. - the voice changed tone sporadically.

_We're all hungry but there's nothing we can do, when we get out we'll seek... something. - MacOwen took a few steps back, forcing the others to do the same.

_But indeed, there is something to do. There's enough food here. - Chandresh kept coming closer. He mixed words with sounds and hisses.

MacOwen did a quick pan with his eyesight. _There's nothing in this place. And you can't eat us either, we're no good to you.

_You think I couldn't digest you? - the skinny Chandresh remarked the words with wickedness.

_Of course not, it's known. - MacOwen replied, and by the end of the sentence, Chandresh had jumped out of sight. The group was on guard, startled.

_Ah! But... Lord Chandresh... can digest anything! - said in a totally inhuman tone of voice, leaping from left to right with sudden speed, causing a sharp wound to the side of the Irishman's head, taking him by surprise and forcing him to throw the torch.

_Move! Dipson, Drescher, run to the opening. Syra, cover my back!

Syra couldn't answer. She was lying on the ground with a huge, opaque black praying mantis-like creature with several limbs, its sharp front claws trying to cut her throat. When MacOwen noticed, he struck a sword at the beast's back, which retreated at abysmal speed into the darkness.

Syra sat up and tried to restore her neck, which hung in grotesque pieces of flesh and muscles on her sides. _He's weakened, but he has the advantage in this site. We have to look for high ground where he can't hide. - she mentioned once that she had regained the ability to speak.

MacOwen grabbed her by the arm and they both ran after Drescher and Dipson. Something hissed behind their backs, but when they were ready to defend themselves, the beast assaulted MacOwen, who lost his balance and fell to the ground. A second lightning strike cut through the right leg above the warrior's knee, spilling blood all over the place. MacOwen held back a scream with all his might, trying to recover the lost limb as a matter of urgency.

Syra stepped away from him, making great leaps, advancing toward the opening. She could see that Dipson and Drescher had already begun to climb, when a black figure approached behind them. With a quick motion he cut Vogel's hand in half, holding the only light source left on the scene. The Dutchman, however, could not contain a pitiful cry as he fell to the ground, defeated. A strong tackle also brought down the Englishman Dipson, who ended up rolling across the floor with sharp wounds in his waist.

Syra wanted to take advantage of the situation to counterattack, but Chandresh had again jumped into the shadows, which stretched out in all directions.

_We have to end this! - shouted MacOwen, limping towards them with his leg half-welded to the rest of his body. Vogel was in a state of shock, feeling in terror the spot where his fingers had been moments before. Charles, for his part, failed in his attempts to stand up, so he crawled to take possession of the light source. When he reached it, he wielded it in all directions, as if it was salvation materialized.

_Charles, turn it off. - MacOwen ordered. - He's guiding by ear and instinct. We're by sight, and we're losing.

Syra, agitated and alert, stood behind him. Dipson hesitated for a couple of seconds, until suddenly the light went out under his thumb, and darkness reigned unopposed. Only Drescher's spasms and gasps were heard for a moment that seemed like eternity. The drops of sweat kept falling, making a scandal every time they touched the ground. Suddenly, a peculiar hissing sound, similar to that which would be made by two layers of scales against each other, was accentuated as it approached from the side. MacOwen slapped Syra on the shoulder, who jumped up with speed, and pinned the insectoid with her fingernails through it all. _Now! – she ordered, trying to hold it still long enough. MacOwen rushed at them, and with a single blow cut through Chandresh's body diagonally, Syra's arms and the rock next to them.

The headless half of the beast shuddered and convulsed until it halted without energy or guidance. The other part crawled as far as it could to find a non-existent security. The Irishman ran towards him, brandishing his steel.

_MacOwen! – he cried out, stretching horribly the last consonant, defiant, until a new lunge of his sword ended the spook.

PART 24: THE MIGHT OF THE EAST

A jocular, sudden chuckle of laughter was heard behind the dull wooden door, the only entrance to the shelter. The shelter was in fact just an ordinary apartment, with heavy curtains that remained closed all the time. The decoration was minimal and with little aesthetic sense. A small, obligatory painting by Yasser Arafat already faded and with a slightly tattered frame, a boring and lonely pennant of Al-Bireh, the favorite local football team, and a pair of grey footed lamps were the only objects that cut the greyish white from the walls. A short, low table was located in the center, and on it rested a couple of old magazines, and the newspaper (on paper) of the day. The headline read "Chaos in Europe" in large Arabic characters. A pair of purple armchairs, clearly purchased cheap from a second-hand furniture store, completed the living room, on the deteriorated floating wooden floor, as had set trend some six decades earlier. No one would suspect anything of that particular apartment.

Sitting in the armchair closest to the window, and with an old laptop over his legs, there was a sturdy, hard-faced man with a thick black beard on his Tunisian skin. He was wearing a dark green vest, pants of the same color, a white shirt and brown shoes. The man was in a very good mood, and typed a response to the news he received in the mail from his contact at *Prima-Gestalt* with a wide smile on his face.

_Hassan, you're not gonna believe this! – the text went impatiently through the encryption software, and he sent it laughingly – Hassan!

From the adjoining room a tall man, almost as stocky as his companion, with a dark complexion, a neat beard and almost perfect features, peered out. He was wearing a slightly tight T-shirt, dress pants, a pair of shiny black shoes. He had an elegant belt in his hand, which he passed through the straps as he walked. Hassan had the parsimony of a millennium of anguish and joy, and his face revealed very little about his opinion of the good news.

_News?

_They're from König, don't you want to see them?

_Please summarize for me.

_I don't think they can be summarized, it's pure gold. – the man on the old laptop started reading as he rubbed his palms and smiled.

_Comrade Lemir – he began to read – the base is in turmoil... blah blah blah... they are evacuating the personnel to Germany... there was a breach in security... probably a Crest agent... the attacker from the Aegis Palace remains a mystery. Not really. – he said amusingly. Hassan nodded his head – the Akkadian is still alive... special unit was eliminated... and here comes the best part. A truce was established between Crest and Menace... broken immediately by the murder of personal advisor of León. It's insane!

Hassan smiled slightly as he buttoned a white shirt. _It's hard to believe, isn't it?

Lemir carefully closed the computer and set it aside. _I can't believe it's been so easy, you make plans for years and then the enemy goes and annihilates itself. It's not fair!

_That's what happens when you sow winds, then you harvest storms. Caucasus sowed betrayals from the time he learned to breathe. It took a while, but his actions finally came for him.

_No doubt brother, but the rest of it? His heirs destroyed each other, now they're toothless hyenas.

Hassan was silent for a few moments as he wore a black coat, almost knee–length and embroidered with gold threads, the style that had become fashionable in Eastern society.

_Where are you going so classy, brother? - Lemir asked, looking for a lighter for his cigarette. - To celebrate the victory?

_I was on my way to dinner, but it looks like I'm going somewhere else.

Lemir made a disconcerted gesture, exhaling a puff of smoke and admiring his chrome-plated steel lighter.

_I'm taking a flight to France. - Hassan replied, adding no details.

He turned his steps back to the room, and searched one of the drawers in the closet., extracting a transparent plastic plate from it, with a photo of his current face and a false name. Looked at himself passing by the mirror, and corrected the separation of his eyebrows to accommodate to the one on the passport.

_What will you do in France? Won't you go after Eylem, right?

_Yes, that's what I'll do. It's a great opportunity to bring her back to her senses and make her join our ranks. She's a very sagacious woman.

_Hassan, brother, I always respect your thoughts but I don't think this is the time to do it. Ultimately, if she wants to join, she will find us with open arms. It is neither necessary nor worthy to go to her for help as if we could not by our own means, especially now that we have paved the way.

_It's not that, Lemir. At this moment, she must find herself alone, without trustworthy allies, without soldiers in her ranks, and with a war that she cannot come to an end. König said nothing about it, but the one who killed the adviser must be one of her Shadows, but one acting on their own. I know her, I'll talk to her, she'll think about it and we'll have added a valuable element to the cause.

_I don't know, I don't like the idea. - the smile on Lemir's face was gone. He climbed to his feet and leaned out of the window, drawing the curtain slightly. The lights of the city assaulted his eyes, and the scandal of the horns his ears. The city of Ramallah was overflowing with cars everywhere, most of them with internal combustion engines. The sky was completely covered with black clouds, sometimes illuminated by the spotlights of the casinos, which had exploded just ten years earlier and had spread throughout the city. Lemir let out one of his last few puffs with some sadness.

_The future looks bright. - Lemir continued after a pause - We just have to make sure we step on León's head for good and the West will fall down. Finish with Perius before it becomes a problem, too.

_And soon. I don't know what he's looking for and I'm not interested in knowing.

_Finally, there is the issue of Xin-Zu, but once we become the dominant force, he will probably ask us on his knees to leave him alone. His allies will be weary of his weakness and will come to us. It'll be the end of him, without even having to fight. – he suddenly turned around – What if the Akkadian gets tough with us?

_That's a good point. – Hassan stopped for a moment and stared at the small picture of the late Palestinian leader. – then I will have to make another change in the plans. I got a favor to ask you, brother. Contact Nasser, tell him he's coming with me, I need him. And also tell Yomir about the situation. Let him know what I'm going to do and why, and tell him to be ready to go with his men to Spain, it will be our first stop. When I'm done with that we'll move on to Germany, I want everything ready for the next step.

Lemir turned with a stern look on his face when he heard of Yomir, Hassan's right-hand man, and Lemir was known for being jealous of him, in a very justified way. He was a much more capable man and had known Hassan for much longer, several hundred years. Perhaps one day, he said to himself. Everything changes. He put his cigarette out in slow motion against a dirty aluminum ashtray.

_I will, no doubt. Do you suspect anything to go with an escort?

_It's better to be cautious. In the West they don't know Nasser and his talents are useful to me. - the strong man from the East replied, putting on a huge coat and wrapping a blue tie around his neck.

Lemir on the other hand liked Nasser much better. He was a very quiet man, always willing to do whatever was asked of him. Even to go for supplies when they were scarce, or to clean up the many shelters where they remained hidden from the now collapsed power of Caucasus. Nasser did as he was asked, period, no protests. He also had an all-proof sixth sense, and had proved indispensable on many occasions.

Lemir nodded, now somewhat bitter. _And then... you're going to France... I think it's a better plan. - something was bothering him about the situation, but he didn't know what. - Can I ask you a very personal question, Hassan?

Hassan stopped in front of the half-open door and turned to listen.

_What's going on between you and Eylem? - Lemir asked, with a mixture of understanding and disquiet, pointing his index finger at Hassan's chest.

Hassan stared him in the eye for a few moments. He closed the door behind him, and left.

PART 25: HASSAN, THE VIRTUOUS OF LOYALTY

Hassan watched from the top of a wall's corridor down, where a huge funeral pyre burned vigorously, as if fuelled by Nusku's anger – the God of light and fire. All around, dozens of soldiers were coming and going in the chaos caused by the sudden acephaly. The heavy wooden gate shrieked as it opened, giving way to a dozen men on horseback returning from patrolling to find the city in mayhem.

Hassan's physiognomy was at that time, two millennia ago, radically different from the present one: his nose was aquiline, his entangled chin had a cleft and two parallel scars ran down his right cheek. His skin was dark brown even though he had not been under the rays of Elagabal – God of the Sun – for two centuries. His hair was black, and he was losing the battle against advanced baldness. The eyes were permanently tired behind his thick eyelids, and he had not yet earned his nickname – Hassan, the Benefactor – by which he would later be known. He wore a newly woven gray robe, and beneath it a studded leather harness bearing the inscribed name of Nin-Karrak, the Protector. A short, opaque bronze sword dangled from his belt, and a solid composite bow at his back, accompanied by a beautiful quiver decorated with images of soldiers holding their bows in high. He walked impatiently, watching the tumult below from the openings in the wall. It had been expanded, destroyed and repaired countless times, resulting in a disorderly pile up of all sizes and shapes, with no design or planning other than day-to-day survival. So had been Mari, the once great metropolis of the river, on the banks of the Euphrates, a cosmopolitan city like few others and a refuge for the sailors who traded on the river, now only a shade of its former glory.

_Nervous? - he heard a voice behind his back. It was Alid-Hur, one of Hassan's comrades in arms, and a disciple, along with him, of the deceased who was now being cremated in the pyre. He was a slim, swiftly moving man, with long, dirty hair down to his shoulders, bulging eyes and violence in his speech. He also wore a gray robe, but loose and held only by his belt, leaving his torso bare. On his back he had a tattoo of Nergal, the winged lion. He wore a similarly short sword, but one of significantly better workmanship - Do you know anything about the death of the master that I don't, O great Aslin? - he asked, calling him by his birth name.

Hassan looked at him sideways. Alid spoke to him in Aramaic, obviously to upset him. He wanted fervently to stick an arrow in his heart and stop him from talking. He had grown weary of his tone of voice, his stench of sweat and his machinations. _Again with that? I don't know anything, he's been poisoned and attacked from behind. For Assur I will kill the man who did it. On the other hand, I told you countless times to communicate before me in Sumerian, and not in the language of the lesser.

_Ah I forgot. It's a shame because it's in vogue, you might as well get used to it. – Alid–Hur wouldn't take his eyes off him. He let one shoulder fall against the wall, grabbed his sword and played slowly with its edge – I didn't come to bother you, Aslin, I heard a few rumors and wanted to–

_I'm not interested in your rumors right now. – he interrupted abruptly – If you don't have something important to say, you'd better leave. – Hassan looked back at the pyre where his master, the High Priest Mecantro, laid. He was a figure of great renown who had returned Mari to the charts, doing an excellent job reconverting it into the merchant and prosperous city of old, and was the one who ultimately pulled the strings throughout the region. He was also the one who turned him and Alid–Hur into *immortal dreads*, but above all, he taught them to bear the burden that it entailed.

_Too bad you don't want to talk, because those are very interesting rumors. You're saying you'll kill the man who took the master's life? What would you do with him?

Hassan shifted his head quickly. Alid was clearly playing for time, but for what? However, he was relaxed. He didn't seem willing to attack, had he set a trap? The situation had everyone disturbed and he expected an outbreak at any moment. He instinctively began to plan a combat in his head between the two of them. Alid was skilled in hand-to-hand combat, but with a sharp arrow bleeding him out he would overpower him.

_Personally, I'd slit his throat. - he continued, mimicking with his sword around an imaginary opponent. He looked outside. One soldier threw more straw and wood into the fire, but halted to contain a fight between two others. The spirits were sensibly warmed up - Just a few more demons to loose and we'll be complete here. - Alid announced sadly. He glanced away at the top of a tower where a soldier gave him a signal by shaking a torch - Well, since you don't want to talk, I'm leaving. But first - he added, pointing his sword at him - I'll tell you what is the word on the walls. They say whoever killed the master did it to win the favor of Sargon in person. And not only that, it is also said that Sargon had one of his advisors killed for fear of betrayal, and that he will soon be looking for someone to take his place. A Virtuous of Loyalty, no more, no less. - he looked sideways at Hassan, pointing out the words. - It would be an irony worthy of a cheap comedy if the new Virtuous was a traitor, wouldn't it? No God would take pity on his vile soul.

In response, he only received a cold, hateful look. An alarm cry sounded in the distance. The columns of smoke indicated that something had caught fire in the southern part of the city, and the villagers rushed to the edge of the Euphrates to fetch water. Mari was falling again, as it had done many times before with the passing of the centuries, but this time it would never recover from the hard blow.

_I wouldn't want to see you among Sargon's advisors, comrade. Because if I do, I'll kill you. - threatened Alid-Hur.

_Shouldn't you be restoring order? Wasn't that what the master commissioned you to do?

_Yeah, that was the last thing he said to me, a few nights ago. You could say he left me in charge of his inheritance. And by the fire of Gibil, I will fulfill my role, or may his wrath consume me.

Hassan decided to calm down and not move forward with a fight he wasn't sure he would win, and toss the matter in another direction. _Would you trample over Jerro, then? - he shot, referring to the *dread*, older than they were, temporary chief in Mecantro's name.

_Jerro isn't even family, he was just an ally of the master. I don't like him and I know you don't either.

277

I'm retiring, I have a lot of things to do before dawn. And I would recommend you to stay here and try to keep order. I'll be watching you. - he uttered, but he spent a few more moments staring into Hassan's eyes with the rush of anger on. Finally he sheathed his blade, and stepped firmly back down the uneven stairs.

Hassan took a deep breath and relaxed. How much had he sacrificed already? How much more was needed? Jerro would soon find out the news, and knowing of his cunning he might even try to claim responsibility for Mecantro's murder and ingratiate himself. It was better then to make a long trip, to Nineveh. Something of this magnitude had to be handled personally. He descended the crude stairs and headed for the north exit. At the stables he asked for the sturdiest horse available, and one was given to him. He rode only a few minutes until he reached the meeting place that had been indicated in the message he received a few weeks earlier, and dismounted. There was no one there. What was going on? Another trap? An unforeseen difficulty? The smell of smoke from the city flooded him, shaking his dark thoughts. If the envoy didn't show up, the plan was in jeopardy. He immediately planned alternatives as he looked and felt the ground for fresh marks. There were no recent footprints. Was he to take the news to the capital himself? He pressed his eyes hard, asking for divine help to guide him to fulfill his Oath. Finally, a rider on the horizon. It was just one man on horseback, most likely the envoy. He waited for him to arrive and greeted.

_I am Aslin, General of Mari, tell me your name and why you came here.

The rider stopped in front of him. He was as exhausted as his beast from the long journey. He wore a white robe down to his knees, a heavy hood over his head and a dagger at his waist. _I am Kamek, and I come on behalf of Sargon. I have been told that you have news for my Master, and in turn I have a message to communicate to you.

_That's right. Mecantro is dead, just like I was asked to. Now nothing and no one will oppose Sargon, I remain faithful to his cause. I bestow Mari to Him as a sign of good faith.

_Excellent news – he said, looking at the new columns of black smoke rising up into the sky from behind the walls – In that case, here is the message. Aslin of Mari, since you have fulfilled the condition imposed, asserted among mortals and immortals, before the Gods, you will become the Virtuous of Loyalty.

Hassan avoided as much as possible to sketch a smile, it would not have been appropriate.

_If you wish, you may accompany me to Nineveh to ingratiate yourself with the great Sargon, Lord of Assur.

_Yes, I do wish. – responded Hassan – I fear that Jerro will use his poisoned tongue to lie about the situation in Mari and try to appropriate something that is not his.

_Agreed. First I must confirm the death of the traitor Mecantro, I will rest my horse for the night and we will leave in the morning.

Hassan showed his confusion. _I'm afraid that won't be possible, I can't make it through the day. – he hesitated before continuing... – I'm a *dread*.

Kamek looked up and down, judging the assassin in front of him. _I am an *immortal* too, but Elagabal is not inconvenient to me, nor to Sargon's servants. Sargon is the chosen one by the Gods, and nothing can oppose him. We'll take another horse and leave immediately in that case. The sooner the better.

_I am grateful. – Hassan replied, suddenly saddened. Were the rumors true then? He had made the right decision, he thought. Undoubtedly Sargon was the chosen one by the Gods. The fact that not even the Sun God resisted him filled him with faith in his posture. And now he was a chosen one of the Chosen One. He rode his horse and followed him.

PART 26: THE BROKEN FAITH

Hassan was euphoric and couldn't sleep. He had arrived after an arduous journey to Nineveh the night before and now, early in the morning, he was waiting for his audition with Sargon, the True King of Assur, the chosen and blessed of the Gods. Huge sacrifices had been the bridge to his place as one of His closest advisors, the Virtuous of Loyalty. He was sorry for his conscience, having betrayed his former master, but it was obviously for the greater good, for the divine will, for his eternal Oath. He apologized to his soul, entrusted it to Alatu – Goddess of Death – and asked her to be compassionate.

He remembered, with nostalgia, the high point of his life, when he underwent the ritual that made him an *immortal dread*. More than one hundred and fifty years ago, around a bonfire fed with trunks of sacred wood, with Mecantro in front of him, under the black moonless night, passing him *the blood*, letting it fall like red tainted threads into the wound of his right hand, and chanting the holy words, which had been repeated for millennia. When he finished, he bandaged his hand and was led into the fire, and there, burning for a few seemingly endless moments, he was finally chained to his new life as *immortal dread*. He swore right there, before all the Gods and his companions in arms, that he would faithfully serve the Blessed One, the King of the World, the Executing Hand of the Gods on Earth, until his death.

He remembered, with infinite sadness, the day he understood that the High Priest was not the perfect man he believed, but just another *dread*, one full of defects, unworthy of being the Executing Hand. He also remembered, now with joy, the first time he heard of Sargon, the true ruler of Nineveh, his miracles, his unparalleled wisdom. The exact moment when in his heart he felt that He must be the King he sought to serve, whom he needed to fulfill his Oath.

He wandered erratically through the rooms that housed him, as he always did when nervous, practicing his speech for the moment when he had him face to face. He noticed his surroundings. It was a double room, two chambers separated by an intricately designed wooden latticed door, the interior neatly decorated with dozens of curtains of fine and colorful fabrics that produced folds of charming textures. The floors were covered with fur and feather cushions. Some rectangular white furniture with gilded paints on the edges rested on the corners. Delicate plaster casts decorated the ceilings. Underneath, somewhere in the Palace where he was, music, tambourines, and some laughter could be heard. Joyful gabbling. The air smelled of incense and spices. Wherever he looked, he felt at ease. Except for the windows. They had been specially walled up for his visit so that they would not be opened by mistake or by a strong wind, but without real care. He suddenly felt unworthy of being at the King's side, and envious of Sargon's host of *immortals*, who wandered freely in the light of the day without hardship. He approached one of the windows and pulled one of the boards to make a gap. A shimmer of light seeped in. He watched the beam of light touching the ground and, after raising a sincere prayer to Elagabal, God of the Sun, placed his hand in between. It began to burn, throwing off a thin trail of smoke and a horrible smell, and had move it away. Undeniably unworthy. He couldn't accept what he was.

Hassan walked away from the window as he rubbed his injured hand and pride. A few knocks on the front door distracted him. Two knocks, one pause, two more knocks. As he had asked his obligated travel companion Kamek to announce himself if he had any news. Precautions are never superfluous in foreign land.

_Come forward Kamek.- Some light leaked in from behind when the door opened, so Hassan covered himself behind a curtain. The newcomer entered and closed the door slowly on purpose, suspicious of the man's absurd weakness.

_Aslin, future Virtuous, I have news for you. - said in a caustic tone of voice as he took off his white hat with beads and metal rings and put it under his arm. He had a similar attire to the one he wore days before, except for some pointed boots and a new belt, both gold-plated. - First, I want to greet you again and welcome you to the city. Second, I want to tell you that you were right, the person you predicted would arrive has been announced during the night.

_Jerro... - Hassan squinted, with deep disdain.

_That was the name he used to introduce himself. He claims to be the one worthy of the title of Virtuous in your place, just as you predicted he would. He is also aware of your arrival and has asked the King Himself to clarify the situation. - he adjusted his belt before continuing, lowering his gaze - He may ask for a trial by duel, so that the Gods may decide.

_I thought so, I'm... surprised he got here so quickly. - Hassan started walking around the room as he spoke. He was nervous and angry. Angry above all - That means that he was already on his way - he raised his finger accusingly - or... he foresaw the fall of Mecantro, but... I don't know how... - Hassan was genuinely surprised, he looked back and forth without being able to set his eyes on any useful place. His mouth suddenly became mushy.

_The problem, is time. - Kamek's tone of voice was similar to that of a healer discovering that nothing could be done for his patient anymore - He arrived a few knots behind us, explaining with exactitude what transpired at Mari. Had it been tomorrow, or days later, it would have been easy to declare that he was an impostor. Now I see only one way out.

Hassan looked up at his visitor. How did Jerro know so quickly what happened in Mari? Did Alid-Hur have anything to do with it? Was that torch a signal for him? He stared into the Assyrian. He did not like the intonation he used for the term "future", when he had so confidently announced his new title before. Neither did the look he gave back, of mistrust. _Kamek – he pointed his index finger in an accusing tone – you too... doubt me. And you've travelled beside me and proved that I was in Mari. And that Jerro didn't.

_Not really, Aslin, General of Mari. What I could see was that the High Priest had indeed died, but not the author of that murder. I didn't see Jerro in that place, but he might as well have acted and run. When my King asks for my testimony, it is my duty to speak the truth.

_Kamek, you can't do this to me, you have to trust me!

Kamek gave out a muffled laugh. _What's the matter, Aslin? What are you afraid of? The King is righteous, just like the Gods. If you have told the truth then you will be rewarded. And whoever has lied will have his head hanging from a wall. Justice is served to all.

He turned around and opened the door, whose lock snapped metallically. Again, Hassan took a few steps back.

_And with this, Aslin, former General of Mari and follower of Mecantro, I have fulfilled my word to keep you informed of your rival. I'll see you tonight, at the audition. - he said in an anguished tone, and closed behind him. A quick hand stopped him.

_Wait, please! You must help me Kamek! - Hassan shouted suddenly in despair.

The visitor stared at him impassively through the thin gap left by the door against the frame. _Understand - he spoke in the most neutral tone of voice he could - I owe you nothing. My duty is to my King.

_I know! - Hassan shouted bitterly, his head leaning against the wood. His plan was falling apart. His sacrifice was being stolen right under the nose. His place, alienated. He felt his whole being sinking away from divine grace - I ask you the following, it is a very small favor. - continued after he understood what was happening. - Get me a sword. I want to practice and be prepared in the event of a duel. That's all.

This was obviously, he thought, a punishment from the Gods for betraying his master. He had to earn his place and forgiveness by exposing his life. The duel was the way they had chosen to prove his value.

Kamek stepped back in and stood in front of the defeated Hassan. After a moment's thought, he drew his sword from the belt and handed it to him. It was short, made of iron, with a wooden handle and round knob – The only condition I will ask is, that you do not use this weapon if there is a duel. You'll leave it here before you're called.

Hassan nodded his head, crestfallen. Kamek said nothing more and left at a steady pace.

The time for the hearing had come. Hassan, flanked by a guard and Kamek, walked down the wide corridor leading to the throne room. Between the salmon columns the cold night air slipped through, and he felt its rigor every time he was outside the aura of warmth of the torches. Before they reached the end, golden double doors opened majestically. The throne room was huge, fabulous, full of white columns and salmon on the sides, very fine fabrics hanging on the walls, and gold. Gold in the sculptures, in the high reliefs, in the jewels. Gold everywhere. Hassan was stunned. All he could see were bursts of light and golden reflections, menacing figures to the left and right. He was ready to entrust his own soul to Alatu for mercy. When they stopped they were thirty paces from the royal throne, covered by multiple veils. Some female figures danced in the back. A figure, standing in the middle, raised a hand and the women ended their dance. The four beautiful young girls came out, drew the veils to the beat of the music coming from shiny wind and string instruments.

The central figure was a very young, slender, dark, soft-looking man with a rectangular nose. His chin was rounded like a ball. Underneath his incipient beard loomed a significant inflammation. Hassan looked at the man's neck, and the first thing he thought was that he was sick, having seen that before. He wore a gleaming crown, brimming with jewels and precious stones, a short purple and gold vest over an impeccable white robe, and a solid golden belt. He was barefoot, and his feet seemed to have never stepped on the sand.

A man dressed in a purple vest, wide white trousers, and golden tipped boots stood in front of the newcomers and announced aloud.

_Here you stand before the Great Sargon II, representative of the ruler of Nineveh, King of all men, conqueror of heaven and earth. Eternal be his name and legacy - All present bowed, including Kamek. Hassan was confused by the situation, but chose to imitate them... What did they mean with Sargon *II*?

_Newcomer, introduce yourself - continued.

Hassan looked at Kamek, trying to get information without speaking. Seeing him hesitate, Kamek stepped forward and spoke, pointing at him. _Here is Aslin, former General of Mari, to claim his place as Virtuous of Loyalty. – Hassan, convulsed, looked around to focus. That man was the Great Sargon? Impossible. And he wasn't the only one present with a swollen jaw, several guards nearby were also affected. In fact, a few steps away from him, one of those guards was terribly thinned, his belly bloated. He could see repressed pain on his face. They couldn't be *immortal*, they had to be ordinary people.

_What merit do you have in claiming such title?

Hassan finally decided to speak. _I... come to claim the title of Virtuous for the merit of surrendering the city of Mari to its rightful owner, the Great King Sargon, and for removing the impostor... the High Priest Mecantro.

_Excellent. – the man stood facing the entrance, which was crossed by three people. Two more guards entered, dressed in leather breastplates with studs, white cloaks and pikes in their hands, and in front of them a tall, dark, broad-shouldered man with fibrous muscles. Black, sagacious eyes, short hair and a beard of few days distinguished his head, as wide as his neck. He wore a gray robe like Hassan's, with an engraving of Adad, God of Tempests. From his belt, an empty sheath hung down.

_Newcomer, introduce yourself – said protocolarly the right hand of Sargon II.

One of the guards accompanying the man announced: _This is Jerro, former Protector of Mari, to claim his place as Virtuous of Loyalty.

_What merit—

_I am the rightful Virtuous of King Sargon, because that is what I have earned. - Jerro interrupted, raising his voice - That man over there - pointing to Hassan - is trying to usurp my achievements, and I ask that the King himself determine his falsity, restoring my rightful place.

_Foreigner, you stand before King Sargon II, reverence yourself and speak with the respect his person demands. - the man and the young king at his side were sensibly irritated.

_I will only bow before the true Sargon, and not his puppet. - he spat defiantly.

Sargon II turned to say something to his right hand in the ear. He spoke again. _The Great Sargon will not be attending this audition, he has left his trusted servant in charge.

_And who are you, standing before me - he said aggressively - with supposed authority?

The right hand was going to speak, but the king interrupted him. _I am Amterié, nephew of the Great Rettla the Virtuous of Generosity, and I rule on behalf of the Great Sargon. I bear the name Sargon II because He has chosen it so. – the words came out with difficulty, pride and anger from his sick throat.

_A Virtuous's nephew? Do you realize that once I get rid of this phony I'll be higher up in the hierarchy than you? I demand to see the King – dropped Jerro disrespectfully.

Certainly a Virtuous had more relevance in the reign than an ordinary man. Sargon II stood furious, but without a sound. Jerro had played a noisy string on Assur's harp. The seconds passed and the situation became uncomfortable. A guard of prominent nose approached Amterié from behind and spoke to his ear, and he answered something. The man in the purple vest approached and spoke to his ear as well.

_That young man – said Kamek quietly, approaching Hassan – was put there by his uncle, a political favor. Rettla is the richest man in the kingdom, he made an enormous contribution to His Eminence in times of need. In this case, the title earned him the right to place him as subrogate. One with little preparation, by the way. The guard standing beside him is called Serencal, one of King Sargon's favorites. You better be on good terms with him. – Hassan nodded.

_The Great King Sargon has already declared. Both will fight a duel before the Gods, who will determine who is the righteous and deserving one. The fight will be held right now, in the Palace Arena.

Not only did Jerro not protest, but he looked at Hassan with contempt before turning around and following his escorts who instructed him to leave. From the very beginning Sargon had decided the duel. Of course, Hassan thought, as it followed the divine purpose and custom.

He moved outward following his escorts, with his mind busy tracing different tactics. Jerro was ahead of him in combat experience, and hand–to–hand was not Hassan's strong suit. His only chance was to wait for him to make a mistake, possibly deliberately leaving his neck defenseless and seizing the opportunity to attack. Yes, knowing Jerro, he might try to win with a single blow by severing his head, for he would have no way of knowing for sure if a blade against his heart would be totally effective. In fact, he didn't even know himself whether he would resist it or not. He had been cut and stabbed countless times but never in the heart itself.

_What will you do, Aslin? – Kamek asked, pretending to be worried.

_Pray to Nin–Karrak. – replied, placing his hand on the chest, where he wore the engraving of the Goddess – She will watch over my well–being.

_Maybe you should do something more solid. I've noticed that this person, Jerro, seems strong and well–

292

trained. You'll have a hard time with him. - Hassan nodded, looking straight ahead - I have also noticed that he is rash and reckless with his words. That might play him off.

Hassan turned to Kamek with prompt suspicion. _What exactly do you mean?

Kamek approached and took him by the arm. _I don't know what they said there, but I understand they were up to something. They already have a favorite. - he whispered.

_Would that be me?

_Perhaps.

At the end of the corridor, beneath the stairs, there was the Arena. It was located at the far end of the Palace's garden, full of all kinds of vegetation, aromatic flowers and tall palm trees. In the distance, in the middle of the large garden, there was a statue of Tammuz, God of spring and plants, surrounded by flowers and various offerings to earn his favor.

The Arena was a simple circle of barren earth no larger than twelve steps, amidst gray stone tiles, surrounded by eight pillars of stone and wood with torches. Four long semicircular stone seats circled around it, so that attendees could comfortably watch two men fight to the death. Two guards began to light the torches and carefully place them on the pillars, granting the place a dramatic tinge.

One of the guards accompanying Jerro explained to him where he should be situated. He stood on the southern edge of the circle. Kamek and Hassan walked all the way to the northern border around it without stepping on the ground, as if there was an invisible barrier protecting it.

_Each one will be given a sword. - Kamek explained - You can only take in one weapon. Once the encounter has begun, if anyone escapes from the circle, they will be marked as cowards and sentenced to death. However, if your opponent pushes you out, you can come back in. - he looked back and nodded his head - Look at that, Aslin.

Sargon II's retinue had arrived and began to settle into the stone seats. The guards were strategically positioned ahead to keep the duelists contained. Amterié, already seated in the most privileged location, gave orders in a low voice to the same big nose guard, Serencal, who had previously appeared to support him. Nearby, the right hand listened to the conversation and nodded.

_Any idea what they're talking about? - Hassan asked.

_No. But if I were you, I'd pay close attention.

Serencal approached Jerro and handed him a sword, while a short, slightly overweight guard walked toward the center of the arena. He announced, after clearing his throat several times and bowing to Sargon II. _Here will duel before the Gods, Aslin, General of Mari, and Jerro, Protector of Mari. Both will receive a sword, which will be their pen. They will both enter the arena, which will be their papyrus. Only one can write his Justice, the other will perish in the attempt.

Serencal approached Hassan and handed him a sword. He wore a regular uniform, but had a silver medallion hanging from his wrinkled neck. His eyes were sunken, and his right eye slightly grayish. He stepped forward and turned subtly. _You better not let go of that edge for anything in the world, or you'll regret it. - he entrusted. The right side of his mouth was paralyzed.

Hassan followed him with his eyes, and turned to Kamek who had walked away for the event to begin. He looked back at him approvingly.

_Let the contestants enter the Arena. - announced the fat guard. Once Jerro and Hassan stepped forward, he trotted out to the side.

Hassan looked ahead. Jerro was there, ten paces away from him, wielding his edge with great confidence. Amterié raised his hand, and after a pause, shouted. _Let the duel begin!

Jerro charged in with a loud scream. He had chosen not to measure his opponent and go straight to the offensive by abusing the difference in power. Hassan dodged by jumping backwards, and then trotted out to one side putting some distance. He actually had an interest in understanding the opponent's moves, and was confident in his defensive ability. Jerro struck again, failing.

Hassan was moving fast. A third attack was stopped by taking Jerro by the arm and pushing him towards his flank. Jerro took him by the clothes making him lose his balance, stumbling a few steps away. The sturdy man slid his blade through the air vertically against Hassan's head, forcing him to roll backwards very close to the rim.

_How much longer are you going to run, Aslin? Face me or give up, but do it now.

Hassan didn't respond, he devoted himself to recover his balance. He decided to set his tactic in motion, purposely leaving his sword down.

_You'll pay for trying to steal my glory, you wretched scumbag. - Jerro insulted, running towards him and brandishing his weapon diagonally at his head. Hassan moved his torso back and defended himself by colliding blade against blade.

To his surprise, a piece of metal flew upward, forming a broad arc and finally falling with a dull sound to the ground. Jerro's sword had broken on impact. He looked at his grip in surprise and indignation. Not for long, as he was caught on a sharp edge piercing his chest, between the ribs. Jerro fell heavily with one knee. The pulling of the blade outwards forced him to ground his hands. A profuse stream of blood rushed down. He raised his head and saw his executioner in front of him. Hassan stomped hard as he cut his enemy's neck with all his might, without losing a beat.

He stood up. The duel was over. Exclamations of all kinds around him were heard, most of them complaining about the short show. He stayed there in the middle of the arena not quite grasping what had befallen. He looked up to look around him. Amterié had risen from his seat and was preparing to speak.

Him. Amterié had prepared this. He gave Jerro a defective sword and he fell straight into the trap. No doubt he didn't mind who won, but the recently deceased had disrespected him in front of everyone and he couldn't forgive him for that. He turned to Kamek. He didn't look surprised at all.

_The Gods have proclaimed themselves. Justice is on the side of Aslin, the brand new Virtuous of Loyalty. – Amterié announced, bowing, followed by those present.

Tired as he was, Hassan slept half a day. He woke up again when the afternoon was already falling. He was in the same room he had stayed in before. Took a jar of water waiting for him on a piece of furniture, cleaned and dried himself with a cloth that smelled of jasmine.

At last, he had succeeded. He had earned his place in the world. He smiled shyly, holding the cloth in his hands. With a little help, maybe. But he had earned it.

Justice was on his side. He would never forget that.

He changed his clothes, a white and purple tunic, a round belt with silver and gold appliqués, and pointed booties. He set aside a diadem and a jeweled bracelet waiting for him in a drawer. He didn't need them.

He heard a couple of knocks on the door, followed by two others.

_Go ahead, friend Kamek. - welcomed the man in a very good mood as his guest entered.

_Congratulations Virtuous. You have written your justice well and obtained your reward. - Kamek closed, bowing.

_Thank you. For a person who distrusted me, you've helped a lot.

_I would call it caution rather than distrust. - he said in a tone between friendly and satirical.

Hassan laughed inwardly, satisfied. He was happy. _I can't wait to speak to His Majesty.

_No doubt, Virtuous. I just came to pay my respects, and to congratulate you on your victory. – he apologized – I won't take up your time.

_Not at all Kamek. In fact, I'd like to ask you something important. That soldier, Serencal. Is he one of Sargon's *immortals*?

_Of course.

Hassan started walking around the place. _I've noticed he's aged, too much. He's sick of one eye. If my experience doesn't fail me, it's because of parasites.

_Is there anything extraordinary about it?

_A lot. We, the *dreads*, don't get sick. And parasites do not thrive in the body. – Kamek followed him with his eyes, in silence – What about Amterié, is he *immortal*?

_Yes. Just like his father, and his uncle. The whole lineage of Sargon. In fact, Amterié is my second cousin on my mother's side.

Hassan stopped short. Sargon's lineage? How could they have offspring? _I'm... astounded. We can't have progeny... do you have sons? – he asked affectionately.

_No, we haven't been blessed with one yet. The royal lineage is strong, but scarce.

299

_Wow, you're so different from me. Yet superior in everything, except perhaps physical endurance.

_Don't grieve, Aslin. You will be a valuable addition to the kingdom.

Hassan smiled with some sadness. _Thank you Kamek my friend. Your words give me encouragement.

_Is there anything else I can do for you?

_Tell me about His Majesty, what kind of man is He?

_A grandiose being! – Kamek rubbed his palms, looking up, thinking of all the goodness of his Lord to put them into words – He is incomparable...

Three days later, Hassan had finally been called. Kamek waited beside him in a rather dark and relatively small chamber, with only two oil lamps illuminating it. Soon he would have an audience with the King, the Chosen One.

Sitting on a wooden chair, Hassan kept his eyes fixed on the ground, his hands squeezing his knees.

_Calm down, Aslin, focus on doing your best to serve your Lord. His Majesty the King, in His vast wisdom, will appreciate your work done in good faith towards the Gods.

Hassan didn't answer, he just smiled nervously. This was happening! Soon he would be at the side of the Great Sargon. One of the doors opened, and a guard spoke to them. _Aslin, Virtuous of Loyalty, you may pass now.

_Go ahead, be confident. – Kamek reassured him.

Hassan nodded, and advanced. He walked down a short hallway to a sturdy, shiny copper door. It was engraved with the figure of Assur, a winged disc, radiating its power and benevolence over all men. The guard struggled to open the door and waited outside.

The room he entered was no bigger than his quarters. The walls were decorated with frescoes, but there were no textiles or fabrics of any kind. There were no carpets on the floor, just the polished stone. Several oil lamps hung from the columns, giving an enigmatic sensation. The smell of incense covered another, rotten one. A long veil hung from the ceiling, behind it a huge bed was visible. Two figures moved to the sides. One approached Hassan. She was a very beautiful young woman, dressed in white and purple. She had eyes of deep tiredness, and her mouth and nose were covered. She asked him with a bow to come in.

Hassan drew the veil with hesitation and fear. He stood at the foot of the bed. Above it rested a decrepit old man, pitiful looking, covered with a sheet of a material that Hassan did not recognize, but was glossy and shiny.

The old man wore no attires, only cloth that bandaged his thin arms, hands, and torso. A few hairs were sticking out of his forehead and cheeks, but there were no others on the rest of his head, even on his eyebrows or eyelashes. Atrocious malachite green veins poked out of his neck. Hassan didn't understand what was in front of him. He couldn't believe his eyes.

The young woman approached his ear. _Virtuous, approach closer to His Majesty if you will be so kind. Please use this cloth to cover your mouth when speaking.

Hassan moved slowly to the side of the bed, and sat down in a chair. He was going to talk, but decided to put the cloth over his mouth first. _Are... are you Sargon? - he asked with astonishment and respect.

The old man turned, but did not fix the eyes on him. He was blind. _Aslin, my new Virtuous. - he said, with a strand of a voice - Welcome, I trust you will perform with honesty and dedication.

The stench grew stronger now that he was near. The smell of death, of rottenness, one that not all the cares in the world could take away. _Yes, Your Majesty.

_So be it. Follow Serencal's orders. He'll tell you what to do. - sighed deeply, and when inhaled, he made an unpleasant noise - Trust Serencal, he is a valuable man. I hope you can show your worth too. - he breathed in making noise and turned around again.

And he stood there, facing the emptiness over him, breathing with whistles.

_Y-yes, Your Majesty. - he managed to answer several moments later.

He rose to his feet, and walked away slowly. Knocked on the copper door and the guard opened it. Kamek greeted him outside.

_Well?

Hassan stood in front of Kamek, unable to speak. The cloth fell out of his hand.

_What's the matter?

_Sargon. He's sick. Badly sick.

_That's disrespectful, Aslin. The King is not sick, he has lived ten lives, ruled Assur for five hundred years. He's aged, no doubt, but his flame is not extinguished.

Hassan collapsed on the inside. The smell of death had stuck to his clothes, he could still feel it invading his chest, his mind, his soul. His own master had lived *twice* that, and was as vital as the first day. And he killed him cowardly.

Sargon could be no chosen. He was a phony. A disgrace. An inferior being.

As a phony he was, Hassan couldn't serve him. The Gods had granted him their favor, but for what? He wondered if there really was someone to serve. What if the Executing Hand was really himself? Justice was on his side. There wouldn't be any one chosen to follow. Just obeying the divine plan.

No! It was impossible! The Oath, he was to serve the Chosen One of the Gods.

He prayed, there, standing in front of the doubt that devoured everything with its demonic maw. He prayed for a sign with all his heart, while his faith broke into a thousand pieces.

_Why me, Kamek? – he asked rhetorically.

_Why were you chosen?

_...Yes. – he sighed without really expecting an answer.

_I'll tell you something, since I see you unwell. Four years ago, the Oracle confided to the Great Sargon that one of his Virtuous would betray him, and that it would be his most faithful servant. His Majesty then mistrusted his servant, your predecessor in Loyalty, a man named Janicus. He spied on him for years, until he finally found a reason to justify his suspicion. He sent for him to be killed. He consulted the Oracle again, who recommended that his new Virtuous to be a person who would earn his title through a fair duel before the Gods. – Kamek put his hand on Hassan's shoulder – Two came claiming the title, one won in a duel. That person is you. Don't hesitate any longer, Aslin. – he patted him, and smiled.

Of course he wasn't going to hesitate. Of course, he had not won the duel fairly but by cheating. Of course that's what was predicted. He thanked the Gods for giving him a sign so quickly. A prophecy that cried out to be fulfilled.▯

PART 27: THE QUEST FOR TRUTH

_Johnny Johnny dear Johnny, I promise you I'll return two favors, big ones. But you gotta help me out on with this. - Fisher pleaded.

_I'm skating on thin ice, lard ass. I already gave you the material I had, what else can I do?

_Yes, I know, but it's raw material, and half of it are formulas I don't get. If we put our heads together, we'll get more out of it, won't we?

Fisher was in a corner standing, in civilian clothes, inside a bar he did not frequent a few kilometers from the base. The music was soft, and in the gloom of the dim lighting the occasional customer could feel as lonely as they wanted to be. Some of them in the rear were playing "bottle billiards", a version of the game that had become popular, which consisted of leaving an empty bottle on the table and whoever touched it with one of the balls paid for the next round. The game must have been exciting because some shrieks were sporadically thrown into the air, to Fisher's distress. In his hand he held an austere assistant, a somewhat old-fashioned model that served him well. On its screen, flashed the face of his old conscription friend, General John Aaron McCarthy. He was a chubby man, with his nose slightly tilted to the right, broad eyebrows near the eye socket, but almost non-existent on the sides. Some strands of shiny hair fell on his forehead, recently treated with a hair loss product.

_I couldn't get anything else Carl, most of the material was destroyed. I know there was a detailed report at one point because I read it, but no one has or knows what happened to it.

_Yes, and I'm very grateful, but I'm asking you this last favor. Look, I'm at Grant's on Washington Avenue, you know which one? Why don't you come over and lend me a hand? I'll buy you a beer too, how about that?

McCarthy grumbled loudly and scratched his forehead. _Yeah, I know which is... fine! I'll tell my wife I'm leaving, I don't think it'll take more than twenty or twenty-five minutes to get there. See you soon, and you better... nothing, I'll tell you later.

_Thank you, Johnny! I'll wait for you here.

He closed the communication and sat back in his chair. The chairs were not really comfortable, or were designed for a much thinner person than he was. Lamented that he couldn't lose those annoying extra kilos, but he really, really didn't have time for that this once. He glanced forward and slid his handbag aside.

At least the table was clean. Fisher ordered a beer of his favorite brand from the man with the long hair and quiet look behind the bar, and unrolled an electronic sheet. It turned on and showed the last page he had been reading, a digitization of raw reports, photographs and data tables, from 1965 to 1981.

He had actually read the report his friend had handed him several times, but there were details of particular interest to him and was unsure of the conclusions he had reached through the data. By the time he noticed, his glass was empty, and someone had sat across from him. He was short, wearing an orange plaid shirt, and on top of it a jacket lined with artificial skin and fur. Underneath, some extremely lowcut pants, and a pair of dull shoes. Fisher could have sworn he was wearing socks in different colors. McCarthy always had lousy taste for fashion. Fortunately, the army dressed him for years, and still does.

_Just in time! – he grabbed his hand with the greeting they always did when they were alone, holding tightly by the elbow and banging fists at the end.

_Let's keep it short or my wife will kill me before the guys at the quarters. Well, what do you got there? Where's my beer? – said, energetic and in a hurry, as he rearranged himself in the seat. He quickly noticed that the chair was not made for someone of his corpulence.

Fisher ordered two extra-large pitchers and extended the sheet. McCarthy quickly flicked through several pages, and snorted. _Now that I have it here, I don't really remember much. I read the report without much care many years ago. Chemistry? No way José.

_I figured it would be like this, so let's take it one step at a time. – he came closer to the table, ready for action and hungry for knowledge – I understand these guys aren't human, but what's affecting them is not a virus, bacteria or contamination – he pointed to the sheet, poking it with his finger – ...so what the hell are they?

_I remember that, but it's not that easy to explain. The report said that... an ordinary human being carries in the DNA a lot of "junk" code, which is an ugly term for a lot of things that scientists still don't fully understand what's for. That code remains deactivated, but it is still passed on to the next generation, in fact we carry DNA from bacteria and many other things that are not strictly... uh... us. Non-humans have enough of that junk code activated, so their bodies behave so differently.

_Okay well, it was pretty much what I... hadn't thought of. I'm surprised. – he kept reading the page carefully – meaning that... anyone could become one. – a young woman with short hair, wide thighs and a myriad of freckles gave them the pitchers. Both friends had a drink.

_Ah, it's very good! - McCarthy said relieved - Yes, it needed to, uh... pass on the active code from an active tissue to a non-active one. There was another requirement, but unfortunately I can't remember. But in theory, yes. You, me or anyone else could be. Oh, wait a minute - he slapped his belly - on animals it didn't work. The code remained active but did not manifest itself. I think that could also happen in humans, in some cases.

Fisher turned several pages, reviewing his own notes he had put over the original data. _I read some of that, I didn't understand why they included a cat in this part.

_Lemme see. - he spent a long minute skimming through the information - This cat, had breeding. Females had the code active, males did not. Likewise, the effects on any of them were not apparent.

_Speaking of which, there's no sexual reproduction? That's what I read on page two hundred and four. - Fisher noted.

_Seems like... no. Once advanced in their... mmh... non-humanism, they can no longer conceive or fertilize.

_This is very interesting, how come you never told me about all this?

McCarthy looked at his friend through the glass of his pitcher as he drank, impatiently. _Because it was top secret. Besides, you never asked!

Fisher smiled sideways. _It's true, it's true. Another thing I don't understand, we've done experiments here, and as I can tell... many. All failures?

_Hypothetical experiments. – he gestured quickly and sardonically – The smartasses of the research team thought it was something like the Rosetta Stone to build the supersoldier. They did the thousand and one tests but failed. All they gave the volunteers was disadvantages. They made them depend on a special serum to live on, and had to stay away from any high energy source. The fire? Deadly. An electrical accident? Deadly. A sunny day? Deadly. – he paused to eat peanuts and have another drink. – Some of those poor bastards endured an hour under the shining sun and then died. Those who had the worst were slowly incinerated. In the shade and with enough clothes they had it better, but the result was more or less the same. The more advanced their state, the more vulnerable they became. It was a gradual effect.

_How do they manage to survive on a day-to-day basis? They seem more useless than they look.

_Ah! The trick is that they get better with time. Unfortunately, it takes too long to see useful results in combat, I'm talking about, I don't know... hundreds of years, or some nonsense. The only good thing was that they developed greater resistance to infection and closed wounds a little faster than normal. The top brass decided they didn't want to wait that long and put everything in a permanent delay. Then someone pushed to destroy the data... and you tell me you know who it was.

_If it wasn't that Perius, it was one of his group. I'm afraid they have an extended network with access to the big shots in the country. Only God knows how far they can go if they've been here that long... how much do they live?

_Dunno. I suspect they don't die, at least not from old age. I think I may have read somewhere that there was no aging, or that it was very mild. Not sure.

Fisher stared out the window. Outside, there were few vehicles on the road. He wondered since when they had been there, plotting, scheming...

_What about hypnosis? He's got over half the men running around like jerks from here to there. Bah, I imagine that's what this is about and not some weird magic spell.

McCarthy hesitated for a moment. _I don't know, dude. No tests were done on hypnosis, at least not related. Before you ask, I have nothing about experiments in that field. By the way, how did you get out of it?

_I didn't, he didn't try anything with me. I think he wants to convince me nicely. – he laughed in a mocking tone – As if.

_Things gettin' tough, Carl. All I heard yesterday were questions here, questions there. Nobody knows a thing, and the worst part is that they're trying so hard to hide it. "Of course we know what we're doing, but if you know anything, call us." – mimicked McCarthy, ridiculing – Those assholes. And did you hear the speech this afternoon? Looks like we've gone back fifty years... damn it.

Fisher took a good drink from his pitcher, and settled as best he could into his narrow seat. _Something's not working out for me. I've been spying on that guy's movements. I haven't seen him eat, just drink champagne and smoke expensive tobacco.

McCarthy would have preferred to change the subject so he could criticize the top dogs in politics, but that night it would be difficult for him. _If memory serves right, they can survive on normal food, as long as it's in quantities. And they can't metabolize anything that comes from another non-human. Weird, huh?

_Did you feed the volunteers flesh from other volunteers?

_Hypothetical volunteers. You see? That's why I never told you anything. It's disgusting.

_Maybe Perius found a way to eat normal food, but I didn't see him do it either. I'll pay more attention. But to get to the point, how do I kill them?

_I'd try a flamethrower. - McCarthy joked with his crop full of peanuts. - As far as we know, a gun works, too. Once dead, they don't walk anymore. I mean, I'm always talking about volunteers. Hypothetical volunteers. - he corrected himself.

_I'm afraid if I try with a gun I won't be able to try anything anymore. What do you advise me to do?

McCarthy snorted, left his pitcher on the table and interlocked his fingers under his chin. _Excellent question. If he's in control like you say, the only course of action is for us to intervene on the base. But as in the previous case, it may be the last thing we try. I don't know what political connections he has, or if there are other people behind Perius.

_Which is likely. - said Fisher.

_In which case, we should consult the Defense Department on the quiet side. I have a friend there, I can ask him without arousing suspicion.

_Great. I still have a lot of questions about this. - he said, shaking the sheet - Another round?

McCarthy laughed. _Thank you, but I'm leaving now. Besides, I've reached the limit. I don't have any more juicy facts to serve you, and I don't understand the notes. But... if you're so curious, I have someone for you. He's an acquaintance of mine who works in Germany. As far as I was notified by unofficial sources, he would investigate something similar there. – he looked up his assistant and showed him the screen. – Copy this contact, and tell him you're a friend of mine.

_Will he help?

_He's too far away to be in the plot, at least he's got that. – the stout General stood up, making the chair squeak against the ground – Well, fatso, I'm leaving. I'm glad you're so youthful. Say hello to your family for me and don't give up. You can count on me.

_Yeah, tomorrow morning I'm going home to spend time with them. I have to work tonight. – he quickly put aside the memory of his wife and daughter – Thank you, man. And thanks for coming, I owe you one.

_You owe me two!

They said goodbye with a hug, and McCarthy walked out the door. Fisher followed him with his eyes until he lost him behind a wall. He was encouraged, at least more informed than an hour ago, his quest for the truth was advancing. He checked the status of his new contact. He was available. Fisher thought it to be very professional of him. So he mentally prepared his questions, and sent him a message.

_Good evening, I hope I'm not disturbing you. I'm Carl Fisher, my friend John McCarthy gave me your contact, I was hoping to ask you some questions if possible.

He waited for an answer from the other side. Finally the communication opened, and a man appeared on the screen. He was thin, light-skinned, with sunken cheeks and a narrow chin. Fisher was surprised that he was so pale, but was not aware of the latest European habits. And besides, that intense look...

_Good evening, I don't know how I can help you, but John is a colleague I appreciate. How can I be of service to you? – kindly asked Matthias Weissman.

PART 28: BEHIND THE CURTAINS

Perius entered the enormous hall triumphantly. Few lights illuminated the central table, and some others shed light on some paintings of important personalities of the last century, insignificant to those who have went through millennia. The doors closed behind him, with his large armed guard outside. He was radiantly dressed in his favorite way, in his classic black suit, an elegant glossy galley, his delicate dragon cane and a crimson silk scarf around his neck. He wore a magisterial moustache under his nose, made by himself just seconds ago and retouched in front of a mirror with some small scissors.

He leaned his hands slightly against the enormous table that dominated the room, made of glass, liquid crystal and steel. Around him, scattered about in no apparent order, five people were sitting in waiting.

_Gentlemen, gentlemen! I'm so glad you are here. I thank you from the bottom of my heart for accepting my humble invitation, I hope you will feel comfortable and to your liking. If you do not mind, I will take a seat with you and we can get started. – he announced in English, respecting the locality, as usual.

The closest person made a cordial gesture with his hand, to formally invite him to begin the meeting he had thought and executed himself. No one was there for pleasure, but rather dominated by circumstances.

_I particularly rejoice that you were able to arrive on time, León. I understand that you are a busy man and that you have set aside a lot of responsibilities to assist in person. I am very aware of this - he continued, now addressing everyone - Gentlemen, I do not want to prolong myself too long as I would be taking up your valuable time. I must therefore sin, then, of little cordiality, to go directly to the problem that afflicts us, and which must be solved in the most expeditious way.

Perius took a moment and a half more to look around, adding more drama to the scene. León was at the far end of the hall, dressed in an extremely formal suit, with a tie that glowed in the dark, as dictated by the latest American fashion. He was crossing his legs and playing with a pen between his fingers, even though he had no means in which to make notes. He wore an impeccably combed blond hair, and an Intelli-Ring in his right ear, with which he controlled the flow of data to his personal computer. A few steps from him was The Genoese, with a taciturn appearance, as if he was not entirely convinced of being in the right place at the right time. He wore a casual suit, with a fake white shirt unbuttoned, his short black hair slightly tangled. He sat crouching, hands clasped together under the table, randomly tapping a lighter against the glass, cutting inconsiderably at the heavy silence that ruled the place.

In front of them was The Cardinal, with his decayed and dull appearance he had for centuries, wearing a simple white cotton tunic, with a silver cross around his neck and a thick ring as his only decorative feature, correctly wrapping up his austere personality. He was calm on the outside, but kept a whirlwind of fear within him. Of those present, he had by far the weakest position, and knew for certain that only the respect for customs (perhaps obsolete by now) was the only reason he had been invited to this meeting.

Away from The Cardinal by several empty seats, there was a sturdy, bald man with a square nose and hard features. His attitude was a mixture of joviality and severity, of a relentless and extremely cunning being. His clothes were real, a modest brown suit, a coat over his legs, shiny shoes, and several gold items that populated his neck and fingers. No one knew his real name and it didn't matter either, as was the case with almost everyone present. His only constant was his first name, which was believed to be his birth name, while his surnames had been countless, as far as his imagination would go. That's why he was simply known as George.

Lastly, the one closest to the door and noticeably away from the rest was a thin, extremely young-looking man with Asian features. Minamoto had worn the same appearance for centuries and centuries, and with the exception of some repaired war wounds, it had been a constant throughout time, as had his name and lineage, which were a source of pride. His impeccable jet-black hair, deep eyes and martial air never revealed more than he wanted, giving the appearance of being an eternal chess player, always ten moves ahead of his opponent. In this case, and for more than two hundred years, that rival had been the same: George, who for the moment won the game. He was clothed in a simple shirt, pants and shoes of his own modified skin.

The Council of Caucasus was complete, with a structure inherited from time immemorial, five Virtuous people who accompanied the leader. No one in attendance had dared to disregard Perius' invitation, the only one who did not possess the grace of the late leader, but who had suddenly become a major player in the turbulent times they were living. A new world order would probably emerge from the outcome of this meeting, whether by agreement or disagreement of the parties. There were two major shortfalls, but they would never have agreed to approach. Who had control of China and many Southeast Asian countries, Xin-Zu, and the Middle Eastern strongman, Hassan, tough rivals to the almost total Western hegemony.

_You may wonder the reasons for my last actions, and it is my deepest wish that you know that I carry only the best intentions within me. - said Perius as he sat at the head, and accompanied himself with grandiose gestures. – Is that w–

_Perius, please, spare us the gibberish. It is known that you have a predilection for theatre, but I don't think it is appropriate at the moment, and I believe that I speak for everyone. – George interrupted, although kindly – There's something I want to know, why now? You never showed political ambition. You might well have been on the right side of Caucasus for your skills and experience, but you chose a different course. Were you waiting for him to vanish from the board? – he stated, firmly.

_I cannot say that I was totally comfortable with the way Caucasus was pulling the threads of the world, and I am more than sure that everyone here had one or two criticisms to make of it. – he replied calmly and freely, never leaving the character – The truth is that his leadership no longer exists, and something must be done in order to avoid the darkness. – he said, raising his voice. The noise of the lighter in the hands of The Genoese continued to pierce the atmosphere – What we have to ask ourselves is, what do we want from this new panorama that is opening up before our eyes? I will tell you what my vision is: a unified, orderly world that respects traditions. Gentlemen, no more conflicts that lead nowhere. We must focus on tomorrow.

_I must remind you gentlemen, there are some missing pieces here that will make that impossible. – said The

Genoese with little tact. Some complex looks were exchanged among those present.

_I understand that both Hassan and Xin have been invited to participate, and have refused or have not responded, is that correct? – George asked.

_That's right – spoke Perius – Unfortunately my words have only found deaf ears from one and the other. But the outcome of this meeting will affect them likewise. I am sure they will soon come to their senses and forget the old differences that stand in the way.

Minamoto raised his hand, forcing a strange, sudden emptiness. He took a few seconds before speaking. _I would like to take us away of the issue for a moment, to resolve first a substantive topic of equal or greater relevance. I have heard countless rumors... about the death of Caucasus, and I would like to know which source has the right information. – no one dared to answer. Minamoto continued – The loudest and most disturbing of these rumors, which I hope not to be real, indicates that some of those present *here* were behind his physical disappearance. – the glances were focused on his person, scrutinizing him from top to bottom – Another, wilder one, indicates that Caucasus has not died, but remains hidden in some location, for an unknown motive.

The Genoese and George began to aggressively hurl questions out loud before being stopped by Perius.

_Gentlemen, please! Let's remain calm. Is it possible to know what evidence of one or the other version exists?

_I cannot present any at this time, but I can prepare them for the next meeting if you wish. - five pairs of eyes incinerated the Japanese, Virtuous of Wisdom.

_What's the point of coming to this place to throw accusations and follies at large? - George shouted.

_I'm not the person who should be sitting in the dock, George. - Minamoto defended himself - But maybe someone here does need to be.

_If I may, gentlemen, I think we're out of focus on the main subject. - injected The Cardinal, Virtuous of Loyalty, calmly and prudently - I am the first to want to know the final fate of my lord, but what most dazes my thoughts is that will be of the world under my feet tomorrow. This widespread chaos must end. How many deaths will it take to settle the matter?

_I agree with The Cardinal. - Minamoto hastened - The actions of León and Eylem have been savage. - he turned to face Perius - but even more savage were yours, Perius.

_Drastic, rather than savage - said George, Virtuous of Generosity, as he leapt back in his seat.

_Barbaric, I'd say. - León, who had remained silent, replied - I have lost many men under your hand,

Perius, as I tried to pacify the circumstances and keep Eylem and her ambitions for power at bay. Nevertheless, I decided to be present at your invitation, since your cordiality and reputation as a man of reason and word are ahead of you. You can't reason with Eylem. Having been under the fist of Caucasus for so long has disturbed her, and now that she finds a shred of freedom, she decides it's time to take it all without stopping to ponder. – no one dared to interrupt León – but what's done is done. Eylem's threat is deactivated for the time being, after the events in the Palace. I propose, as The Cardinal wisely put it, that we first settle the situation for the future, and then focus on the other issues. – he paused, waiting for the others.

_I agree with León. – said George, looking sidelong at Perius, who seemed distracted by the fine details of his cane.

Minamoto and The Genoese nodded slightly, as the only answer.

_So what do you propose, Perius? – asked The Cardinal.

Perius looked up. It was his turn to shine again. _Gentlemen, what I propose is to end this obsolete system. Shall we continue to fight for the empty throne, or shall we concentrate on progress? Caucasus himself invented the law of "the oldest must rule", in case he no longer stood among us. But we well know that it was a law that no one intended to follow, because no one imagined a world without the Grand Caucasus. He did not imagine himself deceased.

George threw a dissonant chuckle. _Oh, that's true. And so much drama has it caused.

Perius continued. _We also know that, if this rule is to be respected, the next to take the throne should be the Akkadian, who has no interest in occupying this position.

_That's why I should be next. – cut León, Virtuous of Cunning, with authority.

_I'm afraid it's not that simple, León – went on Perius. – Tell me, honestly, how long could you last on the throne without the support of those present? How long would you resist the onslaughts of the East?

_I can't answer that, Perius, because what reasons would my colleagues have to not support me? – León took enough time to make eye contact with his five interlocutors.

_Or we could ask ourselves quite the opposite. – Minamoto interjected, no longer so kindly.

_I am more than sure that The Genoese, a person of thought and good will, understands the situation better than anyone else, and that I can count with his support, don't you think? – León said, looking at his secret partner.

_In fact, that's true. My vision of an orderly world is one that follows custom, the rule of Caucasus and common sense. If the one who has the seniority and capacity to rule is León, then he has my support. – seconded the military man, Virtuous of Might.

The Cardinal sought for the Japanese man's approval before opening his mouth. When he was sure he had it, jumped in. _I can't... say I'm in favor of that position. In my scarce but firm knowledge, and bound by my loyalty to Caucasus, I cannot let León take power lightly.

Both León and The Genoese turned to the new bloc that had emerged from the ecclesiastical power and the economic giant of Asia. _What reasons do you invoke? – asked The Genoese.

The Cardinal scratched his eyebrow, making an uncomfortable pause. _I'm afraid I have to deal with assumptions, so I'm terribly sorry. But, suppose León inherits the throne. What will happen from the East? My interest is in advocating for peace, and it is my understanding that not only will the two Eastern fronts not cooperate, but they will also be further opposed and violence will intensify. As an argument, I could argue that they will claim that León is not the rightful heir as long as the Akkadian exists, or even Garim, and refuse to negotiate again, as they have so often declined in the past.

_Garim doesn't count, he hasn't been seen in centuries, so the solution would be to eliminate the Akkadian, wouldn't it, León? – Minamoto asked, with a certain amount of malice – but if I have not been misled, that has already been tried, and it has failed.

León left the pen on the table, and pushed his body forwards. He seemed slightly choleric. _The Akkadian is a constant threat to order. It has been since roman times and will remain so as long as he lives. It's true, I tried to uproot that problem, but I didn't reap a victory.

Perius watched the stage with a smile on his face, as he continued to seem lost admiring the pipe he pulled from one of his pockets.

_And will it not be those same means you used against the Akkadian, which could, hypothetically, been used against Caucasus? – Minamoto threw, without a hint of compassion.

León looked up at the Asian, calmly and with temperance. _Minamoto, are you accusing me of this crime?

_I wouldn't dare, but it's certainly a valid question, León. – he fought back.

_We are going back to secondary matters. - said George - Although I agree with the Cardinal's hypothesis. The East cannot be easily pacified. If you will allow me, I will stand up - he said, as he began the second act - I agree that the throne is a difficult place to fill, but it does not have to be so. Here are the brightest minds in the world, chosen by the greatest leader who ever walked this earth. I am more than convinced that only the best can come out of this meeting. Since we are the Council of Caucasus, let us act as such. Let us carry forward his vision of the world, all together.

_What do you propose, George? - asked The Genoese.

_A fivefold throne, of course! A government of consensus. All voices will be heard. Conflicts, resolved like the gentlemen we are. Everyone will be able to thrive and be free in this new paradigm, as long as they respect their neighbors and maintain cordiality. It is a world model that includes, rather than excludes, the East.

_It is interesting, but challenging to implement. - sincerely added The Cardinal.

_Absolutely not, partners. - Perius mentioned - In fact, it is words more or words less my proposal. I am glad I heard it from an eminence like George.

_In the first instance, it seems less conflictive than the other alternative, but I am also concerned about implementation. Many will reject this proposal, to be free to do as they please without responding to a higher power. They may even use the same arguments as the East to rebel. - Minamoto noted.

_It may seem like a whim, but it doesn't seem like a viable model to me. - León shot - This world can only be led by a firm hand, not a multitude of pacifists. On the other hand - he paused, defiantly - I am not stupid, I understand what is happening here. No doubt you'll make my mission of order even more difficult until it becomes impossible.

_These are hard words that I do not find justified, kind sir - Perius calmed - This model of the world could never be complete without you, a vital cog in the wheel. No one here would ever dare to leave you out, or in an unworthy position.

León seemed to doubt, at least a tenth of a second. Perius continued. _I have not yet gone into my position at length. First of all, I would like to apologize for my actions, perhaps a little excessive but well-intentioned. What I wanted to do was to shake this lost world with a slap in the face, to achieve precisely this, a meeting with the most prominent personalities, and to repair in a short time all the damage caused by the lack of leadership. And not only that, what I intend to do is to make this space for dialogue permanent. May all of us here be able to debate and resolve, be open to more voices if necessary, and correct the course.

The Genoese and León shared glances, before focusing on Perius. _Let's say it is possible, this... space for dialogue. And that it's long-lasting in time. What happens now? - asked León - What practical measures will we take? The world is still revolutionized.

Perius got up as George sat down again. The third act began. _It's very simple. Trade is currently restricted, as is transport. I propose that this be maintained. It will damage regional economies, but there is a reason for that. The structure of interdependent countries is exhausted, only causing collapses that are difficult to solve, as one piece drags the rest with it. In two decades we can have a robust model of self-sufficient countries, each governed by a firm, thinking and capable hand. - he made a gesture, indicating to all presents - We do not need interdependence to keep human greed in check, we are here to guide their destinies. And if a conflict arises, it will be resolved swiftly in this space.

_It's interesting. - said Minamoto, seemingly pensive.

_I like the idea. - seconded George.

_I find it possible. - said the Cardinal.

After a short pause, León spoke. _I can't say I'm against it, the idea of strong and free pieces satisfies me. My people are prepared to withstand a two-decade crisis and resurface with greater firmness. I may not be in favor of theory, but I am in favor of practice.

_But what about the military blocs? They will need restructuring to adjust to the new economic model. - asked The Genoese.

_No one more prepared to answer that question than yourself. - Perius added, politely pointing his pipe at him.

The Genoese took a few seconds to respond. _In that case, the most appropriate thing would be to momentarily disarm the Pacific Treaty and the New Warsaw Pact, to restart the United States-Brazil dialogue, to formally invite China and India to a new alliance, that will create enough uncertainty for at least Xin to agree to approach us. I have no idea how Hassan will react, beyond doubling his spies. If we succeed in engaging in dialogue with China, Hassan and his people may at least come here to know first-hand what we are proposing, at the risk of being left in the wrong corner of the game.

_Two decades of hunger, I understand - lamented the Cardinal - A necessary evil...

_If it is convenient, gentlemen, we will meet again at a place to be agreed in six months. It is early, I know, but we are structuring a new order and it's better to be prepared and attentive.

_I agree. - stated Leon - The others nodded silently.

_I am confident we have a radiant future ahead of us, gentlemen. I am grateful to you for having listened my thoughts. - Perius said cheerfully. - It will be until we meet again, such pleasant company. Farewell - Perius made a greeting, bowing slightly. The rest stood up and headed for the exit. No one said another word, they didn't even look at each other. Everything was said. They all had their plays ready. Perius was the last to retire, followed by his escort. Before leaving the huge government building in Washington D.C., Perius gave an almost unnoticeable signal to one of the soldiers accompanying him who remained relegated, behind the curtains.

The soldier's gaze was empty, as a result of a deep vexation of his psyche. He waited for a while, as had been ordered in advance, spinning around the building, seemingly aimlessly, until he entered an empty room. He waited there for an hour, until a woman with an equally empty look entered and whispered in his ear. _Tell your master that everything went perfectly, that my Lord is very pleased and that he should continue with his agreement.

The soldier nodded, his mind lost.

PART 29: ALIVE

Vogel Drescher looked up. He couldn't believe it. What could be observed, there, in the distance, was the light of the stars. That momentarily distracted him from the current situation, with a deep wound on one shoulder, and below that, a portion of his hand missing, now under several layers of bandages. After two days of confinement, what they fervently wanted was to breathe the night air and shake off the guano from the soles. They were alive.

The four compelled companions continued their ascending path until they found their way out. The horror seemed finally over. The adventure none of them asked for, over. They peeped out. The celestial vault was partially covered. Actually, few stars dared to shine that cold night. Dark clouds loomed dangerously over the punished soil. The storm wind was blowing against them.

_It might rain. – Dipson assured – And if it's radioactive fallout, it won't be convenient for us to travel long distances.

_Aren't we far enough? – Syra asked, disgusted by the real possibility of having to stay, this time voluntarily, in that damned cave.

_From the impact zone perhaps, but the clouds depend on weather conditions. We have to be careful. - answered the Englishman Dipson - If the wind blew in this direction...

_On the other hand, it must be a few hours before dawn. I'm not sure how much time we'll need for... - MacOwen stopped. They all watched what was coming along a dirt road. Three sets of lights, trucks of some sort, drove away from the direction where the Aegis Palace had been.

Syra looked at MacOwen, now with only one pair of eyes, to see if they both were tuned once again. And they were.

_I'm sorry about the users of those transports, but it's an... emergency. We will try to do as little damage as possible. - announced Liam MacOwen - We'll ambush them, we need one of those vehicles.

The four of them moved as swiftly as possible towards one side of the road, hidden by skeletal trees. One of the transports passed by. It was an Italian military truck for troop transport, inside it carried about a dozen men armed and with hazardous materials suits. Definitely a tough target, given the situation. They stood still. The second transport passed. It was similar to the previous one, but it had eight or nine men inside it, with similar gear. They waited for the third. It was a jeep, with three people inside. They wore suits and weapons, but they were outnumbered and last. That was the target. At the signal, Syra and MacOwen jumped on the vehicle, and within moments had killed its occupants. Dipson and Drescher quickly climbed into it. Syra took the wheel and they set off. The short pause and blinding lights of the jeep helped to avoid suspicion. They continued that way for several kilometers, until an intense rain began to fall. The dark drops dyed everything with corruption. When they reached a narrow bridge, they saw their opportunity. They turned off all the lights and changed direction. The soldiers, dumbfounded but more concerned about their own lives, made their way across the bridge.

Now, alone, and trying to remain unnoticed, they continued on a road. It took a few hours until they found a partially evacuated village. The intense rain continued to fall on the last inhabitants who, with tears in their eyes and in a hurry, mounted their belongings in their cars to leave, assisted by some ill-equipped policemen. No one noticed the jeep out of place, nor that they were stopping at one of the buildings, partially rickety due to lack of maintenance, far away enough from the questions of the last to leave, busy with their own business. They parked under roof, and relaxed at last, cannibalized the dead bodies as if they were beasts.

Drescher was deeply saddened to be conquered by that heinous hunger that weakened and pushed him to his darkest side. He looked at his companions, who seemed unconcerned about it, or perhaps at peace with their own demons.

The light of dawn rose from behind the clouds, threatening to conquer the sky for several hours, before falling defeated again at night in the eternal dance.

They explored the place. The old wooden building had, in addition to a spacious garage, two floors. Three bedrooms on the top, and a kitchen downstairs next to a large living room, with a small but cozy room.

_We should spend the day here. Let's rest, we need it. This night it may not rain, and everyone can continue their journey wherever they please. – Dipson proposed, and everyone tacitly agreed. They were too tired to answer.

Dipson and Drescher settled into two of the upper rooms, one next to the other, in case the Dutchman needed help. The latter had barely said a word since they left the cave. He felt extremely useless, exhausted, hurt and betrayed by himself. Wondered how long it would take to be complete again, at least physically, his mind was another completely different issue. The room was poorly furnished, and the lamp hanging from the ceiling was not working. It didn't matter to him.

Drescher lay down on the large bed in great pain, helped by Dipson.

_Charles, thank you so much for your support. I really needed it.

_No need for thanks. In this cruel world, few of us are willing to lend a hand to our neighbors. – he observed his companion's half hand and lamented his choice of words.

_Anyway, thank you. I'll try to sleep now. If you all leave, please let me know first. I don't want to be alone here.

_Sure, good morning, Vogel. Have a good rest.

Dipson left, leaving him alone. It took him just seconds to fall sound asleep.

Charles continued into the other room. It had a light that did work, but the door did not close properly and cracked when it moved. Inside there were two small single beds. On one of the walls there were several photographs of a boy and a girl playing and fooling around. On the floor, orphaned, lay an old plush rabbit with one ear missing. The abandonment was felt in the air, almost as evident as the moisture in the ugly curtains.

He felt angry with himself. After so many years of study, his ability to heal was still minimal. Why was this art so elusive? So ordinary he was that he couldn't even get close to the masters?

He stood in front of one of the two beds with reluctance, looked at his clothes, how dirty they were and how tiring it was to see them removed to sleep with a little more comfort. He put his satchel aside and decided to deal with it later. Yes, afterwards he would. Always afterwards, he thought before falling asleep. All his hopes were in the after. Because now, he was useless.

Syra stayed several minutes in the bathroom on the top floor, soaking her hair in hot water in an old tub while waiting for it to fill up. It was a little dirty, but compared to her, it was impeccable. All the sconces were either broken or crooked. There was a white towel with holes hanging from one of the walls, with a slight layer of dust on top. An ugly moisture stain on the ceiling grew darker, until it finally began to drip shyly.

She disassembled her illusory suit to make it ordinary skin again, and immersed herself in the tub, to lie there motionless for several minutes as she settled her thoughts. She recalled all those times being really close to die, counting a dozen, even had the luxury of classifying them. Put one hand around her neck, remembering how close the last one had been, Chandresh's sharp hand close, very close to finishing the job and slicing her head off completely. It felt awful. Stomped, defeated, forced to depend on someone else again. She hated that. She hated dealing with weak people. But also with people stronger than her. They made her feel again the defenseless state of her youth in which she could only scream and cry, while some random gang of bandits whipped her village, burned down the houses and raped the women. Raped her. She remembered the heat of the fire that burned her, the loneliness, the hopelessness. When she promised herself it wouldn't be like this anymore. She needed to feel powerful again, in control of the situation. Returned to the present, her body under warm water, despite everything, she was safe once again.

MacOwen struggled to get his clothes off and sat down. They had holes and cuts everywhere. They were belongings that had accompanied him for a long time, now he had to get rid of them. How many things had he left behind? And how many loved ones? He thought of those soldiers he killed, and apologized mentally to them again making a sign of the cross on his chest. How many had perished in those days? All because of a conflict between *his own*. Again those of *his kind* conveying the discord. And himself, one more of *them*. He was disgusted by his own nature. Was apologizing really redeeming him, or was it just a mental exercise to make him feel better about himself? Was it just another survival mechanism? What was the use of faith but to help the neighbor?

He calmed down for a few minutes as he took a shower in the small bathroom next to the room on the ground floor. There was hardly space for all the appliances stuffed in there, leaving a functional bathroom but difficult to access and use. At least it seemed clean and in decent condition.

There were fellow others to help today. His faithful companion Dipson, the clumsy Drescher, the icy Syra. Perhaps they deserved salvation no more than the lives he took with his own edge, but he could not judge one man over another. Just as he couldn't judge himself either. Only God could do that. They were all alive. Thanks to him, in part.

He stepped out of the shower, tired and slightly shaken by the internal battle. Looked down at his blade, now full of mud and blood. He cleaned it slowly with a blank mind. The sword was only an instrument, his hand was the executioner. He left it in its scabbard on the side and looked around.

There was a small bedside table against a corner, red in color, which contrasted with little taste with the walls all apple green, as did the small bed in the middle. In the only window, the tapping of the banging drops was heard. On the opposite wall, a set of ceramic plates were the only decoration of the place. One of the dishes was missing. In its place was a solitary nail, and a halo of dirt that indicated what was once there.

He turned off the light and lay down on the little bed. His feet hung off the mattress, but didn't care, nor did for the cold of the night. He closed his eyes, but couldn't sleep. He was awakened by the sound of the door opening slowly.

_Who..? Syra?

Syra stepped in slowly, still naked and much more curvy than usual. Her round, swollen breasts moved to the beat of seduction, for one cannot be a complete Shadow without learning the arts of love as well as those of war, both with their profound similarities. She walked up to him without saying anything, her gaze burning with excitement, overcome with the desire to be in control again. In control of a powerful man.

_What are you...? – he wanted to ask, but an index finger over his mouth stopped him.

She crawled up to him, sat on his lap, and kissed him with passion and lust.

PART 30: HELPLESSNESS

Lohe stumbled for the umpteenth time, now against a root coming out of the ground. She was deeply distracted from the immediate task of surviving and fleeing, in the face of what was occupying her thoughts: what would she do with her sudden freedom and how would she keep it. When would they come after her? Probably soon. The further away she was, possibly the better chance of escaping. But they had Seekers, she had seen them in action, or rather, reports written by them. How to hide from a Seeker? If they knew who you were, they could track you, no matter where you were moving to.

She continued walking, without a true direction. One day had already passed. Her suit and helmet fortunately protected her, without them her escape would have been nil. To the initial feeling of freedom and joy, came a burden of sudden responsibility for her own actions. What options did she have? She stopped to sit up against a tree, and grabbed her injured elbow. The pain was squeezing at intervals, it was probably cracked, or broken. Looked up, saw how the light passed gently through the foliage, she found it to be extremely beautiful. A row of busy ants carried chunks of leaf to their nest, walking near her head. Time passed slowly in those woods, but it still passed. Why hadn't they come for her?

She sat up straighter, leaning her back better against the trunk, kicking some snow and mud in the process. A Seeker probably already had her. Perhaps there were no longer any agents left in France to locate a renegade. Maybe nobody cared anymore. With half the army wrecked, who could be interested in the last survivor of a failed team? Not just the survivor, but the part that had caused the defeat. Why couldn't she do her part? Her twins had fulfilled their duties. The brave Fender, defending them. The lovely Konnex, holding the monster. She was supposed to finish him off, and couldn't. As a gift, she had lost everything she loved. She paused for a long time as she reached that part. Did the Akkadian... have anything to do with her sudden desire for freedom? Was that the gift he mentioned before defeating them? The cruelest gift imaginable, she thought in torment.

Set in motion again, she was not so attracted to her decision anymore. But it was too late to turn around. A few hours passed, the Sun was beginning its decline, and really didn't know where to go, other than forward and in a straight line. Felt somewhat foolish after banging her helmet against a low branch, and broke some of her dark state of mind, when she heard a loud metallic sound at her feet. Intense pain seized her, causing her to lose balance. A huge trap was biting her left ankle above the boot. She cried out in pain first, then in rage.

What was happening to her? She was a failure-making machine.

Struggling to open the trap, she took the leg out of the way. Tried to stand up, but the pain in the ankle was too much. A few drops of blood began to drift to the ground. She leaned against a tree, and shouted again, in anguish, hating herself for not paying attention, for continuing to accumulate bad decisions. For being manipulated by the murderer of her siblings. For gambling everything she had and everything she was in a visceral outburst. Under the helmet, some tears streamed down her soft cheeks. Up above, even the winter sun wanted to devour her. She felt terrible, squeezed by a suffocating helplessness. Maybe it was time to quit, to give up.

Time to surrender.

She plummeted to the ground, definitely.

A voice was heard. Someone was coming. It didn't matter who it was, she wouldn't defend. She entrusted herself to a higher power, if such a thing existed. Now the footsteps could be heard breaking the dead leaves on the ground. It was a man, an armed man. He spoke French and she didn't understand what he was saying.

The man approached Lohe, left his hunting rifle on the ground and helped her to stand up. Lohe watched him without pausing for any particular detail. He was not of León's army, looked like a lumberjack, or a hunter. He kept talking to her, not getting anything.

_I don't understand what you're telling me. – she confessed, in German.

_German? Little German. Me Antoine.

_I'm Lohe.

Antoine tried to get her helmet off, but she stopped him abruptly.

_No, don't take it off, I need it.

_Hospital? Come, hospital. – said the hunter in a lousy accent, but genuinely concerned.

_No, no hospital. No hospital Antoine.

_No hospital? *Pourquoi?*

_No hospital please.

The hunter was perplexed, thinking of alternatives. He wanted to help but didn't know how.

_House? My house? Close.

Maybe she could hide there, at least get some rest and walk on her own. She didn't think it was a bad alternative. For a defeated woman with no options, not bad at all.

_Yes, house. Let's go.

Antoine helped her walk almost a kilometer to a rural truck that had seen better days. He got her in and set out. A few minutes later, they arrived at a small hut in a clearing surrounded by cut logs. The cabin looked like a new construction, with a gable roof, a fireplace, automated windows and a simple wooden door. Outside, a solar panel rotated following the trajectory of the star, providing energy to the house. They parked, and the hunter helped the warrior into one of the rooms of the cabin, and sat her down on the bed. The windows were opaque, so she agreed to finally remove the helmet. She set it aside and regarded, this time with a greater awareness of who had helped her. He was a young man, with a somewhat careless beard, prominent nose, short, brown hair. His eyes were fixed on her, and he seemed suddenly nervous and clumsy. He left and came back in a minute, bringing a first aid kit. Lohe took off the left boot, pulled up the sleeve of the pants to check for damage. The indentations of the trap's teeth were clearly visible. Antoine cleaned the area with clumsiness and dedication, disinfected and tied it with a bandage, while continuing to speak and stutter in French.

He looked at her sideways and smiled. It was finally over. Beyond the initial pain, there was nothing broken and it looked like a flesh wound. Still, it was swollen and it pricked when moved. She lay down on the bed, exhausted.

_Thank you, Antoine.

Antoine smiled broadly, muttered something and withdrew, to come back a few seconds later, say something else and leave. Lohe stared at the ceiling lying down, thinking about what she would do now, and the pains that plagued her. The hunter returned, this time with a personal assistant, a civilian model. He spoke softly to the attendant, and pointed it at her direction.

_Hello, my name is Antoine. – said the device, in German.

Of course, a translator program. A short smile was drawn on Lohe's beautiful, tired face.

_Hello, my name is Lohe. Thanks for helping me.

Antoine put the assistant in his ear, and nodded nervously.

_You're welcome. That trap you stepped in was mine, I'm so sorry. – he replied, technology involved. Lohe was silent. Antoine continued – Why didn't you want to go to a hospital?

Lohe looked at him sideways. He wanted the truth? She couldn't tell him. On the other hand, why lie? She was already defeated. _I'm in the militia, and I've escaped. I'd get caught again in a hospital.

Antoine was surprised at that reply, and thought for a moment. _Why did you run away?

Lohe let out a sigh. _Because I was being held prisoner for as long as I am aware, and I desired freedom. Now I'm not so sure I want it anymore.

Antoine opened his eyes wide. _Freedom is the best thing a person can have. - the gadget dispassionately translated the hunter's cry.

_I'd like to rest a little now.

_Yes, of course, have a good rest, miss. - Antoine walked away smiling silly, almost bumping into the frame of the door as he turned around.

Very strange, Lohe thought. But at least he was friendly. She immediately fell asleep.

Lohe walked through a green field of tall grasses, wearing a gray training suit. The sky was a light blue color, but it changed from time to time to violet. Not a cloud over her head, the grasses tickled her legs. Some low walls of old bricks, scattered here and there, dotted the field. She glanced down, and a line of ants walked along her foot, but it did not bother her, feeling they were nice. She kept walking until reaching a much higher, concrete wall. She wanted to know what that was, so tried to circle it by walking to the right, then trotting. The wall was too long, and never reached the corner. Lohe ran and ran until finding where it ended. It was a hangar like *Prima-Gestalt's*, but painted white as snow. There was no one around. The girl entered through the huge, enormous main entrance, but when she turned around it was gone. In its place were now several doors leading to offices. She didn't wonder why. It was noisy. People walking in a hurry from here to there, doctors and staff, soldiers marching and singing. Attempted to open one of the doors, but she couldn't, it was locked. Tried once more, with great effort, but only managed to make the door bigger. She gave up, and walked on among the people. Were they all big now, or was she small? Lohe asked a fat man where her siblings were, and he pointed out a long, well-lit corridor. Walked down the hall and she got lost, because it was not a corridor, but a maze of doors and windows, all massive. Lohe became saddened, and was about to break into tears, when a loving hand rested on her head. It was Fender, but he was tall, very tall, and his face could not be seen.

_Come on, Lo, we gotta break something. - he confided.

_Where's Konny? - she asked, but without getting an answer.

The giant Fender took her by the hand and walked down a white corridor together.

_This is where we have to go. It's an important mission, Lo. - he said, releasing her and entering through a huge and terrifying-looking black door.

_I don't want to go there Fen, I want to see Konny. - her own voice sounded strange.

_Konny's inside, she needs us. - he said before going in.

She walked through the doorway, scared. Inside, everything was destroyed. There were broken brick blocks and columns by the thousands on the floor. It seemed like a whole city had succumbed. She saw her twins lying on the floor, inert in front of her. Wanted to run, but this time she couldn't. Looking down, she saw that there was a trap in her ankle, tied to a chain. She pulled the chain, but failed to break free.

_Fen! - she shouted - I can't go, I'm trapped.

She pulled the chain, it was cold, and the links were making a dreadful sound as they bumped into each other.

_Konny, help me! - shouted again, but no one answered.

The sky began to darken, and it covered everything. Until all that was left was her and the chain.

_Guys, I can't go! I'm trapped! – shouted in vain.

She felt anguish and a desire to cry, and the chain wouldn't let go. A horrible voice called her by her name. It came from the darkness. No, it was the darkness.

_I can set you free, is that what you want? – the wickedness questioned.

Lohe didn't answer. She was pulling the chain, and it was getting bigger and heavier and heavier.

_Do you want freedom? I can give it to you. – assured the darkness in a low tone.

Lohe cried out, she could no longer move, only reaching to wipe away the tears that ran downwards with her hands.

_ Yes. – she finally answered – but please don't hurt my siblings.

_That, cannot be done. – screamed the emptiness in a flaming voice.

Lohe wiped her eyes, looked down and her chains were gone. Her body was small, so small. Had a long, blue dress, like the doll she saw once and could never have. Stood up, and now she was in a large space, with concrete gray floor. There was no light, but she could see. Ahead, there was a shining cube. Walked up very slowly and touched it with her little hand. Inside was her, but it wasn't her. The other Lohe was an adult, naked and with long, very long hair, floating in the ether. She looked asleep. Lohe liked the way the golden hair floated, like an angel. Noticed that Angel Lohe was trapped in the cube, and couldn't get out.

So she kicked the cube with her little foot, but it didn't have any effect. Thought she needed more strength. All the strength, to help Angel Lohe. She didn't notice, but now she was an adult herself. Went backwards to gain momentum and lashed out with all the strength of her fist. The cube did not break, but simply disappeared in a ball of light along with her alter ego.

_I did it! – exclaimed – I'm strong!

Darkness took over again, robbing her of her victory and joy. And the darkness spoke.

_No, you are not. – said the nightmare.

Lohe woke up startled, and did not immediately recognize where she was. The room remained dark, under the waterproof logs. She lay there without thinking about anything for a long time. It had been awful, but it wasn't the first time she'd dreamed of it. She had already experienced it, but couldn't remember when. Lohe looked out the cloudy window. Outside, the night, crickets and owls reigned. Next to the bed there was a wooden crutch, a little chipped, which she used to move around. Leapt out of the room, where she found the hunter at dinner. He smiled at her, and invited her to sit down with a gesture. She agreed, for lack of anything better to do. The noise of the crutch on the floor sounded loud in that quiet atmosphere.

_You want something to eat? – he translated.

_No, thank you. – Lohe apologized.

_You must be hungry, many hours without eating.

It was true, but the food there wasn't any use. She remembered having a couple of syringes with ProtePlasm, if she rationed them well, it could last a week. _Don't worry, I'll get something to eat.

Antoine continued to dine in silence. The table was dressed in a red, slightly faded tablecloth with white dots. Above it was half of a red wine, two glasses, an empty plate (for her, she supposed) and another one with a stew of meat and various roots that looked tasty. A tray of yesterday's bread and a new candle completed the picture. Lohe watched the entire scene, examining every detail as she held her sore elbow. Antoine took the assistant again. _Does your elbow hurt?

Lohe looked down. It all happened in slow motion. How long had it been since she felt that peace, of not having anything to do? No one to obey? No one to destroy? She had severed her ties with the world, and now she was in a small cabin far from everything. The rules had changed... For good? The darkness had made her chains disappear, demanding in return the highest of prices.

_Yes, I hurt myself in the woods.

_After dinner I'll see what I can do about that.

She watched the candle wax burn. Slowly, the drops fell very gently down the side, until they reached the base where they solidified. The smell of the stew flooded her nose. She craved to share food with this man, in the peace of that forest, even though it would not feed her properly.

_Can I have some stew? - Lohe asked, enthralled by the magic of the moment.

Antoine quickly went to the kitchen, served on the plate and brought her a spoon. The stew was good, and it tasted like spices she'd never had before. The hunter smiled at her, and she replied in kind. Lohe liked his smile. She thought it was sincere.

PART 31: PROMISE OF A NEW WORLD

Amelia looked in the mirror for the hundredth time, this once in a long black dress with sequins on her breasts and shoulders. It convinced her more than the red dress, which she perceived as too revealing, for some reason. On the bed laid a dozen or more dresses and various garments, as were others on the floor. She saw the reflection of the disorder she had caused (and that was to be put in order later) and felt quite discouraged. But that would be a fight for tomorrow. She finished combing her brand new curls, each crowned by a small, shiny bead, and spent a few minutes in her make-up until she was satisfied, put on her high heels and went over the final details. Looked at the clock on the wall, and got frantic again, it was too late! Given the hour, that must have been the final set, no more time for changes. She stood in front of the mirror again watching her image as impartially as she could and tried to calm her heart that wanted to come out.

It was not bad, not bad at all, she looked rather good. In fact... she didn't remember the last time she felt pretty. A faint smile was drawn on her face. Her life was slowly getting better, and despite everything. And it was thanks to Kad. She faded her smile with effort and compressed her cheeks tightly. Again, her inner child wanted to rebel. Kad wasn't a good candidate, stop it! But he undoubtedly made her happy.

And by the way, in any minute he'd jump in from the window, it was about time. She sat in a miraculously clothes-less corner and paused. What would happen that night? Kad hadn't given much detail, only clarifying that they were "going to have dinner with an acquaintance" and for she to "buy a nice dress". She looked at the clock, twenty seconds had passed. Exhaled hard, trying to make her nerves disappear. On the other hand, where was it possible to dine in public? A state of Emergency had been in place for two days and no one could stay in the streets after the 19.00 hours. Unless it's someone important or government agent, of course. But Kad wasn't one of those. What did he have in mind?

She panicked at the sound of the doorbell. Got up confused and answered. On the screen she saw a tall man, dressed in black, with a bowler hat and a slightly lost look on his face.

_Yeah? – she asked puzzled.

_I'm looking for Miss Alba, her limousine is here.

What the hell? _It's me... I'll... I'll be right down.

A limousine, and a chauffeur. Who could afford a chauffeur these days? Only the rich, eccentric, distrustful of self-drive type. She grabbed her purse and coat and rushed to the elevator. Outside she was met by the driver, who greeted her with a slight gesture and escorted her to the vehicle.

_Good evening, Amelia. We travel with style tonight. - Kad said, sitting in the back, making her a gesture to sit beside him. He wore a dark blue jacket, a white shirt and a classic tie of the same color as his suit. True to his style, he wore no adornment or device. His hair was extremely short.

_G-good evening, Kad. - she said, smiling like a airheaded teenager, as she got in and the driver closed the door manually. She remained silent, waiting for him to say something about her image. She picked up a lock of hair and tucked it behind the ear.

_Beautiful dress, you look lovely.

_T-Thank you. - she stammered. Underneath the makeup her cheekbones began to redden. When she was sure that a whole sentence would come out of her mouth without interruptions, she continued. _Where are we going?

_A person who comes from afar is in town and wants to talk to me in friendly terms, so he invited me to dinner. I found it convenient for you to accompany me, as long

357

as you're careful in how you behave. - the kind but subtly alarming tone put her on her guard.

_I'll behave, Kad. I don't know what you mean. - she fought back.

_I know, but remember two things. Speak only if you are asked any questions, and do not stare anyone in the eye for too long. - he smiled, with the usual cordiality. Close by, and light years away, as usual.

The vehicle was advancing smoothly. There was no traffic at all. The streets, deserted. The curfew was total. Since the announcement of a new, world-scale terrorist group, panic had taken hold of everyone and nothing else was discussed. Airports, routes, all closed. The ships did not enter or leave the ports.

They passed through three checkpoints heavily guarded by military personnel mounted on tanks. On all three occasions, the chauffeur presented credentials and they were given passage without question. No doubt the person they were going to see was important.

_This person we're having dinner with, is he from the government? - Amelia asked, almost certainly about the affirmative answer.

_No.

_Some businessman?

_No. - Kad denied again.

_How come we're getting through so many checkpoints without any problems?

Kad looked at her sideways as he crossed one leg over the other. _The law only applies to those who exist. The rest of us are on the outside. – he wrapped up, with a mysterious smile, inviting no more questions.

The limousine stopped in front of a sumptuous building. Amelia noticed that there were several vehicles parked in front, the place was active despite the prevailing conditions. Clearly, rich people have a different way of life. The building functioned as an office tower, on whose terrace there was a luxury restaurant. They got out of the limousine and were escorted by a gleaming red carpet into the interior. Kad gently offered her his arm, and Amelia took it. She thought he was a little shorter and thinner than the last time they met, but that didn't make sense. The situation was straining her, that must be it. Or the high heels. They went up the elevator to the top floor expeditiously. The place was almost packed with people eating dinner, as if the world were spinning normally on any given day. The waiters came and went carrying dishes with food. It was one of those exclusive places where they offered the novel gourmet printed food, with prey of cultivated meat with tastes of a hundred different animals and vegetables, which were four or five times more expensive than the traditional one, but were morally "superior" for using proteins instead of live animals.

They advanced until they came across a man with long hair, very corpulent and dressed in a simple white shirt, black trousers and shoes. Amelia would have sworn he was the henchman of some action movie villain. He greeted Kad frigidly and ignored her completely, to lead them to one of the tables.

_Akkadian, welcome. Thank you for accepting my invitation. - said a man elegantly dressed in a tuxedo, a shiny black bow, and numerous jewels on his hands and fingers. He had a prominent nose, jet hair almost up to his shoulders and hair styled backwards. Amelia didn't know what to think, he was certainly handsome and elegant, but he radiated an aura of mistrust. She didn't like it at all, and couldn't determine his age, no matter how hard she tried. She could determine instead that he was ignoring her in a similar way to the big guy before.

_Hassan, I imagine. You look very different, undercover? - Kad replied, standing in front of his host, as calmly as would a tropical storm about to fall be.

_I certainly look different, but it's a trifle. We are what we are on the inside, the outside changes like the sand in the dunes. Please have a seat.

Kad slid one of the purple corduroy armchairs for Amelia to sit on, and then he sat down. For the first time Hassan noticed her presence.

_Akkadian, who's the lady?

_My companion, I hope you don't mind.

_I see. No, I don't mind, as long as she's behaving as ought to.

Amelia was about to explode with rage! Who was this rude, chauvinist guy? She looked at Kad and he returned an order with his eyes: "Don't protest, be quiet".

_I recommend the lobster with caviar, it's exquisite. - Hassan continued. He gestured and immediately a waiter came over to take their orders on his double-sided screen once the newcomers accepted the proposal. Hassan filled three glasses of champagne from a brand Amelia didn't recognize, but which probably costs more than her apartment - I would like to toast, to the promise of a new world.

The three of them raised their glasses and had a little sip. The drink tasted fancy and totally out of place, she thought. What did he bring her for?

_So, what do you want to talk about? Any news you want to tell me from the other side of the globe? - Kad asked, as he leaned back and crossed his fingers.

Hassan sipped from his glass again, and placed it gently on the silken cloth. He stared sternly at Kad. _You could say that. You should know things are changing. I heard about a... little mishap you had recently. I'm glad you're safe.

Kad just nodded his head. Sitting in that posture, with such calm and bearing, he looked like a king from whom they were trying to win a favor.

_These are interesting times, very interesting times. Those who called themselves our enemies have fallen. And we, moreover, have redoubled our strength. We are already in a position to crush everything in our path. - Hassan was frightening in his gestures, his tone of voice, the words he used - The demon has been defeated by his own minions, the same group that tried to hunt you down and failed. That means destiny has a plan for you. And I daresay that plan includes me. It includes us. Justice is on our side.

Kad held out one hand, stopping the host's verbiage. _Some of your boys must have told you that I'm not interested in current politics. The fact that Caucasus has died surprised me, but the direction in which the whole thing is faring is of no concern to me.

Hassan nodded with some bitterness. _Oh yes, yes, so I've been told. However, it was my moral duty to invite you to lead the change, given your history. But if I cannot, at least I'd wish to be sure that we mustn't count you among those who oppose us.

_I don't. Hassan, I really don't care. Do whatever you want. I grew sick of power games a long time ago.

When you've got a few more centuries under your belt, maybe you'll know what I mean.

_You treat me like an impertinent young man, and I'm a long way from being one. The world belongs to the strong, it always has been and always will be. - Hassan replied harshly.

_I didn't want to make you uncomfortable, just to explain my point of view. - Kad decompressed.

The waiter arrived with the dishes, exquisitely decorated with a golden gloss sauce. The dish itself emitted bursts of colored lights at the same rate as the soft background music. It had gold dust in its mixture. The three of them remained silent as they ate. The tension was unbearable. Unbearable.

_It's de-delicious. - Amelia stammered, choking slightly with her bite. The situation was getting nasty. She didn't know where to look without feeling that she was transgressing something. At least the food was great.

Kad poured champagne into her glass, and squeezed her knee in a quasi-paternal gesture of trust. He smiled at her, tacitly assuring that everything would be all right. Or so she thought at least.

_How are things in the East? - Kad asked - I haven't been there in a long time.

_Excellent. And you are welcome to visit the region of your choice, anytime you like. We've been busy all these years. Is it true what you said? – Suddenly he asked – Were you took by surprise about Caucasus?

Kad finished chewing his bite and looked up expectantly. _That's right.

_Gosh. Well, one of my sources told me a about a gossip that pointed to that end almost two years ago. Since then we have been making preparations in case it happened, and it did.

_What kind of preparations? I'm sure you're dying to tell me. – Kad fired with little tact.

Hassan shot him a hard look back. _We are preparing a shock to the West's finances, and another blow even worse to its war potential. For misfortune or luck, the second was not necessary. The day before yesterday, a local source warned us of a skirmish in Aegis that culminated in a big explosion, saving us the trouble. That source also gave us a clue about the hand that led to that outcome. Someone you know well, I would venture to say.

_If *that source* indicated that it was Perius, I am also aware of it. We crossed paths recently. – said Kad, with little patience for the rumors – and he pointed out that he was preparing something great, worthy of witnessing. He wouldn't speak about it because one of Eylem's kids was spying on us, so I suspect he had something to do with this incident. - Kad took a break - Speaking of Eylem, have you visited her yet?

Hassan did not reply, he spent a minute devouring the delicacy that was depleting in front of him. He wiped his mouth with a napkin, cleared his throat, and continued. _No, not yet. I intend to do so very soon. I also believe that Perius is not only involved in this, but also has the help of someone from the inner circle of Caucasus. Most likely George's.

_George? Have the conspiracies gone that far?

_Occident is rotten, Akkadian. That is why we have come to purify it. With fire.

_It's unnecessary what you do. - Kad said accusing with his fork - We know you don't want to purify anything, just destroy what Caucasus did, and that's fine with me.

Hassan seemed to ignore the scathing comments. _That *is* to purify. To remove the black blot that was that spawn.

_What's this coup you're planning? - Kad asked, with false interest.

_We have been buying shares in companies related to León. A very slow and steady job. Tomorrow Monday, as soon as the markets open, we will sell them en masse and cause them to collapse. By the time they can stop it, it'll be too late, they'll be ruined. Of course, we'll lose capital, but their losses will be astronomical.

_I think it's too simple a plan to be effective. Leon's no fool.

_No, he's not. But my men are relentless and skillful, they left no loose ends in the operation.

_Isn't revealing the plan to me a loose end? – said the Akkadian, defiant.

_It's a goodwill gesture towards you. It's also my way of putting into words the fact that we're not a bunch of improvisers. We are the future, and everything else will be ashes.

Kad tried a bite in silence, and drank water to clear his throat. Amelia watched him without knowing what to do, or what to say. The plot that was woven in front of her, if true, was too large to swallow. She had been observing around, many of the patrons were more interested in Kad and Hassan's talk than in their dishes, and nearly half the waiters were constantly scrutinizing them. A droplet fell slowly down the side of her glass advancing in zigzag, driven down by the omnipotent and inescapable gravity. They all were part of it, she suddenly understood. All these people, the ones watching, were in this game, whatever it was. She looked back at Kad, the very banner of serenity in that whirlwind of glances. And she, in the middle, clinging to his arm as if it were the last bastion.

_Any news of Xin? Under the circumstances, he may as well be thinking of something similar to your plan.

_It's true, and indeed I have. I spoke to his right hand yesterday. He's interested in the direction we're taking. I don't remember the last time Xin was open to dialogue, it must have been already twenty years. I have a hunch we can come to an agreement. At the moment I'm not interested in China against us, if I could at least keep them aside it would be fantastic.

Kad raised an eyebrow, seemed genuinely surprised. _So Xin came out of hiding, that's another one I didn't expect. This is a year to remember.

_A year to remember. – Hassan seconded, with a hint of irony.

The big guy came up to Hassan and said a few words in his ear. Hassan nodded slowly, gave him a brief order, and he withdrew.

_Sorry to interrupt, but I have some news. – he paused, dramatically – We found León's main base, and it's empty. There's no one defending it, so we captured it. Not for long since we're going to demolish it. It is a symbol of power and should not remain. – Hassan smiled broadly, and raised his glass again. – A year to remember. – he repeated cruelly.

Kad and Amelia left the building and waited a few minutes in silence for the limousine that had brought them there. The driver politely opened the door and they set out on their way back.

Amelia let go of her companion, and put some physical distance, as much as she could in the confined space of the vehicle. She stared out the window at the lonely night of the city, and put her thoughts in order. She was beginning to form a picture of what that night had been, and she had a thousand questions to ask, but knew that the "Akkadian" would only answer one, or two at most. She decided on the one that made the most noise.

_Kad, can I ask you something?

_Tell me. - he answered, with no particular tone of voice. The king was once again on his throne, hundreds of parsecs away from her. Of everyone. Of everything.

_What did you bring me with you? I didn't understand much about tonight, but what I did get was that I was out of place. Then, what's the point..?

Kad turned to look her in the eye, and he did so for a few long seconds. He exhaled some air and folded his arms. _One day I won't be around anymore, that's for sure. But I don't want to part without leaving something, a legacy. You will be part of that legacy.

Amelia laughed nervously, slightly affected by the bubbles of champagne, and by a sudden sadness that invaded her chest. _Me, a legacy? What could I-?

_When I found you, you hated yourself, and your life – he interrupted – so I took the liberty of turning you into something that would serve me. You're happy with that so far, aren't you? – Amelia felt small, she only nodded slightly – I will continue to do that, transforming your life into something you had never imagined, or dreamed of, because you had no dreams or hopes. Don't worry, you'll like your new life. – he smiled, with stiff kindness.

Amelia bowed her head. She was worn out, feeling like a slave scolded by her master. Should she fight it? Should she allow it? What were her dreams, her hopes, what did she really want in this life?

_Now you're thinking about what your desires are. – Kad's deep voice interrupted her train of thought – And tomorrow, or next week, you will think about how much of what you really want is yours, and how much was put there by the society around you. Then you'll find yourself empty, but hungry for answers. I'll save you some suffering, since I'll have the answers ready once you have the questions.

Have the questions? Questions was the only thing she had to spare. But they weren't the right ones.

PART 32: THE PRICE TO PAY

Fisher sat on one of the two stools in the downsized Communications Room 4, making sure the equipment he needed was up and running. Calling from his personal phone had been a bad move, he thought later. If someone undertook the trouble to investigate it, they could trace a link between him and Weissman. That mistake could no longer be undone. At least now, from a secure line, no one would know what kind of link there was. He drew his assistant out of his pocket where he had the phone number and dialed. While the system was handling the call and encryption, he wore a wireless headset with a microphone and waited. A minute later, a voice from the other side greeted him.

_General?

_Weissman, Fisher here. I have already made the necessary arrangements, so instruct your friend where to go to be picked up. Please write down the instructions.

_Whenever you're ready. – there was anxiety in his voice.

_A helicopter will pass through today at 2030 GMT+1. Krupp must be alone and carry only handheld equipment. If he carries any more, they'll be left on the ground. If anyone else shows up with him, the pilot has orders not to descend.

_Understood.

_The coordinates where he should be are: Latitude 49.421356, longitude 11.164853. It can be assumed that he has some kind of GPS system.

_Yes... that's right. – Weissman replied as he took notes.

_Good. I recommend that you don't look up for that location unless you have a secure connection, or from a public device. We must not skimp on precautions.

_I have a secure connection. That's... southeast of Nüremberg.

_Exactly. During the journey, he will be given documents to pose as a low-ranking US diplomat in Germany under a false identity, if someone asks questions, he is "being evacuated due to a terrorist threat". No one should ask for more information, nor should anyone give it away. – Fisher's tone of voice was serious and efficient. He was on his element with this kind of mission. Get in, operate, get out. Simple and mathematical – He will be taken to Tel Aviv, where he will take a commercial airliner accompanied by two undercover officers at Ben Gurion Airport to New York, on AEuropa flight 23444 at 1810 GTM+3 tomorrow.

_A regular flight? What happens if the airport closes?

_I see it as unlikely for the airport to close. Israel is still on blue alert until the United States issues a superior one. It may turn yellow tomorrow, but I doubt it.

_Suppose that happens, what's the alternative?

_Agents have orders to stay with Krupp until he's safe. They can stay up to two weeks, or until they get a counter order. That city is safe.

_General - Weissman interrupted - forgive my temper, but today no city is safe. In a scenario like this, the farther the better. That's why I trust a person like you to take active care of it.

_I understand your position. I've given you my word to do everything I possibly can to keep Krupp safe. If air travel is not possible, I will arrange for a military corvette. It'll take longer, but it'll be a safe trip.

_That's what I needed to hear.

_Once in New York, he will be transferred to Rockaway, a small nearby community, where he will establish himself by drawing the least possible attention. Two other officers will check daily for two months to make sure everything is fine, and that no one suspects his true identity. Money and groceries will be passed monthly so that he can live comfortably and leave the house as little as possible.

Weissman sighed deeply. He liked the plan, it sounded solid. Looks like Krupp would finally make it. Now it was his turn to do his part, to make him disappear until the arrival of the helicopter, to find a body of the same physiognomy and bury it. _I am pleased with your professionalism and the energy you have put into this task. I'm grateful to you, General. To show you my good will, I will send you the information I promised as soon as I know that Krupp has left Israel without any problems.

_In that case, if all goes well, it would be tomorrow.

_That's right. I'll open a new data box in a public website and upload the information there. Once that's done, I'll pass you a username and password. I suggest you delete the content as soon as you can and close the data box. This way it will be difficult to trace and leave a minimum of evidence.

_I think it's appropriate. We'll be in touch tomorrow, then.

_Until tomorrow, General.

Fisher flipped a switch with a red tip on the panel under his hand, and the communication went dead. It was done. Tomorrow he would receive precise information about what Perius was, and perhaps how to destroy him. He needed to analyze it too. Leaned back on the stool but found only a void where the backrest should be, so he hesitated, and moved to a wall to support his back. He took off his headphones and tossed them on the desk. Who could help him with the analysis? It had to be someone outside the base, since he couldn't trust anyone inside. It was possible that Old McCarthy knew some brilliant mind. He pulled his assistant out of his pocket and dialed his number.

No one answered. He tried again several more times without success. It was strange, at that time he must have been at home about to have dinner. He searched for his wife's phone, Maria, but hesitated to call her. Maybe he shouldn't have to bother her, or include in this mess. He weighed pros and cons for a minute, and finally made up his mind.

_Hello, Maria? I'm Carl. – he said cheerfully – How's it going out there?

_Carl... – McCarthy's sweet wife managed to say, before remaining silent.

_Maria, what's wrong? – he asked, now worried. But he didn't get an answer – Maria, please, answer me!

_I–It's John... he... my God.

_Did something happen to John? Where is he?

He only received sobs in response. Fisher stood slowly, waiting for the worst answer. Communications Room 4 was almost completely silent. The liquefied gas that cooled the equipment whistled softly, almost inaudible in the background. Again, sobbing. Fisher bolted without closing the door as he held his assistant tightly to his ear and trotted down the hall ignoring the stationed soldiers saluting. He jumped up one floor up the stairs and continued down another corridor. Maria on the other side still did not answer his questions.

He came into his office, tore his coat off the rack and closed behind him. Finally, there was a response.

_John... has passed away.

Fisher ordered his car to park. The street was quiet, with several vehicles parked in front of the McCarthy house. He struggled out with his coat in one hand, and put the other on the roof of his car as the door closed. He looked at the house, then at the floor. He didn't know what to say after ringing the bell. "Johnny's dead because I screwed up"? "I'm sorry, Maria"? He was about to punch his own window, but held back. McCarthy had turned up dead after falling off a watchtower at the base. Alleged witnesses claimed that he tripped and fell. All lies. McCarthy never climbed the towers, he was pushed, out of the way. The question was what harm was he doing? Or was it a message to him? That he was alone, and that if he asked for help he would regret it. That opposing the monster had a price to pay. He found himself walking slowly toward the front, near the door.

Fisher stopped his finger centimeters from the doorbell, suddenly paralyzed. He was to blame, indirectly, and didn't dare to tell them. His pride as a military man took control of the situation, and finally pressed the doorbell. He wouldn't say anything, since it won't do any good, instead he would use his friend's death as an everlasting reminder that he must tread lightly, not neglecting a step in his efforts to destroy Perius's plans. The door opened, a tall young man appeared, with the same nose as his late father holding a little girl in his arms, both with tears in their eyes. A few steps back, the chubby little Maria came out to meet him. They embraced each other in silence.

PART 33: LEGACY

Lohe heard a command, from a known voice but couldn't pinpoint exactly where it came from. She turned around to find out. It was a man with glasses and a white coat, behind a mirrored window. It was that place where they did the endless tests, the grey room with tube lights on the ceiling, with a yellow inscription: "03".

_Break the next block. - ordered the voice through the speakers.

_ But it hurts. - she replied bitterly.

_Do it or you lot won't get nutrition. - the voice warned, threatening.

Lohe looked at her hands, they were full of calluses and marks. A grimy gray training outfit was her entire attire. She didn't want to continue with it, she was exhausted and wanted to see her siblings. It worried her they might be doing something to them, knowing it was *bad*. If any of the triplets failed, they all suffered. A window opened above her and she felt a tremendous amount of heat, a scorching one. She refused to look up at the Sun, the Ruthless Emperor.

_It burns me! - she shouted, bathed in light.

_Break the next block. - he repeated mechanically.

She turned and saw a solid concrete pillar taller than her. Punched it in rage, and demolished it as soon touching it, falling like scattered ashes. Over and over again, she'd break blocks of habit.

_Here's your reward, keep working as you're told. - a woman with short hair and a white coat injected her with the contents of a syringe. They had all done their duty and earned it.

She walked out a door and down some steep stairs, looked downwards and jumped, falling over some flowers, crushing them. They cracked like dry leaves despite being full of color and life. She knew it was a wrongly deed, but really felt nothing but apathy. Walked to a melancholy black wooden hut, whose door was open, inviting her in. On a long table of cold metal, she saw several weapons of different design and caliber. She knew that only one could be carried. When she could take them all, she'd be invincible. Came closer and took one, checked it and thought it was appropriate, made her feel comfortable and accompanied. She headed out safe and ready.

It was now an underground corridor, which was getting progressively darker. She glanced back, being followed by several armed soldiers. At last! She thought. They were marching towards the most important mission, ending Caucasus. They turned into an even darker corridor, nothing was visible anymore. Suddenly, shots fired. She closed her eyes shut.

When she opened them again, she was tied with chains to a wall. The mission was a success, why were they punishing her? Pulled the chains and couldn't get out. She detested chains. The rigor of the shackles undermined her every time she made mistakes or disobeyed. The woman in the white coat approached her with a pair of tweezers.

_Your siblings will suffer for your disobedience.

Loud screams, it was Konny and Fen, they were in danger. She wanted to scream too, but couldn't.

The woman held the tweezers to her head, and stuck something behind her ear. A horrifying sensation ensued, of having a foreign body crawling over the ear. Everything was horrible. She shook her feet and arms, but the chains pulled harder. On her bare, dirty fingers there was a line of ants, working incessantly, carrying small leaves down amid the heavy links. The woman disappeared through the door. Instead, Fender entered slowly, with an expression of fear and dismay. He didn't move when he walked, floating over the floor.

_Brother, you came... help me!

_Little girl, I'm gonna help you. You have to be strong on your own.

_But how? How? It's the three of us. It's always been the three of us. I'm alone now. - her eyes filled with tears when she found out his brother was dead - why did you leave me alone?

Fender pulled an incredibly shiny object out of his clothes. It was an ice pick, similar to the one she saw last night in the lumberjack's kitchen.

_It's the only way, Lo, forgive me. - he said, and stabbed her. The pain was unbearable, because he was provoking it. Not for betrayal, but for passing on a responsibility she didn't want to bear. The edge entered her body again and again, and she felt more and more alone, more and more destroyed.

_Everything I am, so are you. We won't leave you, we'll always be with you. - he said with infinite sorrow, as he thrust the dagger hard against her body. _What I am, so are you.

Lohe woke up in shock, almost falling out of bed. She regained her equilibrium, not before throwing an old digital clock on the ground, which stopped when its cord was fully stretched. The room was completely dark.

Outside, the wind whistling through the wood on the walls could be heard. She took several deep breaths until calming down. The nightmares had been haunting her more and more since that fateful day. The clock on the floor indicated that it was minutes before five in the morning. The atmosphere was warm thanks to a convection stove on the other side of the room. She lit a lamp and sat there, covering her face with the hands, trying to remember every possible detail of the dream, which were trying to escape in haste. His brother had been tortured by stabbing for years, among other things, why did she remember him just now, and in that way? Her suffering was nothing in comparison. With regard to suffering... her current pains no longer plagued her that much. She removed the bandage from the ankle and moved her foot. The skin was tugging, but it was tolerable. She took out the one on her right elbow and tried to move it. It stung, although it was much less than the day before. Why did it feel so heavy, having to carry on the consciences of her siblings, their longings, their hidden dreams?

She picked up the makeshift crutch and left the room trying not to make a sound. Antoine was sleeping soundly on a folded blanket and covered by two others near the dining room table. It was not very spacious, adjoining a small kitchen. The room where she was now was quite large, destined to be bedroom and storage room for all sorts of things against the wall at the back. The bathroom was not absent, although it was separated from the dwelling by a few meters, under a fibrocement roof and wooden slats. That lumberjack's life was very lonely, she thought. She watched him sleep peacefully, his cheek squeezed against the small pillow. It was all peace there, in that snowy forest. She turned around to go back to bed, but stopped halfway, touching behind her right ear with the hand of her healthy arm. She squinted her light blue eyes. Yes... she could recall. At some point many years ago something was implanted there. She suspected it might be some kind of tracking device. In fact, the wristwatch she destroyed must have been a secondary system in case the other one failed, or vice versa. Had to keep moving, she had no choice. Really regretted having to leave the cabin and Antoine, but the peace was short-lived.

She returned to her room to meditate on what to do. On the edge of the bed she sat down, but couldn't stay still, feeling restless, unsure whether to wake Antoine up in the middle of the night, or to wait until the morning. She decided to wait on her back, with her hands gently tapping on the belly and shaking her healthy foot from here to there, to use that time to think. What if she tried to remove the device? She explored with her fingers the area behind her ears to note disparities. Clenching hard behind her right ear a spherical mound could be felt. Something artificial. If an incision was made there, one may be able to remove it and destroy it, or better yet, use it to mislead. She made the decision. Limping to her host, stopped nearby without daring to touch him.

_Antoine, I need your help. - she called, resolved.

Antoine shook an arm and babbled incoherently as the only answer.

_Antoine, wake up.

At last the lumberjack turned face up, wiping a fine thread of dribble from the corner of his lips. _ *Que se passe-t-il?*

_Forgive me for waking you up, but I require your assistance.

Antoine took a long minute until he could find his assistant, press on the correct application and get some of the crusts out of his eyes. _Could you repeat that? I didn't understand.

_I need a sharp knife and support.

_A what?

Lohe turned on the light in the dining room, put a chair where the light was brightest, and sat down quickly. _I have a tracking device behind my right ear. I have to get it out of there as soon as possible and get rid of it. What I need you to do is to make a cut here. - she mentioned, drawing an imaginary line with the index - and take it out. The task may require pliers.

Antoine was already standing in front of her, with the device translating in his palm, with a typical expression of someone who is dying of tiredness and is unable to process what is being told. Lohe understood the situation perfectly, and wanted to speed things up.

_I'm not kidding, we have to make it urgently. In fact, it might be too late.

The Frenchman left for the room with laziness, and a couple of minutes later he returned yawning with a toolbox, a knife and a towel. _Are you sure about this? It's going to hurt a lot and it could fail. – he translated.

_Very sure.

The man left the box and the device on the dining room table, and passed the flame of a lighter through the knife several times, his tired body moving automatically. He had no medical experience, but living alone in the forest teaches one to do many different things, and it wasn't the first time he had to remove a foreign object inside a person. He felt the area, sensing the sphere. _Is that it?

_Yes. Quickly, please.

Without a word more, the edge sank into the skin, blood began to pour out on the old towel. No particular expression could be seen on Lohe's face while being cut.

Using the fine tweezers he removed with some hardship a small purple capsule and placed it in a tiny bowl. From the first aid box he pulled out a medical stapler and carefully closed the wound by holding the dermis. He cleaned the area with an antibacterial liquid and the blood stains with a cotton swab. When the work was done, he broke the silence. _What do you want to do with this? - he asked annoyed, pointing to the capsule.

_To buy time I should take it far away, make it move in the opposite direction to me.

Antoine was studying the capsule without taking his eyes off it. _I'm going to help you, but under one condition. I want you to tell me everything. Why you're running away and from whom. - he waited for an answer, not daring to look at her.

Lohe thought about it for a moment. She wasn't sure if it was correct to involve this man any more. She would hate to see him dead because of her, but right now had to dispose of the tracker. _All right, I'll tell you everything. But we have to get rid of that right now.

_Let's go to the van. - sighed the Frenchman.

They traveled a dirt road for several kilometers, took a lonely route and followed a long way. Finally, they parked in a barren lot by a stream. In the sky there were only clouds and no aircrafts, for Lohe's peace of mind. Antoine dug a small hole in a piece of polystyrene and put the infamous capsule inside. He leaned it on the water in the shape of a barge, and let it float along the stream. Both watched silently as it drifted away until it was out of sight. They retraced their steps and set out on their journey back.

Sitting in the passenger seat, with a borrowed hooded coat on top, and her thumbs drumming nervously at each other, Lohe decided to begin her story. She owed him.

_I don't know where I was born, but I grew up on a base. I think it was always the same base, but I'm not sure. It's called *First Form* – said the digital assistant translating literally – I was trained my whole life to be a soldier in a triple unit, composed of me and my siblings. Their names are... were... *Defense* and *Connection*.

Antoine didn't say a word, inside the cabin only she could be heard, the echo of the assistant and the rhythmic roar of the electric motor. _We were sent on special missions, to eliminate new-human targets. – she paused – I suspect it didn't translate that well. The targets aren't human, they're like *me*.

_That you're not human?

_No.

Antoine turned to look at her. He didn't understand what his exotic guest could have of "non-humanity". He saw her so beautiful, with her rounded nose, her deep blue eyes, a fragility only a strong woman could have. He was bewitched, watching as the movement of the van bounced up and down her golden, scrambled hair, and her breasts in a comical and sensual way. He noticed that he had a foolish expression on his face, so he fixed his attention on the road. _Didn't they... *make* you believe you weren't human? It's a very cruel thing to do.

_The training was very cruel, I understood that years later after talking to other soldiers on the base. They tortured us. But beyond that, I'm not wrong to say that we're not human. That much is true. When we get to the cabin, I'll show you. – she waited, scrutinizing his gaze, expecting a reaction of disgust or repulsion. She didn't find one – Three days ago they sent us on a mission and it was a failure. My twins...

The pause grew longer and longer. The suspension of the vehicle was squeaking with the potholes of the road. _They fell in combat. – continued – They were all I had, the three of us were always there. I... I got desperate, so when I saw the opportunity, I ran away.

_My condolences, Lohe. – he mentioned somewhat off-balance. He certainly did not expect such a story. – I don't know what to say, it's the strangest story I've ever heard. I didn't know they did such things in the German army.

387

_It's a paramilitary force, not dependent on the government. Or almost. I never got to know the political background, it was not my task and they never told us anything, only rumors circulating. Unverified information.

_But... explain to me what you are then.

_I don't have details, I just know that we have to take special precautions against heat, electricity, fire, excessive sunlight. We're vulnerable to all of those. To feed us we use ProtePlasm, it is a special liquid but I ignore its composition. Normal food does not nourish us enough to live, although it can supplement a shortage of fluid.

Antoine grimaced. He regretted what was going on inside him. _Uh, where do we get that?

_I still have two syringes, I don't know where else to get them from. Except going back. – she looked out the window for a moment. It was dawn, but the gray clouds covered the whole sky – Forgive me Antoine, I... I didn't think it through. I shouldn't have involved you. I'm sorry.

_You didn't, I'm helping you because I thought it was the right thing to do. I still believe that, huh? In fact, I know where we can go so they won't find us. It's safe. – he smiled.

_It's dangerous. You don't owe me anything, you don't have to. You'd be at risk.

Antoine shook his head with a chuckle, it was a little late for that. He looked into her eyes, saw his own reflection in them and understood. It was the second time in his life he had experienced that, to feel his heart warm, his stomach floating in his belly, his hands trembling. Being in love. So he knew what would happen: he would accompany the lonely and mysterious young woman wherever she went.

They arrived at the hut and got out of the vehicle. Helped by Antoine and covered by the hood, she hopped along the way. She halted in front of a felled tree, of which only the trunk protruded from the ground. _I promised you to show you what I am. I think this is a rapid and effective way. Step away, please.

She clamped her feet as comfortably as doable, taking several deep breaths and drawing wide circles with her healthy arm. She exhaled with a scream, blowing up the trunk with a falling fist. Shrapnel flew in all directions, some of it stuck in her hand. Antoine jumped back, speechless.

_This is what I was trained for. – she explained when the dust cleared from the air, shaking her dirty coat. – Even with the little energy I have accumulated at the moment, it's enough to destroy this.

The shards of wood in her hand gained her attention, and she removed them carefully. To her amazement, the wounds began to heal. As she noticed the slow healing process, it stopped. She couldn't stop thinking about what the nightmare told her: "What I am, so are you".

PART 34: WOMAN'S PERFUME

Things were not going swell for Anzhelika. Her last –
official – mission had not ended as she wanted,
receiving as a gift some lead on her back, which,
although far from being mortal, hurt like hell. Her last
mission – unofficial in this case – had ended poorly,
discovered by León before receiving any useful
information to find this Antoinette Soleil. Battling the
lions was not a simple matter and she understood that,
but this was an exaggeration. Since then she had not
allowed herself to sleep, something she now needed
more than ever. She looked at the mirror in the white
hotel room she paid for with a stolen card, naked, in
the way her body remembered to be, without conscious
modifications at all. It was a method she developed
some time ago to rethink her situation. She wasn't sure
if it worked or not, but it had a cathartic effect that
suited her. After an hour of looking into her eyes,
decided that she was under a lot of stress, and that she
would allow herself to play for a while on her next job.
It was not a professional attitude but one urgently in
need.

Fortunately, there was a glimmer of hope in the whole
deal. After a systematic search of the contacts in the

digital assistant of the late Budem Edelstein, she had found several candidates to track, but one caught her attention. First, because she was cute. Second, because she was a systems engineer specializing in data encryption, which was a handy way to finish reading all the information that was stolen from *Prima-Gestalt*, and if she got very useful data out of it, she could go back to Eylem on better terms. And third, because she was single, lesbian and very liberal. That fact was not a minor one, because it was the basis of her anti-stress plan.

It would consist of: Get in, seduce, and get out. No tricks. Or almost.

The fundamental basis would be to do it the easy way. No threatening, no forcing. A game of pure seduction... That sounded good.

Since she was not going to use several of her favorite tools, the action plan required prior research. She found out about some of the target's tastes, and more intel about her, using the current trendy social network, HapPic. Lika never understood exactly why people liked to publish their lives, leaving so many juicy facts to use, but it didn't stop her from rejoicing. The subject in question was called Erika Persson, Swedish, thirty-eight years old, rich, living by herself? in a house full of luxury, she loved to vacation on the beach (always with a different female company). In short, she was living the dream. It was particularly interesting to her to see a long series of photos, each one with its own explanation, with a particular lady, a former couple of the aforementioned. Slim, radiant smile, brown curls, big breasts. Erika seemed madly in love, at least for a short time.

She made a risky bet. To create the best version of that woman, better curves, prettier, but copying the fundamental aspects. From the videos she was able to understand her basic personality, so she only had to complete it with some details that would surely interest her. Erika liked intelligence, and that was no problem. Although she also liked women with curls, and that couldn't be done unless she wore an ugly wig... Lika could change her hair color on the white-blonde-brown-black scale, but not in shape. It always came out straight with a few slight waves, a trick that always slipped out. Nothing to do in so few hours. Her new creation would be a blonde with straight hair.

What if the chick saw someone very much like her ex and ran away? Well, she'd waste a lot of time putting the plan back together, or she'd even have to resort to unholy trickery and lose the game she played with herself, but if it went well she'd save a lot of time and effort.

She checked the details of her new look several times, mentally reviewing what should be said and how. So she called the target as soon as ready, pretending to be the executive director of a well-known technology company that wanted her services, concluding the video-chat on a Sunday night date, as she expected. Not just any date. The curfew forced early travel, and since no restaurant or night club would be open, it had to be intimate, close, homey encounter.

When Sunday the 30th arrived, everything was ready. Lika, disguised as her new incarnation, "Amanda", wore an elegant grey dress, to contrast, even slightly, how easy it had been for the engineer to hook up a date. This one seemed to like fast girls, but she was driven mad by the difficult ones. There wasn't time for that.

She travelled by taxi to the place, and charged the expense on another stolen card, which she discarded. No waiting was required, as someone was expecting her at the door, rose in hand.

Erika was tall, thin, with somewhat rectangular features on her nose and cheekbones but with a rounded jaw, her tanned skin was noticeable and her hair was very short, shaven on the back of her neck. She had a fibrous appearance underneath her tight white shirt, and a warm, eager smile on her face.

_Welcome Amanda, you look lovely in person, more than by video without a doubt.

_Thank you very much, Erika, nice to meet you. – she stopped to smell the rose, with a movement studied and executed to the millimeter. This evening would undoubtedly be a manual of seduction. And the class was starting right now, with stage one: beauty. Because it all comes through the eyes.

_I hope you didn't have any trouble getting here – said the hostess as she took the newcomer's coat and hung it from the perch – I don't know what's going to happen, but I hope it's over soon.

Erika Persson's house looked like a miniature mansion, the black and white tiles on the floor glowed with neon light in their joints, at regular intervals that followed the rhythm of the soft background music. On the walls there was little decoration but very tasteful. A pop painting dominated the main room, showing the figure of a woman throwing a top hat backwards, that produced an effect of light simulating a rainbow moving from left to right. In a shelf several objects formed a collection of the exotic places she had visited, and that was what Lika was glancing before answering, very sparingly.

_No, no problem fortunately. – she said at last. With the curfew still four hours away and the afternoon cloudy and cold, there had indeed been no problem.

_I prepared a special dish for you, spaghetti a la carbonara, I hope you like it.

_I hope so too. – she snapped with a simply overwhelming smile.

The purpose of the dinner was to elude and create a halo of mystery about every detail of Amanda's invented life, as the fool fills what is unknown with what they like the most. The ingenious deception that sums up stage two would be just that: to create mystery.

_This is delicious, you're a fantastic cook. - she lied.

_I'm glad you like it. Would you like some white wine? I've got one that'll go great with the food.

_Yes, please. Your house is a very cozy place. No doubt you have very good taste... I wonder if you have good taste in other areas... of your life – she revealed, looking down below Erika's waist. Stage three was the best fit for her: flirting.

_That you can find out without any difficulties, beautiful lady. - she replied laughing as she opened the cork from the bottle – But, I would like to know more about you. So far I know incredibly little about you and I find it unreasonable, don't you think?

Lika smiled broadly, leaning forward to reveal more of her cleavage. _I'm prepared to tell you anything you wish. But... you'll have to earn it.

With the end of dinner, stage four began: unattainable promises.

_Oh, yeah? – she was slightly surprised, even clumsily tipping over an empty glass. – What do you have in mind?

_You see, I've been told you're very good. The best.

_At least I get paid like one. – Erika joked.

_I want to know how good you really are, Miss Persson. In fact – she continued, crossing one leg – I came specially to acknowledge that, in a very personalized way. – she took a few seconds to taste the wine – Ready for the challenge?

The woman took a sip, put the glass down and held her hand gently. _I'm all ears, I accept.

Lika rose from her chair to grab something from her purse and returned. _Here it is. It's a little Airdrive. Inside you'll find two files. One's a dumb thing from work. The other is a video. Although... – she paused for another subtle moment to continue – not just any video. It's something I recorded before coming here. Before I actually changed my clothes. – simulated a genuine laugh – It is a special prize for you. The trick is they're both encrypted, and I won't say which is which.

Erika picked up the light gray memory device that she extended to her and walked to the wall–mounted stereo. She gave an order and the music changed to something more appropriate for a challenge. She turned to her centralized command computer, lowered her giant screen and curved it slightly towards her for peripheral vision, dropping a winning look in the process. Finally, she placed the Airdrive on the table, which was immediately detected and scanned.

Lika stood behind her, caressing her shoulders. Two files appeared on the screen, both with a series of numbers by name, which looked identical. _Here they are, which is which?

_I won't tell you, you rascal, that would make the task easier. I'd start with this one. – she said, pushing Erika's cheek with one of her breasts and pointing to one of the files.

Erika was momentarily distracted by biting the surface of her dress, smelling her lustful woman's perfume. _In that case... I'll start with the other one. – she mentioned with a big smile, opening several encryption analysis programs, and ignoring that both were in reality the same. Within a few minutes a lengthy, almost unintelligible report came to light. The engineer spent quite some time browsing through the contents. As she read, her face he became less cheerful, more professional. _There are some very interesting things around here. In fact...

She was quiet, drumming her fingers as she continued to read another report of results in a dark gray window. _I've seen this before... – she slipped focused.

Erika opened a black window, wrote a few commands, and stopped for a moment before executing, with a strange grimace on the mouth.

The window stood still for a few seconds, and then a progress bar emerged from underneath advancing with speed. _No way, it's going too fast.

_What does that mean?

_The decryption is being done in record time. So I got it right on every parameter. I already knew that algorithm. This was written by the doctor... what was it... Edelstein.

Seconds later, the process was over.

_Yes. – she pitched, incredibly serious and disturbed – it has to be Edelstein's. Where did you get this, Amanda?

Lika took control of the pointer, ignoring Erika's questions. She went to the contents of the file. Thirteen new files had been decrypted from the recently opened, one video chat, three accounting files, and nine other text documents. Immediately addressed one of these, whose German name was "Orders – Blinding Plan – Aegis Palace". The text was quite short, just five pages.

_Amanda, are you listening to me? – she said in a somber voice, as a drop of sweat fell down her neck.

Anzhelika did not answer. She just read as she licked, psychotically, the little drop of perspiration that slid down. _Shhhh. – she silenced the prisoner with a sweet gesture.

The moments passed, and the military plans paraded on the screen. _I–I shouldn't be reading this, no? – Erika stammered in fear.

_Probably not, dear. – dropped, without spending too much attention – So... León ordered to limit the damage... to withdraw before losing.

_Is this military espionage?

_How about you relax and go to the bathroom? While I'm copying this. – she wrapped without patience, stroking her hair.

Erika was finally able to stand up, and as she walked away she heard her captor speaking to herself with great concentration.

Once locked in the bathroom, standing in front of the door, Erika ordered quietly. _Computer, call Edelstein, Budem.

After a few moments, she heard a phone ringing nearby, a few meters away. It was Edelstein's phone, ringing inside a lady's purse. _Darling, I had so much fun tonight, I hope you'll invite me back soon. – Anzhelika's soft voice was heard from the speakers –

Unfortunately I have to leave, there's something important I have to investigate immediately. Thank you for being so kind. Don't wait for me. – she whispered, and closed the conversation with the sound of a kiss.

And so began the sixth and final stage of the manual of seduction: to vanish.

PART 35: EXPENDABLES

Crashes and shouts woke up Liam MacOwen. He slid from under the blankets and hid behind the rough window frame. He cleaned the fogged glass as he felt the afternoon chill creep into his bones. Below, several dark green uniformed men in black vests, helmets covering their eyes and large guns walked by and gave instructions. They were combing the place, looking for refugees. Whether it was to kill or rescue them, it didn't matter, they were a big problem.

He glided down the hall to Dipson, still asleep without even taking off his coat or shoes. He touched his shoulder and gave him a silent signal to keep quiet. _There are enemies below. We've got to scram out of here. - he whispered.

_How many? - Dipson was incredibly awake to have been sound asleep seconds ago.

_I don't know, maybe a dozen or more.

_Let's go for the others. - he said as he stood up - Would they be the teammates of those we killed?

_Go get them, I'll go fetch my things, I'll be ready in a minute.

They both ran out of the room with as little noise as possible.

By the time MacOwen was ready, Dipson was back.

_Drescher's awake, I can't find Syra anywhere.

MacOwen frowned at him as he finished tightening his belt. _She's gone?

_Perhaps. – Dipson looked out the window to see. The situation downstairs had become tense. A soldier had taken a woman with a little girl in arms and a child out of the house across the street. The boy, no more than fifteen years old, got rid of the man and started running down the street. The screams of the woman, apparently her mother, were in vain. He fell under the fire of a rifle.

_We have to go. Now.

They rushed out into the hallway, where the Dutchman waited against a wall, seemed to be asleep standing up, or almost. _What's going on?

_There are soldiers downstairs, we're leaving. – MacOwen said, pushing him firmly towards the stairs.

_I heard gunshots. And Miss Syra?

_Looks like she's gone.

Drescher didn't seem surprised at all, he barely let go of a little air from his nose, confirming what he thought of her.

Dipson, already on the ground floor, retraced his steps to give some news. _Not only is she gone, I think she took the jeep.

_Damned Shadow... - the Irishman MacOwen didn't have much more time to complain. He was interrupted by the noise at the door. Several voices were heard, and then knocking - To the garage, fast!

The large garage was made of chipped wood and dirt. Wherever no boxes or jars rested, the floor was covered with grease, motor oil and sawdust. On the walls someone hung a rusty old bicycle, and on one side a shelf overflowed from ceiling to floor with various tools and old paint cans. However, a vehicle was conspicuous by its absence.

The three men leaned silently against the gate to try and strike something out of their situation. A gentle wind was blowing through the little broken glasses of the window. Above, black clouds covered the sky. _Vogel, please have a look. - Charles Dipson asked - See what weapons they have, do you recognize them?

Through the window he saw two soldiers distracted, smoking in the middle of the street, watching as their companions attacked the front door with a battering ram.

_Yes, they are AGER–25. From the general appearance and the fact that they speak English, I'd say they're some kind of American paramilitary force. Or British? No, they're American. I don't know what they're doing here, but it won't be any good.

_But... – only got to say Charles Dipson.

_I don't know if they have explosive rounds, Charles, by the noise just now they seem like standard 5.56 mm... that is, common bullets. – he stated – That model allows for a lot of modifications, so it's not sure.

The sound of banging against the wood was replaced by that of wood shattering to pieces. The soldiers were already inside.

_What do we do now? – Dipson asked hopelessly.

_We will have to fight – MacOwen snapped before being interrupted.

_Hey you idiots! – Drescher shouted in English – Stop looking at your dicks and watch the corner, they're getting away!

The men outside jumped into action and looked around the corner, suddenly alert, to run, a little confused and without cigarettes.

_Let's go now! – said the Dutchman.

The trio ran out the other way. They had barely covered a hundred meters at full speed when they heard a loud voice. They managed to take refuge behind a troop transport truck when the shooting began.

_Keep moving! – MacOwen ordered.

_But where? – Dipson asked for the obvious.

_Those are common bullets but they can kill me! – Drescher pleaded.

_Stop shooting! – A desperate voice shouted out several times inside the cab of the truck.

Liam MacOwen opened the door on the passenger's side and lunged his sword at the unfortunate driver's flank, who hardly complained as he was violently dragged out to the side. _Climb up!

_Do you know how to drive, Liam?

In response, the Irishman sat down in the driver's seat, moved the lever to position "D" and pushed the pedal to the full throttle. As the truck began to move, the shooting resumed, making several marks on the reinforced glass. As they gained distance the shooting subsided, and finally ceased.

Drescher, sitting in the middle of the cabin, started laughing out loud, hitting the dashboard with his healthy hand. _I can't believe it! That was great!

Dipson looked at him sideways, somewhat concerned about his partner's state of mental health. _We could have died there.

_Yeah, I know, but we didn't. And we have a transport now.

They continued at full speed up to the road out of town. Nothing or anyone could be seen on either side. And so far, nobody behind either.

_That way. - pointed out the Englishman Dipson - we would be going in the direction of the explosion, I recommend we take the left.

_This doesn't end here. They're going to report that we stole this and to come after us.

_Then what?

_I don't know, let's keep going as far as we can.

They continued along the empty road, with the night already falling. The clouds discharged their potentially radioactive content in some stretches, turning the moor into a depressing, stygian wasteland.

On the side of the road they found a vehicle with its lights out. A man in green uniform was signaling for them to stop. They slowed down as they approached.

_What do we do? - consulted Dipson - It could be a trap.

_But on the other hand, we need to get rid of this truck. - Drescher backed.

_I'm in doubt. I say we go on, someone will come for him.

_Isn't that our jeep? - said Vogel pointing outside as they passed by.

_You! - a familiar voice sounded.

MacOwen slammed on the brakes, and the three of them looked at each other in surprise.

_You were just going to leave like that? - Syra said, slowly changing from a makeshift soldier to her more familiar appearance and peering in from the Irishman's side.

_Unbelievable. What the hell are you doing here?

_The battery died.

_I meant why are you here *without us*? - MacOwen was really angry.

_Last night you said we could leave after we'd rested, and that's what I did.

_But with the car!

_I, uh... I know, sorry. I felt there might be danger nearby, and I saw you lot too tired to follow me. - the Shadow was doing her best to win over her former partners with words, and failed to do so, to Drescher's delight. – Besides, I'm going to Marseilles. I doubt you'd be interested in that.

_We don't really have a clear destiny, miss. – said Vogel maliciously – What could you possibly say to persuade us to go down that road?

Syra fulminated him with her eyes before answering. _There's a Crest's headquarters, it's the last location where Eylem was. I want to present my report and regroup, a lot has happened since then.

The men looked at each other, and decided quickly. _We'll go. Get in – ordered Liam.

_Wait, we could switch to the jeep. It would attract less attention. Do you think we can? – Dipson asked.

Fortunately the jeep had a hybrid engine, and after filling it with fuel from the reserve tanks of the transport truck, they set off quickly.

_So Marseilles. What will we do there? I'm not really sure I trust Eylem. – MacOwen hesitated.

_Why do you say that?

_León deliberately stopped his assault with a motive. That's very strange, not to mention the nuclear attack.

_I don't think Eylem knew about that attack. – Syra noted.

_What if she knew? We saw who was there at the Palace... no one said it but I'm fed up of hypocrisy. The ones that went that day, we included, were the pariahs, the ones Eylem holds in least esteem. - continued Liam, taking advantage of the silence of his companions - I had problems with her in the past, and she has regarded me as a fanatic and a madman.

_Well... she has called me useless on more than one occasion. - Drescher confessed, squeezing his bandaged hand.

_I don't think she knows me. - Dipson assured.

A few minutes passed. The raindrops began to fall on the ceiling, briefly cutting the silence off.

_That's true. - slowly said Syra- I too have had problems with her because of insubordination. But I promised it wouldn't happen again. And I've been reviewing the troops present, and... it's true... I guess we were... expendable. But that outcome? Who would benefit from that? Certainly not us, neither did León.

_It's a Caucasesque move. - Drescher threw in the air.

Those present stared at the Dutchman. _What, what's wrong? - he asked, suddenly upset.

_What did you mean by that?

_Ah, that's the kind of thing a madman like Caucasus would do. Erase enemies with one stroke of the pen without anyone suspecting anything. And with an enviable display of power. – he paused as he still felt the gazes fixed on him – I mean, I read about his history. He's been putting sides to fight each other since forever. I suppose that to fake your own death, make them split into two groups that start fighting and then returning is of a genius worthy of him.

_I need answers. – MacOwen sentenced.

PART 36: THE ROAD TO DISASTER

Kad looked out from his large balcony and watched proudly as the moonlight washed over his fields with its tenderly imprint, lands given to him by the kings of Rome and now rightfully his own. He wore a white robe and a purple one on top, tied with a fine string around his waist. His long, coppery hairs covered his shoulders and beyond, and a lock of them was braided and tied with a small red ribbon. The villa in which he lived was beautiful, finely decorated and spacious, with new paint, carvings and the best that money could get. Kad had worked hard for the Roman cause, and it had paid him generously. A servant handed him a tray of grapes and a glass of wine, which he politely refused. He was completely happy, just as he was. He breathed in the night air and smiled out a puff.

_Where are you, Dad?

He heard a little girl's voice calling him from downstairs. The girl ran up the beautiful marble stairs and ran to the balcony.

_There you are, Dad! – she shouted, almost to his ear.

The little girl hugged her adoptive father's legs with great affection, and he kissed her forehead.

_Did you miss me, Porpé? I wasn't gone that long this time.

The girl nodded and smiled showing her teeth, and some gaps between them. Her hair was black and shoulder-length, with a few braids on each side of her face, topped with red ribbons. A pair of brown eyes, puffy cheeks and a round nose like a little ball. She seemed physically unable to stop jumping and jumping with infinite energy.

_And your sister?

_Downstairs. Let's play! Let's play! – she repeated.

Porpé dragged Kad by the hand down to where Circe and another girl, a few years older, were waiting. Circe wore a stunning, thin, slightly transparent white robe that revealed her beautiful legs, a golden gown around her waist, and lots of fine-looking jewelry on her wrists. Behind her, a little girl carefully braided her hair. She was almost identical to her younger sister, but with a bit more calm, a speck more of experience and a palm taller. She was dressed in the same way as her adoptive mother, but with more opaque fabrics, embroidered with figures of various animals.

_Jano! You could have announced your arrival, I heard from Refonte. We missed you so much. – Circe said, turning to look and immediately disassembling an unfinished braid.

_Hello dad! - The eldest, Mejai, shouted happily as she tried to rescue her work.

_My princesses, what good is a surprise if I'm going to spoil it myself! I decided to come back early. - Kad kissed Mejai fondly on the forehead, and passionately kissed Circe on the lips.

_That's right, we're very happy to have you here. How'd it go? - Circe asked.

_Not as well as I'd like. The Etruscans are sitting on a pile of spears, and from up there they want to negotiate. Tomorrow night I'll talk to the kings myself, and we'll see what we can do. - Kad replied, with a hint of bitterness.

_Do you think there's going to be a war?

_I hope not. Before coming back I had a very pleasant talk with Descénidos, and I didn't see in him a motivation to fight. Unfortunately, he is not the only one with a voice among their ranks.

_Descénidos has always been an honest and cunning person. A war is not in anyone's best interest, and he knows it.

_That's true, but people change... - Kad looked out through one of the openings in the wall, just below the

414

ceiling. He was worried about something else, in the back of his mind, and he never neglected a feeling like that – And you, what have you been doing? – he asked, trying to be a little more cheerful.

_We went for a walk this morning to the city with Refonte and Aramea. – said Mejai – I think they're up to something! – she mentioned with a flush on her cheeks. Circe and Kad smiled complicitly at the girls innocence, and the obvious affair between two of their servants that they tacitly allowed.

_Anything interesting?

_We climbed a tall tall tower! – shouted Porpé.

Kad contemplated his new family proudly. Mejai and Porpé were two Sabine girls, orphans of the war, that Circe and Kad had adopted three years ago and taken to live with them. Kad felt particularly guilty about the situation, as it was Rome, in its eternal eagerness to expand, that had trampled the girls' village, savagely burned their fields and murdered their men. When the abducted women arrived in the city by cart, Circe saw them and rescued them from the slave seller for a few coins. Since then, they tried to give them the most normal and happy life possible, within the limitations. And above all, never to pass *the blood* to them, as they had agreed.

And Circe... they had spent many years together. If there was anything alike love between those *who are*

415

like them, this must be it. They enjoyed each other's company and what they had achieved. However, all good things come to an end. They had agreed to split up once the girls were older and knew for sure that they were living happily and smoothly with their own families. Maybe one day they would meet again and spend more time together. Only the Gods knew.

A respectful cough interrupted his thoughts. It was Refonte, his trusted man in the villa, standing in front of the hall. His belly was bulky and his extremities were very thin for the size of his torso. He wore a short beard over his face, a wide forehead and an attentive and eloquent look. A simple long robe, sandals and leather bracelets were his attire. Kad nodded his head, apologized momentarily and went with him to a secluded place.

_Is there a problem, Refonte?

_Lord, I hate to interrupt you, but a rider has arrived from the city. He's coming on behalf of Remo and wants to talk to you right away.

_I see, let's go with him.

Refonte and Aramea were technically slaves, but everyone in the house treated them as if they were free, and even received a weekly wage. They both recognized Kad's kindness and gave him a steadfast loyalty in return.

The two men headed for the stable at a steady pace, half a mile away from the house. The rider was inside, giving water to his horse. Refonte bowed and withdrew.

_My lord, my apologies for disturbing you. I bring news from the Palace, King Remo wants to discuss the Etruscan situation as soon as possible. He thinks the matter is serious.

_Tonight? – Kad was worried.

_Yes, right now, actually.

Kad prepared one of his favorite animals himself, saddled and mounted it. They both parted quickly for the city. The whole thing was getting out of hand. The relationship between Remo and Romano sparked more than a blacksmith's shop. It was the first difficult step Rome faced and already threatened to shake its foundations. The financial problems were chasing behind them, harassing the poorest, victims of the landlords who charged excessive rents, and they had begun to riot, provoking uprisings and requesting the head of the puppet human king who was sitting on the throne. More soldiers guarding the city were fewer soldiers on the battlefield, generating constant protests from Argosio, the Chief of the guard.

After riding for an hour, they arrived in the city. The excessive growth had left more than half of its inhabitants outside the walls, so they had almost completely disarmed it brick by brick, using that material to build more houses. The buildings were scattered all over the place leaving little room to walk under the dirty awnings and crates of merchandise that crowded the way. The guards had often forced the streets clean with beatings so that they could be used, effectively, for transit.

Kad and his companion rode to the Palace, but entered from the side instead of the main entrance, where they announced themselves and gave them way. The rider waved respectfully and left.

Kad advanced down a long hallway, barely lit by distant torches. Numerous shadows moved around, more than he would have liked, and he could feel invisible eyes on the back of his head. His arrival was not unnoticed, nor was out of the plans. The Palace, so beautiful and promising, had undergone countless changes of arrangements, constructions and remodeling following the whims of the true kings. This was done so regularly that it had become customary. The Palace was the representation in stone of the joint thought of Remo and Romano.

A soldier dressed in leather and with a sword on the belt stepped up to Kad, and when he recognized him he let him pass into Remo's quarters. They were divided into three parts, the main room, the bathrooms and the last one a closed compartment where he rested and kept his most important effects, treasures gathered throughout his life. Gold chests, slender marble statues, fine fabrics, the room overflowed with beauty, perhaps too much, with objects piled on top of each other. At the end, a figure sat alone on a beautifully carved wooden throne, waiting for him. He wore a tunic of embroidered linen, a glossy leather belt, and an unusual crown of gold with precious stones. He held a copper cup in his hand with some ruby inlays. The vision was funereal.

_I'm glad you accepted my invitation, and I apologize for not letting you rest as you deserved after such a long journey, but the matter is delicate and requires urgency. – said Remo, without moving.

Kad stepped over to where he was, and bowed a short, not too effusive bow. _Yes, I understand the situation, that's why I didn't hesitate to come forward.

Remo took a drink from his glass, snapped his lips freely, taking his time. _So, which news do you bring?

Kad didn't find Remo's attitude amusing. He just took a deep breath and tried to get it over with. _I was in Curtum for a week, I was not allowed to enter Velathri, but it was more than obvious that there were a large number of troops stationed there. From the quantity of camps I'd say they have twice as many men there as we do, but it might as well have been a farce for me to see. – Remo let out a sigh, between entertaining and sarcastic, while having another sip. – Unfortunately, I didn't have any glimpse, even fleeting, of their triremes.

I did notice that their guards were well fed, and in good health, at least those who were close to me. Needless to say, I was in custody the whole time.

_What about your friend, Descénidos? - Remo cut without any kindness.

_As far as I can see, he doesn't think the war is worth it. He's never ceased to prove that he's a reasonable person. However, he made me aware that Rome would lose in open conflict.

_Interesting... what about Caprico, did you talk to him?

_Briefly, he is a man of few words and preferred to leave me with Descénidos. Still, I had the impression that he is waiting for the right moment for an attack, a distraction from us that would turn his victory into a great victory.

Remo stood up and approached one of the busts on his right, on a column painted blue, light blue and gold. He gently ran one hand over it, going over the details of the curls in it. _Caprico is the real enemy, but he's an advantage rather than a liability. He's desperate for glory, and will commit a mistake. We must try to make that mistake cost him dearly. What do you think, Akkadian?

Kad narrowed his eyes with mistrust. _I think it's best not to go to war. Rome has riches, it is better that we give them away in exchange for goods than risk losing them. They have iron and wheat, so let's buy them iron and wheat. Descénidos believes that if this moment of tension is postponed, there is a chance that no conflict will occur, and I think so as well.

Remo seemed bored with his statue, and moved into a beautifully decorated vase with orange and yellow lines. He stroked its surface gently for a few moments before speaking. _Sometimes you're a little short-sighted, Jano.

Jano? Now he called him by the nickname Circe gave him so many years ago, and by the same he was known to the locals. It had never particularly bothered him, as he had used thousands of names over a millennium. But said by him, it sounded like an insult.

_I'll tell you what's about to happen. We're going to war, and Rome won't lose. Nor will it have victory either. I'm not a daydreamer, nor deluded. We will have so many casualties in our ranks that we will no longer be able to expand, at least not to the north. But I don't care, we'll keep growing by taking the islands to the south. We will wait a generation or two, Argosio will train more men, we will build enough triremes in that time, and those islands will be ours. Because a stalemate, for us is a win. But for Caprico it's a monumental defeat – he remarked, with a frightening smile – and not only that, but later, I'll kill him. Or rather, *we* will kill him. When we go to negotiate peace.

421

Kad was not expecting that, it sounded like a drunken man's delusions, if he didn't know they came from one of the kings. Attacking Caprico in the heart of enemy forces? _Remo, I don't mean to sound disrespectful, but it's not feasible. We're not going to get a stalemate. We will lose, and there will be no turning back, it will be the end of Rome.

Remo appeared bored again, and began to play with a heavy gold medallion that he lifted from one of his overflowing chests. _Jano, Jano, please. I'll tell you why it's going to be like this, just like I said. Because when you talk to Romulas, which will be very soon, he will introduce you to his twisted plan. - he crossed his eyes briefly with Kad, for the first time since he came in. - He'll tell you it's true, they're more than us, and they'll beat us. And he will also tell you that we don't have to go to war, but that we have to surrender the city, let it be filled with those disgusting pigs, and that we must conspire from the shadows. - he sat down again on his throne and threw the medallion against a wall with his eyes fixed on Kad. - That is his wish, and he will try to convince you of that. But enough for today, you're still green. Once you've talked to him and matured the idea, I'll call you back. - he raised his index finger threateningly - And rest assured knowing one thing. It will be his vision or mine that will prevail. None other. Now leave, I need to think. - he said, with a rude wave of his hand.

Kad turned and walked away, doors closing behind him. He had never felt comfortable with Remo, but now it was the worst. Was it true what he said about Romano? It was a pitiful plan... to give up the city without a fight. He shook his head with sudden repulsion. He had to tell Argosio everything, wine in hand if possible.

He moved down a different corridor from the previous one to avoid prying eyes. Folded his cloak so that it would serve as a hood, and covered his face with it. He got on his horse and left at gallop. Turned around to rarely used streets, but it was futile, he felt the eyes, those eyes, like daggers on him. He reached a dark tavern that he visited sparingly, but it was the place he needed now. He tied up his horse, tossed a coin to the ragged guy sitting on the staircase and entered. He asked for a glass of wine and waited. Soon, what he expected made an appearance.

_What a beautiful night, isn't it? – said a skinny man with half his teeth missing and dirty hair, limping down from his leg.

_Maybe. Do you know who I am?

_Everyone knows, you're Jano the Ambassador.

Too much fame, he didn't like it at all. _Possibly, you want to earn a few centums?

The ugly man smiled at him and nodded firmly.

Kad handed him a copper on the palm of his hand and clenched it holding his fist. _I imagine you also know the chief of the guard, Argosio.

_Oh, yes, I know who he is. - he listened attentively as he tried to take his hand out.

_I want you to go look for him, he must now be at the Crunchy Plank, or getting drunk in the tavern that is facing it, the Clumsy Rooster.

_I know 'em, yes, yes.

_Excellent, go and tell him that Jano wants to see him urgently, and to give you another copper. He'll protest, but he must remember he owes me money from the last time. If you find him and he comes, I'll give you another copper. - he promised, letting go of his hand.

The sparsely toothed man smiled broadly and ran down the street with a speed that a real limp could never reach. Kad's cup finally arrived, and he rushed it in one go.

The candle in front of him had burned almost completely when he heard a familiar voice behind him.

_You wretched dog, I already paid you everything! - Argosio put his heavy hand on the Akkadian's shoulder and sat down next to him. Glued like mud to a wheel came the messenger, waiting for his third coin. Kad extended one and gestured to him not to disturb them. The toothless man happily left.

_No, you awful baldhead, you still owed me four silvers. You drink so much you forget where you stand. I already ordered you a drink to save time.

Argosio laughed and punched the bar in front of him with his fist. _It's possible, I'm too busy and my memory is failing. Good to see you back in one piece. How was your trip?

_I've done better, but I wanted you to come for something else. Things are going to get ugly, and I want to know if I can trust you - Kad did not continue, a figure had come forward behind them.

_Akkadian, I have a message for you. - said the hooded figure.

Kad turned to face the figure, but he didn't recognize him. He watched his companion's reaction, who was angry at having his conversation interrupted. He glanced at the toothless man, who shrugged with cowardice and guilt. _From whom? - he spat.

_From Romano. - the hooded man extended a small scroll with a wax seal, which he opened reluctantly.

The message called for him to meet Romano immediately in his private villa. And that he would not accept delays.

_What will you do, chum? - Argosio asked.

Kad squeezed the message and threw it on the floor. He didn't need this now. _Go there, I'll have to tell you tomorrow.

_Whatever it is, count with me. Now go, I'll take care of these pitchers myself.

He rode with the hooded man to Romano's villa, it wasn't long before dawn. The villa was large, had its own fields, irrigation channels, and was in an unbeatable location. He was surprised by the large number of guards stationed, what assassin could make his way and strike a fatal blow against Romano? Himself, perhaps?

A couple of them, well-armed, stopped them at the entrance of the gate. They looked like mercenaries, well-trained and silent. The hooded man crossed over a few words on the quiet, and they let them pass. They left the steeds in the stable in charge of a groom, and the hooded man told Kad to follow him. This strange individual must have been trusted by Romano, because he played a more important role than just a messenger, he followed him closely at all times, but who was he? How did he never hear from him?

Another pair of guards at the entrance to the mansion scrutinized them from head to toe before letting them pass. The mansion was not too different from Kad's, which was not surprising, as it had been designed by the same architect. Of course, it boasted details peculiar to the owner's mind. The columns were carved with riders holding lustrous spears and shields, illustrating a fictitious combat.

The interior of the main hall was completely carpeted, the center of the hall was governed by a solid oak table with legs carved like wild beasts, and eight armchairs of the same material and finishes, covered with purple silk fabrics. Four torches on each corner illuminated taciturnly the place, yet gave a peaceful feeling of well-being. The hooded man accompanied him down a wide corridor to the farthest room. He knocked gently on the door, and an invitation to enter was heard. Kad came in, this time alone.

The room was large, and the walls were clean of decorations, with only a luminous calcareous white. On the back wall hung a lone round wooden shield, without a speck of dust on its surface, a small stand with short swords beneath it, and two portholes facing the outside on either side. The dim lighting came from six small burners.

Kad stopped in front of his host, who smiled at him with false kindness as he played with the edge of a short sword in his hands. He wore a light leather outfit with shoulder pads over a linen camisole, and thin-striped sandals. Simple, but refined.

_Welcome Akkadian. I apologize for calling you suddenly, but the situation is delicate. – Caucasus mentioned with a phrase almost copied from his pair.

Something was out of place, but he didn't know what. Was it the surroundings? A hidden danger? He looked around, but nothing caught his eye. _There's no need for apologies, I understand the hurry.

_I gather you've made a... stopover... at the palace.

_That's right, Remo asked me to go.

Caucasus nodded calmly. He took a few steps away, turning his back on him, brandishing his blade, cutting through the air. He approached the stand quietly, and lifted another sword.

_Fancy a little friendly duel? Something quick, at first blood.

Kad raised an eyebrow, but agreed. Caucasus threw the second sword at him, which was deftly caught.

_One thing I've always admired about you, – said Caucasus, putting himself on guard – is your ability to read a combat.

Caucasus swung a lunge at him, which Kad avoided with a swift motion. He turned and countered, finding Caucasus' iron and causing a clash.

_You're not the most skilled with a sword, but your technique is perfect, at least for you. The right move at the right time. No one else could use that extra step, that extra ounce of strength – he let out a scream as he attacked him three times in quick succession, each one flawlessly avoided. This time there was no counter-attack, he simply backed off several steps and changed hands with his weapon – The years have forced me to become a skilled warrior, a survivor. But your capacity... you certainly have talent. A gift from the Gods.

Kad lunged at him with a feint. Where Caucasus waited for an edge, there was nothing. Instead, he struck with the pommel on his wrist, sliding the defending weapon away from where it was meant to be. With another quick glide, he slid to his back and cut Caucasus forearm almost to the bone. He lost his balance and staggered, and by the time he was on his guard again, he found Kad crouched, elegantly pointing his sword at his throat. The fight was over.

_You've beaten me! An excellent combat, I needed the exercise. – Caucasus arm was already closing the wound, leaving a slight scar, dark in color, and he turned his attention to the process until it was completed, when he sheathed his blade – If I had your talent... and Remo's miraculous healing I would be unstoppable, wouldn't I?

_Thank you for the compliments, Romano. - Kad could not completely hide a sardonic tone, while he left his sword on the stand. - Everyone has their tools, to try to spend one more night alive.

_No doubt about it. Now, what news you bring from Etruria?

Kad commented again on his experiences and impressions on Etruscan soil, for a Caucasus listening attentively, with his arms folded and his back against the wall.

_An open confrontation is madness, we won't get away with it. - said Caucasus, with a crafted concern.

_What is the alternative? - Kad asked, with some aggression, knowing roughly the answer, which was long awaited. For a moment, the concert of deafening crickets took over.

_Tell me Akkadian, do you know what's so special about these Etruscans? What is it about them that makes them grow, to be so hardened, even more so than us?

Kad took a moment, surprised by that question. _No, I don't.

_Neither do I. - wrapped up. He pulled away from the wall and began to walk slowly through the room with one hand on his chin - But I want to know. - the tone of voice became severe – What they possess, why, how. I want to take it for myself. The plebs in Rome no longer satisfice me, they're useless idlers. – now he said with fury, looking him intensely in the eye – They... the Etruscans... think that I will give Rome away, that they will take her and make her their whore. Let them think that, they couldn't be more wrong.

Caucasus walk pretended to be frenetic and passionate. _Instead. – he continued – I will seize them all. I will make them my labor force, my slaves. And best of all, they'll never know it. When they believe they have the perfect victory, they will have the perfect defeat in return. Maybe I'll know one day why they were better than the Romans, or not. I don't care. Or perhaps, the Gods will show me a superior populace, and I will lose interest in playing with their souls. – the energy radiating from Caucasus was brutal, majestic, magnificent, distressing – Rome is not a city, it is an Empire. What do I care about losing one city, if I get the means to conquer ten in its place? Do you understand Akkadian, what Rome is? – he made a paused so sublime that the world itself stopped – the eternal Empire.

Kad didn't know what to believe or disbelieve. Caucasus was undoubtedly a genius. An important part of him was now in agreement with this megalomaniacal project. Fortunately, the sanest part remained skeptical. But alas, the psychological attack was not over.

_There's another big issue, partner. -the change of pace in Caucasus was notorious- There are insurgents in Mesonia.

_I didn't know that. How many are there? - Kad cared little, he had his mind set on finding the best course of action. He didn't like it at all. Maybe it was best to take his belongings, his family and start over somewhere else. He regretted that his pride did not allow him to leave his own Roman project to the divine will. He knew he was going to stay after all. At least a little while longer. Just a little while longer.

_Just a hundred or two, but it's in a terrible time. They're behind our lines and thwarting any kind of plan. But I think I have a double solution. I'll ask Remo to negotiate personally with the insurgents. He'll have them eating out of his hand in a few hours. And besides, it'll be a rapprochement between him and me, after too long. Which will allow me - he said with an accomplice grin - to go to Curtum and talk to Caprico, I'll fill him with compliments and play the loser. Then the second act will come, but better to not go too far ahead. - he finished, with a wide, spectral smile - Will you come with me?

_Sure, Romano. - both kings leaving the security of the city? Too odd.

_But for now, rest, when the moon is full you will leave. Enjoy your family in the meantime. - Caucasus ended with a smile.

Some plan he hadn't figured out yet was being cooked up. He had to go along with them for the time being, and agree to travel again. He had to do it himself, save Rome from the madness of these kings. There was no safe road on this journey, only one to disaster.

PART 37: WAR DRUMS

_At last I find you. - Kad said as he entered a newly erected tent just two leagues from Mesonia, a small settlement southeast of the city. Outside, in the village, a few bonfires cut through the afternoon sky, and a mob was thundering some improvised war drums.

_I'm not exactly hiding, dog. Although I think you're coming at a bad time, we'll soon have to go in and it will be a massacre - replied the Chief of the guard, the huge Argosio. He was paying more attention to sharpening his sword than to counting the clay tablets with reports of troops and potential insurgents resting on a crude table with easels - I doubt you'd want to participate.

_That's exactly what I wanted to talk about - he began, removing a heavy hood and picking up his enormous cloak, which protected him from the damaging daylight rays - The kings are now discussing this matter, and if everything goes as planned, Remo will come here personally to try to calm them down. He may even convince some of them to march under your command.

Argosio looked up from his weapon to face his companion in surprise._ Damn it, why do I hear about this now? When would he come?

_It can be at any time, if they use a roofed carriage so he can get out during the day.

_It would be the best solution, Remo is most convincing.

_I wanted to tell you something else, too. There are... strange inconsistencies with both kings.

_Like what?

_Until a year ago I could say, without mistake, that the four of us were working for Rome. I don't know today. You saw me, the day before yesterday I was in a meeting with both of them. Romano wants to give up the city to avoid the fight, and Remo wants an open conflict with the Etruscans.

Argosio was silent for a moment, making sure the blade was perfect. _Look, man, I'm gonna tell you something. I agree that something's wrong, and I don't like what you're saying. I want to trust you, but now you come in here telling crazy stories. Before you went on your trip, I was given a papyrus. – he got up from his bench and went by Kad, tapping him with the blade on the top of his right shoulder. – The papyrus told me to watch out for you, that you were conspiring with the enemy.

435

Kad became irritated and brusquely withdrew the soldier's arm away from him. _How could you say that to me?

_I know what you're going to say, dog. I don't believe that stupid papyrus. I've known you a long time and I can see you want to work for the Roman bounty. But don't give me that bullshit. Both Remo and Romano are astute, and they don't want to lose. What you told me just means defeat in one sense or another.

_That's what they told me. I give you my word of honor.

Argosio exhaled hard. _Then I don't know what else to tell you. I will not allow neither, and I ask you not to allow it too.

_On that we agree. – Kad was about to turn around, but he retraced his steps. – Who do you suspect was the author of the nefarious papyrus?

_No idea, it could have been anyone. Or not so anyone... there are some new folks around here, did you see them?

_If you mean the hooded men who look like mercenaries, yes. I've seen them. I thought they were under your command.

_No, they are not. I don't know who they are, they arrived five days ago and still haven't done anything useful. I had them followed. And they *carry the blood*, I don't know if everyone, but at least most of them.

_Who pays them?

_Good question, I haven't had time to find out yet. As you know I have been busy – he said, pointing his thumb in the direction of Mesonia.

Kad leaned his back against one of the poles, chin up and look worried. He took a moment before he spoke. _On another note, Remo asked me to go back to Etruria and talk to Descénidos. He wants me to distract them while he sets things up here and marches against them. I'm going to go, but to propose a trade pact that will be useful to us. I didn't discuss it with them because in my opinion they're insane. The problem is, if Rome awaits at their doorstep on my return then my efforts will be useless.

_I see Akko... I can't promise you that we won't march, but I can promise that I'll delay it until after your return. If you come back with an alternative like that, it may be what we are needing, making the scale tilt towards sanity.

Kad approached the table to check, without much emphasis, some of the clay tablets. He took one at random and shook it up with intrigue. _This smells really bad. Argo... I think they're tr–

He was going to keep talking, telling him that he suspected someone was trying to sabotage the city, but was interrupted by two soldiers who suddenly broke into the tent. _Chief! The sentries have seen Etruscan horsemen! – one said.

_An advance party, to the west. – certified the second.

_Shit, bad timing, bad timing! – said Argosio in a bad mood, running one hand over his head.

_Any carriage has come from the city? – Kad asked overwhelmed.

_No, lord. But orders have come from King Ancus Marcius for Ambassador Jano. – the first soldier said, extending a papyrus to Kad, referring to the man who served as a monarch for the plebs.

_I'll have to send a centuria of men west. Maybe more. – the Chief of the guard grumbled. – I don't have that many people.

_I have a solution, Argo. – Kad said as he read the document – I'll go. It says here... that Descénidos might arrive today with a convoy, in which case I'd better receive them. The strange thing is that he didn't mention anything to me about it when I went there... and assuming it's not him, if you lend me fifty good men on horseback I'll stand up to them, or see what their intentions are.

Argosio smiled, as in the best days. _I like that. I'll give you ten, you slacker.

_Thirty, you big ugliness.

_Done!

In a few minutes Kad and thirty well-armed horsemen set out to meet the Etruscan advance party. They rode for an hour with the afternoon sun just hidden behind the mountains and the first stars peeking out their majesties above their heads, until they found them. No one approached or signaled to parley. Far from it, they continued to advance in their direction, wielding their weapons high and shouting war cries.

_Prepare to fight! Formation! - Kad ordered, drawing his blade.

With the riders in an arrow formation, they moved forward boldly. The fifty-five Etruscan horsemen broke their formation at the last moment and split in two to flank the Roman group, taking too long, for the misfortune of three of the rear horsemen who fell pierced by the spears. Soon the group was surrounded. The Etruscans on the left flank galloped at full speed, trying to break the few rows, claiming seven casualties, while those on the right flank feinted and stopped suddenly to confuse their opponents.

_Don't turn around, move forward! - he ordered pointing to the right side, and then to two of his closest riders. - You two, to my sides!

Kad's men, with him watching their backs, continued to gallop against the right Etruscan group, which without speed or direction due to the failed feint, were promptly crossed, only three managed to escape and did not return. At the same time, the leader of the enemy party, in front of the left flank, gave the order, and they rushed at Kad and his small escort. He caught them getting off his horse and making it run parallel to the enemy's straight formation, which took them a few valuable seconds to avoid. Already on foot and with sword in hand, he took momentum and made an inhumane leap forward, skipping and flipping over the first rider who approached him unaccompanied at his sides, knocking him down from his mount with a tackle and destroying his neck in the process. The surprised Etruscan leader, misjudging the resistance that a lone man could offer, ordered him to be surrounded, ignoring the escorts who were defending themselves in closed combat one by one with all their strength. Kad severed one attacker's arm and destroyed another one's helm and skull in two rapid onslaughts. A third buried his metal in Kad's shoulder, only to see his hand flying in front of his eyes and be dismounted in a trice. The group leader yelled an order, and the riders fled, barely twenty-one surviving in total.

Outraged, Kad smashed the heart of the one-handed soldier writhing on the floor, and left the other fallen to his men. His wound had already closed, leaving a slight purple scar visible through the hole in his clothes.

He ordered the wounded to be killed, and the bodies to be stripped of any valuables, when he saw something curious. He walked over to a small leather handbag recently dumped in the field. Inside there was only a scroll. Little had it written, just an order to investigate the west of Rome, and a count of troops to attack from the north: twenty centuries on horseback, ten centuries with pikes, twenty centuries of archers. Those numbers were twice as many as the total number of Roman forces. There was no mention of anything else, not even triremes. But he was more concerned about something else, the suspicious way in which that information had come to his hand.

_Grab your effects and let's get back, moving! – he shouted. Still, it was precious data to fail to report.

A little more than an hour later Kad and his group were galloping toward the palace of the kings, but their advance was impeded. A crowd had gathered on the narrow street to throw stones and shout for food, insulting Marcius' name. He immediately noticed that the air in that place was full of gray smoke. In the distance, two fire spots devoured the straw and cloth roofs, and the alarming voices of the guards were heard. The city was beginning to convulse. Two soldiers trotted past him, and he stopped them to inquire.

_Halt! What's going on in the city?

_Agitators, Ambassador Jano. They're calling to rebel.

_Repress them. – he ordered – Etruscan gold runs here, stop those charlatans and question them, let them spill whoever is paying them.

_Yes, sir! – they said in unison.

He assumed that the road to the palace would become even more difficult, and decided to change course to the outskirts, and see if Argosio was still in the tent near Mesonia. He ordered his group to find agitators and put out the fires, and he went mounting.

He rode in the opposite direction, dodging merchants and peasants. A man in rags tried to block his way and pulled a pale dagger between his clothes. He was greeted by Kad with an accurate kick in the jaw, and continued his journey. Already in the suburbs there were fewer people and animals, so he continued at speed. Near a water well he recognized several of Argosio's trusted men with torches in hand, organizing the insurgents' reprimand. When they saw him arrive, they received him with respect, and indicated that the Chief was about to arrive. He hadn't even got off his horse, when he saw Argosio arrive at the front of a score of riders from the south.

_Dog! I'm sorry I can't stay to hear about your exploits. The city's about to burn.

_Yes, I've seen it, I'm afraid they're Etruscan agitators. I'll be brief. The advance party attacked us but was defeated, Descénidos was not among them. I think their leader recognized me and that's why they ditched. However, they left this on the way. Sounds highly suspicious to me. - he shouted to him, riding on his beast, and when he was near, he handed the scroll out to him. Argosio ordered a stop while reading the contents.

_If this is real, we're at a severe disadvantage. - he snorted - The only thing left for us to do is to gather all the men to the encounter. We still have time to take the hill and assault them with arrows by surprise. Height would unfortunately be our only advantage.

_What if it's a fake?

_It's too risky to leave it to chance. - he said with a sneer - Rome no longer has high walls, so a defensive position is useless with our numbers, they're going to slaughter us. I'll send three groups of sentries east and southwest and northwest. If they come in triremes across the Tiber, we'll see them.

_What happened in Mesonia?

Argosio shook his head bitterly. _It was a disaster. Remo didn't show up, there was no negotiation, just blood. The agitators did an excellent job there, to their disgrace.

Kad stared at him, silently judging the killing.

_Understand, I couldn't afford to assign anyone there, we're short on hands!

_All right, I see. - he said looking down - I'll come with you, but on one condition.

_Anything, Akkadian.

_Assign ten men to my house to take care of my girls and Circe. I have a grim feeling about this.

_You'll have to settle with four.

Almost seven hundred Roman horsemen quickly arrived at Mount Quirinale, a few leagues north of the city, and sixteen hundred soldiers, including pikemen, archers and swordsmen marched behind them. A few others had to stay behind to make sure there was a city on their return. They formed lines, with Kad and Argosio in the center discussing tactics, and waiting for any sign of the sentry torches. The Roman banners of the troops on foot were getting closer and closer, at a good pace. Minutes passed and still nothing happened.

_What if it's a trap? – Kad asked, dressed in leather armor reinforced with metal plates, a helmet with a red feather and a sword on his belt.

_Hush, dog. I got it the first time, you wanted me to disregard that information you gave me? – said the Chief reluctantly. He wore a similar outfit, but with a round wooden shield and a red emblem on his chest. – Causto! Come here. – he ordered one of his trusted captains, who approached him until he could speak to him in the ear – What is known about kings? The real ones.

_Nothing yet. I sent a sentry into town and he's not back yet.

_A thousand demons! We're risking Rome's future and they're not here to fight! All right, get back in line, don't let your men get distracted. If there's any sign, I want you to be the first to ride.

_Yes, sir! – asserted Captain Causto.

A generalized murmur among the soldiers was heard from the back rows. Kad and Argosio rode for a better view. They would have preferred not to see. The city was in flames, with these being worse in the west, but spreading to the rest. Shouts and screams for revenge multiplied among the troops. Many riders broke ranks to ride to Rome. The captains were trying to maintain the straightness with little success. A man on horseback rode backwards up the hill, shouting at the four winds

445

and carrying a torch. When he got close enough, his message was finally understood: The Etruscans are burning and killing everyone, he repeated over and over again.

Both *blood carriers* looked at each other, and without a word advanced to the sentry.

_What's going on over there? – Kad asked, exclaiming so his voice would be heard over the background noise.

_The Etruscans are advancing unopposed, entering from the west, already taking the port and the slums, and perhaps more.

Argosio leaned over his horse and grabbed him by the shoulder in a firm, choleric manner. _You're one of Epestu's men, aren't you? Tell me something, do you know the founding kings?

_Romulas and Remo? Of course. – the sentry was sensibly confused by the question, far from the critical situation they were going through.

_Have you seen anyone like that up there?

_But the founders must be crumbling old men, if they live, what does that have to do with anything?

_They don't age, soldier. And you've seen the faces of the founders in the palace frescoes. So tell me, have you seen any of them today?

The soldier thought for a moment, and replied. _Now that I think about it, it's possible. A man followed by an escort of about twenty hooded men on horseback went to meet the Etruscans, I thought he was a Romulas' bastard, because of his resemblance to the old king.

_Indeed it was a bastard, but one who surrendered the city. – Kad stated with fire in his eyes – We must return, urgently. – sentenced, herding his steed at full speed.

PART 38: ASHES

Kad and Argosio, followed by the army marched towards the captured city, entering from the north side. However, there was no resistance in sight. Few residents went, most of them had barricaded themselves in their homes or were hiding in the alleys. They rode in front of the soldiers on foot and entered towards the city center. A small group of soldiers stepped forward and paid their respects.

_Where is Captain Epestu? – spat Argosio.

_Ambassador Jano, Chief Argosio, they've besieged the palace and must have entered by now. Epestu was slain, I don't know who's left in charge.

_Have any of you seen Romulas, the founding king?

The men looked at each other in strangeness, and did not answer.

_Bah, good–for–nothings! Let's go to the palace, everybody, march! – Argosio barked.

_Argo, I'm going to take a detour. I need to check on Circe and the girls. – he announced, turning his stallion over.

_Akko, now is not the time! The city is being captured. – he gestured with his hand, pointing to the smoke rising to the sky.

_I know! – he shouted furiously.

_They'll be fine, this is more important. I need you over there, man. – he said, trying to calm down.

_No, it's not more important. I'll be back as soon as I can.

Argosio insulted him cruelly until he couldn't hear his voice.

Kad rode fast without finding antagonism. The villa was secluded in the southeastern part of the city, and Kad trusted that no one had yet reached there. Upon arrival, he was glad that he had not seen even a sign of confrontation, moved smilingly toward the stable, and stepped down without tying his beast, hurling his helmet carelessly.

He opened the wooden door and ran in. The candles and torches were out, barely the starlight and the rising quarter of the Moon were seeping in. No one in sight. He continued and climbed the stairs to the first floor with agility. A lump was lying on the ground. It was a person, hooded, with three arrows nailed to the forehead, looking like a pincushion. He stumbled upon a dagger that glowed softly. It shook as it was kicked, scratching the ground with a frightening sound.

Mercenaries. Assassins.

The same ones who were escorting Caucasus. Kad got desperate. He searched the first room quickly without finding anything out of place. He went out to check a second one, when, in the darkness, he saw something that knocked him to his knees.

The mortecine light of the Moon that entered through the window was cruelly reflected on two bodies that were mutilated, with cuts and perforations, like lambs in the slaughterhouse. He crawled into the room, staggering. He held the head of the sweet Mejai. Her eyes swollen and out of their sockets, the result of a heavy blow, had cried blood. Vile stains of vital fluid desecrated entirely her delicate dress. He took her in his arms and placed her carefully on the cot. He couldn't close her eyelids when he passed his hand over her. He turned and moved, very slowly, to the body of her little sister, Porpé. Her head hung from her neck, joined barely together by a deformed shred of skin. She was completely drenched in blood. He stepped into the puddle that stretched out in all directions, causing a muffled, sad sound. Kad lifted her up and laid her beside Mejai's mortal remains, trying to keep the head on her shoulders and her eyelids closed. He placed the four innocent little hands on their chests. Sitting at the side of the cot, he stroked the red hairs of his adoptive daughters one last time.

He peeped out the window, leaving bloodstains on the frame. Below he could see that there were several foreign bodies lying in the grass. He turned for an eternal moment to take a final look at his little ones, forever lost in the meek and relentless peace of death. He jumped down and took a long time to get up. Checked the bodies reluctantly, the closest to the wall was from Refonte, whose face had been shattered by the edge of several daggers. Further afield he recognized Aramea, downcast with her limbs curled up, and lifeless. Three others he could not recognize, they were hooded men. All of them had arrows nailed to their bodies and heads, the latter being lethal. He followed an imaginary line formed by the bodies of the invaders, into his fields. A flash of light caught his eye, it was a gold bracelet. For they had not come for jewelry, as they were not thieves. They were executioners, desiring instead to deprive of life to his family, to his home. Circe's remains lay face down on the bushes, which swayed in the placid wind, beside a finely crafted bow that had been trampled underfoot until broken. Her lover's head was gone. He didn't dare touch her. Kad just crouched down and swung on his fists, sick with rage.

He retraced his steps and climbed on his horse, riding at full speed toward the city center. It wasn't hard to notice that Circe had put up as much resistance as she could on her own. And that no guard had ever helped. That Argosio had failed him. He did not notice, however, that a figure was slipping through the shadows, bringing news of the events that had taken place.

Arriving in the vicinity of the palace, Kad observed with surprise that the Etruscan soldiers were not only not attacking the population, nor him, but were distributing jewels, statuettes and other valuable objects, the spoils obtained from the palace. The crowded mob cheered for the name of someone called Tarquinius.

He resumed galloping, but towards the royal villa of Caucasus. Continued unobstructed, perhaps because no one recognized him or because he no longer mattered. Rome had fallen.

The royal villa was strangely deserted but with lights on, no hooded in sight. A man stationed at the window went inside when he saw him. He dismounted and advanced briskly to the front door. Stepped in shaking it with all the violence of his right foot, blowing away the small bronze rod that was used as a lock. Inside, four soldiers were surprised and on guard. Obviously they didn't expect any trouble.

_Jano, what are you doing here?

_Just tell me where Romano is and you can leave. – he said with incredible serenity.

_Inside, but we're not allowed to let anyone in.

_First and last warning, or I don't answer for my actions. Go away now. – threatened Kad, sword in hand.

The soldiers lined up in a row, fainting with fear, blocking their way into Caucasus' chambers.

Without wasting a moment, Kad crushed the two central soldiers with his body against the door, grabbing them by the throat and throwing them to the ground. That earned him two stab wounds on his flanks, which he completely ignored. He slit the throat of one of the standing soldiers, and without losing impulse, turned on his heels and severed the arteries from the neck of the second one. The body of the mortally wounded soldier fell against the wall, dropping one of the torches and scattering ashes in all directions. The two soldiers on the ground shouted in panic, and only managed to escape.

Kad, bleeding from his injuries and overlooking the dust of the ashes in the air and the last muffled cries of the men lying there, opened the heavy oak door, dodging the legs of the fallen man still twisting like octopus tentacles.

Inside waited Caucasus, with a short sword in each hand, in a defensive pose.

_What the hell are you doing? You are supposed to be battling the enemy. – shouted Caucasus furiously.

_What do I do? - Kad stopped, giant, occupying the entire threshold of the gate, producing a spectral shadow inwards - I came to end you.

_What? Why? - he asked nervously - Remo sent you?

_My woman and my girls have been killed by the hooded men that follow you. I've seen them with my own eyes. You... you ordered it. - he threw defiantly.

Caucasus raised an eyebrow and lowered his defensive stance slightly, trying to lower the spirits. _Those hooded ones? They're mercenaries hired by Remo, they respond to his orders.

_It is late for deceptions, I saw you when I came here last night, right here. - he declared, covered in blood and completely still, with no fighting stance, his sword firmly clutched in his hand.

_Akkadian, I plead guilty to deceiving you, but not to what you think. It was a necessary deception for the Etruscans to make a mistake and–

_Silence! - he cut short.

_No, wait! - he stopped him, almost begging - It's the truth, we pretended we were disagreeing with Remo, while I was making preparations outside the city, Remo stayed here and pretended to be me. We traded places.

_Liar! I was with both of you the other night, you weren't wearing masks, and I could see you perfectly well. – he finished, and rushed in with unleashed fury.

The king defended himself from the attack with both weapons and leapt backwards, only to jump again after another attack, remaining dangerously close to the wall. He escaped at one side, taking a cut in his arm. Kad stood still, staring at the wound. Caucasus, noting the pause in the duel and the attention he paid to his cut, observed it as it closed, leaving a scar behind.

_Remo leaves no scars when he closes the wounds, you must necessarily be Romano. It's the end of lies, you fraud.

_Wait, no! – shouted Caucasus simulating despair as he dodged an attack. Kad took several strides forward to close the gap and strike with his sword, missing the blow. In return, he received a stab wound behind his right armpit, causing him to lose his balance – in that case, Akkadian, I will send you to your fake family you love so much. – he sentenced.

Caucasus changed his composure to an aggressive one, and charged twice at his challenger, failing to connect against his flesh. He then launched three ferocious attacks, sticking his sword deep into the waist beneath the Akkadian's armor, lifting him one and a half feet with tremendous force and hurling him back.

Kad, using the wall behind his back, thrust himself and half-turning, attacked with his weapon drawing a downward arc. Caucasus deliberately exposed his left shoulder, where Kad's sword penetrated and was blocked, to his surprise. As he struggled to wrest it out of its imprisonment, Caucasus unleashed several slashes against his rival's arms, each producing a cut. When the Akkadian was finally able to remove his weapon from the king's back, the latter dropped his swords to the ground, which shrieked against the stone, and grabbed him tightly with his hands. The veins in the monarch's arms swelled tremendously and burst, but the blood, instead of falling, formed fine red fibers that began to seep, forcibly, through his opponent's wounds. Kad let out a high-pitched cry of pain, suddenly feeling his torso being paralyzed little by little, his arms, shoulders, and then chest squeezing, being devoured from within. His heart was pumping hard, nearly popping out as he resisted this internal invasion. With fire in his eyes, Kad held him by the elbows, trying to head-butt him, but he was too far away to do it. Kad, totally cornered, shook himself in vain, his arms felt so weak that he dropped his weapon.

_This will soon be over, your strength will be mine. - sentenced Caucasus, mockingly.

Kad leapt up and embraced the king's waist with his legs, getting close enough to wipe away Caucasus' triumphant smile with an unrelenting head-butt, succeeding in its brutality in sinking his frontal bone, sending both contenders down. Caucasus, fallen on his back on the ground, crawled as far as he could away from his enemy as he tried to rearrange his skull by hitting his temples hard. After several attempts, the bone repositioned and stopped sticking into his gray matter, allowing him to stand up with difficulty.

Kad used the little force remaining in his hands to remove the remnants of the fibers hanging from his arms, releasing blood from the wounds that were not closing.

_Stupid Akkadian, I'll have you killed later. – Caucasus hardly stated as he staggered outward, bumping into one of the walls in the process.

_Coward! – Kad insulted, being able to take his weapon from the ground and leave in pursuit.

A mistake, given his affected eyesight, led Caucasus to lose his balance and stumble over a step, giving Kad enough time to get to him. Unable to get up in time, he was approached with a kick that broke one of his ribs. Caucasus simulated great pain, but as his adversary approached, he inhumanly extended his arm, and with his sharp fingernails he severely cut Kad's neck, falling flat on his face as he recoiled. The roman king stood up willing to escape, and passed exhausted over the body of one of the soldiers.

He heard footsteps behind him and turned, to find Kad almost upon him, bleeding profusely from his throat, sword in hand, launching a relentless quadruple attack aimed at different heights. The fourth offensive in the series could neither be dodged nor stopped, and from the outside in, it severed the man's calf, it hanging grotesquely like the weight of a pendulum. Caucasus, dejected, collapsed to the ground, where the other fallen lay. Unwilling to surrender, he took the deceased's short sword and aimed it at his enemy.

Kad slammed the sword, which Caucasus was using to protect himself as best as he could, trying to recover his lost limb by holding it in place, until a blow to his hand caused him to release his main fortification, leaving the king defenseless and with two of his fingers missing. Immediately, Kad pressed one knee against his chest and took him by the short hairs without a word. The blood flowing from his throat fell on the defeated man's left eye, forcing him to close it.

Caucasus, taking him by the throat and nailing his thumbs to the wounds, felt the breath of death coming to him. _No! I'll give you anything you want! - he managed to scream, before his head rolled away.

PART 39: DIVIDE AND CONQUER

Kad, barely recovered, still stained with his blood, that of enemies and loved ones alike, climbed up to his brute and rode in haste to the villa of Remo. His thirst seemed to be unquenched. A group of Roman soldiers passed by, staring at him, but daring not to stop him.

He didn't make it to the villa. Argosio came out to halt him, leading a large but battered group of soldiers, the reconquest had been a short failure. _Akkadian, I need to talk to you. Now... – he shouted.

_Lead on. – answered Kad, whose heart and mind had been tempered by the fire of suffering.

The two rode at a prudent distance from each other, to one of the main squares. The square was relatively intact, with its grass trampled and uprooted, but with its stone benches standing, as well as the trees. The villagers and some soldiers ran through the streets. Many carried bags of grain and flour recently looted from the kings' barns, while continuing to cheer for the savior, the generous Etruscan puppet and king Tarquinius.

Finally they both dismounted and moved closer until being ten paces away. They kept staring into each other's eyes, all confidence shattered. A faint bubble of silence and stillness was drawn around the two men, while chaos and violence reigned outside, the strong against the weak. Kad finally destroyed the calm.

_Argosio - he spat out - Circe has been murdered. Mejai and Porpé, both dead. None of your men protected them.

Argosio took a long time to respond, tightened by his own hatred, with a knot in his throat. _I'm sorry.

_You ordered your soldiers to leave.

_I didn't order that. - he defended himself serenely.

_What did you order then?

_To... leave if they thought the area was quiet.

Kad took a few moments before continuing. _When I needed you, you failed me. - he sentenced with bitterness.

_We're outnumbered, what did you want me to do, huh? Look around you. I did something to remedy it. You, on the other hand, were busy with your little games, or your conspiracies.

_Conspiracies?

_I'm told you went after Remo's head. Why did you kill him? For revenge? Or was it to keep the Etruscan gold all to yourself, traitor?

Kad looked at him in awe. _I went for Romano's life, and I took it. His hooded men were the perpetrators of my family's crime.

_You have gone mad – he remarked with sadness – who was in Romano's villa, was Remo. He hid there when the city was taken. The hooded men responded to him. And I can affirm this because until just a moment ago I was with Romano and I spoke with him. He explained several things to me.

_That's impossible, you're lying. – Kad denied.

_I'm not lying, you've simply gone mad as a doornail. A dangerous madman.

Kad advanced two more steps and faced him screaming in anger. _And what did the so-called Romano tell you, huh? You insolent idiot, wretched bastard! My family's dead, that's all I asked of you.

_You piece of horse dung! I'll tell you what he told me. – replied Argosio, burning in anger – He told me something that makes sense, that you made up that scroll to deceive us, to get my men away from the city, and so allow the troops to pass, just as the plan of the deranged Remo was. That you were both plotting with

Descénidos to deliver the city to Etruria, and that you did it all for some filthy riches.

_That's wrong! The one who planned that is Romano, who is now gone. – Kad defended himself pointing his sword at his former partner.

_You say it's wrong but it all checks out. I can't trust you anymore.

_Imbecile, you say that after you fail me. – he insulted with his weapon held high.

Argosio looked down on him with deep contempt. _I'll tell you what we'll do. – he suddenly cut off with his arms folded – And you're going to accept it, no matter what. This war, if I may call it a war, is lost. They are more than us, they are better organized and we are scattered here. So you're going to get on that colt, and ride to the villa. I'll follow you behind. You're gonna talk to Romano, and then you can go collect your filthy gold. Nobody ever wants to see you around here again.

Kad, wrapped in an insane fury, climbed on his steed and rode at horseback toward the villa, followed closely by Argosio. Arriving at the fields before the dwelling, the soldiers set out to avoid the passage, but they moved away when they saw the sign of their Chief's raised hand. Kad dismounted and headed for the entrance. The soldiers flanking the door looked at him with deep grudges in their eyes, his treachery having already been rumored, but they did not stand in the way. Kad entered, followed the brightest corridor into a large, perfectly lit room.

The walls of the shimmering hall were decorated with figures of horsemen and women with pitchers, the columns painted in a candid blue with yellow details, beautiful vases of lustrous shine of various bright colors adorned one of the corners with taste and style. The furniture, chairs and armchairs were lined with fine fabrics and covered with cushions. Everything was glowing, everything was beautiful. In the center and dominating the place, Romano waited with a gorgeous copper cup full of wine. He was clothed in a light tunic of linen, unadorned, his feet barefoot, seated with his legs crossed one on top of the other, for a King requires no jewels, nor a crown. Greeted Kad with a cordial but short nod, he looked majestic, eternal, omnipotent.

Beside him, sitting casually on the stairs and dressed in war attire, a man of dark complexion, short black hair followed him with his gaze, one of total victory. At his feet rested a bronze helmet, a leather bag and a cup. A curved sword hung from his waist. It was Caprico, the Etruscan Commander.

_Akkadian, you finally arrived. Leave us alone, please gentlemen. – he asked the soldiers present, Romans and Etruscans alike – Would you like a drink, traitor?

Kad did not respond, he stood still, looking confused at the return of a deceased man.

_Apparently not. - closed the king when the guards withdrew, taking a sip from his goblet - I will not invite you to sit down because this will be a brief meeting, I must attend to more important matters with the gentleman present here. - he said, pointing to Caprico.

_We meet again, Akkadian - Caprico greeted without a hint of kindness. His voice was hoarse, consequence of a wound on his neck that he could never close properly, centuries ago.

_As you know, Rome has lost. - continued Romano, with a deep voice that echoed with itself - It had lost a long time ago, even before your intrigues with Descénidos, before Remo's insanities that would have killed us all. - he marveled, drawing a wide circle with the cup, without a single drop of wine jumping out - Fortunately... you've already taken care of the madman of my former companion and co-governor, that's what I've been told.

_And fortunately as well, Descénidos has already paid with his life for his conspiracies. - laughed Caprico.

Kad raised his menacing edge, dripping with the blood of his victims of the day. _I gave you death, only moments ago, how come you're here?

Caprico and Caucasus looked at each other, curious. _Evidently madness is contagious, Akkadian. – said the Etruscan in a mocking tone.

_No doubt, my friend Caprico. This man has already lost his senses. – lamented the king.

_Enough of this babble! What sorcery is this?! – Kad shouted angrily.

_I'll tell you what happened, and I hope you to understand in your insanity. – Romano continued – In an act of treason, perhaps justified or not, you have murdered one of your kings, Remo. I don't know why you did it, maybe you confused one with the other and you were actually after my neck. It doesn't matter anymore, if it hadn't been for you, I would have gone tomorrow to expire him. – he took a nearby pitcher, and poured wine into two cups, offering the second to the Commander of Etruria – In fact... I like it better this way, serving justice on Remo myself, the founding king who sought our annihilation – he nodded resolutely – and so it will be told. Your presence in the history of Rome is not necessary.

_You... you both... you planned it all! – Kad yelled swinging his sword from one monster to another – Your ambition is sickening. You are not aiming for glory or dominion, but to dispossess, to subdue, to destroy, for the sake of pleasure. You disgust me.

465

_The feeling is mutual, Akkadian. – dismissed Romano with anguish in his eyes - You don't know your role in... - he made a gesture, looking for the right term - this theatrical piece. You are content to go out on adventures and do what your heart dictates, without realizing that this is a story about power, where the winners split the world among themselves. You don't have the flair for it, therefore, your character is either superfluous, or a pawn for the protagonists. Us, in this case. – he closed, looking at Caprico, who replied with an accomplice smile – I know what you think, Akkadian. You want revenge for being used, but on the other hand, if you fight us, you'll lose. And even if you do achieve a victory, it will be brief. Because you'll come out battered and many soldiers are waiting outside. There is also Argosio, from whose grace you have fallen, and will have no trouble finishing you off – he said with a huge smile.

Caprico drew his sword from the sheath, but he was held back by Romano. _There is no need, he will do nothing – he stood up, radiant, to approach Kad. He approached until the tip of the sword was less than a palm away from his neck – he won't do anything because he knows he will die if he fights, and deep down... he doesn't care about Rome, or us, or anyone else. All he cares about is himself. He's selfish in extreme.

Caucasus, standing in front of Kad where only he could see him, slowly changed his face to Argosio's, a fact that was greeted with an expression of total confusion, retreating. _I know because I know him as if I were his best partner – said the copy of Argosio – or better yet... – he changed again, imitating the Akkadian's own physiognomy, laughing – I know him as if he were myself. Now leave, infamous. Your services are no longer useful. – spat the demon with contempt, adopting Remo's face – I have everything I need right here. – he stole the face of the late Romano again and returned to his seat next to Caprico.

Kad snorted in anger and frustration at the scene, but then tried to calm himself by slowly exhaling the grim air from his lungs. He slowly sheathed his weapon and approached the door. Turned around, determined, to face the conspirators before leaving. _Maybe you're right, this is all about a battle for power. That this is a story without heroes, only villains. In that case, I will be a villain for you, too.

He left the house and surrounded himself again with dark stares. Argosio, still mounted, raised his hand as a sign to not move. Kad walked up to him.

_We've been deceived, bewitched. – Kad snapped at the unpleasant look on the face of the Chief of the guard, responding in kind – They wanted to divide us.

_And they succeeded, without a doubt. Like I said before, I don't want to see you again. And if I do, I'll bury my blade in your throat. – he hurt, with his hand still raised.

Kad stared with sadness, perhaps dismay, at his former companion, now a deadly enemy. _Neither do I, and the same threat weighs upon you.

He turned, but he couldn't find his horse. Instead, a soldier with a raging temper approached him and gave him another one, rested and sturdy. Kad mounted it and rode away, never to return.

PART 40: KNOWLEDGE IS POWER

Carl Arthur Fisher paused for a moment to open his umbrella. Not because he resented getting wet from the rain that had begun to fall, but to put some distance between McCarthy's widow and her son Freddy, who were now walking a few steps ahead of him. Behind the group carrying the coffin to its final resting place was his own wife, Carmen, a short, blond-cheeked woman with bulging cheekbones, and bright, sad blue eyes. A little further on, taken from the widow's elbow, his daughter Lara walked forward, a young woman with wide hips, who had inherited her mother's eyes and nose, and her father's jaw. Fisher, looking at the scenery, felt embarrassed and suffocated.

Guilty.

He would rather walk on glass with his bare feet than on that place. The gray Sunday threatened to dye everything with sadness. He deeply hated the fact that it was raining, it seemed like a disgusting cliché of a bad war movie. The cemetery, a tree-lined place with dull green pastures and tombs of all sizes and shapes in granite, marble and steel, extended in all directions.

After a long journey along the concrete tiles, the procession arrived at the final resting place of the warrior. They gathered around a small podium, where a man in a black suit helped an elderly priest with scarce gray hair to climb, while holding an umbrella over his head. As he reviewed his notes and tested the microphone, the crowd, about thirty people, became quiet as they waited for the service to begin.

_Ladies, gentlemen, comrades in arms, colleagues, family and friends, we are gathered here to honor and celebrate the life of General John Aaron McCarthy. - began the religious.

Even now, Fisher had preferred to keep a prudent distance from his family and his great friend. The umbrellas covered his expressions, but at least he knew they weren't looking at him. Except someone.

_A regrettable death, no doubt. - said Thomas Hendrich slowly, positioning himself to the left of Fisher, who did his best to ignore the comment - But there are deaths that have a purpose. All soldiers die for one, for their nation.

Fisher looked at his side. Hendrich was dressed in black from head to toe and also carried an umbrella. Just arrived at his other side, and pretending not to pay attention, the personal lackey of the above-mentioned,

Ashton. Fisher slowly began to boil in anger, and clenched his fists to the point of harm. But he didn't say anything.

_Of course - Hendrich continued - one cannot help but wonder... - he almost whispered in the ear, without looking at him- how many more? How many more sacrifices are enough?

_...where he met his wife, Maria Elizabeth Cohen, and who would be the mother of his only son, Frederick McCarthy. - spoke the priest.

_That's up to us, Fisher. We, who have the power of decision. - Hendrich pecked.

Fisher couldn't contain himself anymore. _In that case, why don't you decide to go to hell for once?

Hendrich smiled fleetingly. _Because I want to pay my respects, and I have orders - he turned to look him in the eye, to get a burning, hateful look in return - that are basically to talk to you, and to give you information so that you may understand. Please - he asked with one hand on his chest - do not misinterpret our intentions. We just strive for what's best for our country, same as you.

_Working for a monster is not the best thing for anyone, but the monster.

_I understand your position, but you're wrong, you lack the facts to get the full picture. I'm going to reveal something interesting to you. – he said quietly, looking at the podium – We know that you've been in contact with someone. From Germany.

Fisher squinted his eyes and let his jaw drop slightly.

_Don't be surprised, Carl, and please don't underestimate us. We've been tracking your movements. You are a great strategist but your security measures against espionage fall short of being too basic.

_What the fuck do you want from me? – he insulted as low as he could, getting some disapproving looks from people close by. His wife reproached him silently. He didn't care.

_...an impeccable military career, where he won both awards and friendships – was heard through the loudspeakers.

_This is no place to discuss these matters, how about a little distance? I have something to offer you that I assure will be of your interest.

After pondering for a few seconds, Fisher followed the Chief of Intelligence under a small roof over a mausoleum several meters away. The fat droplets hit the metal roof making a scandal.

Hendrich loosened his tie slightly after closing his umbrella. _See, Fisher, we identified your contact. His name is Matthias Weissman, and he is not what you think. He's non-human too, are you aware?

From the General's reaction, he had no idea. Hendrich continued. _Not only that, but he's part of one of the factions I told you about. That faction is looking to get hold of the levers of power that you fear so much, with those ramifications of terror that only God knows where they end up. You must realize... you're negotiating with a potential enemy of this country.

_What I may or may not have talked to him does not concern you - Fisher defended himself - it's not a security issue, nor a threat. It was a private affair.

_Do you really think he's not a threat? Everything that comes from one faction or the other, or what remains of them, is dangerous. That's why we planned their demise. I advise you to approach the right side, General. Ours.

_The one who kills their own soldiers? You will deny it Hendrich, but I know you had something to do with McCarthy's death. So why don't you just accept it and tell me what the fuck you want?

_There's nothing to accept, that was just an accident. But about the other thing... here it is. Mr. Perius asked me in particular to bring his words to you. He wants you to meet him.

_Never! - closed Fisher.

_To meet him - he said again - because he will offer to be at your orders.

Fisher looked at him strangely, in his visceral hatred, out of balance at that phrase. _Who? The monster at my orders?

_If you want to call him a monster, that's up to you. But yes, that's right.

_What is he plotting now? - he asked in confusion.

_As I told you, it's a sign of goodwill. He wants you, from now on, to be the head of the operations, and he'll do as you wish. See?

_It's a trap.

_Quite the opposite. That's the best gesture he could have. If you agree, tell me where and when you want to meet with Perius.

Fisher took a long moment, looking at the dark green grass growing carelessly in a bronze vase beside him. A slight grimace surfaced before replying. _All right. I'll meet him, at the place I'll instruct. I'll get in touch with you at the end of the day, so you can have it delivered.

_Good. - Hendrich smiled casually - I'm glad of your disposition. I'll wait for your call then.

Hendrich made a formal military salute, and went over to Ashton's, said a few words in his ear, and they both set off along the tiled path. Fisher returned near the podium, where he had been before. He was scheming something new. What Hendrich didn't know is that his ...non-human colleague... had sent him a lot of encrypted data about the research in a secret laboratory, and had already translated it thanks to a free – and anonymous – program on the Internet. It wasn't perfect, but it was understandable. He couldn't wait to get to a quiet place and read it through, knowing it had accurate information about resistance and behavior to various stimuli. Weaknesses. What if he found the right vulnerability? What if he set up a meeting in a controlled location? If by any chance, that damn monster fell into a trap? That information was power. He carefully felt the roll-up screen in his pocket, the key to everything.

No, he couldn't wait.

As soon as the formalities of the meeting were over, he left his wife and daughter at home and, with a cheap excuse, left again. He let himself be guided to the other side of town by the self-drive, and programmed it to go around a few times before being parked, in a small effort to mislead. He entered and sat down in a slightly crowded coffee house, whose tables were separated by partitions, giving some privacy. There he began to read carefully all the material translated along with the referential, in those cases where he had doubts with the words. He skipped most of the performance graphs, statistics, insignificant percentage variation sheets on several different topics, while taking notes on paper of everything he could think of. From there, the answer he needed would stand out. As the hours went by and several coffees with milk later, he sighed deeply, and dedicated himself to completing the final and perhaps more arduous step: sorting his notes into something coherent.

Exhausted, he got up to stretch his legs, went outside for a moment and phoned home announcing that he would be back very soon. He gathered some steam, and returned at a steady pace to his improvised work desk. He slowly went through his second notebook, now sorted into themes.

The first part had been devoted to everything that converged or made mention of elements that he had already read in the North American report, and later on, those that had a tangential connection. Weissman's report confirmed many of the hypotheses presented in the crude paper he had reviewed in his late friend's one.

The subject of the activated code was the main one. They called it a "control code", but he didn't understand why. It was certainly more professional than just "junk code". Effective methods of transmission, including a hundred or so similar forms of blood-borne transmission, by tissue grafting and from which part of the body they proceeded, considering the less likely, not too conspicuously, flakes of skin, saliva and other body fluids. By the way, there was no mention of any kind of sexual reproduction, as if it were understood that it was not possible. Maybe it was part of other reports not included. Mysteriously, there was an egotistical component in the contagion, without it there was no manifestation in the carriers. The component, however, could be supplemented by presenting the test subject with a life-threatening hazard, in which case it increased the likelihood of manifestation. It was remarkable that, at least in part, becoming a monster was a voluntary decision of someone who wanted everything for themselves, or had a fervent sense of survival.

One section, a little out of place from the others, reported on the problems that the climatic conditions gave to the "troops". He was not surprised by the heat and solar radiation, but by the fact that it no longer spoke of experiments but of combat troops. Unfortunately, the report was a paper scan, the dates of which (among other things) had been scratched off with a marker, preventing them from being read. There, it mentioned other obvious weaknesses, but did not describe them, which he found strange. In addition, it considered the performance of these regiments in extreme conditions, such as the desert, jungles, and even radioactive areas.

The next part was devoted to the most interesting notes on experiments on test subjects (who were again subjects rather than troops, although he did not know whether it was before or after the previous section) in terms of exposure to various pathogens and how organisms fought against them. The list was immense, in most infections with bacteria, spores and parasites, the results indicated, to a greater or lesser degree, a substantial difference against an ordinary human. The differences were smaller in comparison to viruses or harmful chemicals.

And this is where his notes came to a standstill. The report listed three different types of test subjects: the "infected", who had been previously exposed to the control code, and two others that he had a hard time understanding. One he wrote down as "accelerated", whose explanation he found meaningful much later. And the other was "superior human", an incognito that he left until the end. The "accelerated" ones were much better than the "infected" ones, and initially he did not understand what the difference was. But all this was overshadowed by the "superiors", whose results were... unprecedented. In all categories, they far outperformed the other two types. Fisher scratched his eyebrow again, as he had when he first read it, cursing from within, as he suspected that the wretched demon Perius might well fit the description.

Continuing with the notes, he began with what was new. There was a long file on the benefits of a certain special serum that they named Proteplasm in its new standardized version, a **P–R17**, largely superior to the previous one, **P–R14**, which offered extra concentrated doses so that any *new-man* (term he quickly understood as a synonym of non–human) could feed without depending on other external sources. He wondered where the chemical would be obtained, and what properties he could exploit to his advantage. He recalled that his countrymen had ventured into the manufacture of serums to feed these spawns, but did not reach so far in their research. This line of investigation would take a secondary position for the time being.

He reread the following section of notes: in which he had compiled everything related to these "accelerated". As he was able to rescue, using more common sense than scientific data, they were different in that they had been exposed to a type of designed ...phagocytary? cells that changed (or devoured perhaps, the terminology was not clear) more quickly normal to... non–normal cells. This significantly reduced conversion times and provided faster results.

Then, Fisher came to the most puzzling part. These strange *superiors, Überlegener mensch*, in their original terminology, were not infected, but, as he was able to elucidate, already had all the innate properties, or rather were born that way. The cause was obviously genetic manipulation of embryos that, by means of an artificial uterus, had managed to build babies with the same capacities as an *advanced adult*, a term that he did not fully understand, as it was a given as obvious, but which clearly seemed to indicate a monster of the scope of which he himself knew. Another long section made sporadic mention of different methods that, strangely, not only did not try to improve these individuals but, on the contrary, to limit them as much as possible. The reason? Hard to determine. The only apparent cause for this was the original composition of the embryos, which were derived from two mysterious entities: the *alpha* and *beta* subjects, whose characteristics were repeatedly censored throughout the documents. And only once did it mention a *gamma* subject, in a totally different context, that suggested a tactical need. The number of question marks he drew next to these notes was exaggerated.

Another strong area of doubt was the allusions to an elite unit called *Spearhead*, whose composition seemed to be purely and exclusively of *limited superiors*, although it did not say limited in what way. The report recklessly pitched out the proposal not to limit them, creating an improved version, tentatively called "*Hellebarde*" (or translated, Halberd), this being the easiest way to the main objective of the whole affair: the creation of the ultimate being. As to the fate of these recommendations, there were no indications. Anyway, the conclusions were devastating. These people had finally found their super soldier, and were already testing their most effective combinations. He feared he would succeed in destroying a monster, only to have seven more take its place, as if it were the head of a Hydra, and himself a quasi-heroic Hercules. He drummed his fingers on the table without finding a satisfactory conclusion to that terrible scenario, and so he continued.

Underneath it all, he wrote his own conclusions, to see if now, a few minutes later and slightly wiser, he agreed on what to do. The difficulty of planting an explosive attack was extremely high. If the monster itself was unaware of the existence of detonating material, some of his followers would do so, leaving him in serious trouble. The same thing happened if he decided on a fire trap. Electrify the floor or a door? Didn't seem like an option either. The use of firearms was flatly ruled out, as he could only carry a concealed pistol that did not raise suspicions because of its size, which greatly reduced his offensive capacity. In addition, he doubted the effect that a lead miniature would have against a century-old aberration... or perhaps a millennial one.

Then, an idea came in half a sip from his mug. He went over his notes frantically, until he found the phrase. And there it was. Of course! So hard to detect, so powerful at the same time. Radiation.

Something that wasn't even supposed to be there... invisible, undetectable, deadly. Yes! That would work. A soft smile began to slowly creep into Fisher's face.

He had to take all the necessary precautions but it was possible. He outlined several courses of action, listing possible places to plant the artifact.

Not just any artifact: a High Power Microwave Emitter, which was stored in the Special Weapons area of the Base. The potency of the microwaves, and their capability to be concentrated in a limited area made them perfect. No noise, no lights, no nothing. He could transport it himself with a cart. Install it nearby, and even stay in the same room as the target without fear of being burned.

The monster, as he knew, was particularly weak to high energy doses, so it should have a greater (and faster) effect on him than any other. A few moments of doubt, as he's absorbing the radiation, would be all he needed. And he himself would see to it that Perius stood still, exploiting another of his weaknesses, his tongue. Question by question, word by word, believing that he had bought the game, Perius would find his end. And once he had absorbed enough, there'd be no turning back.

He tipped all the weight of his back against the backrest, really happy. He finally had a plan.

PART 41: REBELLION

It was not until Syra was finally satisfied with the security measures to approach the collapsed base of Crest in Marseille that they finally entered. She first, followed behind by Vogel Drescher, Liam MacOwen and Charles Dipson. There was not even a soul in sight, watching the door, or inside the mansion. The cold of the night dared to slip through the holes in the windows, whistling furiously and causing the blinds to collide, so that even the most irreligious would spontaneously believe in ghosts and the hereafter.

Syra stopped a few steps away from the reinforced trap door leading to the basement, a little hesitant.

_What's the matter? – Vogel whispered.

_I'm not sure what code to call out. It's a... delicate moment we're going through. – she mumbled in reply.

The four of them looked at each other for a moment, doubtful.

_There is not a generic one? – inquired Dipson.

Syra squatted down, took the metal ring from the trap door and shook it three times, then twice, then twice, then twice more, making echoes all over the building.

Seconds passed by without any news. Vogel turned to see MacOwen, who simply shrugged. A full minute had passed, when the Irishman finally decided to lay one hand on the Shadow's shoulder, but before he could tell her to try an alternative, a series of faint blows were heard below. Three quick hits, then three more spaced out.

_Yeah, it's me, damn it. Open up already. – Syra snapped, irritated by the situation. – Who's there? Silfo? Open up.

Steel against rusted steel shrieked in protest as the door was lifted, and the silhouette of a head poked out of the blackened background. _I had to make sure, you know how it is. – said the silhouette of Silfo.

_If you have such passion for security, you would have waited until the sequence was completed, you idiot. – insulted Syra with particular familiarity.

_And what about them? – pointed to the silhouette.

_They're with me. They helped defend Aegis. – Syra turned to look the Dutchman sideways. – *Some* of them helped. – rectified.

One by one, the newcomers went down the poorly lit corridor of Crest's basement, following Silfo, a wide, bald, muscular man, with long pants and a t-shirt made of his own hardened skin, albeit in actual boots.

_Wait, Silfo – MacOwen begged – Before we go on, we have to know, is Eylem here?

Silfo stopped short, and pressing a fist against the wall he responded, strangely spacing his words, wearily. _No... she's... not here. And that's the biggest problem right now.

_What do you know about the whole deal at Aegis? – Dipson consulted.

_That it went very badly, that they all died. We were just discussing that. Come on in. – he invited, opening the door in front of him.

Within the southern chamber, sitting on boxes, ramshackle furniture, and any chair-like objects, were seven Shadows in silence, inspecting those who had entered. Cigarette smoke filled the third highest portion of the place. Silfo sat down on two stacked boxes, took his cigarette, and motioned with a wave of his hand to the quartet to take seats, in nonexistent places.

_Good evening, sorry to interrupt your meeting. – greeted Vogel.

_It's no bother, you're just in time. I have a lot to ask you. – said a voice in the background, which Anzhelika considered her ordinary, unchanged voice.

_All right, so do we. – said the Irishman MacOwen.

485

The columns of smoke continued to rise slowly to the ceiling, being, for the moment, the only thing that dared to move in the tiresome tension that reigned. Drescher felt, as so many times before, that inexplicable sensation that ran through his spine that forced him to act in moments of tension to try to decompress it. _Ladies, gentlemen, we have a lot to talk about, how about I start? - he said, with a charismatic smile.

_Go ahead. - a shadow sitting on a bench near the door said, with a cigarette hanging carelessly from his lips. His hair was short, reddish, with a bushy beard of the same color, and a black overcoat that reached his heels.

_Know that the battle at the Aegis Palace was one of those, that forever, define the spirit, temper the mind and body in the fierce struggle. - Vogel Drescher paused in his speech, looking around and reading the general annoyance. Nobody wanted to hear that. Instead, he decided to go for an ultra-short version, without details, or odes to bravery - ...Well, I'll leave the details for another time. What does matter - pointed out - is that when León's troops arrived they did it by air, we noticed that they were using "unsuitable" weaponry to fight us, including - he wanted to stress but could not continue, two Shadows began to protest with shouts, being silenced by another three with the same tone.

486

_Stop it! – Lika asked for the fourth time, finally being effective. – We already know your opinions, we want to hear the facts.

Vogel rasped to clear his throat. _Continuing, after we managed to sneak out of the enemy, was when the worst happened. The nuclear attack.

_How's that you sneaked out, huh? – Silfo asked impatiently.

_There are a series of underground caverns under the Palace, thanks to which we were able to get out of the situation. – commented Liam MacOwen.

_Let's get back to the point. – said a Shadow sitting to Lika's right, a woman of extremely white skin, jet hair down to her shoulders and a frown that lasted forever. – Who the hell dropped the bomb?

_No, that's not the point, Ginebra, but whether or not Eylem knew what would happen! – accused the androgynous shadow sitting in the western corner, dressed in a leather jacket full of belts, a woolen hat and a nervous dagger that flew between the fingers.

The screams flew chaotic in all directions, like paper planes in a whirlwind. Suddenly, a clang of broken boards stopped all the voices. Dozens of small and medium-sized objects began to dance on the floor, stumbling against the feet of those present. Everyone watched, somewhat astonished, as MacOwen re-sheathed his enormous sword after destroying one of the nearby shelves with a single blow in a visceral act, which completely diverged with his calm voice. _Enough, gentlemen. This outburst must not continue.

A piece of a machine gun, which had fallen on the only table in the center of the room was waving, rebelliously, a small spring with a screw in its tip, producing a singular metallic sound.

Dipson raised a hand, in a respectful gesture to ask for permission to speak. _I see that we are not agreeing on the interpretations, but if my hearing does not fail me, I have been able to determine two main approaches. One that resolutely defends Eylem, understanding that she would not deliberately expose her elements, in order to win a prize, which would still be diffuse, something that would not make complete sense. The other one accuses Eylem of some sort of pact with León, although I do not quite comprehend what it is based on.

_It's simple. – Lika said shaking a personal assistant. – I stole this from one of León's main bases, *Prima-Gestalt*. After some effort I managed to decrypt the files. – she waited a few seconds, in order to gain dramatic momentum. – And here are the results.

_But how to know if they're real? – added Ginebra Annet in a mocking tone.

_You already asked that. – spat another, a thin man sitting on the floor against a wall, with deep brown eyes, a thick black and gray jacket, and apparently the only Shadow who dared to wear white sneakers.

_She still won't answer. Plus she said getting in and out was easy. They could have planted it on purpose.

_I know what I said, Ginebra. – Lika spoke – Yes, I mentioned that it was relatively easy for someone of my level, but the security wasn't bad. It was suspicious, though. – she took a moment to leave the device on the table and grimace. – Anyway, it's a matter for another time, the important thing is the contents.

_Can I see it? – asked Syra before taking the assistant. She stumbled upon an extremely long open file, lengthy enough to arch an eyebrow. _I won't read all this now. What does it say?

_That we were betrayed. – Silfo accused.

_It's a strategic analysis of the forward strike against us, reporting the use and type of weapons. They were limited, on purpose. – Anzhelika explained.

_So they wanted to harm us less! – shouted the androgynous shadow.

_Why would they do that? – shouted a woman with short, curly hair, rounded features and a long, extremely low-cut dress, standing up at the same time.

_Calm down, please. - Liam asked - In fact we, after the fight, thought about exactly that, to come to a similar conclusion.

_Well, well... let's say it's true. That León and his men limited themselves on purpose, why did they do it? It indicates nothing more than a bad decision on their part. - said Ginebra in a hoarse voice.

_We don't know, but the fact that Eylem's missing indicates something. It is undeniable. - stirred Silfo.

_Did you Seek her presence? - Lika asked.

_Yes. - assured Ginebra - I already did. She's somewhere in eastern France, moving in a way that makes it hard for me to know where. It's on purpose, obviously.

_Speaking of which... If I give you a name and a picture, could you find a person?

Ginebra looked at her strangely. _Possibly, has it anything to do with this?

_No, it's personal. You owe me a favor... - said Lika with an accomplice smile.

_Let's get back to the subject, please! - said the red bearded Shadow.

_I think Eylem's behavior is extremely suspicious. In fact, I refuse to follow her orders until the matter is resolved. – the androgynous Shadow sentenced pointing a knife threateningly.

_I agree. – seconded the man in the jacket – My loyalty at this moment is to Crest.

_Or what's left of it. I mean, us. – lamented Silfo, pointing a circle at those present – including them, I suppose. – added, pointing a finger at MacOwen, Drescher and Dipson.

_I think the same, what about you guys? – Lika shot, shaking her head at those who were not yet proclaiming themselves.

After a few seconds of hesitation, the long dress Shadow raised her hand. _All right. I understand your position and although by no means I like the whole thing, I agree that we all deserve an explanation. A good explanation. – specially pointed out – And until that happens, I agree with you, I won't follow anyone's orders.

A kind of tacit agreement was beginning to be woven into the eyes of those present. Continuing with Syra who gave her support, she was seconded by everyone else. Ginebra was the last to speak. _If everyone agrees, I'll have to, as well. We are a team. And I also want an explanation.

_Now that we agree, what do we do? – the reddish beard Shadow consulted in general.

_Spy. - said Silfo.

Liam MacOwen slowly pushed Drescher out of the room a few steps away, approached his ear and whispered. _Vogel, please be careful not to say anything about what you mentioned on the way back here.

_What, exactly? - the Dutchman muttered, staring at him.

_What you said about Caucasus. That he may still be alive.

A handful of minutes later, while in the basement the next steps were still being discussed, under a lonely, broken lamppost near the mansion's entrance, Ginebra approached with ease despite the low temperatures.

_What's this favor I'm supposed to return, huh? - consulted the Seeker.

Lika extended a photograph. _This.

_Who's she?

_The fucker who fell on Lykaios. - said with a grudge as she removed the strands of hair that had fallen on her face due to the wind.

Ginebra looked down at the photo. It was from a military file. Underneath it, handwritten was a name:

Sergeant Antoinette Soleil. She glanced at Lika again, waiting for an answer as to why she was bothering. However, she understood without asking. She placed a hand on the photograph and closed her eyes. _Give me a few minutes to concentrate.

PART 42: A RAINBOW CAGE

The Astro GT was a particular car. It allowed its user to be controlled by voice and regardless of distance, since it links up with a personal assistant perfectly. Among the commands it included interaction with other devices with humanoid presence simulation. Basically, you can ask it to leave your garage, travel across town, pay for groceries automatically at the supermarket or elsewhere and go home. The only thing it can't do is put the boxes and bags in the trunk by itself. But the fact that it was a mobile receptacle of permissions to use bank accounts, access to housing, to real items was undoubtedly revolutionary. Not because the technology didn't exist, but because of the *concept*. A machine designed to operate on its own in a human world. The company that made it was really bold.

After the bursting of the cryptocurrency bubble in 2028, and then the sharp fall in mortgage lending all around the world in 2033, the global economy had become incredibly conservative, and was raising its head as slowly as it could, trying to keep as much gold in its hands as possible, a historic haven of value. Innovative products were the exception rather than the rule. Industries with a promising future, such as space mining or robotics, had been frozen for an indefinite period. For, as economists now say, value can be created simply by not going out looking for more, by abusing artificial scarcity.

But the Astro was the ideal vehicle for a person like Commander Matthias Weissman, who detested using his men as small-time juniors. Those who put their lives at risk for others deserved respect, and he made sure that those at his charge felt and knew so. That had not been different in his normal life, nor in *the other*. Despite having been *converted* almost a century ago, he never got used (and never wanted to) to a nocturnal life. The work had to be done early in the morning. His own weakness to sunlight was no obstacle, it was sufficient to render the windows opaque.

And that's why the GT was a fundamental tool. And that morning, on a Monday totally distanced from a normal one, he let his machine drive him to the Waldorf IV tower in the center of Berlin, where the person who could answer the questions that refused to leave his head, Beatrix Virtanen, was waiting. León's favorite Seeker... and his own.

He never took an in-depth interest in this arcane art of finding people through magic gimmicks, even after having empirical proof that they were not charlatans. Or actually, they were, except for a select group of particularly talented beings whose predictions were statistical anomalies. No two were alike, each had a different method and varying degrees of effectiveness, but they definitely set a reliable course. Some used pendulums, others rituals, others sacrifices, but the mechanism was similar. Some intel on the wanted person allowed the Seeker to locate a clue to their whereabouts.

Beatrix Virtanen was special even in that select group, as she was also a talented Seer, and it was extremely common for her predictions of future events to come true. In fact, her effectiveness rate was low because of the measures taken to modify the outcomes of the visions.

The Astro slowed down in the underground parking lot of the building and the voice from his on-board computer told the Commander so, cutting off his train of thought. On his way out, he met with his escort, two soldiers of León's paramilitary forces, uniformed in blue and black, who greeted him and accompanied him to the elevator. One of them marked the Reception button, explaining to the Commander what he already knew, that he had to undergo an electric field scan before proceeding, a routine system that he himself had helped to establish with his collaborator and fugitive General Krupp. Had it been correctly executed at *Prima-Gestalt*, this system would have saved him considerable headaches.

Once he arrived, he was invited to check his biometric data, fingerprints, retina and secret password and measure the electric field his brain generated when typing it to confirm that he was who he promised to be. After the usual greetings, he was taken to another elevator behind the public ones, with access to the floors from the forties onwards.

It is strange, Weissman thought, that fate is like a gentle blizzard that pushes men slowly but evenly. A long ago he had decided, some years after his *change*, that matters of the heart had taken a back seat. That a partner was necessary to procreate, and then not effective, nor desirable. That once he completed the cycle of his normal life (the global average life expectancy, about ninety years?) he could devote himself 100% to his passion, the strategy. Yet here he was, approaching one meter at a time to a woman that his mind did not want to face, but his emotions did. Ironically, it was his own mind that had agreed with his heart, given the moment, with a tricky but effective ruse: information he needed. In person.

A sound announced the arrival and the doors opened. He was greeted by two security guards, not soldiers but agents of a private company owned by León. They were also under his orders despite being civilians.

_Good morning, Commander, unusual time for a visit. – one of them, in a satin jacket with a huge *Securitas* logo on his shoulder, greeted him with respect and affection.

_Good morning. Yes, possibly.

_Miss Virtanen is not usually available in the morning, how did you manage to do it? - asked the other one with a little comedy.

_Moving some influences, of course. - he closed somewhat sharply, albeit with kindness. In other conditions he would have preferred to continue the talk with his men, but he did not have the time.

_Please come in, we'll announce your presence. Take a seat in the lobby, the lady will be with you as soon as possible. - said the taller of the two, as he picked up the phone. After opening the door with two magnetic keys, they let him in.

He entered a dazzling room, decorated at the whim of its resident (or prisoner, lately). The floors glowed softly with the colors of the rainbow, filtering their soft light to the vaulted ceiling and the multitude of plants with beautiful flowers, most of them genetically designed, which dotted the place with life.

It was, without a doubt, an unblemished fusion between a home and a garden. The perfect cage. After enjoying the view of the surroundings, he took a seat in a comfortable white velvet armchair near the door and was silently grateful that he was not as irreplaceable as Virtanen.

Getting an interview with her had not been easy, leaving aside his mixed feelings. First: if he wanted to use her services, there were official channels for that purpose. And that was not the case, not even remotely, because Second: there was no one in particular to follow except the Persons of Interest who were monitored daily, and the important predictions were communicated as soon as they occurred. And Third: all communications were recorded, and what he needed was necessarily unofficial and the less record of the events the better. His own arrival at the Waldorf IV building was already too much exposure and suspicion would arise. Fortunately, recent events justified (although not entirely, to his concern) his presence.

A few minutes passed, perhaps the ideal amount to wait for, when she appeared. Beatrix was the same as when they met, decades ago. Thin, long, elegant legs hardly covered by the cloth of her black dress, a flat abdomen that fell just below her delicate breasts. Narrow shoulders caressed barely by her short brown hair crowned a face of rounded cheekbones, dimples on her cheeks and slender chin. Some filaments of her Eye Augmentation (the bionic technology that had given the graceful shot to the old-fashioned glasses, for those who could afford it) over her brown eyes glowed dimly each time the intensity of the floor light changed spectrum, striking each carbon nanotube differently.

A huge smile was drawn, out of habit, on the woman's thin lips. _Matthias, what a nice surprise.

Weissman suddenly forgot what he had planned to say beforehand. _Thank you, it's... a pleasure. - came out of his mouth, betraying him.

Beatrix put her hands together and gently sat down at a perfect distance between them, taking into account so many factors that a supercomputer would have taken at least half a second to calculate.

_Thank you for attending to my special request, Beatrix.

_Don't mention it, I'll always be there to help you. We promised, didn't we?

Weissman felt his tie suddenly tightened and had to untangle it. _W-we did. I'll try to be brief.

_No need - she answered sweetly - may I offer you some tea?

The military man waved a negative hand gesture, recomposed. _No, I will simply explain the reasons for my visit.

Virtanen smiled sadly. _Before you start, I want to know something.

The stillness began to seep in between them, locked as they were in the rainbow cage. _Do you remember the first drawing I made for you? - she said. They were both silent, staring at one another - We didn't know each other well. That time, I asked you to trust me.

_Of course I remember it. I've apologized to you for that occasion, many times.

_I know. But afterwards – after a long and uncomfortable pause, she added – years later... did you ever really trust me?

Matthias Weissman sighed out loud. _I didn't have a choice, did I? Your skills are evident.

_That has nothing to do with trust.

Weissman lowered his eyes, surrendered. He would not come out of this battle unscathed. There was no chance, really. _Beatrix, trust wasn't our problem. I trusted, and I do.

_I still keep that drawing you gave me back, you know?

A cold sweat came down the Commander's back as he felt the low blow. _No. I didn't.

_When I draw a picture, a small part of me gets impregnated in the paper. I understood that relatively recently. – she stood up serenely, went to one of the walls and after touching a panel, a hidden shelf was revealed without any sound. The woman took a drawing folder from there and returned to her place. She handed him one of the last sheets, a freehand drawing of a young girl kneeling (and crying) in a room. It seemed to have been drawn a long time ago. – Have you ever seen this person before?

_Yes, it's... Diana Monseratti? The wife of the Lithuanian president who was kidnapped by a terrorist cell. I didn't know they asked you to Seek for her.

_They didn't ask, I just did. See that painting behind the woman? - she asked, pointing to a huge mural, very detailed about a rose garden with a shack on the prairie. He waited for Matthias to assent - That painting doesn't exist. When Diana was found in the place I saw, the room was just as I drew it, except for the mural of the prairie. That came from myself. It is not the only case, in most of my drawings, I see the scenes as they are, except for one detail, big or small, which is out of place. Some told me that those are visions of things as they might have been, as they might be, others said that were the desires of the person I was Seeking. But no. They are my own desires. That's what I think.

Weissman couldn't help but appreciate the level of detail in the illustration. _Is that what you meant by a part of you remaining in your works?

_Yes. The... drawing I made of your brother was the same. - Matthias left the paper on his lap, trying to keep his anger, nostalgia and bitterness from attacking his rear. - I'm sorry, it was actually my fault. All this time.

_No. No, it wasn't. He was buried exactly where you said he was. We were late because of logistical complications. I don't even give you an iota of guilt in that operation. You did a lot more than we expected. - he let go, proud of his military pragmatism.

_Thank you, but it was my fault. I delayed the operation. The railroad tracks I drew didn't exist, but I wanted them to exist. - the awkward silence was filled by a duo of tears advancing like conquerors down the woman's cheeks - and perhaps you don't know it but a few years ago, those rail roads were built, in the place I had seen.

Weissman could feel the enemy artillery impacting fiercely on his barracks. _ Did you... did you see the future?

_It turned out to be my first prediction...

_I see. - he said, not really understanding. It would take a long time to process that information. He returned the paper, swallowing with difficulty. - Beatrix, I... I think it was a mistake coming here.

_Perhaps. I still don't know why you're here, to be honest.

_To get details of the Aegis Palace operation. - he mentioned getting up and putting his coat on.

_Oh, I see. I couldn't do anything about it, could I? - she got up, too, but her figure was dwarfed.

_Yes, but why?

Beatrix threw herself back in her armchair to gaze at the ceiling over her temple. _I don't know, Matthias. I didn't see anything.

_It was a catastrophe, with major repercussions.

_Don't get me wrong, I understand that such an event, I should have predicted it. Wait. - she went to the wall and touched another panel. This time she had to pass a retinal scan and a fingerprint before a shelf was revealed, from which she extracted another drawing folder. - This was my vision about that event - she announced, extending a sheet of paper.

The illustration looked like an aerial view of the Palace, but it was fragmented, with pieces of it floating in unusual places. Everything seemed to gravitate towards a huge black pit. By paying more attention, some figures could be distinguished in this pit. Sore faces, disembodied limbs, sorrow, grief.

_Even knowing the outcome, I couldn't relate the event to your drawing. It's very cryptic, far away from your style.

_That's right. I simply couldn't see.

_And nothing else?

Beatrix left her calm melancholy to get tense. _I... - she remained quiet a few long seconds - please don't tell León. Or anyone else, okay?

_I won't say anything.

_I... I felt that someone was preventing me from seeing, on purpose - Matthias frowned, in deep discomfort at the surprise - I felt that someone was holding a veil in front of me, that was obscuring everything. I can't explain whom, or how.

_Why don't you want to say anything? - Weissman was genuinely concerned.

_I don't know, I feel it won't be good for me to know the truth. Please, don't comment about it!

_I won't. But it leaves me uneasy, it could be an active enemy weapon that we know nothing about.

_You're going to investigate, right? - fear was tangible in her inquisitive contemplation.

The soldier stepped forward but stopped short, unable to go and comfort someone who was so special to him, a life behind. _I'll investigate, without putting you at risk. I promise. - he turned around to leave, but he spun again. - Can I ask you in return not to divulge something?

_Y-yes. Whatever you want.

_It's a small thing, and I swear I won't bother you anymore. Remember Alex Krupp?

_I think so, he was a friend of yours.

_Yes, he's a very close colleague. In the unlikely event that someone asks you to Seek for him, please report that you have seen him dead. – Beatrix opened her eyes, full of melancholy and guilt, to follow Weissman with her gaze as he walked towards the exit – Is that feasible? – he asked puzzled by the reaction.

To all answers, Virtanen nodded meekly without taking her eyes off him.

A slight, but real smile finally appeared on the lips of the man leaving. _Thank you, Beatrix.

The door closed by itself after Weissman, who was surprised that the guards were not attentive. He walked to the security desk and stared at the screen. _Is something wrong?

The nearest guard turned to see him just a second before explaining, absorbed. _The markets all over the world are falling, they say it started because of Cynatech shareholders. It has spread everywhere and there are riots in the main cities.

The other guard pivoted to see the Commander's reaction, who had not fully grasped the extent of the severe attack they had received, to the very heart of León's empire. _Our company is part of that group – said the man resignedly, wiping the sweat away under his cap – I think we are all unemployed now.

PART 43: COLLAPSE

Anxiety is a really funny thing, and it's not just about biting your nails. One recognizes it almost immediately and soon discovers, if one has any introspection, that it is useless. But getting rid of it is more than complicated. That was the torment that Amelia Alba was going through that Monday morning at the end of October. She had barely been able to sleep because of that feeling, nice by the way, that her life was taking a positive turn. Trying to control anxiety wasn't new to her, but wanting to do it because it was the right thing to do, sure was. Now she had a new job and new responsibilities. The night before was especially hard. On one hand, the strange evening with Kad's odd acquaintance, Hassan, where she participated in a conversation where she didn't comprehend a thing.

Or rather, she didn't want to. She wasn't afraid it would be dangerous because Kad wouldn't risk her for nothing. Or would he? It was unlikely, to say the least. On the other hand, like every night and when she had some free time, she devoted herself to hypnosis. She searched the Internet for hundreds of pages dedicated to it, and tried to focus on what she was learning through Kad's method, which consisted of self-deception and trying to grasp the feelings she had. She chose, on his advice, something simple: to hypnotize

507

herself in order to forget her hatred towards peaches. She really hated them. That hairy peel, the blackened and horribly grooved pit touching the red pulp, always gave her the impression that she was eating a live animal. The first few days she didn't quite understand what was doing, just looked in a mirror and said that she loved the damn peaches, with zero advance. As the week went by, she gradually discovered conflicting thoughts of favoritism and demonization of the fruit. As a result of this she had changed tactics, silencing the anti-peach thoughts, or reinforcing them each time they appeared with gentle, soft, forgiving words toward the object of conflict. The fact that she bought some at the market and was willing to have them in the fridge was an extraordinary development. There is, in the depths of the mind, a space where one can write and erase at will. Writing or removing there is not easy, but now that she knew about that space, it was a matter of finding the right method. She was getting the knack of the basics, and Kad congratulated her before leaving her at the apartment. Wow... her whole life was orbiting around him. It is dangerous to stroll like this, she thought.

Another curious thing... is how one gets used to seeing soldiers stationed on almost every corner, or tanks in traffic as if they were just another bus. The sense of tension of the first few days of the curfew had passed, to make way for one of "everything will be back to normal". Arriving at Sinolta's building, she pushed all the personal issues that beset her to the back, put on the more professional face that she got on and went in. She was well aware that she had not earned that position, but intended to deserve it with effort and dedication. Greeted her colleague whom she had become very close to since her arrival, Roxana. It could be said that they were like day and night, she knew herself to be sullen and frequented friends very little, which by the way, were no longer *real* friends. She had always found it difficult to open her deeper self with people. Roxana however, was always vibrant and with a word of encouragement about to fly off her tongue. She really liked her. Perhaps, if all goes well in her new life, she could count on a friendship again!

Immediately behind her Mr. Ruberte showed up, the company's human resources manager, who she greeted with a wide smile. He was like day and night too, but in his case, with himself. Amelia knew, or at least had a notion, of what was going on with him, so observing his behavior also served her practice of hypnosis. From the first day, when he was out of focus, a little euphoric, and seeing "good ideas" everywhere, he went through a period of silence, where it was difficult to extract a word from him even when asking him questions related to work. After his silent stage, he moved on to another crestfallen, slightly depressed one where she found him more than once doubting things he had done or said, having to confirm himself with Roxana and Amelia whether or not this or that event had happened. On the

Friday before the weekend, before leaving, he had told her that "despite everything, I am happy with your work", that would have unsettled any employee in a new position, but that she quickly linked to a half-hearted change of heart about the "good idea" of hiring her. She wouldn't give him any reason to regret it. For the moment being she liked to be there, and began her morning tasks without preamble. It was difficult for her to do so, as she was distracted by some people jogging down the corridor to the main hall. She looked up, curious, only to stumble upon Roxana's stunned look.

_Where's everybody rushing to?

_No idea. Did something happen?

A familiar face peeked through the opening of the door. It was a young man in his twenties... how come she didn't ask his age? Tall, thin, handsome. Everyone called him Frik, perhaps because of his freckles, but in truth his name was Federico, Federico Galo. He had been extra extra nice to Amelia, to the point where she thought he was flirting. Or that maybe he talked like that to every girl, or that he flirted with everyone. She still lacked a self-esteem high enough to buy the idea that someone was attracted to her. Yet there he was, staring her straight in the eye, barely taking a fleeting glance at her partner Roxana. Directing the attention to *her*.

_Good morning! How's it going in here? - greeted Frik full of energy.

_E-excellent, and you?

_Very well, I was wondering why you weren't in the main hall and came to take a look.

_What's going on in there? - Roxana interjected.

_Didn't you see anything? - he asked in surprise as he stroked his chin - A scandal in the Asian stock markets, moved on to the local markets, and spread everywhere. It's chaos! - he shouted jokingly.

A few more passed down the corridor quickly behind Frik. _Go see and tell me - Roxana said - I'll finish this spreadsheet and be right there.

Amelia and Frik left for the hall, a huge space with white walls, a floor that resembled wooden boards, and large windows facing the main avenue. Inside, everyone was crowded around three screens on the same news channel, with a reporter throwing questions at a well-known economist, a man named Viggliani. He was in a bad mood.

_Frik, at last. - a woman greeted him - and you must be Ruberte's new girl, a pleasure. - the woman was quite wide, had curly hair and perhaps too short for the shape of her head, with chubby, red cheeks. Bright blue eyes, which matched her semi-permanent smile.

_Amelia, this is Guadalupe, she works in accounting. – and with a sneer, he said later – well, she works in being my mother, too.

Guadalupe reached out her hand to Amelia with a contagious laugh. _Welcome!

Wow, she still had nothing with Frik and had already met his mother. She clamped that last thought and plunged it into the mental garbage can at breakneck speed.

After the usual greetings, Amelia set out to listen to the news. The red "Alert" and "Breaking News" banners undoubtedly helped to create a panic atmosphere. Some of the attendees cracked jokes, others were making gloomy predictions about the future.

_Amelia, you seem to have come at a difficult time. – said Guadalupe as she shook her head.

_Is Sinolta also listed on the stock exchange?

_It is. But that wouldn't be so bad. The worst news is that they have already named several companies that have fallen hard, some of our major clients. Even though we're getting it off cheap, it's gonna be hard to work through.

_I never liked the new stock market system, and then things like this happen. – said Frik with his arms folded.

_What new system? – Amelia asked.

_The one from the WTO. – Frik mentioned, but seeing a certain bewilderment on Amelia's face, he continued – All the countries in the World Trade Organization committed themselves a few years ago to a lot of things, including keeping the stock market open around the clock, every day. This causes the money flows to be even, but it also made them more volatile. There have been falls, as always, but this one is tremendous.

_Twenty-five percent in a few hours, globally. – Guadalupe explained – That hasn't been seen since '33.

Amelia felt displaced, not by her interlocutors, but by herself. At times, she was afraid to admit everything she didn't know and believed that at her age she should already know about how the world worked. It was another thing she wanted to change about herself. _Won't it go up again as usual? After all, they are cycles, aren't they?

_Sure, but how long will it take, huh? And what caused it?

Amelia went over the events of the fancy, surreal dinner in her mind, and a phrase slipped out of her mind. _Some guys from the Middle East, they sold stock on a massive scale.

Guadalupe and Frik looked at her with surprise. _How do you know that? - consulted the young man.

_A... a rumor I heard. - she evaded, preferring to keep all the details to herself.

The clamor in the background grew, several cries of surprise were hurled through the air, accompanying the images on the screen. A mob began to attack the reporter with stones, forcing him to flee. The drone filming him quickly took height as it continued to capture images. Antiriot wagons arrived throwing jets of cold water at the protesters, getting a rain of debris in return. Underneath the events, the red banner changed to different ones: "Thousands of layoffs announced" and "Bankrupt companies". The three of them looked at each other, wanting to be optimistic but failing to do so.

Ruberte appeared in the room with a frown on his face, his tie sideways and sweat running down his back. _Ladies and gentlemen, I'm attentive to the news and I understand your concern. But there's only one way to keep Sinolta afloat and that's with hard work. Everyone in your offices please, let's work for all of us. - he announced with grand gestures of his hands.

As the crowd scattered to their posts, Amelia greeted quickly and left. Frik was about to do the same, but his mother stopped him. _Where are you going in such a hurry?

_To work, where else?

_And what are you going to do about that girl?

He laughed and stood up with his arms akimbo. _No idea, what are you up to?

_I think she's a good catch. And considering it's the All Saints' Day holiday tomorrow, you could ask her out.

_That's exactly what I was thinking. – smiled the young man.

PART 44: IMPOSTOR

_But what a pleasant surprise! – the figure on the screen lively greeted – What do I owe this honor to?

_Good morning, George, I hope I'm not disturbing you on your... resting. – Leon calmly replied in front of the giant screen hanging from the ceiling of his even bigger office. He was dressed in an elegant black and grey striped suit, a spotless white shirt and a red tie of refractory material, with a ruby ribbon in the bow.

_My dear León, I haven't rested in a millennium – George exaggerated. His hair was extremely short, shaved to the sides, a complexion than resembled a Caribbean tan, which perfectly matched his clever eyes and radiant smile. He was dressed in a simple blue T-shirt, with a logo of *Penta*, the most famous men's clothing brand in the world at the time – that's for the riffraff.

_It's true. Still, thank you for answering.

_What can I do for you? – said as he joined his hands under the chin, waiting.

León raised one of his eyebrows slightly before responding. _I imagine you're aware of the financial misadventures of the day.

_Misadventures? Gee, buddy, I lost a lot of money today. But you, my friend, you have gone into meltdown – said George, the driving force behind the United States since its very inception, true founding father of America, after the separation from his former partner, León himself, with whom he had so many disputes over the control, always under Caucasus, of the Western levers of power.

_It is true that I have lost my main assets. – he answered without raising his tone a single pinch.

_The ones you needed to pay for your militias, and keep a tumultuous Europe under your fist, not to mention it's the territory and power you need to justify your seat on the Council that Perius has so kindly reformed. – George said with a wide smile full of charismatic teeth – I'd say you're in trouble. Do you need a loan?

_No, but thanks for the offer. What I wanted to ask you, is to temporarily close the stock market operations under your control, until the situation calms down.

_All of them?

_All of them.

_Oh, well. This situation may subside, but it won't transform your company's shares from garbage to money.

_It would limit my losses by approximately eighteen percent, provided it is done immediately. Which makes me curious, why haven't you done it yet? You're losing fortunes.

_My friend, you've hit the jackpot! I haven't closed them yet because I took advantage of the situation for a little experiment, since this was already a trainwreck.

_An expensive experiment, no doubt. - Leon noted.

_Very, but useful. Hey, don't think anyone's winning with all this mess. The perpetrator of this attack is paying lavish sums to cause you great damage. Shall I tell you who did it?

_If you're going to aim for Hassan, I've noticed.

_And you didn't suspect anything until today? - George pretended to be surprised.

_To be frank, no. He did his homework very well.

George snapped his lips, in negative. _Are you going to take revenge? You could use a loan - he added, mockingly.

_I will, in time. Could you tell me what this experiment is about?

_You see... friend... I'll tell you a story - began George, leaning back into his rolling chair with the hands clasped in his belly, swaying from left to right as he told

518

it – George and León have been partners for a long time. They've had their differences, of course, but the relationship remains... between its margins. George has known for a long time that León is a greedy being who loathes losing, unlike his fellow man who believes that sometimes one must lose in order to gain wisdom, experience. Knowledge. – he paused melodramatically – knowledge, for example, that León would never be so calm in a situation on the edge, like this one.

Leon listened impassively, with no chance to distinguish even the slightest expression that betrayed him.

_Don't think I'm not applauding this... new facet so serene. So Zen... of León, one I've always recommended. To take things easy, but it's just not in him.

_I don't understand you. Are you accusing me of something?

_Accusations? No. In any case, congratulations. Your imitation is excellent. Top-notch. My only criticism is that, as I see, you never had a chance to witness the real León in a situation where he loses so much and so quickly. Otherwise you'd know how he reacts: Furious, screaming out loud. – George waved his fists up, pretending to be angry – What must have happened to the good León... we'll never know, will we?

_I have lost the plot, I don't get what you're talking about, but I hope you'll stop being ridiculous, I'm not in the mood for this.

_Bah! – dismissed George – friend... don't take it like that. As for the closure of the markets, don't worry. In about twenty minutes everything will be inoperable for at least forty-eight hours. As for the other subject, my experiment seems to have been a success. So, stranger, we'll be seeing you in about six months for the Council meeting. See you soon! – George cut off communication, leaving his huge smile on the screen for a millisecond.

Leon ordered the computer to shut down completely and sighed deeply.

_He knows. – said a voice from behind.

_He suspects. It was a necessary risk to stop the losses. Are the safety deposit boxes in Switzerland being removed?

_Forget the damn boxes... all this happened because of your fixation with the Akkadian. We've been chasing him instead of paying attention to our main target. Could we just cut it out for good? That Akkadian doesn't want anything.

_No. I can't. – denied León.

The Genoese rose to his feet in a spur. _What? Why not?

_I had a dream about him.

The Genoese remained silent, seemed to weigh his options. _You didn't tell me about that dream.

The León impostor also rose to his feet, and wandered wearily toward a pitcher of water, to pour himself into a beautiful, finely crafted crystal glass. _It's the end of one you know. After climbing up the pillars of the Council, I reach the top of the tower, and go through the roof using my arm turned into a spear. So, my Spearhead destroys our enemies, and I arrive at the room full of gold and light.

_Yes, I remember it perfectly.

_I've... omitted a part. – León made time drinking the water slowly. – That room of gold and light has a carved door. A huge grey door, covered with horrifying scenes, disease, putrefaction, death. That door won't let me move forward, I know it represents the Akkadian.

_And what happens next? – asked the Genoese, trapped by the premonitory dream.

_I don't know. The dream ends right there. With me in front of the horrible gray door.

The Genoese walked slowly toward the window. _Nothing to do then. We will continue the plan as it was. Then we'll dedicate ourselves to rebuilding our assets. In any case, everything should be speeded up. We can't keep the war machine running for much longer without money. We've got to hit the nail on the head now.

_I agree. - closed León, thoughtful - Except... there will be a slight change of plans. Someone who no longer has any use for us.

PART 45: FUGITIVES

It is no coincidence that the nature of time is one of the most elusive for science and philosophy. It is not linear, nor does it pretend to be. It flows in a capricious way, even for two witnesses located next to each other, the same event takes place in a different, unique way. And there, as Antoinette Soleil ran quickly to her chosen position, just behind a massive tree from where she had control over the main entrance to that small, lonely hut in the middle of the forest, one can feel the seconds stretching overwhelmingly. Even the breath itself sounds alienated, foreign to our own lungs, an unknown force running through your throat and pharynx. What is the main reason for this change in flow? Fear perhaps? Knowing that in *there* is the deadliest one-third of a weapon created after decades of experimentation to finish off extraordinary beings? The latent possibility that herself or one of her three agents might perish?

Perhaps our understanding of time is completely wrong. Maybe one can take a second, kidnap it, and stretch it out like placed in a medieval torture machine. Maybe we're just ignorant, simply. And then another event occurs, as simple as a voice coming out of the headset, which has just been transferred by radio waves and decoded right into your ear, causing another whimsical change in the flow. _Everybody in position. – she heard the voice of his companion Ramirez, stationed a few meters behind her, in a sober black combat suit just like Soleil's, which protected them from external forces of extreme violence, such as bullets, or the morning sunshine.

_On my signal. – she finally said, feeling the time flow becoming a little more normal. It was almost over, she'd be face to face with the deserter and her host. A fleeting thought went with the bad luck of the host, a lumberjack whose survival aptitude was dangerously close to zero. Not because his death was strictly necessary, but because he was in the wrong place.

Death is a curious thing. It is a void that drags us to it, but only by paying close attention can we feel its strength pulling us into the abyss. She could feel a slight pull in her mind, weaving words she would have considered cowardly in another situation. _Ramirez, *in the lead*, gain access and go to the left, I'll follow to the right. Armstrong, behind me – on second thought, in this situation she considered them coward words as well – use lethal force. – she ordered.

Lethal force. It was the order she had received from León himself, changing the very purpose of her mission there in France. She was aware of the problems that the whole organization was going through, the golden goose had succumbed. So the big boss didn't want to leave any loose ends: Lohe would not be caught, but annihilated, which made her job suddenly much less difficult. Smart girl if there are any, the trick of the locator floating downstream had cost them valuable time. She couldn't waste anymore.

A thunder sounded in front of her, after a blast at close range from Ramirez's shotgun against the door lock, a signal for the other two to rush in. The fourth agent, Weins, was stationed covering the only window large enough for a person to pass through, waiting for an escape. Three, four, five bursts inside, and then silence. A giant drop of sweat came down Weins' forehead, waiting. With the dust still flying everywhere, came a transmission of a string of unexpected words: _Clear... no one's here.

Soleil, Armstrong and Ramirez stepped out, walking away with a mixture of disappointment and relief.

_What do we do now? – Weins consulted.

_There were tracks in the mud, I saw them as we approached. – Armstrong said.

_Are they recent?

They investigated the tracks in the mud, sinking their fingers into the walls to see how resistant they were. They looked fresh.

_They got away from us... how did they know? – Ramirez protested.

_This is Sergeant Antoinette Soleil, the bird is not in the nest. We'll proceed to follow tracks of an unknown vehicle. – she radioed the base.

_Proceed. – coldly returned the voice on the other side.

_Any idea what it might be? – mechanically translated into French the old-fashioned personal assistant of Antoine.

_No. The van is old, has no on-board diagnostic system, just says it's not running, which we're already aware of. – the lumberjack replied, fanning the white smoke that kept coming out of the battery compartment. Stopped by a dirt road, Lohe under the shade of an oak tree and Antoine trying to get rid of some of the smoke that was slipping through his eyes, were invaded by the sounds of the winter forest. Some snow had melted that day and turned the earth into mud, which now splashed on the chassis and boots of both of them.

_We'll have to walk. – Lohe lamented – Could you look at the map and see what's near here?

Antoine nodded and switched from translator to map on the screen and after a brief consultation reported, via software. _There's a... gas station about six kilometers from here. It was wise not to stray too far from the main roads, if that's any consolation. Let's see... wait. It's a CPF station, I have no idea if it'll be open for business.

_What's that acronym?

_French Oil Conglomerate. - *Conglomérat de Pétrole Français* - I didn't know they still existed. - he said as he took one last look at the van, with some apprehension.

_I don't know what that is.

_A company from the time of the energy dispute in France. It fell into disgrace when lobbyists pushed for nuclear power and electric motors. The European Union won against the local "patriots", so to speak.

_I wasn't aware of any of that.

_It's in that direction. - he said as he grabbed his coat, put a small box of ammunition in his backpack and took his hunting rifle. - Will you be okay? It's not cloudy like yesterday.

_As long as I keep my cover on, I'll hold out, let's go. - she spoke before undertaking the long walk, feeling with her fingers her precious ProtePlasm syringes in the pocket and her handgun.

_Not many people remember the Conglomerate, it happened fifteen years ago. - the lumberjack began, hanging his gun over his shoulder - But I was particularly involved, since my uncle worked at CPF. All employees were given a brand-new combustion engine car to support the declining oil industry. He gave it to me, it was my first car. I had to convert the system the next year when the company lost the battle for energy and a barrage of electric cars came along. The price of oil went through the roof as production fell and it became impossible to maintain a gasoline car. - he paused to grimace and scratch his nose - Sorry, I'm boring you.

_No, it's fine! It's not boring at all. - Lohe didn't know exactly how to go on, she was interested in hearing about the world. She decided to do the simplest thing, tell the truth - I actually like to hear about the things that happen. Or happened. - noted - The militia told us almost nothing. It was all training.

_I see. By the way, what's the name of that militia?

_It doesn't have a name.

_Weird. Does it support a cause?

_We were told it was necessary, to maintain the level of secrecy necessary to operate openly. And... the only cause we support is the leader's wishes, he's called León.

_Just León? He doesn't have a last name?

_Not that I know of.

Antoine smiled sadly. He found it unbelievable that such things could happen in the Western world nowadays. He wondered if what she was telling was a hundred percent real, or if it was painted with an important part of fake colored varnish. He looked her in the eye as they walked. If she was lying to him, she was excellent, a professional cheater. He didn't think so, he'd rather believe she was a girl in distress, and that he was helping. The minutes passed, and Antoine could feel the distance between them increase with a wall of silence building brick by brick. After all, they were just two strangers in strange circumstances. That's why hearing her voice took him by surprise.

_So what were you doing...? I mean, why did you live alone in the woods? – Lohe herself did not understand why she was so clumsy in her communication.

_Oh. – that question...

He swallowed spittle as he reviewed the answers he had prepared in case anyone did. He wasn't convinced by any of them, unfortunately. With no answer to give, he described the memories as they rushed into the mind. _Three years and eight months ago I married a woman. The marriage didn't last long, as you can see. – he covered his melancholy with a fleeting smile – We had a little girl, we called her Geraldine. She was so pretty and joyful, loved to laugh. She... – he had to pause because of a sudden lump that seemed to have been shot in his throat – She became very ill. A rare type of leukemia.

–What is leukemia? – she asked innocently.

_Don't you know? It is a type of cancer that attacks the bone marrow and blood. She didn't respond well to the treatments... I wanted to resort to experimental medicine, but my wife didn't. We fought, we fought a lot. Anyway, looking back, I think it was too late. – he remained silent as the assistant finished translating his last and pitiful sentence.

_Did she die? I'm sorry.

_After that we decided not to be together anymore. I particularly wanted to get away from it all. So I spent almost a year and a half alone, to think and be at peace.

Lohe stared at him, with some guilt in her eyes. _I'm sorry I ever bothered you, Antoine.

_Oh no! Please don't! It's no bother. I... – he couldn't say. So he remained silent and let the bricks of silence cement each other again.

An hour and a half later, they were near the gas station. The site was still operating, serving fossil fuel to the villagers with field equipment that, for some reason, still refused to switch to electric motors. Fifteen years after the battle, fuels had slowly become cheaper to accommodate the low demand.

_Do you mind if I go alone? – Antoine asked – It could be dangerous if they see you.

Lohe thought briefly and agreed. _Affirmative. Can I have the rifle?

As she watched the man walk away, she took shelter in the shade of a small brick altar in honor of St. Benedict, decorated with posters of various shapes and sizes with religious inscriptions and acknowledgements. She rubbed her ankle carefully. Although it was now partially healed after yesterday's event, it still hurt. She had tried several more times to replicate the healing effect experienced, without success. Hopefully she'd have more time to practice. But would that ever happen? Should she be a fugitive forever?

If they found her, it was surely because of the Seekers... those unintelligible beings she only knew from reports and data relevant to their missions, but never face to face. They were like a myth, an invisible enemy. Was she supposed to take them all out? She exhaled deeply drawing herself further under the hood. Impossible. Almost as much as going after León. They wanted her back that bad? She felt so incomplete, and unable to achieve completeness again.

A movement captured her attention. A black minivan with tinted windows arrived at the gas station, like the ones they use in the militia when they want to go unnoticed. Lohe slipped away limping through the shadows for a better angle, rifle in hand.

Someone got out of the car. A tall man, dressed in a black business suit, a large overcoat, a ridiculously large hat and sunglasses, standard militia *neomensch* protection. He seemed to be the driver. By regulation and logic, the vehicles in service had a driver because of the need for evasive maneuvers and pursuit if necessary, to take decisions for a number of cases difficult to program. The suspicion was confirmed. Was it impossible to mislead them?

She kneeled on the floor and mounted the rifle, trying to make as little noise as possible. From where she was stationed, had now a good shooting angle of the driver, but it was not convenient to fire until knowing how many were in the minivan, and confirm if they were really following her, or if it was a coincidence. Maybe they could evade them. Inside the station, where they sold food and hunting supplies, they would find only one man on foot and nothing to indicate that he was involved with her. The man in black looked inside the vehicle, said something she couldn't hear, grabbed the cable that hung from the side of the charger, chose the most appropriate plug for his model, and plugged it into the minivan's external connector. There were still no unusual movements, nothing betraying their disposition. The man in black searched his pockets for something, and pulled out a pack of cigarettes, which appeared to be empty. He knocked on the window with his knuckles, pointed to his empty packet, turned around and started walking towards the station. Lohe followed him with her sights, though more concerned about the mysterious occupants of the vehicle. The hunger grip made its appearance, reminding her that she might well find more syringes in the minivan to help her escape.

Antoine finally came out, and without paying attention he walked past the man in black. And he made a rookie mistake. He stared at the minivan for too long before pretending to be distracted. The man in black stopped with the glass door handle in his hand, following Antoine with his gaze. Lohe's finger on the trigger, stiff as a metal, spasmed slightly. The man walked after Antoine for a few steps, and shouted at him to get his attention. Not only did he not turn around, but began to walk faster. Lohe wished earnestly she could warn him of the disaster he was about to cause. Another yell, which caused the frightened lumberjack to accelerate. The man in black reached into his coat, pulled out a gun and pointed it at his back. The sound of the shot thundered with fury.

Antoine fell to his knees, his heart suddenly stopped.

PART 46: IMMORTAL DREAD

"When the goal that drives a person is as powerful as the one to be overthrown, one must tread lightly. Extremely lightly. So it seems that the fabric that is woven is for the benefit of the sovereign. That way they do not suspect, believing that the effort, the dedication, the tears, the blood shed, is all for their benefit. When in fact, it's the exact opposite. But, you can't do everything on your own. It is necessary to resort to the strength of others. They must be convinced with good arguments, with gifts, with good will, with a smile. Never with threats. Because those you turn into allies, are your pillars, pillars on which you will rebuild later. For rebellion against the deceived sovereign, however absent-minded they may be, always leaves chaos and destruction in its wake."

The teachings that the Great Mecantro had left him so many years ago had been engraved with fire. That's how wise Hassan thought his master was, who at the time still used his birth name: Aslin. And he still held the position of Virtuous of Loyalty of Sargon, that King of Nothingness, Ruler of Pestilence and Rot, Bearer of Evil and Corrupt Blood, Usurper of Assur. How remorseful was Hassan for having slain his master, a dead so unworthy of such a wonderful mind, to be now in the service of the moribund Sargon, for almost ten years. He looked up at the night sky outside of the old Jerusalem with infinite nostalgia, swallowed with difficulty, to immerse himself again in the memories.

"And what should be done with those who do not want to lend their strength voluntarily? There is no need to be angry with those hardened ones for being loyal, or for being afraid of change. Anger leads to nothing useful, only to waste. What should be done with those who do not respond to good bargains of the real world, is to offer them better bargains in the world of illusions. Let them believe that they are fighting for their Lord, when in reality they have been set to collide with others hardened ones, cheated, deceived to fight one another. Let them bear the banners they yearn, but to fight for you."

Words that would never leave his head, nor would a thousand, two thousand years go by.

He turned to look around. Hassan never grew tired of measuring his dignity by the number of men he commanded. Flanked to the left and right, hundreds of soldiers marched, already accustomed to the fact that with an *immortal dread* as General, they would march at night and rest during the day. They had learned to respect him, to understand that his condition was far from being an impediment, turning him into a legendary being. To be far from the God of the Sun

Elagabal did not end up affecting the *dread*, whose name had been earned by means of perils, of cunning, of traversing, of living. Of trampling on his enemies with alacrity and cruelty, supported by hundreds of years of battle experience. By force of force.

He looked to his right at Kamek, who had become a friend, if there was such a thing, and did his best to conceal his disdain. Kamek was a good man, honest and honorable, qualities that would turn him against Hassan one day. He was too loyal to the Emperor. He disliked the idea of having to kill him, though the fact that he bore the *twisted* blood of Sargon's lineage was an important drawback.

Because Sargon's lineage weakened with the passing of the centuries, while a *dread*, on the contrary, became stronger day by day. His fame as a ruthless warrior had spread throughout the civilized world, fed by the charlatans and drunks, but fed nevertheless. The caravan of Aslin the Virtuous was gigantic, worthy of the position he had earned as the Most Loyal among the Loyal, the Great Loyal, the Hunter of Traitors. That had quickly set him against the other four Virtuous, and many influential figures in the Palace of Nineveh, but it was a cost he was willing to pay, as it had bestowed an unquantifiable value on him: popularity in the Empire, and beyond the borders.

The huge delegation advanced until they were stopped at the gates of the city, so that the villagers feared to be under siege. But they soon stirred up rumors that the night visitor was the Blessed Aslin and fears became isolated scuffles. The doors opened to make way for the personal guard that accompanied him.

Behind the doors awaited a tight group of monotheists, each adorned with gold beads and precious stones, newly made robes, beards tangled like roots and frowned brows. His arrival in the city was controversial, to say the least.

_Welcome be, great Virtuous, in good time your feet touch Holy Land.

Hassan took his time in silence, annoying on purpose, to look around. _I am grateful for your attentions – he finally said, stressing the words – honorable and gentle men. Please, I'm just passing through and I intend to mobilize my men tomorrow evening. I implore you not to take ill my short visit to your beautiful city, which my predicament has to do with time constraints and not with your lack of hospitality, far from it.

_We understand, that be of no problem. – the head of the group closed the brief but still protocoled greeting, necessary fanfare towards a man of Aslin's position, as representative of the true Emperor of Assur, Sargon I. After the customary greetings of individuals for whom he had no patience, and the usual refusal for overnight accommodation after the arduous journey, he was led to his destination: The Seat.

He rode on horseback escorted by his soldiers and surrounded by the locals through the most humble places, where the need was greatest. The glances stood out among the precarious dwellings, with faces of hunger and disease. Kamek approached riding by his side, and spoke as softly as he could to him.

_Aslin, we're circling around in vain. I've seen where The Seat is and we're not getting anywhere near it.

Hassan looked at him, suddenly alert. _Is that true? - he asked, trying to see far into the distance through the meager roofs of filthy cloth and straw.

Kamek raised his hand and the procession stopped.

_Is something the matter? - the guide consulted innocently.

_Why are we passing through here? It's not the shortest way. - Kamek grumbled.

_Dear guests, we have taken the path that we consider the safest, where the inhabitants are more faithful to you and show you more of their affection. - the head of the delegation stated with diplomacy and lies - Other places are inhabited by goyim, and I cannot ensure your well-being in those areas.

Kamek and Hassan exchanged glances, and after gesturing bitterly, nodded and signaled to continue. Hassan preferred to remain silent the rest of the way. It seemed obvious to him that they wanted to show him how poor they were. Because they thought he came for something he wasn't. He smiled broadly, had suddenly won an important card.

The procession reached a wide avenue surrounded by rich merchants' stalls. At the end of it, in front of a beautiful fountain of rock water, which smelled of desert flowers, was the Temple, the place where The Seat was practiced, a congregation of patriarchs of the Hebrew tribes, who held the local domain. After deciding to go alone, leaving Kamek in charge of the guards, he was taken to the Temple on foot with pomp and ritual, something that secretly delighted Hassan, who tried to keep his head high and dissimulate.

The light of the Temple's candles formed phantasmagorical figures on every surface where the eye stopped settling. The very air that was breathed did not seem normal, but rather gave the impression of coming from the lungs of some deity. Before going down to The Seat, he entrusted himself to Nin-Karrak to protect his innermost dreams, and allow him to carry them forward.

Inside there were four men awaiting, whose reactions to the newcomer were heterogeneous. The place was a room made up of a single block of carved and skillfully polished stone. Six equidistant columns supported the ceiling devoid of any decoration. On the walls could be seen scriptures in Hebrew that Hassan did not recognize, and in his excessive pride, was not interested in understanding either.

Whoever looked a little livelier in the dancing shadows stood up to welcome him. _Aslin! Blessed are my eyes when I see you again, please have a seat. – he invited without much conviction.

_Thank you, Feliah, gentle men. I dare not entertain you too much away from the affairs of the city, so I will waste little of your time to continue my journey westwards. – he said with protocol, because among centenarians, amid the biggest surliness was to waste one's neighbor's time on purpose.

He received no further response, nor did the echo on the walls of The Seat penetrate the prevailing muteness. Hassan deliberately dragged the chair against the ground, making the biggest scandal possible, until he was finally surrounded by those patriarchs.

Hassan looked at them one by one, returning their defiant glances, knowing exactly what was going to happen. If his passage through the city had taught him anything, was what the exact antidote for such a poison was. He smiled broadly and struck his hands against the thick central table.

_Lords, lords of mine. I didn't come here to collect tributes, quite the contrary. I have come to forgive. To help.

His words had an immediate effect on the features of those present, who relaxed sensitively.

_I am aware of the injustice of which you are victims – he continued – and my presence here is to give each one what they deserve. Neither Jerusalem, nor its people, deserve this undignified and despotic treatment.

_Aslin... please forgive us. We have received you with coldness and instead you turn out to be a golden ally. Let us serve you as you ought. – apologized the one who seemed to be the oldest. – Bring wine and dates! – ordered, turning to the front door.

_No, my lords, it's not necessary. My duty is towards you, Hezekiah – he answered to the old patriarch – and not the other way around. I wish to hear what you have to say, which will reach the ears of Sargon or whoever must listen.

_We fear an attack from Assur. In fact, seeing your columns approaching seemed like a sure sign of an incursion. – complained the patriarch to his right.

_Fear not. My army is for my protection, I intend not to do the same here as I did to Merodach in Babylon. – Hassan mentioned deliberately, to remind them the

military victory that had brought him the most honors –
I swear by Shamash God of Justice, or may I be
condemned right here.

_Our sentries have informed us that there are
suspicious movements in Nineveh, that they fear
Sargon's death, and with it the instability of the empire.
– lamented Feliah.

_We don't know whether taking that as a positive or
negative omen, it could distract Assur from its desire to
conquer until we get our commerce in order, or bring
about our ruin quickly. – said another.

_Calm, please. – Hassan tried to quiet them by raising
his hand.

_A new emperor could start a ruthless campaign. –
pleaded the patriarch to his left.

_Sargon is not going to die. – Hassan guaranteed – He
is very ill, as he has been since I learned of him.
There's no indication that his condition will change, the
Gods don't wish it so. That is why I make the effort to
come in person to resolve the obstacles before you. I
count you as my valuable allies and require your
support.

_You got it, Aslin – Hezekiah said – we just need a
good harvest season to stabilize the city's growth. This
will imply having the optimum number of men
guarding the borders, and will allow us to be useful to

your purposes. I know that you intend to form a great alliance to shout your name to the four winds, and that with such might on your shoulders, you will march victoriously to the Palace of Nineveh to replace the dying emperor.

Hassan nodded slowly, curious as to how his plan had been correctly read. _That's correct, in part. Do not misunderstand me. I wish for the prosperity of my Empire, that is why I understand that it requires a strong man in charge. Serencal and Sennacherib's conspiracies have reached far, they only manage to destabilize, as long as it puts sticks in my wheels.

The matter of those two men was actually the reason for Hassan's sleepwalking. After the death of Amterié – nephew of the Virtuous of Generosity, the immensely wealthy Rettla – that honest and intelligent young man, but undoubtedly misnamed "Sargon II", had created a small power vacuum for being one of Sargon's favorites, and also favorite of his number one confidant, Serencal. However, that death had provoked a reaction that ended up turning the most influential in the Empire against Hassan. The conspiracies thus led to the rise of one of Sargon's most distant and little-known relatives, Sennacherib, who quickly became the favorite of almost everyone, including the emperor himself, and who had shown tenacity and cleverness.

Hassan knew that the animosities toward him were in part because he was considered a foreigner, but mostly because he was a *dread*. They feared him for his ability, just as they saw in him their own weaknesses, revealed as if he were a mirror. It was this internal front that ultimately forced Hassan to seek allies outside, who he considered sufficient to crush the capitol and seize the crown. When he returned, he would have gotten the proper power and momentum. Even more so. Those who feared him would soon bow their heads and kiss his feet. Hassan gloated over the shrewdness of his plan.

_Excellent, for Gibil I will burn the city if necessary to conquer it. I entrust myself to Nin-Karrak to keep my life and yours until the appointed time. - Hassan sang with joy.

However, no one responded to his comments. The patriarchs watched each other, impatient. _Foreigner, these walls are not for blaspheming at will. - Hezekiah warned.

Hassan turned around in confusion. _What?

_You are in The Seat, blaspheming the One God - he stressed - Jehovah, is a crime.

Hassan lost every token of joy, his eyes turned grim. He rose from his chair slowly and menacingly. _Blasphemies? What are these absurdities? The Gods are not blasphemies, they are the divine powers that control this world and the other.

Hezekiah and two of the men stood up in response.

_My lords, please! – interceded Feliah with a leap throwing his seat back – Let us not take this any further. We are not here to discuss religious issues, but worldly ones.

Hassan kept his eyes on Hezekiah's angry eyes without even blinking. Mumbling, the patriarch finally sat down, followed by the others. With a wave of his hand, he quietly invited the foreigner to take his seat. After a few moments of defiance, he accepted.

_Certainly, we're not here to talk about religion. – Hassan agreed – And going back to the previous topic, do I have or not the support of The Seat?

The glances flew in all directions, with more doubt than certainty. Finally, a tacit agreement was formed, and Hezekiah spoke. _Yes, you have the support and blessing of The Seat. What are the next steps, Aslin?

Hassan nodded, confident. _It's simple. On my return I will send a man with news of my campaign and instructions. Depending on the progress of my caravan, you will send writings to the cities of Tarsus, Hama, Damascus and the Nineveh itself, expressing your full and complete support for me in a Holy coalition against the corruption in the capitol. It should be phrased as a threat, but not as a declaration of war. In each of these places I already have people who stand with our cause, and will do the proper. If timings are respected, my return to Nineveh will be in conjunction with heated rumors of massive support from the entire civilized world, my emergence will be unstoppable. That same night I intend to execute my plan and eliminate all my sworn enemies at the same time, the others will surrender promptly. After that... I'll take control of Assur, and reward your efforts with it. - the people present listened attentively, without losing a word. - As you will appreciate, if my plan is followed, neither Jerusalem nor others should send men to the battle, although they should prepare, so that the spies can see that the hornet's nest has been shaken. Not a soul will be left unmoved in this Empire.

_What if something goes wrong? - interjected a patriarch.

_It will not fail. I've accumulated support everywhere. I'm very confident of our victory.

_Giving you our support openly puts us in a complicated situation if things don't go as you propose.

_Maybe, but no more than you are now. Remember, you haven't paid any tribute, and I'm supposed to be the one to collect it. As far as I know, I won't take a single sack as soon as I put my foot away from here. - the attendants nodded, understanding themselves to be a blatant insurrection to the Emperor.

_One last question – said Feliah – why go through Egypt? It's too far away to offer the celerity your plan requires.

_Because it is the kingdom that I intend to be my western border, as long as I pacify internally I need peace with Egypt, and for they to contain the incursions of bandits and barbarians.

_Agreed. It's settled then.

After the tense meeting, Feliah and Hassan walked alone under the night veil, circling around the rock pit. Dozens of Assyrian men rested, following them with their eyes, expectant of the last phase of the negotiations.

_Do you know what my fear is, Aslin? If something shakes the foundations of Nineveh your plan becomes impracticable. – Feliah said, walking slowly beside him.

_Like what?

_At this very moment the Virtuosi and their allies must be conspiring to outwit you. They know your plan, get support from the cities and surround the center. But if the center changes, so should your actions. And from one city, changes happen faster than in a dozen. Your play is necessarily slower.

547

_I understand – Hassan held – but they are cowards. My popularity continues to grow, trying to defenestrate me without evidence will turn against them. And by harboring fear in their hearts, they will not dare to wiles that really affect me. Feliah, please don't divulge it, but I've made plans for the military conquest of Nineveh. And I don't even need a vast army behind my back. I know where and how to plant misinformation and falsehoods, I will have them fighting each other, and before they realize what is happening it will be too late.

_You think of everything, Virtuous.

_An observant man is worth seventy.

_No doubt about it. – smiled the patriarch.

_On the other hand, your comrades are somewhat... bellicose about heavenly matters. What, all the descendants of Enoch are like that?

Feliah wiped the joy off his face. _You're somewhat right. I will be frank with you, my people give too much importance to the sacred texts and to God, but this path leads to nothing. Our lineage will never be what it was.

_In what way? – Hassan consulted with real curiosity.

_In the days of Enoch, our people lived long lives, more than any Assyrian *immortal*, stronger and more dignified than any *dread*. No offence – he remarked –

but the day was ours as much as the night. However, the blood thinned. Efforts to contain it seem to have been in vain. The laws for avoiding marriages with goyim, useless. The blood of Judah has weakened from being legends among men, to what we are now.

_I regret not knowing your people's history in depth, Feliah.

Feliah nodded bitterly. _It is fine. And what is worse, our zeal to defend our heritage has earned us the enmity of other peoples, who look at us with thorns for eyes. A twofold evil, then.

_And what does this have to do with your sacred texts?

Feliah put one hand on his shoulder, making him immediately uncomfortable. _Aslin, listen to me carefully, for what I am about to tell you is the truth of this world. Religions, beliefs, Gods... all this is nothing more than the dominance of man over man. They are instruments of control, to control their thoughts, their hearts, and ultimately their actions.

Hassan stopped, shaking Feliah hand vigorously. _Watch your tongue, Jew. Because what you just said is true blasphemy. I understand that you deny the Gods, by taking only one, but to refuse the existence of each and every one of them, attributing it to a purpose of dominion is foolish, to say the least.

_This is not foolish, Aslin, I tell you not to procure your hatred, but for you to make use of this for your purposes, for from the prosperity of your kingdom we too, your allies, will be nourished. But it's the truth. It has been so since the beginning of time, it is now, and it will always be so. I know because I practice it. We practice it. – he corrected – Our methods are refined era after era, with proposals of fictitious things, attributing magical properties to this or that person, to this or that object to obtain veneration, to obtain fear if they dared to go against our laws, all in pursuit of control because the hearts of men are malleable, and treacherous. Your reign will be unstable, at first. You'll need a powerful tool to hold it together. I'm offering it to you as a token of friendship.

Hassan looked at the man from head to toe, disturbed. _It's time for me to leave. – he spat.

PART 47: THE ORACLE OF MEMPHIS

Life tastes like nothing when you doubt everything. How can new experiences be built when the foundations of your soul are faltering? This is how Hassan felt, riding at a man's pace near Memphis, well within Egyptian territory, the last stop on his official tour as ambassador of the rotten Sargon, and the last of his machinations to conquer all. "Religion is nothing but a tool of domination": he could almost hear the words of Feliah resounding in his head, as they had been spoken ten days before, in Jerusalem.

The lights of the torches of the men on horseback around him landed on a magnificent monument, a stone tower with the figure of a pharaoh, painted in bright colors, and adorned with care and grace. In its hands it held a double scepter, the symbols of which now escaped from his grasp, and he didn't run after them. It wasn't the first time the caravan had run into one. In other circumstances he would have enjoyed the fine art of the artisans, eager to please their Gods. Now, navigating in unknown waters within the confines of his heart, it was impossible.

Gods.

He had already lost count of how many there were. Fatal sin to forget those whose power governs us, whose gaze judges us, whose silent orders guide us - were there, perhaps, hundreds of them? In his long nights at the campfire, and his dissertations hidden from the Sun's rays, he had often discussed and debated the true nature of the gods with many people of diverse origins and ideas. About what they wanted, who they were. Told and heard thousands of stories. Sometimes, reaching agreements if this or that god was in fact the same, given the legends that were told, their characteristics, their divine sphere, their personality, only to change the name by what the mortals knew them. Others resembled, but varied in their legends. Perhaps for helping, or being very temperamental against the hero of this or that tale, others for having abandoned him to his fate, but raised doubts whether it was the same deity, or two different ones. Hassan looked up, and wondered how many had power over his heart and his erratic thoughts. A dozen? A hundred?

And in that light, he couldn't help but feel that everything was absurd. That the wind blows because such is the nature of the wind. That the fields become fertile because the river silt caresses them. That fire burns because such is the duty of fire. That lives come and go because that's the law of the world. And it's true for dogs, sheep, birds and men. All alike, no magic hidden behind. That there was never any god, or if it did, long since they left the heavens. And he turned to look around, surrounded by men willing to kill to protect him, yet still feeling alone. Inexorably alone. Cowardly alone. Just like he never felt before.

They passed through an inscribed wall, surely singing praises to some local leader; Does not every building, every monument, every stone laid over stone by man serve any other purpose than to dominate the will of man?

His horse stopped, perhaps twinned by his heavy heart. Behind him, those in charge of carrying the wagons with gifts quietly surrounded him and moved on. All those precious metals and fine canvases, carried league after league for the sole purpose of bending the will of the Egyptian leaders with gifts. For if there is anything that the Egyptians love more than their pharaohs and their gods, is gold. Even to the point of desecrating tombs knowingly of the wicked curse that falls on their heads. Gold, too, was an instrument of domination. And of that he was absolutely certain.

Kamek distracted him, moving one arm in front of his eyes. It took him a while to focus on that man he had learned to call a friend.

_What's the matter with you?

_Nothing, I'm fine.

_Are you sure? Didn't you hear the alert? - Kamek asked.

Hassan turned his head frantically in search of clues about something important that had ensued. He quickly noticed how rigid they all had become in the caravan, and that in the distance, several bright spots were approaching them. Kamek stepped forward, and calmly ordered them to prepare for hostiles. Nevertheless, the dozen newcomers rode quietly, and made signs of peace. It was the official escort, quite late in the attention to their duties. Hassan did not stop to think about the political consequences and causes of this delay. He wasn't in the mood for it. In fact, he skipped the pomp and protocol of the usual greetings in a bad way, and was content to let his horse advance. Fortunately, Kamek had taken the role of chieftain in his place, and his rudeness had soon been forgotten.

An hour later, they were face to face with the majestic gates of the city, whose colors he could hardly guess from the deceptive light of the candles. These were opened, while a duet of horns rang out, singing a welcoming melody.

Unlike other cities, Memphis ceased to exist at night. No one trading, no one walking, no one poking their noses out. He could not even tell if any curious person was coming out of the curtains to spy on his entourage. Nothing. For a moment it occurred to him to think whether the city was inhabited only by silent souls, shadows, and guards.

Upon arriving at the main square, they were invited to wait. All around them, well above the black clouds, were surrounded by giant columns of a beautiful bright amber color. Even the sand under the hooves of the beasts felt soft and delicate. And in front of them, an enormous palace, almost as high as it was wide, dominated almost absolutely with a masterfully carved staircase, which rose to the sky, with doors at its sides that extended as far as the eye could reach. And down through these, a lonely figure.

Kamek stepped off his horse, and patted the hindquarters of Hassan's horse gently.

_So, Aslin, are you going to tell me what's wrong with you? Someone is coming to see us and I want to know before then.

Hassan kept his eyes on the little figure approaching, purposely avoiding crossing them with those who scrutinized him. He dismounted the animal slowly, to buy time. _I have been touched in a sensitive fiber. – he finally snapped, hoping to be left alone. But that didn't happen.

Kamek raised an eyebrow as high as he could. _Does the great Aslin have sensitive fibers? Hard to believe, friend.

_Yes, I know. It's something I've brought back from our stay in the Judea.

_And what would that be?

_A shipment of doubts. About the gods. - he paused, which only served to further hook the Assyrian to the response in the waiting. - On whether they exist, or whether they are a tool, not unlike a chisel. That instead of sculpting the stone, it sculpts the hearts of men.

The Assyrian looked at him, very quietly, and soon he observed around, passing by every nook and cranny, trying to find inspiration in that foreign land.

Egypt was special. One of the few major realms where a mortal reigned. And not just in name, as was common, but in practice. The Pharaoh, master and lord of Egypt, was a god in himself, and it was dangerous to doubt the Gods in a land ruled by one.

The Pharaohs were extraordinary beings. They had been chosen by the holiest of these lands. They were more than chosen, they were *descendants* of Gods. But, by divine whim, or to the misfortune of these men, they had paid the price of a short life in return. A human life, or even less so. And this fed the most

556

monstrous palatial conspiracies, which undermined the kingdom from its base. The only thing that prevented total collapse was the Horus Priesthood, whose members were *the destined*, or, as they were called elsewhere, *blood carriers*, *touched*, *dreads*, or sometimes *demons*. Some of them were even *immortal*, such as those of Sargon's lineage, such as Kamek. And in the priests of Horus, Egypt took refuge when the kingdom suffered, and it suffered greatly. One of the issues that had come up in his discussions with Aslin was how and why the Priesthood had not definitely seized power, or why it allowed instability. They had not agreed on the reasons, but they had agreed to investigate the matter, look for a weakness and exploit it.

Kamek glanced over a beautiful statue of Amon, which appeared penitent on the other side of the square, finally finding the inspiration he needed. _But, what's to doubt, my friend? What else could such beautiful monuments, such fine art, such devotion be destined, but for those who transcend us? Throughout the world and here, men try to win the favor of others, that much is true, but even more so of the Gods, who watch over and guard us. If not, Aslin, what else could such works be intended for?

Hassan shrugged, somewhat dazed but unexpectedly interested in Kamek's words. _Vanity? – he suddenly dropped.

Kamek could not contain a laugh, having been taken by surprise. _More than one, without being afraid of making a mistake, is the work of the vanity of the powerful, but it is not the common, but the exception. You don't have to worry. We all see our beliefs in doubt at some point in our long lives, such is the nature of man. But the Gods know us better than we know ourselves, they know the oxen with which they plow their land. Cheer up, give it a try.

Hassan looked straight ahead, already recognizing the solitary figure descending the infinite steps. _All right, I'll give it a try. We have unfinished business.

_Welcome to you all. - the voice sounded deep and powerful in the distance. By his ceremonial attire, his beads of precious metals and stones, his pace and bearing, and the fact that he ventured alone to receive the foreigners armed to the teeth indicated that he could not be anyone else: The High Priest of Horus, Ankh *the eternal.* His hair was short and white as snow, and his wrinkles shaped his impassive face, of impeccable shavings. It was the second Priest of Horus, successor of the first, whose legend bestows upon him being the founder of Egypt, among other more and better kept secrets. And if there was anything in surplus for Ankh, it was secrets.

_You, gentlemen, must be Aslin, Virtuous of Loyalty, and Kamek, descendant of the Great Sargon. Welcome, welcome to you.

Both men mentioned greeted with careful protocol, followed behind by every man in the caravan.

_High Priest Ankh, we appreciate your gesture. We brought presents for the Pharaoh.

_Your presents will be accepted with honor and returned with hospitality and the highest gratitude. Will you please follow me, my lords? – said as he drew a bow in the air – My men will escort yours to give them food and drink, and offer them deserved rest after the journey. And I myself will take care to offer those to you, if your majesties permit me to do so.

Faced with such words, the guests were only able to accept the offerings with a smile.

They followed the High Priest through the fourteenth door on the right, past several beautiful halls, to what appeared to be the personal temple of Ankh. It was rather modest, decorated with red tones on its walls, phrases that they did not understand, and the statue.

The statue was the size of three men, one on top of the other. Its enormous falcon head bore powerful eyes, whose brightness indicated the presence of something divine, something overwhelming. It was a statue of a God. Of Horus. In his left hand he held a scepter, and his right hand was outstretched, reaching the center of the room, from whose clenched fist a crimson cloth, a clear symbol of the divine blood, descending. Underneath, with his wrist tied to the cloth, a figure of a man was bent, kneeling before the divine in perpetual submission, recipient of the gift of the Gods.

Seeing how amazed his guests were, Ankh offered a brief explanation. _All priests are descendants of Horus, in one way or another. You too, are descendants, for you bear His blood.

Hassan looked sideways at Kamek, knowing him to be different. The blood that ran through his veins was not the same. Hassan's blood had forced him to escape from the Sun, while the Assyrian's had condemned him to a death as slow as it was irreversible. He wondered if there would be any difference with the one given by Horus to the priests. Or if it was all a fable.

_And as *carriers* of his blood, you are welcome in these quarters – he continued.

_Thank you again, High Priest. If it's not inconvenience – said Kamek somewhat hesitantly – can I ask you something?

_It's not inconvenience at all. – the most powerful standing man in that kingdom mentioned with a huge, friendly smile.

_It is known that the Pharaohs are descendants of the Gods, is this similar to what happens with *us*?

_I understand the doubt. It's similar, yes. But different. In the Holy Scriptures it is clearly stated that those who *carry the blood* should not lead, because... our motivations – he stressed – can be selfish, and that we only learn to offer ourselves to others after many lives, lives that have been given to us in exchange for that service. The Pharaohs are descendants of Amon-Ra, the One Who Is Above, whose gift was to lead men in exchange for short lives. For if they lived many lives, they would divert the divine purposes and confuse them with their own.

_We have asked ourselves at length, and please correct us if we have stepped on land that is not permitted to us – Hassan said – why Egypt is being scourged by terrible conspiracies, having such a worthy pillar in the Priesthood upon which to stand. – he mentioned gently pointing to Ankh – So the reasons are the Scriptures?

Ankh nodded. _That's right. If I may be so bold, I knew this subject would be touched upon, sooner or later. I then chose that it should be early, so that my lords may better understand the Egyptian soul.

The two foreigners looked at each other and nodded with a melancholy smile. With such a profound belief, it would be close to the impossible to foster the ascent of the Priesthood to royal power, another of the possibilities they had discussed along the way, enabling them to gain a powerful ally. Since that powerful ally was content to be the foot of the kingdom instead of the head.

_May the Gods not allow it – said Kamek – but what would happen if Pharaoh Shabako suddenly fell ill and there were no worthy heir, while his son was still a child? Would not the kingdom sink into chaos? Would not darkness be conjured by the ascent of a person that is as well-prepared as is wise, like the High Priest of Horus?

_Without hesitation, my most esteemed guest. Fortunately that will not happen, my duties will not conflict over such a scenario. Shabitko will succeed him peacefully.

_How to be sure of it? – questioned puzzled Hassan.

_Because the Oracle of Memphis has confirmed it.

_Oh... I have heard legends about the Oracle and the Temple of Apis – explained Hassan – but I could not separate certainty from falsehood. Who is the Oracle?

_It's not just one person, it's two at the moment. It is a position that is passed from priest to priest. To those who are prepared and have unambiguous traits and faculties. At this time the Priestess of the Oracle is preparing her successor after predicting that her own potencies are about to fade away. The young woman who will succeed her has shown unusual charm and talent. If you wish, I can introduce you, she's in this palace right now. Being my guests, you can even consult with her.

_It would be a great honor. – said the Assyrian, and then he added – Can it be right now? We intend to keep our stay short and return to our duties in Assur.

Ankh smiled showing his perfect teeth. _Clearly. Follow me, please.

The Hall of the Oracle was very different, its floors were entirely carpeted, as was the southern wall. The northernmost wall was dominated by a massive sculpture of a beetle, on whose back was a gigantic eye, just like the one they had seen in the statue of Horus. The beetle shone like gold, for it was covered with a thick layer of that metal. It sparkled ingratiated in its own existence, a milestone of craftsmanship. To the right of the beetle was a large bull, representing Apis, from whose horns hung dozens of necklaces of precious stones and silver. In front of the bull, a stone table carved to the bone rested, which was so smooth that even a sigh would slide off it. On that table the sacred spells were performed. Hassan noticed that there was a stone pillow on it, and he couldn't help but think that it was out of tune with the place. In fact, other things did too. There were some cloths scattered on the floor, as if someone had left them there in disarray. No, not left. Someone messy lived there. What kind of person could treat a sacred enclosure lightly? The cloths were colorful women's garments. A young woman's.

_Here she comes. - Ankh announced.

Hassan turned around.

And he was amazed at the figure that came in. Her robes seemed to float by the art of some sorcery, while her jewels echoed like the heart of a desert genie. The young woman's hips swayed gently, like the wind of the oasis. And those eyes, they looked supernatural, black as a cloudy night.

When she stopped in front of Kamek and Hassan, bowed long and labored, and the veil was finally lifted. She was the priestess, successor to the Oracle: Eylem.

PART 48: A SAND STORM

The desert nights are certainly hard to endure. The sand is treacherous, and storms can come and go without warning. But inside a palace it becomes much more manageable. Especially in good company. Or in Hassan's opinion, the best possible company. He'd spent the last five days with her, and thought he'd never get enough. The candlelit talks, the touch of her skin, the magical effect of her gaze. Eylem seemed like the perfect woman to him. He wondered if she was a gift from the gods, but he did not understand why such a gift would be given to him at the moment of greatest doubt. Could it be to get him to trust them again, precisely?

He stopped daydreaming and sat down on the bed. Some of the veils that hung from it flew as if possessed by melodious souls. His nose was filled with incense and the unmistakable aroma of good oil burning. And he drew a huge smile. Through the single window of his chambers, where he was housed in luxury, a soft, dry breeze came in, and he could almost sense the presence of the omnipotent Nile. His new and best female friend wasn't there for him. He looked for her under the bed, behind the furniture, between the curtains, but she wasn't there. He peeked out the window to look underneath. His smile suddenly faded. Below, gazing up at him, stood Kamek, and even in the distance he could sense the flares coming from his eyes. Hassan shouted at him to wait for him to put on his clothes and would come down to exchange a few words with him, but received no reply.

Already dressed, he went out on the black night that had already taken over the sky several hours ago. He looked for his partner until he found him leaning casually against a column, smoking cannabis in a simple wooden pipe. He wouldn't even say hello.

_I understand you're upset about something, but I don't know exactly what.

Kamek gave several quick puffs to keep the grass from quenching, and released a mouthful of smoke into the air.

_The negotiations with Ankh have been encouraging. – Hassan defended himself – He has accepted an alliance with Assur, and to protect our border from incursions.

Kamek lit a straw on the torch hanging a few feet above their heads, and used it to give his pipe new life. Hassan was beginning to doubt whether his conversations with Ankh had leaked out, or whether he himself had told Kamek the true motivations for his visit. Indeed, to secure an ally, but not for Sargon, but for him, in exchange for lavish gifts in metal. But if

Kamek knew about it, wouldn't be so calm, he'd have accused him directly. Maybe he was just suspicious.

_Tell me, Aslin... don't you think it's time to leave already? The men are uneasy. You and I were treated like princes, but they weren't. They eat the rations they are given, because ours are exhausted or close to. We need to stock up or we'll arrive hungry.

Hassan relaxed. _If it's for food I think our good host will be able to offer us a solution. We will ration it in the last stretch of the journey in order to arrive at the capital without the need to starve, already safe at our borders. - Hassan lied, knowing that there was no safe place on the borders of the Empire for him or anyone else following him, but he could always resort to theft.

_I don't think he'll give us anything but crumbs or stale bread when he's done with you.

_What does that mean?

_That you don't seem to realize you've been set up with a spy – and he added later, looking under Hassan's belt – or if you've set up a spy in her.

_Eylem's not a spy, she's–

_She is a priestess of Horus – he interrupted – therefore a disciple of Ankh, one of the most clever men in this land, who has shown you exactly what you wanted to see so that you can spill everything you know.

Hassan swallowed the string of lewd words he had to offer, but stopped to think. No doubt he had addressed thorny issues in his long conversations with the woman. And it was true what Kamek was implying, both she and Ankh were astute, and could draw more than one conclusion from what he had chosen to speak, to complete what he had chosen to keep quiet. And for someone who's weaving the Emperor's mortuary habit, it's a huge blunder.

_And now you see your mistake, "Great Aslin". - the Assyrian said ironically.

Hassan searched for the Moon, and understood that it was too late to leave the place. It would have to be the next night. _I'm going to give you some credit, friend Kamek. I have loosened my tongue too much, and it is better to leave as soon as possible, if only to cut off further damage.

Kamek let out another puff looking up at the night king, and nodded heavily. _Did she at least tell you your future? - he asked sarcastically.

When Eylem returned to the Virtuous of Loyalty's quarters, Hassan was collecting his belongings in a chest for the servants to carry out. She walked up to him quietly and caressed his neck and back. _What are you doing, my love? Putting your things in order?

568

Hassan wanted to be upset, but he honestly couldn't. _No. We're leaving.

Eylem opened her huge eyes with surprise and almost childish disenchantment. _Oh no! And so suddenly! Why? What happened?

Hassan grabbed her face aggressively, but she did nothing to defend herself, she simply stood still under the yoke of his steady fingers.

_Because of you! – he began shouting, but then lowering his tone word by word – you are someone who listens to me, and then tell on to others. Ankh in particular, and that's not nice. – even he understood how silly his phrase sounded.

_I'm sorry, my darling – she babbled to him as best she could with her mouth tightly between his fingers, in a playful tone – But Ankh is High Priest, he must know what's going on with his guests, no?

Hassan released her and slammed a punch into the feather mattress, which obviously made no noise and was not the least bit threatening. _You... you don't understand... you've been spying on me, asking me accurate questions about the military power I have, about my captains and allies.

Eylem rested one of her hands gently on Hassan's clenched fist. _My love, I didn't compel you to do anything. In fact, we've even discussed tactics on the battlefield. Is that sharing Egyptian military secrets with you? I don't think so. It's just conversation.

Hassan suddenly felt unarmed. Not even the anger that he had tried to build was with him. All he had left was an immense love for that woman who had seduced him to steal his secrets. All he had left was to confess what was inside him. That which was a true gift from the Gods, the heart in love of an *immortal dread*. _You seduced me to steal my things. - he got stuck putting his words together - I mean, my secrets. Assur's secrets.

Eylem sketched the biggest smile a man had ever seen. _No. I seduced you because I liked you. But... - she began to say, with her bright smile gradually diminishing - now that you have the unique opportunity to win my heart, you just walk away. Do you have any idea how rare is genuine love between *blood carriers*? I am doing my best to show you my best smile, because inside I feel that my fire is extinguishing.

Hassan had a huge lump in his throat. _I-I'm... I'm sorry, my beloved. It's just that I'm at a very delicate moment in my life, for things I haven't told you yet.

_Nor you will.

_No! Or I might. I don't know. You of all people should know the moment I'm living. You told me you saw my future.

Eylem nodded with a mixture of childish charm and discomfort.

_Well? Because when we talked about it, you told me you weren't in the mood.

_And I threw a pillow at you.

Hassan laughed, and hated himself for being defeated with such impunity. _And you threw a pillow at me.

Eylem suddenly turned to meet him face to face. _All right, I'll tell you your future. As a parting gift.

Hassan nodded several times, with a funny grin on his face. _I'm all yours, what should I do?

_Nothing. Let me concentrate. - she ordered him closing her eyes.

Underneath her breath the magical spells intended for Apis could be heard, to provide her with the foresight to see the future, with that touch of teatrality that Eylem had for things that were half a joke and half serious issues. Suddenly, she squeezed the man's hand to get his attention.

_Oh! I see your destiny, my noble lord. I see you conquering the world, bringing it to its knees before you. I see you defeating your enemies who are too tired to fight you and are trampled like insects under your feet.

571

Hassan laughed heartily, for he had temporarily forgotten that outside those walls he had to wear a mask again. One that he could probably never take off again. _And that's it? I get the whole world just like that? – he jokingly asked.

_No, no, wait. I see something else. Mmmm..." – she expressed as she shook her head back and forth, as if driven by some mysterious power – I see... that a beautiful woman will be your ruin. You'll lose everything. So watch out for pretty maidens, huh? – she said as she hit his head with a pillow.

Hassan responded with another pillow, and they both laughed and enjoyed each other's company, perhaps for the last time.

By the end of the afternoon of their sixth day, the Assyrian caravan was ready to leave, awaiting the order of the Virtuous. He had strayed to say goodbye to his beloved, to the impatience of all, but as much or more so to Kamek.

Eylem and Hassan were hugging each other behind a large, beautifully decorated vase, which lay on one of the corners of a long corridor, away from the eyes of servants and soldiers.

_You're not coming back, are you? – asked the woman with tears streaming down her cheeks.

_Yes, I'll. As soon as I achieve my goal.

_And what is your goal?

_I'm sorry, but I can't say it.

_Then kiss me and go.

Hassan did not think twice, and passionately kissed the owner of his heart.

Once outside with his conflicting feelings, he set out for the caravan to leave. If all went well, he would soon return as Emperor of Assur, and take her as his wife, against the will of anyone who stood in his way. His soul was relieved to know that his victory was near, he only had to stretch out to reap the fruits of his hard labor. He heard some men screaming for him, so he raised his hand to be found.

_Who's calling me?

_Me sir, am a servant of the High Priest – a very thin young man came running in his direction. – He urged me to come to you, for you to meet him because he has some important news.

Hassan didn't have to travel much to find Ankh. He was awaiting him on the edge of the majestic steps of Memphis Palace, with the night veil looming on the horizon.

_High Priest – greeted the *dread* effusively. – I'm told you have some news for me.

Ankh's gaze gave him a chill that ran down his entire back. He had seen it many times before. It was like the cold and fake pitiful look that is cast on the sick with leprosy, or on the punished to death who repents at the last moment when it is already too late.

_An Assyrian messenger has arrived looking for you. I'm sorry I had to torture him because he didn't want to reveal anything but to you. Very noble boy.

Hassan couldn't believe his ears. _What? You tortured one of my messengers? What's with this outrage? And telling me without shame, to my own face!

Ankh raised his hand to stop the angry man's verbiage. _Put that away, please. Sargon is dead, I don't know how or why. But Sennacherib has taken over the throne and is the new emperor of Assur, with broad local support. An army has left, apparently for Jerusalem, to collect tribute or destroy them for insubordination. And that's not all, but now a reward hangs from your neck. You're a pariah, Aslin.

Hassan was petrified. His wrath ceased suddenly, all his thoughts were lost, even his heartbeat stopped in an instant that seemed to have no end. If a man could be stripped of everything but his body, to throw it all into a black pit, that's what happened to him.

_I am not interested in that reward – continued the priest – although I confess it is more than interesting. If only for the fact that I am your host and concerned for the safety of my guests. However, the moment you cross the doorway of the city you will be just like any other. You are warned not to return to this land, at least not until your... situation is resolved. Now, get out of here. May the Gods have mercy on your soul and grant you a good journey. – he said, to immediately turn his back on him and head to the Palace.

Hassan's remains walked to the caravan, where several hundred men waited for him. One of his captains asked for instructions, but found only silence.

He continued to advance past the gates of the city, followed at some distance by the confused Assyrian soldiers. Kamek got off his horse and ran to Hassan to grab him by the shoulders. _Hey! Aslin, wake up! What's going on? What did Ankh tell you?

Hassan raised his head to look without seeing his companion, and let go of the few words he could let loose. _That Sargon is dead, that I am a pariah. That I'm too late to be Emperor for staying here with Eylem.

Suddenly Kamek boiled with anger and bewilderment. _You tell me my Lord is dead, and you talk about being Emperor? What nonsense are you speaking about? Answer me!

Hassan took the person he once called a friend by the arms, and answered him with brutal sincerity. _I wanted to be Emperor, yes. Because Sargon was a moribund and useless sack! They all ruled in his place. All your blood is vile, and it should be over as soon as possible!

Some enraged voices were heard from the Assyrians in the caravan, some of them drew their sabers from their belts. And so did Kamek. _You have until I count to ten before I cut your head off and give it to the dogs. – he shouted, mumbling his anger.

There was no need to count. Hassan turned around and left. Alone.

PART 49: TOTAL SURRENDER

The new Crest command center, set up in the most hidden and forgotten bunker, was extremely dark, mounted in some lost basement on the outskirts of Jesenice, Slovenia. Above the basement, a sad hut against the mountainside stood, barely touched by a snaking dirt road. Not only was the wind blowing, but it was determined to remove the roofs from every construction in the area, which were scarce and sturdy.

The faded paint was marked by the humidity and several families of fungi that grew on their surfaces, whose preferred place was under the concrete straps of the roof that floated from time to time letting pass huge bursts of cold air. Outside, a half–hidden gray van swayed with the storm's roar, next to a pair of leafless trees. The scene itself was grumbling, trembling. Shivering.

In that sad basement, only one person stood in front of a computer screen on a wooden table, drumming the fingers against each other, waiting. Except for a few standard icons left after a clean installation of an operating system downloaded from an illegal site, it was all black, the only movement of which was the dots that separated the hours from the minutes, 14:34 from that dark Monday, October 31, 2050.

And everything, absolutely everything, was covered in the dust of carelessness.

The person seemed lost in fleeting thoughts, with a young face but without joviality, with marks not of age but of passage of time, without wrinkles of aging but of experience, eyes that seemed supernatural, black as a cloudy night, that were not opaque by the darkness of the place, having lost their brightness day after day, year after year, layer under layer of suffering, one on top of the other. It was Eylem, the leader of a faction in ruins, Crest.

Suddenly, her face lit up and the brightness of the screen glowed brightly, bouncing morbidly all over the small place. From the speakers there was a sound that pretended to be a phone call. And in the middle, an anonymous figure. And this anonymous figure had a banner, which ironically prayed as a label: "YouKnow WhoIAm".

Eylem watched with what seemed to be infinite calmness that letdown of a name, listening to the mocking sound that hammered echoing through the dull walls of gray stone and mildew. And she let it ring, unmoved.

And when the call was about to end automatically, she pressed the green button.

_It took you a while to answer. - said the face on the screen.

_I was busy. You're calling at a bad time.

Hassan laughed, stroking his beard gently. He seemed to have put extra effort in animating highly expressive brown eyes, a friendly face, rich black hair as shiny as oil. On each of his fingers was a ring, all of gold, each adorned with a huge gemstone of different color and shade. _Busy looking for a job? I understand that today is a challenging day for many, who have lost their source of income. But a person of your talent need not to be afraid, *bonami*, you will find one right away, sooner than you think.

_I'm not in the mood for cheap jokes, and I'm not looking for an employer, Hassan. - the woman answered seriously with her arms folded.

_No? May I ask, then... what is the leader of Europe's deadliest group doing?

Eylem did not respond immediately, it looked like she was going to speak, but she swallowed her words and looked down. She breathed deeply before continuing, with a hint of bitterness. _Picking up the pieces of what was once my pride, my labor for centuries. You surely more than anyone know the effort involved in forging a group united and with a purpose.

_No doubt, my dear.

_And you of all people should know what it's like to lose it all in a battle.

_It has happened to me.

Eylem narrowed her eyes, staring at the camera that was taking her image and transmitting it to the hideout of the Middle East's strongman, who was pointing its weapon at the forehead of the entire Occident, demanding total surrender. _You worked for Caucasus, and you know how it is.

_I worked *with* Caucasus, never for him. That's what differentiates us, dear.

_Whatever. You understand what it's like to have your efforts be a piece on someone else's board, which can be traded at any time in a game you don't fully grasp, because it comes from the brightest and most frightening mind in the world.

Hassan nodded his head slightly, awaiting for the torrent of emotions coming from across the line.

_How many times did I think he was crazy...? or that he was doing it out of simple malice, out of contempt for... everyone and everything. Nevertheless, he demonstrated to me that his plans had a purpose. He was always like that, always four steps ahead of anyone else. We all danced in the palm of his hand.

_But he's gone, my dear. The terror is over.

_He's gone. – she bitterly pressed on– It's hard to live most of your life in a fist and then feel it come loose.

_That, I do understand. – nodded Hassan's kind face, who continued to caress his soft beards.

_When I feel this sudden freedom, I see that the one who has loosened the fist intends to impose another one on me. Fucking son of a bitch. That wasn't going to happen. And I fought. And I plotted, and planned to defeat that one who had proved to be better than... – she stopped to swallow spittle – better than the owner of the world! – she left a short space, to breathe a couple of times. – Maybe I pretended too much.

_No. You did well, Eylem. I've tracked your progress. In fact, you came very, very close to defeating León. – Hassan laughed – It was so, so easy for me to give the *coup de grâce* to his power cores that I couldn't believe it at first. But of course, it was to be expected with you as an enemy.

_León is not defeated. Actually, Hassan. – she said angrily, pointing to the middle of his nose – You haven't finished beating anyone. That scoundrel is still out there, plotting. I heard he went to America to negotiate with George and Perius, the ones who bombed our asses. With them! Can you believe it? I don't know exactly what they got to, but they've tried to split the planet between them.

_I was aware of that. The five Virtuous of Caucasus, gathered in Congress, splitting the world among themselves, in the name of the late leader, because the alleged successor wants nothing. Oh, and Perius, that old rascal. – he closed with irony. And he waited such a precise amount of time that atomic clocks could be set using it, to finally say: _And you were not invited.

Eylem sank into her wicker chair. The stance of her arms fell, as did her gaze, and apparently her willingness to go on. _What do you want?

_You once told me I would rule the world.

_I remember it.

Hassan laughed hard. _You said other things too, but we both knew you were a fraud. Anyway, I want you to be with me in my hour of triumph. You're right about one thing, I'm winning the game but it's not over yet. In the next few days I must bring about the final closure, it must be very soon. And that's why I called you.

_Why me? There are groups of mercenaries ready and willing. I'm not, and my group is less so.

_Yes you are, you lot just need the proper motivation. I understand that cutting the throat of a lion will be to your complete liking, a task to which you will put your best efforts. And besides... I'm not interested in those other groups. – Hassan's graceful and enlightened fabricated face approached the camera with almost divine grace, so that he could take it in all its splendor–I am interested in you.

Eylem smiled sadly as she stared into the void above her head. _Again with that? Cut it out. It's been millennia.

Hassan denied, with a full smile. _I won't. It's destiny. We should be together.

_Please, say no more.

_In that case I'll continue when we meet in person.

_In person? – she asked mockingly.

_Think it over, you've got ten seconds... that's how long the next offer will last, ready? – Hassan interlocked the fingers of his hands, showing the ten beautiful rings in front of him – Crest will be reborn, strong as ever, it will be my armed wing in Europe. The whole continent under your control. I'll provide you with weapons, recruits. You'll get everything back, and more. You will have the freedom to do and undo as you wish. If things go well, I'll entrust you with the whole Occident. But you must be with me now. Respond to my orders, fight my fights. The first thing is to bury León, George and the others. No one left alive. And then... we'll rebuild. – he stretched out his hands, like a prophet before his people. – Your turn, my dear Eylem.

Eylem ran her hands across her forehead, removing the short hairs that had fallen on it.

She wiped away the dry perspiration that was invading her, closed her eyes and exhaled. letting the noise of the iron sheets against the wind rule the situation.

And when his interlocutor was about to declare the end of the deadline, she stated: _I accept, but... – she said with a defiant index finger – with one condition. You're not forcing me to do anything, on a personal level.

Hassan smiled with the most genuine smile he had had in centuries. _Done. We should close this deal in person. Would it be stupid to ask where you are?

Eylem lifted her chin, jolted suddenly. _It would. What wouldn't be stupid is for you to point me in the direction of the meeting. And I hope it's in a neutral place, where no one will bother. And I emphasize that, that no one bothers us.

_Good. I totally agree with your observation. You must still be close to France. In that case, I think Greece would be more appropriate. It has been neutral territory for enough years, and there will be no problems moving around or getting there. – In the absence of opposition, he continued – More precisely, Athens, I appreciate the architecture of the place very much. We have to enjoy it now, before it disappears. And sooner rather than later, tomorrow night is fine with you? Will you make it on time?

Eylem nodded, somewhat absent. _And where exactly?

_That's for me to define. I will send you the exact position three hours before the meeting, it is more than enough time for you to show up. Alone.

_I'll be there.

_No traps, Eylem, please. My men will be nearby, I'd rather not have to warn you, but you're a... special woman.

_Warnings are not necessary.

_Much better. Till then. – he made a few spins with his finger in front of the camera, down to the button that ended the friendly chatter of total surrender.

Eylem was again locked in the almost full darkness, drumming her fingers, giving the appearance of being completely immersed in her thoughts, allowing the meek light of the monitor to seep through her pores.

After long minutes, she opened a small drawer under the wooden table, and shuffled through a dozen and a half different phones until she pulled one out. It was an old cell phone model from the late 20th century, and she dialed the only number on the phone book.

_Get everything ready, the meeting will be in Athens. – she decreed.

PART 50: SURFACE TENSION

Lohe leapt to her feet, watching the body fall to the ground. For a moment she stood still, not knowing how to continue.

_Antoine! - She yelled loudly - *Renne*!

The lumberjack stood up in a daze, looking back and running as fast as he could. Four well-armed figures in combat suits quickly stepped out of the black minivan, and after a few seconds of deliberation, stormed out in formation after Antoine, jumping over the driver who had collapsed with a shot to the temple. One shot shook the air, forcing the agents to take cover. They soon triggered the retaliation. Explosive munitions were buzzing in the air to shatter what they touched. Chunks of splinters filled the air near Antoine, who was sprinting at full speed.

_*Hier*! - Lohe shouted to him, removing the empty bullet case and loading the next one. When Antoine came close she got up. The man took her by the hand as he screamed incoherently, and the shock was such that he almost tripped her up. Running this way by the hand made it uselessly difficult, so she shook his arm in an outburst to break free. Antoine slowed down and looked at her, with surprise and sudden disenchantment in his eyes. She was angry with him for the unprofessional manner in which he had behaved, but remembered that he was only a civilian who was being pushed too hard.

_I'm sorry. Trust me. – she asked, not knowing if the little German that the agitated man handled was enough to recognize that phrase.

Antoine did not respond, and his gaze revealed neither understanding nor confusion. What he did do, was point his finger to his right. Lohe turned and saw in the distance what looked like a shed, perhaps abandoned.

They ran that way. Suspiciously, the bursts of gunfire had stopped, and as they turned backwards, their pursuers were nowhere to be seen.

They arrived so fast that slowed down only as they hit their backs against the outer wall. The shed was a rectangular construction of cement and humidity, surrounded by a barren field, with metal sheets, remains of building materials and a road that opened up between the mountains of rubbish. It had few windows, all near the roof made of broken fibrocement sheets where only one arm passed through, and a single double-door opening that occupied almost the entire narrow part of the rectangle. A huge padlock was hanging from the chains that circled several times over the door handles. Lohe poked her head out in the corner. The pursuers didn't show up.

_*Entrer?* - Antoine asked, holding the padlock in his hands.

Lohe's mind was racing. If they were out of sight it could indicate that they were fanning out to close the exits. Alternatively, they could have separated to cover ground, and hiding would give them valuable time. Having the enemies separated also gave them both a certain advantage. However, if they knew where they were and expected reinforcements, entering the shed would be their sentence.

_*Ja.* - Lohe finally affirmed.

She carefully positioned herself in front of the padlock, measured the correct movement by spiraling her healthy leg several times, concentrated her strength, and kicked down the rusty padlock, making a noise so distinctive that it could have been an onomatopoeia. The left door refused to open, while the right door gave way, crawling across the floor. They entered and closed the gate with a rusty latch on the floor. The only sources of light were the multitude of holes that splashed into the shelter, whose light fell irregularly causing more shade than vision of the rickety boxes, obsolete equipment of all kinds, tools in poor condition, cans of all sizes, under a thin and even layer of fine dust, which was tempted to fly at the slightest intervention.

Lohe unconsciously analyzed the best place to hide and counterattack, but in the current condition, a single bolt-action rifle with ordinary ammunition, against the enemy's *Lichtbogen II* superior firepower, the chances of getting out alive were slim. Unless...

She turned over to evaluate the frightened lumberjack. Using him as bait increased the chances of catching by surprise the first agent entering, and perhaps giving her an edge on the second. But Antoine would die in the process. The logic dictated to make use of an asset at your disposal. But she couldn't. It was simply wrong to abuse the person who helped her until now. The old Lohe would have acted differently, she thought.

She yelled at him as quietly as she could and pointed out a place to crouch behind some stacked boxes. She had somewhere else to go.

Outside, Soleil followed by three agents surrounded the old shed. By gestures they discussed the best route into the building, quickly agreeing that the main entrance was suicidal. Instead, they would open a hole in the back wall with a hand grenade, throw in a tear gas canister and shoot anything that coughed. The group's skinniest agent, Weins, stood behind a tree trunk near the main entrance to prevent an escape, while Soleil and the agent Armstrong waited for Ramirez to throw the grenade on her signal.

Soleil lowered her hand and the corpulent agent released the grenade, causing a blast of sheets, hollow brick and cement in all directions. Ramirez was about to throw a tear gas canister, when the three of them were distracted by the sound of an electric motor accelerating to the maximum.

_Look out! – cried Armstrong, firing at the danger.

The car passed through the mountain of metal sheets almost flying the meters that separated it from the shed, crossing through with violence and speed. It first struck Armstrong, who was crushed under one of the wheels, and left Ramirez and Soleil temporarily on the destroyed windshield, to be thrown forwards immediately when the brakes were applied, already inside the building. Both bodies fell like rag dolls in the middle of the shed, scattering boxes, weapons, various objects and pieces of building material that had been blown up by the grenade and the car crash. The red car driver's door opened, and from the cloud of smoke and dust a figure emerged, whose first action was to take one of the square rifles that had fallen to the side and aim it at the fallen ones.

Soleil crawled out as far as she could to hide behind a barrel, pulling her handgun out of its holster, trying to lower her heart rate and clutching at her broken ribs.

She removed her helmet in a futile attempt to improve her breathing. The other downed agent tried to move his bulky body but was shot with an explosive bullet that nearly severed his right leg cleanly. The limb remained attached by a thin strip of skin and reinforced cloth, floating in a pool of blood that grew wider and wider. Among his cries of pain, the figure that had entered crouched down using the car door as a shield.

_Nobody move. – the order of a former Shadow of Crest, Anzhelika, sounded firm. She removed the magazine from her appropriated rifle, checking that the information on the small display was correct, there were only two rounds left.

Notwithstanding the warning, and noting that her tactical position was now irrelevant after the recent events, Lohe dropped down from a roof beam, rolling immediately into the illusory safety of the space between iron shelves, pushing the shocked Antoine into the process.

_Where is Antoinette Soleil? – Lika demanded in German to know, assuming that it would be the language most likely to be understood by León's soldiers. – Whoever tells me, I will let go. You; the one who jumped off the roof. Who are you?

_It's none of your business. And if you withdraw now, I'll let you go. – Lohe threatened, pointing the hunting rifle in her direction.

Lika ignored her own words thrown at her. _You don't seem to be who I'm looking for. The one behind the barrel, who are you?

_What the fuck do you care?! - Soleil shouted to her in fury and the pain of every breath - And who the fuck are you?!

_Just a vengeful Shadow. - Lika replied calmly, pointing at her.

_ She's Soleil! - betrayed Lohe seeing a new possibility, to put a new enemy against an old enemy.

_Damn bitch... - Soleil muttered, pointing as she could in Lohe's direction, but not daring to fire - She is an agent of León, from a secret division against high-profile targets. You're going to be more interested in her than you are in me.

_Is that true? - asked the Shadow.

_I no longer have anything to do with León. That's why all these guys came here, to get me.

The fallen agent tried to get up, and in a thoughtless act influenced by the torrent of chemicals the suit was injecting into his arteries, he managed to pull his handgun out of the holster, to be shot in the neck by the fugitive, and receiving another explosive round in the middle of the chest by Lika. He stopped his movements permanently.

_Ramirez, don't! – Soleil shouted in vain. She leaned better against the barrels, trying to reduce the pain in her ribs that was pulsating horribly. A big drop of sweat had descended to her chin, but refused to fall until it had reached critical mass, to break the surface tension – This... this doesn't have to end badly. – she lamented deeply, knowing herself to be in a weak, ill-armed position with fewer and fewer allies. Words were to become her shield as she sought a way out other than by kicking the bucket. She glanced at the agent on the floor, bleeding out and unconscious, and knew right away that this was already ending badly – We can all go home, no one has to die today.

Lika looked sideways into the hole through which the car had passed, at the agent who had been crushed and was no longer moving, then at the one she herself blew up. _Some have already done so.

_Hey, Lohe! – yelled Soleil – Look, I have nothing against you. On a personal note. – lied – I'm just following orders, you know? I'll say it's not worth going after you. León has more important things to think about than a fugitive. If you kill that Shadow, I promise we'll leave you alone and also I'll share a secret with you.

_This is a joke, right? – Lohe was puzzled – What secret?

_About your siblings.

_Hold on... What siblings? - Lika asked, suddenly suspecting that it was *that* secret division, the one she had found in the archives of *Prima-Gestalt*, Spearhead. Which meant being extra cautious.

_What could you possibly know about them that interests me? They're already dead. - she said surprisingly cold - Besides, I have nothing against this Shadow. In fact, she did me a favor by killing those agents of yours. Less work for me.

_No, no, no. You see... here's a new offer. Face her and let me get away. You don't have to kill her, just distract her, okay? And I'll tell you something you really - emphasized - want to know about them.

_Why don't you stop talking nonsense? - Anzhelika accused - She won't do anything strange, she'll leave quietly without disturbing us while you and I settle our differences.

_What differences? I have no idea who you are. - Soleil protested.

_The one who came to finish you off for killing Lykaios.

_And who the hell is that?

_Don't you remember? He confronted you a few days ago in Barcelona.

Soleil reminisced a little, looking for connections. _Barcelona? That guy on the rooftop?

_I don't know exactly where. But you and a bloke named Chambeaux killed him.

_No, it wasn't me, it was him! - the agent disengaged herself.

_It seems you have things to discuss... we're leaving. - Lohe said, pulling Antoine's shirt to make sure he was attentive for the right time to run.

_Don't go! - Soleil was trying to keep the momentary balance of power from tipping against her. - I have a third man outside. He'll shoot you if you come out, he's well-armed. - and she earnestly hoped it would be so, and would not have rushed to the vehicle to call for reinforcements.

_I'll know what to do when I see him. - ignored Lohe.

_Wait! Your siblings... are alive! - Soleil shouted with all her strength.

Lohe lowered the weapon, with confusion in her eyes. _What do you mean alive? I watched them die in front of me.

_Yeah, I know. But I saw them alive yesterday.

_Stop lying!

_It's not a lie, I'm telling the fucking truth! All right, all right... I... I didn't see them personally, okay? But they told me so. But if you want to know who told me, you must defend me.

Seeing that a potential threat was hesitating to attack her or not, Lika intervened. _You're not buying that. She's lying, obviously.

_You shut up.

_Make me.

_Stop it! - Lohe shuddered. - This is absurd. I just want to leave in peace.

_I agree with that - Soleil said - we can act like civilized people.

_I didn't come to leave in peace. - threatened Lika.

_Here's what we're going to do. - Lohe organized, tired and astounded - I'm going to cover you until you get your helmet and make a call to your man outside. You're going to order him not to shoot. To anyone. Then you'll come in my direction and we'll go out together. If you betray me, I'll blow your head off with a punch. And you know I can do it.

_All right! - Soleil answered quickly putting on her helmet and opening radio communication.

_You think I'll vouch for that? - asked the Shadow with irony.

Soleil took the opportunity to think of a new plan. _Sergeant speaking. Weins, give me your position. - she called in a whisper.

_In the vehicle, calling for backup. Status?

He was gone, but it wasn't that bad. _At least two hostiles. I need immediate extraction. Pay attention...

_I don't think you have a choice. - Lohe noted.

_I do. Here's my offer. Between the two of us, we kill Soleil, and go home. If you're no longer on the Léon team, I don't consider you an enemy.

_Tempting, but I don't know you or if you'll deliver. You're part of Crest, famous for doing whatever it takes, regardless of the promises given.

Lika chuckled with a false laugh._ Perhaps, perhaps. But I'm kind of a fugitive too, a renegade rather. I'm not in Crest anymore, and I don't want anything to do with Eylem.

_Why not?

_Because I suspect she's been cooperating with León instead of confronting him properly.

_Are you independent then?

_More or less. Those of us who were against Crest are getting organized. You are invited to participate if you wish. It would do you good to have allies, since they're still going to be after you. Think about it carefully.

_I already talked to my agent. I ordered him not to shoot. And you don't either! – Soleil said – Are you ready? I'm on my way there, but tell me if you're ready.

_Hold on. – Lika cut out – I'm talking to the lady. Besides, there's no guarantee to know what you told your agent. It could be a trap.

_It's an interesting offer, but it will have to wait. Now I need to get this person out of here. – Lohe announced.

_Who?

One hand slowly leaned out beside the fugitive. The man could only smile and greet. _Bonjour.

_Is that your boyfriend?

_I don't know what that word is.

Again the sound of an accelerating electric motor was heard in the distance, and it was getting louder by the second.

_I hope not to intrude – Soleil interrupted – but my taxi is here. And Ramirez – she added, addressing the fallen agent in the middle of the shed – I'm sorry.

The crashing sound of the impact shook them all, with the black minivan driven by Weins slamming furiously into Lika's car, moving it forward and covering the sergeant with its armored bodywork, crushing Ramirez's body and Anzhelika's ankle mercilessly in the process. Soleil wasted no time and leapt to the door of the companion that opened for her. The driver reversed the vehicle, but not before receiving the last explosive round of the Shadow, which chipped the windshield and smashed the top, but without affecting the machinery.

_Damn it! – Anzhelika insulted, limping as fast as she could towards the red car, sitting on the seat and trying to close the crooked door, it bouncing back and returning to the open position. The lights on the dashboard of the car shrieked like a Christmas tree indicating that critical damage had been done, and that it was dangerous to use. A fine white smoke began to come out of the battery chamber, confirming that the car would not move even a hundred meters.

Lohe came out of hiding, pointing the lumberjack to stay. She hung the weapon on the shoulder and walked slowly with her palms facing forward until she stood beside the renegade. She glanced at the board carefully before speaking. _You won't be able to pursue them on this.

Lika hit a hard blow to the steering wheel with such violence that she broke her fingers. _I know. Shit! She slipped out.

_And you're hurt.

Lika turned to see her with an annoyed face. _I noticed. Thank you for your comments. - she fixed her attention on the wounds on her hands and legs, and to Lohe's curiosity they began to close and reform, just as she so wished to be able to do.

_What are you going to do? - she asked calmly, trying to lower the level of tension they were experiencing.

_I could steal another car, but not a lot of cars come through these parts. They'll be a long way ahead. - she got out of the car completely recovered and tried to close the door again, without success.

_It's not that serious, I located her once and I can do it twice. Although, I'll owe a favor...

_Do you have a Seeker?

_Yes. - she affirmed as she searched the ground for weapons or ammunition. - A moody lady Seeker. She's part of the group I told you about earlier.

_And is it true I could join you?

Lika stood up to observe Lohe, not expecting such sudden interest. _It depends. If you really are from

Spearhead you should be an interesting element to incorporate.

Lohe sighed deeply. _I was. I'm the only one left.

Lika returned to the vehicle, picked up a small backpack from the back seat and kicked the door shut. This one bounced a third time.

_I'd like to meet you all. – added – I must then also ask for a favor, to that Seeker.

Lika was not sure whether to let her go with her, whether she had spoken too much, whether it was an elaborate trap or perhaps a good opportunity. She let herself be guided by female instinct.

_Okay – she nodded several times – and who do you want to find?

_The Akkadian.

PART 51: SCORCHED TO ASHES

Nerves were eating away the last remaining sanity in Carl Fisher's mind. He was mentally reviewing the plan over and over in his head. The basement of the military base was strangely cold that winter afternoon on Monday. The day Perius would die.

He wiped the sweat, which kept running through the parts of his head where he used to have hair years ago. He watched the moistened handkerchief under the dying lighting of that small room that was like his second office since the monster appropriated his base. And this time it would be more than just any office, it would be a direct witness to the destruction of a millennial monster that has traveled the earth since antiquity. And he would be scorched to ashes by his own hands. Or rather, by the machine he had posted on the other side of the wall, in the next room. The night before, taking advantage of the absence of the spawn and bringing up his rank, he took on the task of clearing every guard and meddler from the entire underground, leaving him to maneuver at ease and the shelter of solitude. He pushed the microwave emitter from the lab to the other wing. The device, despite having wheels, was extraordinarily heavy, and it resisted powerfully being dragged to its strategic location, but he did so without hesitation or doubt. And that position had been calculated and recalculated to exhaustion, because that plan had to be perfect. He palpated the remote control that would activate it in his coat pocket to make sure it was where it was meant. It took only a minute to get a dose of energy into the monster that could not compensate, as indicated in the documents he had received from his great and deceased friend McCarthy whom he would avenge, and from the one who cooperated with him, the unusual Weissman. He looked at the clock again. It was almost time.

He suddenly rose to his feet in an impulsive boldness, to millimetrically rearrange the desk that was to separate his own body from the deadly microwave beam, his own chair to be placed exactly in front of the victim, and the seat of executions, destined for the monster. He regretted using "victim" in his strategic statements. Perius was no victim. He was an enemy, of his, of his country's freedom. Of the world.

And as he had been trained for so many years, the enemy must be destroyed. He sat down again. Barely managed to interlock his fingers when he was caught by the only door of the place opening. One of his soldiers poked half a length in. Or objectively former soldiers, those who had been brainwashed by the alien.

_General, Mr. Perius has arrived, he will be here shortly. – said the man's monotonous voice, to exit again.

The moment of truth had arrived. There was an element he hadn't thought of, where to receive him. Sitting? Standing in front of the door? Would it make any difference to the outcome? He stood and sat down several times as he struggled in vain against the uneasiness, ruthless ruler of his neurons. But it was too late now. Suddenly he could perceive a powerful aura enveloping him. Fisher was not a believer, but since the arrival of extraordinary beings into his life, they left him no choice but to keep an open mind. And now he could not shake off that powerful feeling that he was coming. Him.

The door opened again. Behind the glazed glass there was an imposing silhouette, perfectly cut out.

_Sorry I am late, Carl. – the gentleman's deep, melodious voice sounded – May I have a seat?

Fisher stood still and speechless. That powerful aura was negating him. It seemed as real to him as the light generated by the light bulbs, as the buzzing of the computers in the back room. As real as his own hands. That omnipotent aura that caused him to panic.

_Carl, are you doing fine? Maybe I should come back another time. – said the millennial monster with a big, friendly smile. He was dressed in an expensive, elegant, shiny black suit, a snow-white shirt, a delicate black bow with gray streaks, spectacular shoes, platinum cufflink topped with lapis lazuli in each cuff. For the occasion, a pompous moustache had been fabricated and a haircut had been perfected, combed backwards that shone healthily under the majestic light of the room.

_I-I... – He managed to say, without being able to finish the sentence.

_No problem, it will be another time.

Fisher finally saw himself released from the terrible aura that held him prisoner. _No! – shouted – It won't be necessary. I... I feel fine. Sorry about... my attitude. Have a seat, please.

_Oh! – Perius exclaimed with satisfaction – That is much better. In this chair, right?

_Yes. Yes. – he nodded several times, indicating with a hand gesture to sit down. Fisher didn't understand what was going on.

Perius took a few steps forward and placed both hands on the back of the chair. _So in... this chair. All right.

The seconds passed by and the monster was still standing, incinerating him with his eyes, as if he could scrutinize the darkest secrets of his soul standing there, two meters away from him.

Finally he pivoted and took his seat, crossed one leg over the other and put his beautiful cane on his lap. _My friend... we have so much to talk about. I would like to start with the obvious, to thank you for listening to my offer, to apologize for the crudeness of the people who work for me, and to say that I hold you in high esteem, friend Carl. - the act had begun, for the umpteenth time.

Fisher barely managed to nod at the kind and terrifying words.

_I've invited you here for a word, like the well-meaning men we are. I have to admit something to you. You are extremely crafty. I like that. It is the kind of quality I strive for people around me to have. Ah, but that's not all. You are also a pillar of honesty, and loyalty. I said I held you in high esteem, I am afraid I fell short. - Perius leaned forward, slightly correcting the curvature of his perfect black mustache to the right.

Fisher was immobile. He felt his plan was sinking, but he didn't understand how or why. He wanted to press the button on the remote control in his pocket but felt that a rope was holding him prisoner. It was in his damn pocket, but he couldn't get it. He didn't even have to take it out, just needed to get the hand in. Damn it, one finger was enough. But there he was, incapacitated, like a rabbit on the road lit by the headlights of his destiny.

_You also are a man of military talent – continued the demon – one of particular weight in these times we live in. Do not you think..? Oh... – suddenly the elegant monster smiled.

Something vibrated softly somewhere nearby. Fisher couldn't determine what. Obviously it wasn't the machine, since it wasn't activated yet. Neither were the computers in the other room, although he did not know enough about them to discard it.

This powerful feeling of immobility gradually ceased. Fisher moved one foot, then the other, and both hands, which he was able to lower down to his waist. He felt freer.

It was time.

He put one hand in his pocket, and pressed the button of the ultimate weapon. Now he had to distract him for a minute.

_Hendrich has told me that you want to put yourself under my command. Why? – as Fisher talked, he pulled himself together.

_As I told you, your military talent is of interest to me. Do not believe I do not possess my own, friend Carl. After so long you learn a thing or two from the battlefield. What I need is an update, you see? A quick course on modern weaponry, what is useful and what is not. Strategies I have no knowledge of because I have not been involved in a conflict for at least... fifty years? And things moved fast since then. – Perius gave him a masterful smile.

_Do you realize that placing yourself under my command implies that I will give you orders?

_I'm aware, obviously. And I accept the consequences of my words.

_And will you obey as if you were military personnel, and not a civilian? – Fisher's gaze had changed like the day of the night, he felt in charge again, his plan going as calculated. Just the final scourge to the beast was ahead.

_I will carry out your orders like a common Joe.

_In that case, I accept. My first order will be to release all personnel on this base from your mind control.

_Ah... Carl... believe me, I knew that would be a requirement. Please continue. – he interjected amused.

_The second, you will never set foot in the United States again. Choose another country as your center of operations, this one is off-limits to you.

_That second order hurts, but I will abide by it. What else? – Perius moved his foot playfully.

_As a third measure... – Fisher was about to open his mouth, when he came up with the obvious: the minute was almost up and nothing was happening. He was silent, looking him in the eye for several more seconds.

_Well?

Fisher started sweating profusely. His plan wasn't working. He had no way of seeing the microwave cannon on the other side firing at the beast, but he must have seen its effects at this rate. And nothing had happened.

Perius shook one of his hands in front of the soldier. _I knew you were not feeling so well. Did you catch the flu maybe?

_No... I... - Fisher didn't know what to do. Panic was taking over every section of his mind. He had to consciously resist the urge to run out.

_My - friend - Carl - Fisher. - every word of the gentleman was carefully highlighted, as he leaned his head back in a grand gesture of announced victory - I hope I was not mistaken in my diagnosis. As you know, as in the case of military expertise, you do not spend as much time on your feet without knowing some trick or two of medicine. That is why I hope I do not miss my observation that... you do not have the flu, Carl. What you have is a severe case of a failed plan.

Fisher's eyes almost jumped out of their sockets. His lower lip began to tremble.

_Do not get so tense. You see... do you mind if I smoke? - he dropped casually, as he pulled out a pipe and a container with fine tobacco decorated with Hindu motifs - I do not know what plot you had in store for me, but you obviously failed.

Perius filled the pipe with tobacco, and used a silver lighter to bring fire to his vice. He took a couple of puffs of air over his head, perhaps trying not to disturb his host. _You are not to blame - he added pointing the pipe at him - It is very difficult for a child to surprise his father. Mmmm... maybe that sounded too complacent. My apologies, Carl. What I mean is, I do not know you directly, other than our short dialogues since I arrived for a visit, a few days ago. I understand you though. I know you, Carl. To say that more so than yourself would be arrogant, but... - he showed a perfect smile before continuing - it is very close to reality. When I got here today, I felt something strange, my friend. I felt there was danger. And one does not spend so much time with you head over your shoulders ignoring these kinds of sensations. So I kindly asked one of my followers to check around while I was here. Yes, I could have done it myself, but I would have been late for our meeting. - he stopped to take another puff of his pipe.

_And my caution seems to have stumbled upon something of a truth - continued, releasing smoke as he talked - My boy has found something, deactivated it, whatever it is, and reported it to me. - expressed by taking a small personal assistant out of his pocket, the device that had vibrated minutes ago – Now that the game is over, would you be so kind as to tell me what was it about?

Fisher closed his eyes, defeated. Totally beaten. How can one fight a monster like that? He surpassed him in so many different areas that could not even count them. But what seemed to him most spectacular and unjust at the time, was the undefeatable, unbreakable armor of his sixth sense. The monster had acquired such an instinct for survival that it could smell a trap from afar, perhaps even before it was laid. How could such a thing be defeated? It was simply impossible.

Defeat. Total defeat. A final struggle was taking place inside the General, not to shed a single tear. He almost lost it, too.

_Carl, please do not get upset. It is hard to beat me, not grieve about it. Come on... come on, please, tell me what you have planned for me. – the monster's paternal and sweet tone tasted like insult. And it was, in a sense so subtle and harmonious that it deserved a standing ovation.

Fisher swallowed saliva several times, raised his forehead to avoid crying again, and spoke. _I've set up a microwave machine to fry you up. And I have failed.

_Wow! That is inventive. I cannot discern how powerful that device could be, but it might have worked. You have extra points for your imagination. – he said in a friendly tone – Well, now that this part of the talk is behind us, let's get back to the main topic. You asked me to leave this place, and I said I was willing to. I have not had your counterpart yet, how are you going to help us?

Fisher looked at him with infinite sadness, fearing to be the devil's toy for the next few minutes, and then a corpse. _What do you want from me?

_I told you, to join us voluntarily.

_I don't understand. – the phrase was intended to the fact of being used as a toy, rather than the previous sentence.

_It is simple. We have a war on our doorstep. Another war, I mean. The attack we executed was fine but it was just one piece of the board. The next move is pending.

_War against whom?

_Against a chap named León, and his partner, a fellow named The Genoese. They have been plotting behind the Council's back and that is not right.

_I don't get it at all. – Fisher's confusion was total.

_There is no need to go into details now, friend Carl. I will ask Hendrich to prepare a dossier with the information you need. For now we will say that the Council is the last banner of order, and it is in my interest to preserve it. And that León and The Genoese are part of it, or used to, it is still not certain. What it is certain, is that they are playing against us. Among other sins, they have tried to murder a good companion of mine. But perhaps the most unforgivable is that they have caused the fall of a great leader to appropriate his throne. Which would not be... so serious... if it were not for this León, moreover, not being the *actual* León. We still do not know for sure who took his place and personified him, or how long ago. Are you following me?

The General only nodded, his eyes fixed on the ground.

_And the danger of this unknown is that he possesses some kind of secret weapon, the nature of which we are unaware of. But we know that it has a very peculiar effect, to avoid prying eyes on some event. When he wants to attack, we shall not see him coming until it is too late. We will not stand by, and push the investigation as far as we can.

Perius paused to look closely at his destroyed interlocutor, grimacing compassionately.

_Carl... Carl... maybe it is best to leave all this for later. You have a lot to digest from what transpired today. Just remember: You cannot beat us, so I urge you not to waste your time and cooperate.

PART 52: A HAPPY ENDING

Things were going great for Amelia. Since she had crossed paths with that being full of mysteries, she had finally come out of that deep pit into which life threw her. And she could see how quickly her situation improved day after day. That powerful feeling of growing, evolving, learning, improving, in short... of winning... was becoming addictive. She would never let herself fall into the black paths of her own soul again. Stone by stone she would build her own destiny. By the hand of her new mentor, the strange and lovable Kad.

That Tuesday morning was special too. She woke up with a lot of energy, arranged the whole room in record time, had for breakfast her favorite cereals full of extra sugar, dressed in the clothes she had prepared the night before, congratulated herself on that effective technique she had to repeat from now on and that allowed her more time to concentrate on her makeup (which was on point!), and walked out into the streets vividly to meet a new component in her life: dates.

It wasn't the first time she'd gone out with someone, but she had to reminisce about the times she'd done it, and the result her brain returned from those meetings was not positive. She wondered if she had ever been with someone she *really liked*, or if she had always been chosen because she looked easy, or depressed, or knowing she would say yes without much insistence.

Never again.

Never again would she allow herself to feel so insignificant, to trample on her self-esteem, or allow others to do so. She had value! She would have run to get it tattooed, but it would have to be another day. She wanted to arrive early for her date with the tall, handsome, friendly-eyed guy from work who few called Federico.

After walking several blocks she reached her favorite square, where the Magic Fountain of Montjuic was located. She had always liked its laser, water and music shows, because it helped her not to think. Now she liked it because she could really enjoy it, without having to hold the door where her demons insisted on sneaking in. She didn't have to wait long, soon her company arrived.

They had lunch in a nice place, and she found out she had a new magnetism. Who had ever smiled at her so much before her change? Who had ever acted so nervous when she told them that they looked handsome? No one. Maybe Frik was a particularly shy guy, but frankly she didn't think so. No, he wasn't shy. He was rather intimidated. He told her he was nervous about not wasting his chance with her. She thought that was *so* cute.

They walked about a hundred times around the square, talking about everything and everyone. Of how the world seemed to collapse, of how the tanks lined up at traffic lights as if they were rush hour cars, of how terrorism had turned governments upside down, of how protest marches were multiplying all over the world, of how the color orange favored her, of how the birds sang. About serious things, about silly things. But despite the laughter, the people around her suffered. Some had already lost their lives in the protests. Things were getting pretty messy out there. Amelia wondered if she was the only one having a wonderful time. Even if Sinolta closed and was fired, she had an interesting savings fund, courtesy of her beloved mentor.

And she still had one wish left. She was not sure what to ask for, but she was almost certain that if she asked for the Moon, Kad would get it for her one way or another. She couldn't stop comparing Frik to him, even though she knew there was no comparison. The guy next to her was twenty-six (finally asked him) and the naivety that matched that, and he was an ordinary, though charismatic, person who made her laugh a lot. He had a pretty smile, and liked the way he looked at her. Not particularly her type, for that he lacked musculature, some more tattoos and a nose ring, but... this was the new Amelia. And after much laughter and flirting, the young man said he wanted to kiss her, and she agreed. He let her hair float to the winter wind, sketched the most pleasing of smiles, and they kissed. It was the beginning of the rest of her life. It was her happy ending.

Things were going awful for Crista. Since she had crossed paths with that millenary being full of horror and the smell of death, she had entered a deep pit, the one that she had dodged with greater or lesser skill since she was born and *reborn*, but could no longer avoid its unstoppable gravitational influence. Her dealings with that late Crest agent whose name she hadn't even discovered had led nowhere. That moron who called himself Shadow had finally bit the dust, courtesy of someone from León's side. In fact, that same Crest organization seemed to have suddenly disappeared. And in short, they had only given her a little money to live on, breaking their verbal agreement.

After the curfew following the terrorist attack with nuclear weapons, no less, hunting had become an impossible task. Too much danger. If they saw someone crouching in a dark alley sinking a knife into some bastard, they would have shot without a second thought, any of the hundreds of military personnel who tirelessly patrolled the European nights. Hunger reminded her of its imposing presence, the effect of relying on ordinary food that fed her little but was very expensive. So the few savings she had were dwindling.

Her scams had to become more risky, and her wretched suppliers had become shoddier.

And now she was there, waking up in a shithole the owner called a "hotel room". She got up from the disgusting bed, kicked some of the plastic wrappers of various processed foods furiously, and immediately began to count whether her belongings were still in the same place where she left them. She heard banging outside in the next room. Screams, insults. Someone who was forcibly thrown out for some reason that didn't interest her. A gunshot put her on alert. A horrid voice was heard reprimanding someone for having pierced the roof. She had to get out of there, but her movements were slow. She was tired... so tired of fighting giants and always losing.

How unfair it all was.

She clutched her face tightly with the hands, trying unsuccessfully to squeeze out all the hatred and sadness against this motherfucking world that was causing her ruin. She didn't have the time or the desire to put on makeup, or to wear her filthy, unlucky scarf. She threw her scarce things into a spacious purse, looked at the pronounced dark under eye circles in the broken mirror of the repulsive bathroom, and glanced out the window. It was late afternoon and it was time to leave. To go out and try to earn a living by any means possible, by trickery, cheating, deceit, to deprive a wealthy person of the resources to survive one more night.

She hated going out with the daylight still in the sky, it made her feel insecure. It would be the same for anyone if heaven itself wanted to hurt you, because there was no safe place for her anywhere. But she had no choice, because after the 19.00hs anyone outside four walls was arrested. She had little time to try to earn a coin, a card, a purse with or without an owner. She picked a corner she thought fit, spread out a blanket, adjusted her long gray skirt as she sat down, and pulled out her primary tool: her deck of tarot cards. By habit the first throw was to herself, as she looked around out of the corner of her eye, weighing her chances of scamming here or there. She looked at her cards and clung to the first sensation they gave her. The Empress, The Wizard and the Wheel of Fortune seemed a little elusive, but they went hand in hand with some new business or enterprise to get her out of her infinite ordeal, a magic?, special?, component in that reversal, and a markedly feminine dye. So for today, she'd be paying attention to the women passing by.

After an hour and a bit more of fortune telling some passers-by and picking up some wallets, she moved elsewhere before arousing suspicion. She stretched her blanket under a streetlamp, wiped away some tears caused by the cold wind, and waited. It wasn't long before the appointed time. In the distance, she saw a young woman coming. She was well dressed, and walked happily. That wasn't inconspicuous in those days when they were living. Closer by, she also noticed that she was smiling. With that kind of smile from someone who's doing *great*. That indicated money.

_Hello beautiful young lady, would you like to learn today what fate has in store for you? - she said while evaluating her more closely, and shuffling the cards. The girl smelled of new perfume and success. A clear candidate.

_Yeah, why not... - Amelia answered, too happy to discover a potential scam. - How much would it cost me?

_I like your energy, it's radiant, you know? So here's what I'm proposing: if your destiny turns out to be something encouraging, you'll pay me my usual fee of five euros, but if something comes out that isn't so good, it'll be free... plus you'll be warned to change it. What do you say?

_All right. - she replied, pulling out a bill, revealing in the process that there were several others accompanying it, to the delight of the gypsy woman - I hope it's something positive! - she radiated brightly, placing the valuable paper in a small wooden chest decorated with plastic pearls in front of the woman.

_Excellent, that optimistic attitude is important... here we go - Crista shuffled with efficiency and energy, thinking about how to procure the rest of that money -

now cut the deck, wherever you like, the next three cards will indicate your future – she said, extending the deck. After cutting, she repeatedly ran her hand over the cards in an exaggerated manner, to extract one after the other, placing three face up on the blanket. The Emperor, The Wizard and The Wheel of Fortune had been revealed to the curiosity of Crista, whose initial feeling was that they all pointed to one person, and a connection to herself – This card... is The Emperor, it indicates that you will come across a masculine figure, very compelling and that will change your life. I see he will be central to your immediate future, seems to be pulling very strongly.

_Oh, that's no surprise. I know who he is.

_I see, so he's a person from your present?

_Yeah. It's got to be Kad.

Crista shook her smile and dropped her hands slightly. _Who might that be?

_He's a man I met recently. He's helped me a lot in everything. I practically owe him my life.

Crista didn't know what to think, but she knew she had little time to do it. Kad as in the *Akkadian*? That old monster helping someone? And some random gal? He must be playing with her, the poor thing. However... she didn't look miserable at all.

On the contrary, she herself was the miserable one, and the "poor thing" looked flourishing, magnificent. What did that mean? Were the rumors false? Wasn't he a savage madman? Crista had felt his suffocating and atrocious power, they could not simply be superstitions. The Akkadian was a beast. But now she doubted about what kind. And more importantly, how could she gain anything from it? She could feel her own Wheel of Fortune shyly starting to spin. She needed information! _I love that! Do you know what that means? That it's a fated bond. By the way, my name is Crista, what's yours? - she consulted, showing the most affectionate smile that came out in between the envy and despair.

An hour later, Crista was behind a streetlight column, making sure that not even her shadow stood out. She's got a lot of juicy data, but no extra bills. If she was going to get something out of that girl it wouldn't be a few filthy euros, but a much bigger prize. If her cards were right, this was her business related to a woman: follow her, make the most of it, run away. In that order.

She watched her walk to a beggar and give him some money, then to buy food and colorful knick-knacks. She watched her cheerfully greet some acquaintance of hers, play with love with a neighbor's dog, and then go up to an apartment. Fortunately, it faced the street, so Crista immediately wrote down which one it was, underneath all the things she had been learning from her.

There, hidden behind the cold and darkness of the night, her troubled mind dared to imagine a change in her life. It was risky, but had to try. She glanced downward, noticing the stains on her jacket sleeves, and realized that she could not feel her toes, barely protected by the boots whose soles had come off halfway.

Crista understood that she was already finished, and decided to be honest with herself: she was worthless and had little to lose.

She looked up, like a child peeking into the window of a toy store she couldn't get into. Like a sick man watching the hospital where they could save him if he could afford it. Like... a soul in sorrow who is shut out from the Gates of Heaven.

Up there, the Gates of her Heaven might be waiting for her, if only she could get to them and push that happy imbecile out of the way. She'd do anything to achieve that. Bit her lower lip, determined.

To kill. To destroy. It didn't matter anymore.

PART 53: HIDDEN IN THE DARKNESS

The full Moon had appeared as a witness in the night sky for that exceptional encounter, accompanied by the visible stars that shone despite the light pollution. Sitting quietly on a stone bench with her legs crossed, was Eylem, her arms stretched out over the backrest, looking up at the vast heights. She wore a thick purple jacket and a woolen hat, not because she needed them but because it was easier to have them than to recreate them using biomass to pass for an ordinary civilian. Everything else had been recreated by her hardened and textured skin simulating clothing, as was her custom.

The site chosen by Hassan for that obligatory gathering was the Monastikiri Square in Athens, recently renovated after being sold to an Arab construction company. Everything had been on sale in Greece for several years, since it was expelled from the European Union. And the countries of the Middle East, in their investment frenzy as the oil business neared its end, had acquired a lot of assets, especially there and in South America. The Greek rulers had since then juggled their public accounts in vain in an attempt to be accepted again, for the amusement of those who held true power. The irony was that after recent events, the Union itself was close to disappearing. All countries, loose to their fates, would once again be lone wolves after carrion, and perhaps war.

Around Eylem there was not much, some tall columns of grass clods not yet placed, rows of tiles waiting to be laid, some old stone buildings, some newer aluminum and glass buildings with closed shops. The curfew had also been implemented by the local authorities, but was simply impracticable. The number of troops in the armed forces, even combined, was not even enough to cover the capital, and most of them had been destined to reinforce the maritime border with Africa and ensure that no unwanted boat reached the coast. However, the streets of the city were almost empty at that time. Only a few drunkards and unconscious people dared to wander, unconcerned about the danger they were in, or on the contrary, offering even more danger hidden in the darkness.

The crickets ceased to be the woman's only companion when she observed a figure approaching. From the way he walked, he could only be one: Hassan.

The lights of the lampposts illuminated the gait of his triumphal bearing. In his finest garb, he wore a custom-made black two-piece suit under an elegant grey overcoat, and shiny leather shoes. A black tie with red and yellow fluorescences around the neck. Already in the distance it was possible to observe the play of

625

lights caused by the jewels in their rings when they were struck by the luminaires. He had adopted the same appearance as the last time they had communicated, but in person the effect was very different. It was accompanied by an incomparable stately aura, one that cannot be transmitted by digital means. The plaza itself seemed to change color as he walked.

When he was close, he stood in front of her with measured movements, dedicating himself to observing her exhaustively. Eylem, underneath the cap that rounded her face making her look more innocent than she was, looked up at him with expectant eyes, giving almost the appearance of a deer waiting for the final claw. Time passed and the face-to-face dialogue they had waited so long for did not take place. The tension of a thousand years apart, of millions of things to be said, of hundreds of frustrated sexual encounters, of decades of truncated shared stories increased instant by instant. Second by second.

_You look gorgeous. – the newcomer finally broke the silence, giving a wide smile of the caliber that only a world champion could have.

_ Thank you. You're more handsome than usual, good job on those modifications. – she rebuked him, but with such subtlety that it seemed like a compliment. Her body language changed, she crossed her arms and gathered her legs, trying to take up as little space as possible.

_Can I have a seat? – he asked, receiving an affirmative gesture in return.

Sitting side by side watching the stars, it seemed like a romantic encounter, if not for the environment, the continent's unsteady near future, and the unattainable thoughts inside their heads.

_I'm glad you came alone.

_And how do you know I came alone?

_Because I've had some of my men in control of the place since before I mentioned where it would be. – explained the man – Besides, I have one in particular that has an incredible sixth sense. And if I had a bad feeling myself, I just wouldn't be here.

_How clever.

_Did you expect less?

Eylem smiled at him sideways. _No. Well, what did you come to tell me?

_I want to know what you want.

_So many things... – she seemed to start, but kept silent, perhaps weighing her thoughts – I want to be able to free myself. Of what's keeping me tied up.

_My dear Eylem – Hassan clasped his palms to highlight his words – I am not here to imprison you to anything. I offered you the whole Europe, you can do whatever you want.

_But you told me I ought to fight your battles.

_And I'll fight yours. It is fair, don't you think?

_You would never be there for my battles, Aslin. – she replied with his birth name.

_I'm not that anymore. I've changed.

_Frankly, I don't care what name you use, inside you're the same.

Hassan opened his arms, and looked down. _Don't you think I've changed? Take a good look at me. More than two millennia have passed and I have learned so much that I cannot be the same. It is simply impossible.

Eylem showed herself irascible for the first time, pointing at him coarsely with her index finger. _You are the same degenerate who pretends to feel like the hero of the story, when all you have done is try to conquer and destroy everything and trample over everything.

_Are you accusing me of wanting to rule the world? – he laughed out fakely. – All of *our own* do it. Your beloved Caucasus, the most.

_But neither he nor anyone else pretended to be the good guy. On the contrary.

_I am fair. I treat people fairly by giving them what they deserve. How is that not good? – Hassan raised his voice – And that's why I'm different. That's why I'm better.

_You're a fraud, Hassan. That's why you abandoned me, that's why your plans fail, because you can't build a real future with lies.

_Woman, what kind of a joke is this? You were the crawling dog of the most lying and manipulative man of all times!

_A hypocrite in addition to a fraud. You accuse me of being a crawling dog, but you brazenly stole his ideas, copied the greatest and most brilliant of his lies... using religion as mass domination. And you still do.

_It wasn't his idea, he took it from someone else and improved it. But, what's wrong with using someone else's ideas, if they're good? – he defended himself with a violent hand gesture – I also picked up strategies from him, in our many conflicts. I retained his territories for hundreds of years, in case you don't remember, thanks to my skill. His crusades were his failure.

_You lost them, in the end. You were kicked out of Europe. You were always a second in this story.

Hassan's gaze blazed with fire. _The loser in the end *was him*, as one of his own dogs ended up biting his hand. And I'm still here, to–

629

_I know. - she interrupted, looking at him with overwhelming eyes - We were the ones who killed him.

Hassan was going to continue, but kept quiet. _What? We?

Eylem stood up to face him, letting out steam like a vengeful dragon. _León and me. We have been scheming this plan for sixty years, to put a definitive end to the wars between *our own*. Between all peoples. And to this purpose, it was necessary to put an end to Caucasus in the first place, the one whose plots have led to countless conflicts. And it happened now because we discovered recently that he had a plan, one to disappear for a while and wait for a massacre for power to occur among the groups, and then reappear to encourage the growth of the winner, for years later to invent a new conflict, as he always did. We got tired of it, we had to act. We took advantage of that plan to attack, and destroy him once and for all.

_But... you... you and León are sworn enemies. - the man seemed genuinely confused.

_I'm a fraud, too, Hassan. And I confess I have always been. In fact... *all my work* was based on teaching the art of deception, of living in and for the shadows. Now... today... it's time for you to know the truth, because there won't be any second chances. - she stared him in the eye, speaking slowly so that every word stab him deeply – I've never loved you. Never, not even when I was an innocent girl. I was fond of you, yes, but not in love. I wanted you to fulfill your dreams, and your dreams made you my enemy. But even that affection vanished long ago. And today, when you're next on the list of people who prevent a lasting peace... I'm the one who planned your demise.

Hassan was speechless, inert. His jaw barely dared to move at all.

_Because with you alive – continued the woman – there will never be peace. We brought you out of the hole, made you think you'd won. When you've actually fallen into a trap.

Hassan arose out of instinct rather than awareness of what was happening, wrapped in rage. He grabbed the woman by the neck, but she quickly broke free and nudged him on the forehead, knocking him to the ground on his knees.

From behind the clod columns, three armed figures jumped out in black combat suits. They ran with flawless speed and professionalism the short distance from the target, surrounded it and fired a dozen rounds of explosive ammunition from their square rifles. The impacts shook Hassan one after the other, tearing his chest, shattering his arms, destroying his legs, and blowing his left ear off.

Eylem raised a hand to stop the fire. The uniformed changed positions, two on either side of the victim, and one on the back, who had the task of executing him.

_Wait, please. – Eylem crouched in front of the defeated Hassan, and waited a few dramatic moments before continuing. _You have no idea how tough it was, the sacrifices we have made, the years of dedication for this very moment. The painstaking effort necessary to infiltrate our agents into yours, including your little psychic friend who hasn't warned you of anything. Nasser is one of the agents I planted among your people. And León also prepared a trick so that no one could see this outcome, not even you, although I don't know how he did it. – she shook her head in disbelief – I see you here and I still can't believe it.

Hassan kept bleeding, staring his captor in the eye, panting and shaking. His body was making no effort to recover, as Hassan himself was actively surrendering. Part of it, because of his pride shattered to pieces. Partly because of the crushing empathic attack he was subjected to. Partly, because of his stomped heart. _I... I love you, Eylem. – he said with a thread of voice.

_Yours is not love, Hassan. It's obsession. – the mournful face of Eylem slowly relaxed– A long time ago... I warned you that a woman would cause your ruin. You ignored me, you fool. – Eylem lowered her hand, signaling the end – Farewell...

The agent behind Hassan's back planted her feet firmly, drew two wide circles with her arms, accompanied by rhythmic flexing of her muscles. And in a flashing motion, she struck him with a punch of such violence that she pulverized the man's body. Remains of flesh and pieces of organs splashed onto all present, leaving a smoking red and black circle on the floor.

Eylem stood there, still dirty from the charred flesh and blood of the man who claimed to love her. She did not take her eyes off Hassan's final resting place.

_Target neutralized. - sounded a Fender's voice in German, still aiming at the pit that was a threat instants ago - Spearhead extraction in ninety seconds.

The other two agents visibly relaxed. A Konnex agent hanged the weapon on her shoulder, took off the helmet, and smiled at her brothers. _You've done great, congratulations.

_Very good job keeping him in line, Konny. - congratulated Fender - and an impeccable task, sis. Our first mission came out perfect - he said, removing his helmet and smiling at the third agent.

A Lohe agent leaned one knee on the ground, drained of energy. She took off her helmet, laid it on the floor and brushed her short hair back. _Thank you! - she exclaimed happily for the success.

PARTE 54: A NEW ERA

Matthias Weissman woke up frightened, with this inexplicable but oppressive feeling that something was not right. Sitting on his bed, trying to stop his neck from hurting, he started checking messages in his personal assistant. He just discovered a suspicious hollow. Apparently *nothing* had happened since his visit to Beatrix the day before. Nothing. In a convulsed world, in a battle against Crest, against Hassan, and now against the unholy alliance between George and Perius. He decided to clean up while he was putting his thoughts in order. He could not, no matter how hard he tried, shake off the feeling of something biting his heels. Even half-naked, he ordered his computer to shut down completely, while pulling out a small laptop from inside a false bottom of the drawer. He turned it on and connected it to a secure network (or what he understood to be the safest thing he could have, under the circumstances) and checked one by one the clandestine mailboxes he kept hidden from the militia. In one of them he found a new e-mail. It was from Beatrix, sent about thirty minutes ago. It was extremely short, and came from her official account, so his own mailbox was now compromised. He didn't get why she had exposed himself like that, until he opened it and understood. The message said: RUN FROM THERE NOW.

His body moved on its own, his eyes found in a fraction of a second the objects he had to take with him. But his mind needed answers. What had happened? Was it related to what he found about the "Veil" she mentioned when visiting her? That this weapon was at the service of León and not the enemy, confusing his own rather than others. He dressed up in a matter of a minute with the first thing he found available, rescued some money hidden in one of the spots on the roof, took his official personal assistant, an alternative one and another that he had hidden under a loose tile in the kitchen. Turned on the oven and threw in all but one of the devices. It had a new message from his friend living secretly in the United States, General Alex Krupp. There was no text or images, just audio. He took the gadget to his ear in confusion, and pressed Play.

After a few seconds of silence, he heard his unmistakable and lamentable voice: Matthias... they're going to kill me, I'm sure. They're out there, I don't have any guns here. I don't want to die!

In the next nine seconds there were only a few background noises to be heard, and the desperate cry of his friend. The message had been sent four hours ago. It was obvious that Krupp was no longer alive, and he would be next.

He jammed some belongings into a backpack, put on sunglasses and a hat, and left his apartment heading to the service elevator. There was nobody in the hallway. He went down to the ground and walked as fast as he could to the security perimeter fence, greeted the guard at the sentry box curtly and continued without looking back. It was early morning already, the city was getting ready to start the day. Weissman waited for at least two taxis to pass by and stopped one, as there was no way he would get into the first cab waiting outside. He needed to put distance between him and the tower that served as wireless communication to the area. After he had already covered several blocks, called on the phone and vehemently wished that there would be an answering voice on the other side. And it did.

_Fisher, is it you? - Weissman asked almost whispering.

The answer came in slowly, and when it did, it was muffled, with no desire for life. _Yes, what do you want?

_I want to know what happened to Krupp.

_I'm... I'm sorry. Krupp's been murdered, I couldn't do anything.

Some veins in the Commander's sore neck swelled. _You promised me his safety, you gave me your word!

_I'm sorry. There's no way to win this game, Matthias. There is no way. They're too powerful.

_Who did it?

_I don't know, I don't want to know anymore. I've given up.

Both men remained silent, having nothing to say, their thoughts blank in the face of the abyss of defeat.

_Fisher, why have you given up? You're a man of fortitude. – he said when his analytical mind could take control.

_Perius... is invincible. I'm still alive because he took me as a toy. I have family to look after, please understand.

In Weissman's mind, new possibilities were forming that would get him out of trouble. _Do I have a way to communicate with him?

_He's not here anymore, he's travelled to Spain. But I have a phone number I can give you.

_Yes, please.

_Again, I'm sorry. I beg your pardon. – he lamented before hanging up.

Seconds later, he received a contact number. While he was booking and calling, asked the driver to go to the bus station. The airports were closed, and the roads were under constant surveillance, but it was his best option, as long as he could convince or bribe his way out. The ringing tone sounded over and over again, not reaching anyone on the other side. And suddenly...

_*Aló?*

_Are... are you Perius?

_Intriguing! – sounded the cheerful voice on the other side – That's right, with whom do I have the pleasure?

Fifteen hours and a tiring journey later, Weissman arrived at the coordinates that had been delivered to him, in some secluded restaurant for wealthy people on the terrace of a building in Barcelona, away from the political conflicts, but not from the scandals. He went upstairs, and after announcing the false name included in the message, they let him in. He looked around, and overcautiously preferred to sit near the bar. Took off his glasses and hat, and dedicated himself with care to try to recognize those present. The place was half empty, perhaps a dozen people, a third of whom were waiters. A group of three at a table, a loner talking on the phone against the window, and those two. *Those,* in a semi–closed circular area formed by tall and elegant armchairs, with a table of synthetic fiber with gold and silver details in the middle. Some pipe smoke was rising towards the ceiling. A few bottles of various fine liquors accompanied them. He couldn't hear what they were saying, but he could feel the hairs on the back of his neck stiffening in fear. Because those two were *monsters*. He took a deep breath, clenched his fists, and headed toward them.

_Oh, by the way, my dearest partner... I forgot to warn you that I brought a guest to one of our meetings once more. My apologies, but it might be enjoyable to meet him. - the voice of an unequalled old-fashioned gentleman sounded jolly. Dressed in white, with a cognac glass in his right hand and his lovely dragon-headed cane in his lap, he followed the man with his eyes.

_Again, Roman? We went through this a few days ago. - replied the other voice, full of rich nuances, a titanic confidence, an enviable calm. Kad had instead made himself a simple grey suit with a fake black overcoat with the biomass he had accumulated since his encounter with *Speerspitze*. He dedicated an ambiguous look to Weissman, between approval and disinterest – Don't just stand there, boy, sit down. Have a drink.

_Before we talk to our guest, I want an answer, Kad. - Perius went on as if nothing had happened.

_To what?

_Whether or not you're coming with me.

_To see Xin-Zu? I don't know... - he seemed hesitant.

Perius shouted in amazement. _Ah! I thought I had convinced you already! Maybe you need one more drink. - he laughed as he poured more whiskey into the glass.

_Sorry to interrupt, gentlemen. - Weissman's tone of voice was a little erratic, still trying to keep his fear in check - I came just as you told me, sir.

_Yes, indeed, I am glad you got here in one piece. Things got tough out there, huh? - smiled the gentleman - Whiskey? - he asked rhetorically while serving him a measure - I will fill you in, last night old Hassan got his bottom handed over to him, so we finally know what Eylem and that guy who claims to be a León were up to. We do not know how much longer this alliance will last as it has fulfilled its purpose. They've done well, for a change. - he theatrically raised his glass as a representation of Shakespeare - By the way... to be or not to be León... do you happen to know anything about his true identity?

_I... no. - Matthias replied in confusion - As I said, I have information about what you called the "secret weapon", the Veil Project, in exchange for protection, hasn't it? - he spoke in automatic, because confusion reigned in his head. If León and Eylem were plotted, they had deceived everyone into a false conflict between them, but then why had Krupp suffered for it? It didn't make sense. So... León himself hindered *Prima-Gestalt's* security upgrades? And if so, why condemn Krupp for it? Was there a hidden war within the agreement between them?

_All right, I will keep that. Yes, I have already given you my word, so you are in *my custody* now. And keeping up with the news, my partner here will be joining us.

_Me? - Kad laughed - I haven't accepted yet.

_Ah! But you're about to.

_Let me get this straight, *compadre*. You promised me that if I allied with you and "the good George" we would form a new era together. Blah blah in the middle, me as the supreme leader. Was it so?

_You have left several important blah blahs on the road, but yes.

Kad bowed his head to the side. _You get bored with George, don't you? - he said in a mocking tone.

_Yes, he is too somber a bloke for my taste. - lamented Perius - But backing to the topic... remember that there will be no Council, and no Genoese, Cardinal, Minamoto, nor that-who-is-not-León with it. We have no need of them. We do not have Hassan's spoilsport around here anymore, only his friend Xin-

Zu would be left. The age of Caucasus is over, and the age of the Akkadian is coming. - he exclaimed.

_What do we do about Eylem? I don't dislike her. - Kad asked with a grimace.

_Me neither, we shall see. She will probably have some troubles putting her ranks together for the time being, so I do not mind.

Weissman couldn't remember the last time he felt so misplaced and lost in a conversation. He felt like a child sitting at the adult's table by mistake.

Perius rushed his drink and snapped his lips. _Kad, do not you think your plan for a new religion with you at the head has a lot to do with it? You will need political power at some point. Gods have power, as you can tell.

_Yeah, I know. I've already considered it... in fact you're about to convince me. - he closed with a warm smile.

_I knew it! Well, here is my last argument in favor: it will be a lot of fun. - he said, stressing his words.

Kad burst out laughing, perhaps touched at the right spot. _All right, you convinced me. I'm with you and that annoying George. A toast?

_Excellent! - exclaimed the gentleman - Come on boy, you are part of it now too, are you not?

Weissman wanted to react, but his arm was simply too slow, and he was left out, watching the overwhelming scene unfold in front of him.

_For a new era. – the *monsters* toasted.

www.ingramcontent.com/pod-product-compliance
Lightning Source LLC
Chambersburg PA
CBHW072006020726
47501CB00006B/1712